SECOND
MARRIAGE

SECOND MARRIAGE

*'There are none so blind
as those who will not see'*
Traditional

GEORGINA MACKIE

PIATKUS

In memory of my husband, Alan
with love and my thanks.

This story and all its characters are entirely fictitious,
but without his patient support – and his ability to make
delicious cucumber sandwiches – it could never have
been written.

As it seems to me that writers are merely
transmitters that deliver words on to paper, much as,
one step further on, actors deliver them to an audience,
I would also like to thank all the 'stagehands' who have
helped this novel into being. This includes everyone at Piatkus
Books, my daughters Roo and Sarah-Frances,
my extended families and my friends – all of whom
were only ever there when, for whatever reason,
I needed them most.

Copyright © 1996 by Georgina Mackie

First published in Great Britain in 1996 by
Judy Piatkus (Publishers) Ltd of
5 Windmill Street, London W1

The moral right of the author has been asserted

A catalogue record for this book is available from the British Library

ISBN 0-7499-0339-2

Set in 11/12pt Times by
Action Typesetting Ltd, Gloucester
Printed and bound in Great Britain by
Mackays of Chatham PLC, Chatham, Kent

Chapter One

Amy Kenworthy surfaced slowly from her afternoon nap in the sheltered corner of her daughter's garden, and opening her eyes, narrowed them against the strong September sunlight.

There was a man standing amongst the dappled shadows under the lilac trees at the end of the lawn. A tall, dark-haired chap, standing particularly still, hands clasped behind his back as he looked away across the paddock to the woods and the moor below Dunkery Beacon.

Amy was old now; gaga, her daughter Anthea had said to that young upstart of a woman doctor. But she recognised that man under the lilac tree. Before he had divorced Anthea to marry the woman he'd brought down from London, he had been Amy's son-in-law, and this garden had been his garden, this house and this farm his home. He seemed larger than she remembered and around him there appeared to be a bright aura of light. But it was definitely him.

Lawrence Seligman.

As if he had heard her think his name, he turned to look at her, and meeting the gaze of his fiercely blue eyes she felt a strange surge of energy. Felt, for a moment, as fit and as strong as she had in the days when she'd walked out over Exmoor to gather the plants and the minerals she'd made into potions and oils for the folk who had come to her for healing.

What are you doing here? she said to him in her mind. *You, who laughed at the healing. Never believed in any of it?*

These days she was past being of use to him or to anyone else, herself included, but curious, she glanced down as she

1

eased herself straighter in her chair – and when she looked again he had gone. The garden was silent and still in the afternoon heat and the lawn under the lilac trees was dappled with only empty pools of sunlight.

Barely a mile away across the Vale of Porlock in the orchard behind the house at Tivington, Beth Seligman continued to kneel beside his body in the trampled grass. Lying, eyes closed, his head turned slightly towards her, one arm outstretched ...

A nursing sister until she had married him, she was no stranger to death or its procedures. She knew what she must do. Walk back across the yard to the house and phone for an ambulance. An accident. She must remember to say that it had been an accident – and glancing at the syringe in her hand, she set it down in the grass.

Later the police would come and she'd need to make a statement. There would be a post mortem, the funeral and, in a week or so, an inquest. And then it would be over. Seven years of a marriage that should never have begun.

In the meantime she would have to tell his family. She knew what to say both to them and to the police. She was perfectly calm. Her anger had died with him and her thinking had never been clearer.

'I'm sure he was there,' Amy said aloud to her husband Arthur – and in her mind she continued, *I'd know that man anywhere. Once seen, never forgotten.*

Now, now, Mother, he seemed to caution from inside her head.

'Who's she talking to?' asked Wanda, the younger of Amy's two granddaughters.

'Search me,' said Anthea. 'She's gone downhill a lot since you were last home.'

Who's gone downhill ...? Suddenly aware that she was sitting in her high-backed chair by the fireplace in the tiny living room, Amy realised that, unable to get out of the low garden chair on her own, Anthea and Wanda must have helped her indoors. Arthur, of course, was not there and, talking quietly, her girls were seated at the table by the window –

Anthea tucked behind her cashbox and the big farm ledger; Wanda, Amy's favourite, though she'd taken care never to let it show, dressed as always entirely in black. Black blouse, a long black skirt and black laced boots. Even her dear little face was a hideous mask of black and white make-up. Since Amy had seen her last she'd also dyed her hair black and had had it cut so it stuck out in spikes. She looked like a lavvy brush.

She'd been so pretty as a child, with her blonde curls and her big blue eyes.

'Hello, Granny. Have you had a nice sleep?'

'Cut her a slice of fruit cake, Wanda love, can you,' Anthea said. 'She likes a slice of cake with her tea. Take the nuts off or they'll get under her teeth.'

The indignity of age, thought Amy resentfully, but Wanda did as she was asked, and when she placed the slice of cake on the arm of the chair, Amy was again uncertain.

'You don't live here ...?'

'No, Granny love. I had a day off work so I've come home for the night to see you and Mum.'

That's it, Amy thought, sucking her cheeks. Wanda lived in Taunton and her elder sister Vivien, the brainy one, she lived and worked in Bristol. Was something quite important in that big shipping company, Hall, Thane and Daniels.

'I'm Wanda,' the child added, smiling down at her through black-painted lips.

'I know that, my dear,' said Amy softly, nodding her head as she smiled in return.

'You've done well then, Gran,' said Anthea. 'Looking like that you could be forgiven for thinking she was a zebra crossing. She's written off two cars this year with drivers crashing into her – and are we surprised? You're a wild thing, Wanda – on and off the road. Ask your Gran if she wants another cup of tea. And help her drink it, love. That dress was clean on this morning.'

She had her father's eyes, did Wanda – though it was Reggie Pugsley, a pure-bred moor man, who should have been her father. Anthea, dismissing him as dull, had laughed at the idea of marrying him, but he would never have left her as that other one had. *And look at you now*, Amy thought, watching

3

her. *Nights in a lonely bed, long days that exhaust you and a face lined with sorrow. You have worked every minute God gave to make a success of this farm since the day that one left. And now you have me to look after as well. I, who am old, whose work here is done, and who am well ready to pass on to join your gentle brother Anthony and my Arthur, your father.*

Instead, it was Lawrence who had gone. Lawrence, who had never been quite the man folk thought he was and, sensing that Amy had known it, he had kept his distance. So why he, of all people, should have come to her now, she had no idea.

Though surely that had been him out there in the garden?

Or had it been merely a memory ...?

Hard to tell. Had Wanda been there, *she* would have known. Regardless of who her father was, Wanda had the sensitivity to know these things – and to learn about healing if she'd a mind to do so. But to Amy these days the past so often seemed clearer than the present that it was difficult to know one from the other. Time and place were, it seemed, as elastic and elusive as was Wanda all done up in her black and white – her clothes from an era long gone, her make-up and hair, for Amy's taste, rather too modern.

In any case, day after day imprisoned in her bed or this armchair, why should Amy want to live in the present when the past and the future had so much more to offer?

And if he had been in the garden, they would know soon enough. Soon there would be a great clamouring; a storm of telephone bells and talking, and the uneasy rumblings of conscience and upheaval that followed a change of any kind.

What was more, if and when this particular storm broke, she also seemed to know that it might well change the form of this family as surely as a storm of weather could change the shape of a forest.

'My deepest condolences, Mrs. Seligman,' said the policeman who had come to take Beth's statement. 'We all liked him down at the station. Met him at auctions, cattle shows, that sort of thing, and he'd always come over and pass the time of day. We appreciated that. He'll be sadly missed.'

'Thank you.'

She had answered his friendly questions about the race

horses Lawrence had bred in Australia before coming to England twenty-five years ago, and had listened politely while he'd marvelled at his ability to build, as a second career and from nothing, a highly successful chain of agricultural auctioneers and estate agency businesses throughout the South West of England. Then she had thanked him, watched him walk to his blue and white car, waited until he had driven out of the yard and, immensely relieved to be alone again, she had gone back into the house.

'Your children,' he had said. 'Will one of them be able to say with you tonight?'

'I have no children,' she'd replied, repeating easily the exact words she'd said to Lawrence at lunchtime. Though at lunchtime she had fired the words from her mouth like bitter gravel. Dear God, and had he been in some temper ...

Not wanting to think about that, she had looked at the policeman's hands. Clean and unmarked as a boy's ...

'You have stepdaughters?' he'd said. 'Mr. Seligman had daughters?'

And, anxious for him to be gone, she had agreed to phone them.

At least, to phone Vivien. Vivien, as strong, intelligent and efficient as her father – she could tell Wanda and the rest of the family.

'I'll come down,' Vivien insisted. 'You can't stay there on your own. I'll clear some leave with Thane, go home and pack a bag and be with you as soon as I can.'

But even as she replaced the telephone receiver and looked at the pile of files on her desk, she regretted having been quite so hasty. This was their busiest time of year, added to which they were short-staffed. Every one of those files represented a cargo for which the paperwork had to be done and shipping arranged as soon as possible. What was more, since neither she nor Wanda had been down to Tivington very often when Lawrence was alive, it seemed rather pointless to rush down there now that he was dead – particularly as Beth hadn't sounded any too keen on having her there.

Nor did she want any of her work to be dumped on Martin. Unbeknown to Martin, although he was older and

5

more experienced, Thane had more or less promised her the coveted Senior Export Manager's job on the basis that she'd done exceptionally well since she'd been with them. He had also said that she was the sort who would expect to climb the promotion ladder fast, and that they didn't want to risk losing her to a competitor. Thus, in these few weeks before the interviews, the whole office was working overtime to clear the backlog of work, and she was working harder, longer hours than any of them to prove herself capable and worthy of promotion.

She really didn't need to be taking time off to go down to Tivington.

'I am sorry,' she said to Thane when she'd explained.

'Good heavens, Vivien – no, of course you must go.' And himself a man in late middle age, he added nervously, He can't have been any age either. What was it – a heart attack?'

'No. He was fifty-three. And he was trying to castrate a young race horse. I can't think why he was keeping a race horse in the orchard. I can't imagine what he was doing with a race horse in England. I thought he'd left all that in Australia. He still has a financial interest in stud ranches out there. I don't know. My stepmother wasn't too coherent but it seems the horse must have spooked just as he was about to give it an anaesthetic. The injection went into my father's leg. A massive dose for a human. There was an antidote, but it was too late.'

'My dear Vivien,' said Thane, shocked. 'I never did like horses ... And such a tragic waste! I read an article about your father in *Business South West* not long ago. He was an extremely able man. In fact I've always been rather surprised that he didn't want you to work for him.'

He did. Persistently ... He had sent her to business college expressly for that purpose and had nagged her about learning to run his set-up in England every time they'd spoken. Which was why she hadn't been in touch with him for months. The nagging had started as soon as he'd left Mother for Beth, while Viv had still been at school. Though he had never nagged Wanda.

'He did want me to work for him,' she said. 'But I couldn't. It wouldn't have worked.'

6

He would have questioned her every decision and checked every letter she dictated. Would, in the end, have turned her into a Lawrence Seligman clone. Because that was what he really wanted – and she had wanted a life and a career of her own.

Employ Wanda, she had suggested. Employ a punk and cheer up the office a bit. But Lawrence had not been amused. Anyway, Wanda didn't have a business brain. In fact there were times when Viv wondered if Wanda had a brain at all. She was a backsliding little swine, was Wanda ...

'Anyway, Vivien,' said Thane, 'I mustn't detain you any longer, but do please give my condolences to your family.'

I must call Mum, she thought as she went back down the stairs to her office on the floor below. It must be seven years since Lawrence had left her, but it wouldn't do for her to hear this on the grapevine. And it was quite some grapevine down there in Porlock Vale. When Lawrence, a respected pillar of the local community, had married Beth and moved her down from London into a house within sight of the family home at Luccombe, that grapevine had glowed hotter and redder than Beth's gorgeous abundance of rich auburn hair. Not least because of his choice of location ...

'You're going to live *where*?' Viv had asked, aghast, when he'd told her. 'You must be joking! What do you want us to do – lean out of the window and wave a white sheet to wish you a good night?'

'That's enough from you, madam,' he'd said, catching the innuendo. 'However, I'm not divorcing you and Wanda. It's your mother I'm divorcing. I want you to be very clear about that. I want to see you girls as often as I can – and I want to make that as easy as possible.'

'Oh great ... And won't the gossips just love that for an explanation.'

'I don't give a damn what they think – and neither should you. Nor do we need to explain. Our lives are our business, not theirs.'

That Lawrence had a pile-driver will and the sensitivity of a block of steel had been amply proven – and even Mum had seemed to realise that she was better off without him once she'd got over the devastation of his leaving, discovered

7

who she was in her own right, and had begun to make a success of turning that smallholding into a very viable little farm.

All the same, she musn't hear this one on the grapevine ...

And before I leave here I must call Robin, Viv thought. *Tell him I can't see him tonight. Another date I'll be breaking – though he really won't be able to argue with this one ...*

Robin – the man she'd been seeing on quite a serious basis for seven months, yet he'd never met Lawrence, or indeed any of the rest of her family ...

And I suppose I must call Wanda. If I can find her. Since leaving school Wanda had changed jobs, addresses and telephone numbers more than most people did in a lifetime – and right now Viv could have done with a reliable sister who would have helped by pulling her share of the family load.

It was, though, just possible that Wanda had handled her relationship with Lawrence far better than she had. Just twelve at the time of the divorce, Wanda had stuck close to Mum, only occasionally allowing herself to be transported back and forth between the two houses like some mute miserable package in a game of pass the parcel. Then later, as she'd grown older, having given the situation time to cool down, she had met up with him again and had come to know him as a friend. Had enjoyed meeting him quite often, as far as Viv was aware. Her backsliding nature had, it seemed, in that instance paid off.

Whereas I was sixteen when he remarried, Viv thought. *Grown up. At least, I pretended that I was ... I guess what I actually was, was cockily overconfident and dead bolshy – because I too was hurting and, unwilling to let them see it, I didn't know how else to behave.*

And thereafter, as self-appointed negotiator of visits and general go-between, the aggression between Vivien and her father had just seemed to grow and became a habit that neither of them knew how to break.

Though he did try so hard to be a father to us. Always made sure we were doing well; never forgot our birthdays; always appeared at Luccombe with presents on Christmas Eve. I could have at least called him occasionally ...

I'm still the bloody go-between, she thought, as back in her office she checked her watch, sat down at her desk and pulled the phone towards her. Though perhaps this would now be an end to it ...

And then, although she had no idea what she expected to find – other than a weeping widow and, quite literally, a shut stable door – she was suddenly in a great hurry to be done with the telephone calls and get down to Tivington as fast as she could.

Anthea listened without comment and, supporting herself against the bench that served as a desk in the little room under the rise of the stairs, she watched the late-afternoon sunlight dancing between the leaves of the hedge beyond the window.

'Anyway,' Viv said, 'as soon as I know any more I'll call you. And while I'm at Tivington I'll come over and see you. See Granny ... Before it's too late. It's months since I've seen her, and when this sort of thing happens it makes you think.'

'Yes ...'

'By the way, is Wanda still working in that art shop in Taunton?'

'She is,' Anthea said and, having told her that, tonight Wanda had come home, she waited, resigned. Viv never lost an opportunity to moan about her sister, though fortunately this time she had other things on her mind and did not.

We have become such a fragmented family since he left, Anthea thought when the call was over, and she drove her fists deep into the pockets of her tatty beige working cardigan.

Dead ... Applied to Lawrence the word suddenly seemed as empty and final as its meaning.

He had liked to call this cubby-hole under the stairs, the telephone room – and on the bench, crammed with boxes, farm accounts and back numbers of *Farmers' Weekly,* was the pair of book ends – tarnished silver-plated stirrups set in wood – that he'd found in an antique shop in Dunster and had bought for her on their tenth wedding anniversary.

Light years ago, when he had still loved her ...

She closed the telephone directory that had been left open on the bench and replaced it on the shelf. From the living room across the hall she could hear the television. Wanda and Gran were watching the evening news. Other people's tragedies ...

9

Except, of course, you never quite knew what Gran was watching – and she often talked to Anthea's father and her brother Anthony even though they had been dead and buried for years.

Lawrence and Anthony had been friends, and thinking about them both, remembering things that she had long since chosen to push to the back of her mind, Anthea remained in the telephone room for some time.

Then Wanda called to her, asking if the phone was free and could she use it. Wanda spent half her life on the phone ...

'No you can't, Wanda,' she said, slowly pushing herself off the bench. 'Not yet. I've got something to tell you.'

Amy watched helplessly as Anthea held Wanda while she wept. Anthea's expression was distant and, concerned, Amy remembered how, for almost a year after Lawrence had left, Anthea'd had no emotion left in her to give to anyone. It had been Amy, still fit and full of energy, who had cared for the child then.

Such very blue eyes ... Her father's eyes ...

But these deep sapphire eyes were Wanda's. The other eyes she was seeing must just be an echo of memory. He couldn't be here. By now he would have passed to a higher dimension.

At least, Amy hoped he had, for if a spirit didn't go obediently when it was called, the moor folk always said that it lost the final vital surge of energy to do so, and in the old days she'd often heard talk about the earthbounds trapped and drifting in the Exmoor mists.

Beth had made herself a mug of hot sweet tea and taken it out to the garden to sit on the log bench that caught the last of the afternoon sun.

He had made this log bench and put it here the first summer they were married. They had been good together at the beginning ... He, and the marriage had been, at the beginning, everything she had thought she'd ever wanted. She had known he was different from the moment she'd met him that long hot August eight years ago at Dunster Show.

Working in London as a nursing sister for American Oil, she had come down to spend a weekend with Liz and Mike who were attempting to scratch a living from a farm they'd bought on the moor. She and Liz had been picnicking with the children and Lawrence had walked up the hill through the heat shimmer rising from the big white marquees and the gaudy trade stands on the flat lands below.

Just a man in his mid-forties, of slightly more than average height and looks, with good shoulders and thick, straight dark hair brushed low across a broad forehead – but there was something about him. The set of those shoulders, perhaps. Or it may just have been that he had seemed to appear from nowhere out of a mirage.

He shared their picnic and, as he had grown up on a ranch in New South Wales and she had just returned from two years working in Perth, they had found a great deal in common.

'That was interesting,' Liz said from her corner of the rug after he'd gone.

'Umm.'

'In fact it was almost obscene.'

Beth looked at her.

'Oh come on,' said Liz, laughing. 'In the course of an apparently innocent conversation, you were practically eating each other alive.'

'Oh really?'

'Oh yes, oh really,' Liz teased.

'He has got amazing eyes. And have you noticed those incredibly dark thick lashes?'

'Not as well as you have, obviously. Nice safari suit, I thought.'

'Exquisitely cut trousers.'

'Nice bum.'

'Well, there you are,' Beth said indignantly, defending herself as she laughed with her. 'You noticed too!'

'Ah yes – but you're blushing. Lord – and I never thought I'd see the day!'

'Okay – he's very attractive.'

'He is also married of course.'

'Of course,' she said lightly. 'By his age, if the best fruit hasn't been picked it's in the process of being handled. Still, there's no harm in looking.'

'And look, my friend, is all you had better do with that one.

11

That one is *very* married. To one of the locals from hill-farming stock. Those hill people feud and fight like cats – and you know what happened to Lorna Doone.'

'He was lovely with the baby,' Beth said, watching Liz shift Danny from the crook of one elbow to the other so that she could pour them another glass of wine.

'Umm. And how are you these days? You haven't said anything so perhaps I shouldn't ask.'

'No, you can ask. I'm fine.'

'Have you seen Ben since you've been back?'

'Absolutely not. No point.'

Ben had been the real reason, having realised that his sporadic reconciliations with his Catholic wife in Dublin would go on forever, that she'd decided to go to Australia in the first place.

'You're looking pale,' he'd said when he'd seen her off at Heathrow. 'A couple of years of good fresh air will do you good.'

'Thanks,' she'd said bitterly. He hadn't thought to ask why she was pale, nor had she told him. She'd made up her mind never to tell him some time ago; even before she'd come round from the anaesthetic in the ante-room to a background of kind voices, tubes, bottles and rolls of bandages. A ten-minute operation and a night in the ward, its eau de nil ceiling and ornate cornices sparkling through tears she'd thought might never stop. It had been more like leaking than weeping. Bleeding at both ends ... But the tears were for the loss of a much-longed-for child, not for the man who had fathered it.

Liz had been the only person she had told. Even before they had trained together at Barts they had been friends for as long as she could remember.

'Oh well, give it time,' Liz said.

'How much time have I got, Liz?'

'Plenty. I didn't have Danny until I was thirty-nine.'

'He's your third,' said Beth, reaching out to stroke her Godson's soft downy head as he slept. 'Maybe I should have had Ben's baby and brought it up on my own.'

Liz watched her with sympathy. 'My God, life can be unkind ... I adore my little rug rats now I've got them, but I was never particularly maternal. You though, you have

12

never wanted to be anything else but a mother ever since I've known you.'

It might even have been the way Lawrence had smiled and talked to Danny that had grabbed at her heart but, whatever it had been, the fierce and instant attraction was apparently mutual – so that when, having had no contact in the intervening months, he had suddenly turned up unannounced on the doorstep of her London flat on a dank night in November, she'd realised afterwards that she had not been all that surprised to see him.

'I supposed you asked Liz for my address.'

'No. You said you worked for American Oil, so I called them. They were a bit cagey at first, so I told them I was your brother.'

'Oh great, so you're a liar as well.'

'As well as what ...?'

An adulterer ...? What else was he doing here, armed with a huge bunch of flowers when he almost certainly knew that the sight of him melted her bones.

'Never mind.'

'Beth – I'm in London for meetings with my Australian business partner, so I thought I'd look you up. I thought if you're not busy, you might let me take you out to dinner.'

Standing on her doorstep in a trenchcoat, its collar turned up against the cold, he looked like a character from a gangster film. She eyed him suspiciously, then wondering if her bones would stand the strain, had agreed. They had gone to an Italian restaurant near her flat and had talked about Australia all evening.

'You loved it there,' she said, amused at his enthusiasm and the return to full strength of his accent as he talked about the friends, the race horses and the life he had left behind. 'Have you never wanted to go back?'

'Lord, no. I was a different sort of chap altogether out there. I left all that behind me. I'll never go back.'

'Not even to visit?'

'No. Anyway, I don't need to. After I came to England and decided to stay I made Tillotson my partner and gave him a half share of everything, so he runs the ranches and decides on most of the breeding and training programmes now.'

13

'Gave him? He's lucky to have such a generous friend.'

'Not really.' His blue eyes clouded and he looked away. 'No, not at all. Actually, a very good friend of mine had just died. His death was my fault – if only indirectly,' He paused, pulled a face, shook his head. 'Anyway, after that I just wanted out. On those isolated ranches things get out of perspective – especially in the heat. In the event, half of everything I owned was a small price to pay for the freedom that gave me the chance of a completely fresh start.' He sighed and put his hands on the table. 'Talking of which – shall we get out of here?'

As they walked back through the cold drizzling rain to her flat, he said, 'As for my partner, Tillotson, we used to be friends. We grew up together – but these days it's purely business, even though it's good to be able to talk about Australia. It's a hell of a country.' He looked at her. 'How about you ...? You obviously loved it too? Don't you want to go back?'

'One day. Yes, I'd love to. And next time I'd like to see your territory. Sydney and New South Wales.'

She would also have liked to continue the conversation, but the miserable weather had returned them very firmly to England on a cold autumn night. And anyway, as they walked he had taken her arm and once again she was acutely aware of him as a man rather than just a friend with whom she was spending the evening. They walked in silence, and she decided that, when they reached the door of her building, she would thank him for a lovely evening and send him on his way.

But it hadn't happened like that. At the top of the steps she had allowed him to take the key out of her hand and open the door. Had allowed him to follow her into the hall and on up the stairs.

'Brandy?'

'That would be nice.'

Even more aware of him in the close confines of the flat, she fetched the bottle and a couple of glasses, knowing that her only defence now would be to get him to talk about the wife he had so far not mentioned.

'So what did you do when you came to England?'

'I really came to visit the family of the friend who died, but I'd qualified as an auctioneer so it wasn't too hard to get work. And then, well, I guess one thing just lead to another.'

'You met your wife.'

'Yes,' he said easily, his eyes holding hers. 'I am married.'
She looked down at her brandy glass.

'The friend who died,' he said, 'my wife was his sister.'

'I see.'

'Beth,' he said softly, 'I have tried to love her. God knows,
I have tried ... But you ... You are something quite else.'

Whatever I am, she thought as he took her in his arms, *you
are yet another married bastard, and here, yet again, go I
down the same dead-end path.*

But he was kissing her now, and she began to respond. Oh
well, consenting adults in private ... After all it was his
conscience that would carry this. He was the one who was
married to the wife he didn't love. The same old story, the
same gripe; the mating call of the married lonely, the married
misunderstood. Though, just for a moment outside the
bedroom, he did hesitate. Seemed, for a moment, unsure.

Fine ... Well she knew what to do about that. His body had
been making promises to hers all evening. Promises that had
started that day back in August ...

Afterwards, lying together, he had asked her what she was
thinking.

All sorts of things ... That their bodies had been born for
each other; that everywhere she had ever been, every man she
had ever known and everything she had seen or done, had
probably been for the purpose of leading her to this evening
and this bed with this man she hardly knew, except for what
he had told her about a completely different life he had led
almost twenty years ago in another continent on the other side
of the world. A life which, apart from a few days once a year
in London, he had chosen to put behind him after the death of
a friend which was clearly still too painful for him to talk
about.

'You – what are you thinking?' she asked.

'That with you, I at last know I'm a man.'

She turned her head on the pillow to look at him. 'That
sounds like quite a compliment.'

'It's the best one I know how to give you. I've never been
able to say it to anyone else.'

15

How many others had there been ...? Quite a few, probably, by the way he'd made love to her.

'I suppose you do this every time you come up to London,' she said, looking at the ceiling.

'No. In seventeen years of marriage, you're the first.'

'Can I believe that ...?'

'Believe it,' he said, meeting her eyes across the pillows.

And then, with them as with him and Anthea, one event had led to another. For the week he was in London they met every night and after that he had managed to get up to London on some pretext or another for at least one day every week until she came down to Somerset to spend Christmas with Liz and Mike.

While she was there, she and Lawrence met as often as he could steal time from his family or from the office. Liz, without being in any way judgmental, was nervous for her – on all counts. And then finally their meetings in lay-bys and woodland clearings – which would perhaps have seemed exciting and romantic at eighteen – turned out at their age, to be cold, uncomfortable and downright sordid.

However, in a small close-knit community where he was so well known, there had been nowhere else that they could meet. Eventually, hating herself for having become involved in the first place, she had ended the affair and, in the New Year, had returned to London feeling heart-sore and tired, but had tried to console herself with the knowledge that, for the sake of everyone involved, she had made the right decision.

It had been February before she'd heard from him again. Out of the blue he had telephoned her in the office, informed her that his wife had agreed to a divorce, and had asked her to marry him.

'Hold on, Lawrie ...'

'Do you want me or don't you?'

'Of course I want you, but–'

'No buts, Beth. Not this time. I want you like crazy. I need you. And there's more. I think I may have found us a house.'

'Wait – what about your children? Have you told the children?'

'Yes, yes. No worries. They'll stay with their mother but they'll come to visit. We'll be seeing a lot of them. That's the other thing about the house – it's near enough for them to pop over anytime on their ponies or their bikes.'

'Oh, right.'

'You won't mind them visiting?'

'Heavens, no! I'll love it.'

She had loved the idea of the extended family as much as she had loved him. The daughters he adored – and about whom he had joked that, given his inability to make love to his wife, must have been conceived by a miracle – would now be the half-sisters to the babies he would have with her. At last, in addition to falling unexpectedly and helplessly in love, a much-longed-for child of her own seemed a probability.

'Don't you want to hear about the house?'

'Go on,' she'd said, happier than she'd thought possible and grinning like a fool.

'It's a beaut. A lovely sandstone farmhouse just below Tivington woods, with an orchard, a few outbuildings and a marvellous view over Porlock Vale. It's just come on the market. Franks had the instructions yesterday and I had a look on my way to the office this morning. It needs a lot of work, but no worries. I can handle that.'

No worries. No worries about the house, or about the girls, or the wife. No worries about anything, she thought now, as remembering his voice when he'd told her, she stood up and strolled to the end of the lawn where the neatly scythed bank dropped steeply into the lane.

He had assured her that his marriage was dead, so she hadn't even been particularly worried about him continuing to live with Anthea until Easter, so that, at Anthea's request, the split would not have happened before his daughters came home from boarding school for the holidays. He could then tell them himself and move out thereafter. Beth, too, had been concerned about the girls ...

And perhaps if he hadn't found this house quite so soon, or if he had given her a little more time to get to know him, everything would have been different. Instead, in those few months between February and their wedding in June, ambitions apparently united, they had charged blindly into the future like two over-excited, love-sick children.

Standing now in almost the exact spot that she had stood

17

arm in arm with him that spring seven years ago, she looked back across the neat garden to the house, its walls fired by the last brilliant rays of the setting sun. Seven years ago the garden had been little more than an overgrown field, one wall of the house had been crumbling, and part of the slate roof and its rafters had caved in.

'Oh, Lawrie, can we really make anything of this? I've seen cow sheds that look more appealing.'

'The foundations,' he'd said, 'are solid as rock. In a couple of years I can make this one of the most beautiful houses in the district.'

No worries. And seeing the sun reflecting from its windows, it was, she accepted, every bit as lovely as he had promised. A monument to his foresight and determination. It was the foundations of the marriage that had been wrong.

Though she had loved him in the beginning. Had allowed the sun to shine and her bones to melt every time the bastard came into the room.

And she had gone on loving him until this spring. Until May, in Morocco – although perhaps the rot had started with an unexpected visit from Tillotson in April, since which he had seemed preoccupied and distant. She had assumed he was tired and that the holiday in Morocco would bring them together again – but he had complained about the heat and hadn't touched her. And a few days before they were due to fly home, after lunch by the hotel swimming pool, they'd been joined at his invitation by a group of exceptionally attractive dusky-skinned young men and girls.

A hot day even for North Africa; they were all drinking more brandy than coffee and, to any save the blind and the senseless, the mounting tension was unmistakable. She had known who it would be. Had seen the eye contact and the smiles that privately acknowledged, the slight incline of the head that accepted.

'Are you going in for a rest this afternoon?' he had asked, in effect dismissing her. *Do as you're told, sheila* ... There was no resisting that rock-hard stare from those very blue eyes – though in any case, she had felt sick and had been only too glad to escape.

And perhaps, really, she had known it for months. Ever

since the day back in November when she'd gone with him to London and had caught sight of him and Tillotson, giggling, falling all over each other like two schoolboy drunks as they came out of a club in a shady little back alley. Their friendship, it seemed, had been rekindled and had burst into flames. They were partners now in an intimate collusion that had nothing to do with their business interests – but only on that afternoon in Morocco had she realised fully what it was that she had seen, and the extent of it.

She didn't sleep. She was too upset, too disgusted, humiliated, angry and hurt. And when she'd heard him come in about an hour later, she had opened her eyes to see him watching her from the cane chair at the end of the big double bed. His look was much softer. A look that belonged to the Lawrence she had loved. His dark head, tanned shoulders and the dark green ceramic tiles on the floor were patterned with dots of bright sunlight filtering through the shuttered window.

He said, 'I make you very unhappy. I think, perhaps, that you should divorce me.' She sat up, swung her legs over the side of the bed. The room was heavy with heat and her head was throbbing.

'Chuck me that bikini, Lawrence, can you?'

'I thought I was past all this,' he said, not moving. 'That married to you things would be different. That you'd sorted me out for good and always.'

'The black bikini. I'm going for a swim.'

'Do you want to divorce me?'

'I love you,' she said, though she was no longer sure it was true.

'Strange though it may seem, I love you too. I care about you very much.'

'How often does this happen?'

'Not often. And I'm discreet. Never on your doorstep.'

'Marvellous,' she said, fighting to keep back the tears.

'Beth ...'

'Don't tell me. I don't want to hear it! I never want to hear it ... I'm going for a swim!'

Because ignoring it had been the only way she'd known how to cope. *Oh, Lawrie ... Why wasn't I enough?* But he did still care about her. He'd swum with her, his manner apologetic and tender, and later that night in bed he'd held her gently and stroked her hair while she'd wept.

So really, it was very simple. He was kind to her and sensitive to her feelings, so she had accepted it. She had let him live his life his way and, having pushed her feelings to the back of her mind, she had been able to ignore them. Even when Tillotson had come to England to gallop round London with him again in July for the third time in less than a year, she'd pretended that nothing had changed.

And until today, although inside the knowledge and the pretence had steadily torn her apart, it had more or less worked.

It was just that today, finally, something inside her had snapped. She had hated him, and he knew it.

Lying in the trampled grass – the needle, silver against his brown cord trousers; his hands clutching his thigh; his eyes, angry at first, then accusing, then pleading, then wide with disbelief and, finally, as consciousness faded, accepting – until he was staring not at but through her ...

Dear God, though ... He hadn't deserved to die. A divorce would have been enough.

It was an accident, she told herself firmly as in the fading light she looked up at the orchard behind the house and saw the horse grazing peacefully amongst the trees. An accident – and in the end, you did do all you could. *He shouldn't have grabbed you. Shaken you like a rag ...*

Remembering it she realised that her neck was hurting. Pressing her hand against it she thought, *this year I shall be forty-five. Will never now have a child of my own.*

Don't think about it. Forget it. Push it down ...

In any case, it didn't matter. Nothing mattered. As she had lived with his other life, so could she live with his death – and turning, she walked back across the lawn to the house.

In the kitchen she turned on the light. Fetched potatoes from the utility room. Began to peel them for Vivien's supper. Beyond the window night had fallen, its darkness solidified – and once again she was perfectly calm. In fact, apart from a sharp pain in her chest as she breathed, she was comfortably numb. Could feel absolutely nothing.

*

'Poor Granny,' Wanda said, practically tripping over Anthea's heels, so close was she following her down the narrow staircase to the living room. 'I do love her. When you think how she used to be, up at Cloutsham, chasing after the sheep with Gramps, waving that thumbstick, and her hair done up in that red paisley scarf. Her hair was black as anything then, and she was so full of energy. It must be awful for her to be as she is now. Does she always go to bed this early?'

'She was tired tonight,' said Anthea, collecting the remains of the supper things and the cloth from the table to take through to the kitchen.

I am tired tonight, she thought as Wanda followed her.

Clearing a space for the dirty plates amongst the clutter on the kitchen table, she turned on the hot tap to run water into the sink. Wanda, like some huge wilting pot plant, was now leaning against the big Welsh dresser. She never seemed to have the energy to stand up straight. Never stood at all if there was somewhere to drape herself or, better still, to sit or to sprawl. No wonder Viv got annoyed with her.

Though you wouldn't catch Wanda rushing down to comfort that woman at Tivington ... Viv had accepted the divorce and Lawrence's remarriage, and Wanda, whose feelings ran deeper, had not. That was the crux of it.

'Anyway,' Wanda said, 'she did seem to take in the news about Dad. You know – I still don't understand what he was doing trying to cut that colt on his own. Why didn't he get the vet to do it?'

Oh, Wanda, Anthea thought, *not again, please!* Understandably, she'd been talking about her father and had gone over and over his accident all evening, her young voice dull with sadness, reverberating in Anthea's head so that it had begun to throb worse than a generator. Of all the days Anthea had longed to see her daughters, and all the evenings she had often longed for company, what she most longed for tonight was space in order to get her own thoughts into some sort of perspective.

'I know he'd cut colts before, but that was years ago in Australia – and why here with plenty of good vets near by? And why was he doing it on his own?'

'You may well ask.'

'He must have known it was dangerous.'

'Of course.'

She placed the last of the plates to drip dry in the old wooden drainer on the wall above the sink, tossed Wanda a tea towel, and began to wash the animals' feeding pans she'd brought in from the yard.

'You'll miss him too, I expect.'

'I lost him years ago.'

'I know, but you always knew where he was if you needed him.'

'I wasn't in the habit of ringing him to come over and change the light bulbs, Wanda.'

'No – but suddenly he's just not going to be there. Not anywhere.'

'Look, pet, I'm sorry,' she said, her head pounding, her patience suddenly exhausted. 'I know you're upset, but it's not only Gran who's tired tonight and I do have to get up early in the morning. We'll have plenty of time to talk now you're not going back until after the funeral. And look – Mary will be in to clean tomorrow, so I'll be going shopping. Why don't you go over to Tivington? I can drop you off on my way to Minehead and Viv can bring you back later.'

Go over there and talk to them about him, Wanda – please ...?

'Oh – you know Viv. She'll have everything running like clockwork. She won't want me there.'

'All the same, I think you should offer,' Anthea said, drying her hands, red and parboiled from the too-hot water, she walked over to the door. 'Whether or not you go over there, you should at least ring up and offer. And you ought to have a word with her anyway. The woman ... Beth.'

'Where are you going?' asked Wanda as Anthea took her faded blue quilter anorak off its peg.

'To shut up the geese.' Aware of the panic in Wanda's voice, she added, 'I won't be long. Ring Viv and I'll be back.'

Outside on the doorstep she pulled the door shut behind her and let go of her tension in a sigh. The cool night air began to soothe her. It tasted of damp heather and of moss, and behind the house in the trees by the pond she could hear the gentle flutterings of a dove.

22

Then slowly she started to walk across the lawn towards the gate in the garden wall. She would not be going to the funeral. The girls would nag and kick up a fuss – but she'd already made up her mind. And Lawrie would have known why she wasn't going.

Perhaps he does know, she thought. Even now ... Because, for a moment, as she paused by the gate and looked into the darkness under the lilac trees, she had the strangest feeling ...

Then, chiding herself for being as daft as her mother, she opened the gate and walked on up the path.

Don't go, Wanda pleaded, watching the door close. As the latch clicked into place she remembered the nights as a kid when, lying awake and alone in the darkness, her small world had suddenly seemed to expand into a vast black void in which she'd either had to scream out for a drink of water as an excuse for a cuddle, or hang on as tight as she could to Harold, her big blue teddy bear.

'Oh, grow up, Wanda,' she muttered aloud. Viv was always telling her to grow up, so maybe she was right.

And she supposed she had better phone her.

She was glad to be here tonight rather than at her bedsit in Taunton. She felt safe in this house, even if it was chaotic and, despite Mary's twice-weekly efforts, none too clean. The cracks and tears in the lino on the kitchen floor – as much as you could see of it for the pots, pans, animal-food sacks and ironing waiting for attention – were black with grime – and probably worse, given the livestock that wandered in and out.

Her room in Taunton wasn't up to much, but at least it was clean and tidy. Realising she must take after her father who had always liked things to be neat and orderly, she wondered how much the domestic chaos might have had to do with his leaving. This whole house – old-fashioned, over-furnished, albeit it mostly with good antiques, and every room in need of a good coat of paint – was as different from his immaculate renovated house at Tivington as was Mum from Beth. Mum had reserved all her energy for the yard and the land – which were always immaculate – while in the house, only the drawing-room, kept for best, was anything like respectable.

In fact, this house was a bit like living in a bubble where

time had stopped – while out in the yard, down in the village and beyond, the months and the years had ticked relentlessly on.

And for Daddy, living in that house at Tivington, the years had raced – although the thought that he might die had just never occurred to her. Not yet. Mum whose hair had turned grey after he left, looked older than he had – and it wasn't much of a life for her here, especially since a slight stroke had turned dear old Granny into little more than a loveable but barely mobile cabbage.

Everyone I have ever loved is growing old or dying – and I can't relate at all to my sarcastic bloody sister, she thought. *Though I suppose I'd better phone her ...*

Moving away from the dresser she went through to the cosy living room that smelt of wood smoke from the large open fire. Whether or not the fire was lit the whole house always smelt comfortingly of wood smoke and it was the one smell above all others that she associated with home. This room always had a good feeling too – and somehow, in here, she seemed to feel closer to her father.

Needing to hold on to the closeness, she sat down on the arm of what had been his chair. It wasn't so long ago that she'd found him again. Almost five years she'd wasted, feeling hurt and rejected for Mum, refusing to see him any more than she had to, keeping every conversation as short as possible. And then, when she'd at last relented and agreed to meet up with him for a drink in a pub one day when he had come to Taunton, it had been like walking out into sunlight. Like meeting a new friend, yet in essence they had already known each other so well. She could say anything to Dad ...

The pity was that she had wasted those first five years.

'Why do some people die when they're young?' she'd asked Gran once, oh, light years ago.

'We don't die, child. We pass into spirit. God calls each one of us when the time is right for us to begin our work for Him in the life that comes after. That is, the next level of our spiritual development.'

Gran had always been keen on the spiritual, though she'd rarely gone to church. Instead, she'd sort of lived it ...

'Don't we get a rest then, even when we die?'

And Gran had laughed. 'A rest? You don't know what work is yet, young Wanda. Have you any idea what you want to do when you grow up?'

'No,' she'd said, and wise beyond her years, added, 'but I expect I'll know when the time is right and I get there.'

'Right on,' Dad suddenly seemed to say inside her head, as if agreeing with her.

You'll have to show me.

'*I intend to, young Wanda. I intend to.*'

She did feel close to him. Incredibly close ... closer, perhaps, right now, than she had ever felt. As if, now, he was part of her – and gradually she began to realise that her feelings of emptiness and loss had been replaced by a glow of peace and wellbeing.

From where Anthea was standing on the path that led up to the moor she could see away over the trees that bordered the drive to the far side of the valley – and in the house at Tivington lights were shining from two downstairs windows and, from a window above, there was just a glimmer.

Like hope ... Because, regardless of what she had allowed everyone else to think, she had never given up hope that he might tire of his fancy woman and come home to her. Moreover, given time, she was fairly sure that he would have.

And little over a month ago he had come to see her ...

She'd been hosing the yard when the white Range Rover had turned in through the gate and, her heart beating faster, she'd turned off the tap and watched him drive towards her, and wind down the window.

'Is that Percy?' he'd asked, eyeing the geese which were approaching noisily from the direction of the pond in order to inspect the vehicle and its occupant. 'He's very lame.' And, taking his time, as though expecting any second to be sent packing, he opened the car door, stepped down into the yard, and answered her unspoken question. 'I was just passing, so I thought I'd look in.'

Passing? Up a track that ended in a wood? He'd never called in other than at Christmas to see the girls.

'The girls aren't here.'

'I didn't think they would be, no.' He leant against the

25

Range Rover and folded his arms. He looked very together in his brown twill trousers, checked shirt and plain crimson wool tie under a green waxed cotton jacket. But he did look tired.

'Are you ill?'

'No. Why? Do I look it?'

'You're thinner.'

'Ah, that's healthy eating,' he said, patting his stomach.

Oh, right – so the food I gave you was poisonous. All the same, I seem to remember you usually had a second helping.

'You haven't come round here for a good square meal then.'

'No. I just thought I'd look in and say hello.'

Lying devil – you never did anything without a reason, and quite often there were at least two. But he had fixed her with his dark blue eyes, and she had to look away. Looked down at the yard broom to which she was holding on tightly with both hands.

'Have you seen the girls lately?' she asked.

'I've seen Wanda.'

'All black and white like a minstrel. Have you seen that squat she lives in?'

'She's happy with it. She tells me her arm's mended well.'

'Yes, well don't you going buying another car for her this time. Last time she broke her arm. Next time it might be her neck. You won't, will you?'

'Not yet.'

'You spoil her.'

'No worries. I don't see enough of her to do any harm.'

'There's more black on that child than there was on old Grandmother Kenworthy in her widowed dotage.'

He laughed, 'Aah, it's just a stage she's going through. She'll come right.' He looked down at the geese that had stopped the furious honking they used to warn of strangers and were now standing in a semicircle around his feet. 'Just the three of them these days, is it? So who have we here?'

'Percy, Gertie and Petal.'

'The last of the feathered Mohicans. That gander really is lame. What's the matter with him?'

'Reg Pugsley backed into him with the truck and the leg never mended properly. He has arthritis in it now. And he's blind in one eye.'

'Umm – well, in a manner of speaking, aren't we all.'

She laughed with him and, feeling more at ease, curious and ridiculously full of hope as to why he had come to see her, she had asked him in for a cup of tea.

'Reg Pugsley comes up to lend a hand occasionally then, does he?'

'He came up to fix the barn door. It blew off its hinges in the autumn gales.'

They were walking through the living room to the kitchen, and as he followed her she sensed rather than saw him looking around. She had guessed what he was thinking.

Everything is just as it was when you left, Lawrie. No extra members of the household. Unfortunately for me, fool that I am, I'm still in love with you. The only shirts in the ironing are the ones you left behind. I'm wearing them out. Wearing them to feel closer to you ...

'I sold some bullocks for Reg a couple of months ago. Got a good price for them too. Matter of fact, I rather thought he'd have had his feet under your table long before now.'

'Reggie's feet under my table would have eased your conscience, would it? If you have a conscience. Tea – or would you rather have whisky?'

'Bit early. Better not. Anthea – I didn't come here just to stickybeak.'

He'd pulled out a chair and sat down at the table while she made the tea. Proper tea; leaves in a pot, not bags full of what he used to complain was plantation dust. She wanted it to be right for him. At Christmas she always made sure there was a bottle of his favourite whisky in the cupboard for his visits, though she'd rather have died than admit it.

'So,' she said, her heart still beating too fast as she fussed with the tea things. 'Why did you come here?'

'I'm very fond of you, Anthea. I like to know you're all right.'

Fond. A limp, lukewarm affection, probably born out of conscience and sired, at best, by regret. The disappointment rose into her throat and made her cough. Seeing him sitting there – his feet very firmly under her table again – fond was no relation to the love she still felt for him.

'I like to know the three of you are safe and well,' he said.

'I did offer to pay Wanda's rent on a decent flat you know, but she won't hear of it. And I suppose Viv's not doing too badly. She could do better if she worked for me, of course ... But how about you – are you all right for money?'

'Is that why you came here?' she said, looking at him, her throat tight with anger now as well as disappointment. 'To offer me money?'

'Not unless you want it. But if you do there's plenty in the bank, so it would be silly for you to go short.'

'Lawrence,' she said, and thumped the milk jug down on the table, 'I don't want your money. I don't want your damned money!' she hissed. 'When did I take anything from you other than this house and the land that was my settlement, and the maintenance you paid for the girls?'

'You didn't. And I admire your independence. As to what you've done with the farm – that is amazing.'

'Thanks. So why are you here then? You might as well tell me. Whatever it is I expect I can stand the shock.'

Dumping the tarnished silver sugar bowl on the table in front of him and wishing she'd had time to clean it, look out the best cups, clear the clutter off the table, she sat down opposite him to wait for his reply.

'Could you? I wonder ...' He looked at the battered cardboard box by the Rayburn. 'More kittens ... Which cat do they belong to?'

'Mopsa.'

'You've changed, Anthea. Toughened up.'

'Yes, well. After you left, I had to.'

'Some of us never change. That can be the problem.'

To avoid looking at him she had looked at the kittens. He sipped his tea, then he said, 'There might be a problem in Australia. Still, if we have to sell up out there you for one would be glad to see the family ties broken for good and all.' He shook his head wearily. 'Oh Anthea – it's nothing new. Nothing you or anyone else can do anything about. Nor am I ill, thank God. In fact, since you ask, I did think I might need a medical, so a couple of weeks ago I had a good going over at a hospital while I was in London. They tell me I'm fit as a flea. Perhaps, if you need a reason for me coming to see you, it's exactly that. I'm fit as a flea, and damned grateful.'

28

So what is it then? Marriage on the rocks? All other possibilities having been eliminated, it had to be – though she couldn't bring herself to ask him outright. He'd have denied it anyway. She knew him and his pride.

You can come home Lawrie, she thought, meeting his eyes. He was fond of her. Just fond. But she could have lived with that – and the hope that, once again, it would grow into more.

In all, that afternoon he had stayed for just over an hour, and when he got up to leave her sense of impending loss was as strong as it had ever been.

'You're a good soul, Anthea. Thank you for listening,' he'd said as they'd walked down the steps from the front door to the yard. The geese had gathered round him again and had begun to squawk. 'Noisy bloody things, crapping everywhere. I don't know why you don't put the lot of them in the pot and be done with it.'

'They're pets. Especially Percy,' she said, suddenly close to tears, although she knew full well he never had been able to abide the geese.

'Sorry, I forgot. Yes, I know they are. Sorry.' He patted her arm and let his hand rest there. 'Good old Anthea, champion of lost causes, me included. Actually, you deserve better than me.'

You can come home, Lawrie, warts and all. Though yet again she didn't say it. And he had squeezed her arm, turned away and got into the Range Rover.

He never had come home ... And now he never would.

'You would like me to come over tomorrow, then,' Wanda said into the telephone.

'Yes I would. There's so much to arrange. The funeral, the hymns, the bank – and what we should do with that horse. So many people have got to be contacted. God – what time is it? I said I'd call Graham Lang. He was Dad's friend as well as his solicitor, so I guess he won't mind – and he does work from home.'

'How's Beth?'

'Incredible ... She's even cooked me a three-course dinner. It's me who's wobbly. Poor Daddy ... I just can't believe it.'

Daddy ...? Viv hadn't called him that in years. Nor had

there been any sign of the usual grudging impatience that entered Viv's voice as soon as she knew it was Wanda on the line.

'As a matter of interest, Wanda, when did you last see Dad?'

'Last week. I met him for a drink after work. Why?'

'I just wondered. I wish I'd made more of an effort to see him.'

Was this Viv? She was usually so certain, so forceful, so cutting.

'Yes, well. He never pushed and badgered me like he did you.'

'No he didn't,' Viv agreed gratefully. 'All the same, I am upset.'

'I can tell you are.'

'Well, aren't you?'

'Of course I am.' But for some reason she also felt extremely peaceful.

'I wish to God I'd called him just half as often as you did. I'll come and see Gran while I'm down here.' Wanda heard her hesitate and then she said, 'Look, Wanda ... I know this sounds odd, but, well ... I think you're an idle slob, and just about everything you like and stand for I hate – but funnily enough, I am fond of you.'

'You *are* gutted. Well gutted.'

'Well – aren't you quite fond of me?'

'I always have been.'

'Thanks. It's good to know that. Thanks a lot.'

'I'll see you tomorrow, then,' Wanda said, as eyebrows raised she replaced the phone. Hell, Viv was feeling vulnerable. None of this sounded like her at all.

Anthea had walked on up the grassy path through the gorse and the heather and out on to the moor at the top of the hill. Both Lawrie and Anthony had loved these moors.

'So this is where Anthony grew up,' he had said one evening in the garden at Cloutsham soon after he'd come to England. 'It's a bit of beaut country. No wonder he was always talking about his home and his family. And you ... He talked about you all the time. When I saw you ... You are very like him. Male and female, but two peas in a pod. The likeness is amazing.'

30

She didn't agree. Anthony, blond and slight of build, had been a far better-looking man than she, stockier and with coarser features, was for a woman. Though she had been grateful and not a little flattered, and something in the way Lawrie had looked at her when he'd said it, his intensely blue eyes hurting at the loss of his friend, had made her decide that for as long as he was around she'd put on a skirt of an evening and perhaps just a touch of make-up.

Strange, the things you remembered ...

'Anthony said you were devastated when he went to Australia.'

'I never thought he would go,' she said. 'Not when it came to it.'

'You were good mates.'

'We were inseparable.'

'Well – how about me as a stop gap? I've never had a sister, but we could give it a try.'

'We could give it a try,' she'd agreed, laughing.

And, to her surprise, the friendship had flourished and had grown into more. He'd started the business, just the one office in Minehead at first, and soon after that they had married and bought this farmhouse and the few acres that went with it. Nine months, almost to the day after the wedding, Vivien had arrived – though, naturally, it was all perfectly proper and right side of the blanket. And a few years later Wanda had come along to make them a family of four.

A happy family. And if it hadn't been for that woman across the valley who had bewitched him, they would have continued to be so.

I never will know how she managed it, Lawrie, she thought, because, you and I, we were like brother and sister, and above all else, we were such good friends.

Graham Lang, stretched out on the sofa in the living room at the back of the house, rolled over lazily and reached for the telephone.

'Vivien Seligman ...? Yes, of course I remember you. No, you're not disturbing me. I'm only listening to music.'

Then as she began to tell him, he sat up and planted his feet firmly on the floor to steady himself. Christ ... He'd had lunch with Lawrie just a couple of days ago, and next week they'd arranged to play golf.

He disentangled the stereo headphones from his neck and threw them on to the coffee table. 'No, the Australian partnership has always been dealt with by solicitors in London. Yes, your father's will is in my office.'

It was habit that made him twist round for a pencil on the shelf above one of the stereo speakers, then lean forward to make notes on a corner of the *Daily Telegraph*. He dealt with this sort of thing quite often in the course of his work though, thank God, until now the death had never been that of a personal friend.

'No, I think that covers it for the moment. I'll see you and Beth tomorrow. Yes ... Anytime after two o'clock. I'm in court until lunchtime. Is there anything else I can do? Would you like me to phone the Australian business partner for you? No, of course not – no trouble at all. I'll be glad to. Anything ... My God, Vivien – I am so sorry. Yes ... All right – I'll see you tomorrow.'

Deo volente, he thought as he picked up the telephone and replaced it on the coffee table. Then he pulled both his hands down over his face. Christ ... Lawrence Seligman scythed down by the ghoul in the black-hooded cloak. He'd been a bloody good bloke had Lawrence. Graham had lost a damned good friend.

Viv dumped her holdall on the bed, laid her briefcase on the desk and looked around the room. Her room – that was almost identical to Wanda's which faced west on the other side of the corridor. Rooms which, like the rest of the house, had been done out predominantly in a very pale peach colour by a firm of interior designers. If her bedroom seemed somewhat soulless, that, like so much else in her relationship with her father, was nobody's fault but her own.

He had tried, and so had Beth – but in all the time her father and stepmother had lived here, Vivien had contributed just two of her own belongings. On almost her first weekend visit she'd brought a practically new, and therefore not all that well-liked furry rabbit to sit amongst the slightly twee coordinated cushions on the wide pine bed. And on the wall above the desk she'd hung a framed photograph of Dad as a young man in Australia. Dad, standing beside a small flimsy biplane, holding a gold and crimson head collar presented to a horse called The Wild Chancer, the first winner of a big race for Tarran Hills Stud.

It was, she realised looking at it now, a photograph of Lawrence The Achiever and, although she had forgotten its existence, she remembered how forcefully, as a child, it had inspired her to be like him.

The room felt chilly and, turning away from the photograph, she went over to close the window. The outside light was on and down in the yard she noticed the back of his white Range Rover parked in the barn where, presumably, he had left it at lunchtime.

The Range Rover he'd bought the year he'd married Beth had been olive green. He and Beth had arrived in it for sports' day at the school where Viv and Wanda boarded in Oxfordshire. Viv had been furious for having to drop out of the fifteen hundred metres halfway round – thus making a right fool of herself in front of his new wife.

'How much training did you do?' he'd said, spotting the problem immediately.

'Never mind, Lawrie,' Beth said. 'It's only a race.'

'How much training?' he insisted.

'Okay, okay. Not much.'

'Right on. So shoulder the responsibilities for your own failures and understand that if you want success, you've got to work for it. Do the training!'

I wish I'd worked at our relationship, she thought. *But I didn't, so I'll have to accept that too.*

'I don't nag you for fun, you know, sheila,' he'd said to her once. 'You're a kid packed with potential, and if you work, anything you want badly enough you'll get.'

He nagged me, but he did it with the very best of intentions, she thought as she closed the window. And when she had drawn the curtains she looked again at the photograph. *I never realised ... Never stopped to think. And thus I hardly knew him ... Never gave myself chance, and I certainly never knew him as one adult knows another, or as a friend.*

In fact, as to why she'd been in such a hurry to get down

to Tivington, she had no idea. There was nothing of him for her here. All her memories of him were at Luccombe while she'd still been just a child.

Still, he would have been the first to say that it was no good worrying about the past – and turning away she wandered back across the room to sit down at the small modern desk he'd provided for each of their bedrooms on the assumption that, as part of their school holidays would be spent here, they would need somewhere to study.

Dear God though, if she'd had to come down here tonight and tell him about her promised promotion at Thane's, there'd have been hell to pay.

Life without him was going to need some adjusting, though it would, at last, be a life that was her own. Reaching for her briefcase, she took out the job application form.

A mere formality Thane had assured her, but as she hadn't yet had time to fill in the paperwork, she might as well do it now while Beth was still in the bath.

Remembering that Wanda would be waiting, Anthea started back down the path. Friends. Just friends, but his second marriage was dead and, given time, having come home, he'd have learnt to love her again. She was sure of it.

Why had the woman allowed him to try to castrate that horse on his own? And why, since she was a nurse and had been in the orchard when it happened, hadn't she been able to save him ...?

Or maybe, as the marriage was rocky, she had wanted it to happen.

Maybe – just maybe – it was murder.

The path was steeper here, and having stopped to glare at the house across the valley, she walked on. The geese, three white almost luminous bundles, were asleep at the foot of the haystack outside the paddock wall.

'Come on then, Percy, my pet,' she said to him quietly as she approached. 'We don't want the foxes to get you.'

There'd been enough sadness today ...

Such an elderly little trio they are now, she thought, as one by one they rose to their full height, stretched, flapped their wings, and waddled ahead of her down the path in the

34

starlight. Poor half-blind Percy moved with a gait that was a mixture of limp and precarious roll, and even Petal, the youngest and latest addition to the flock, had long since forgotten what life looked like from inside an egg.

'Oi!'

The geese had reached the place where a large gorse bush overhung the path, and suddenly, for no reason at all, Gertie had twisted her neck, clattered her beak, and landed Petal a hefty peck on the wing.

'Stop that,' Anthea said as the two geese continued to hiss at each other. 'What's the matter with you?'

Gertie was usually such an easy-going old bird – but having pulled up a bracken frond Anthea swished it at their twitching tails feathers and urged them past the gorse bush and on down the path.

It was easier walking here, and Anthea again looked across the valley. There were lights at only the upstairs windows at Tivington now and, with every step she took, the house gradually disappeared below the line of the trees.

Bitch ...

She might very well have murdered him ...

Tillotson finished his breakfast cup of coffee, picked up his wide-brimmed hat and his grip and went out on to the verandah, allowing the fly door to slam shut behind him. A long time ago Lawrie would have been walking beside him. Would have been coming with him to the city. A long time ago ... Even so, the news of his death had settled in Tillotson's stomach as a raw lump.

In the distance the Tarran Hills showed blue through the early mist, and the path, the lawn, and the stretch of grass beyond the white fence where the plane was waiting, were silvered with dew. *Jeeze*, he thought, *spring is no time to die. I hope to Christ I don't chuck in my chips in the spring.*

'I'm booked to come to England in November, but there's no way I can make it to the funeral,' he'd said to the solicitor who had phoned. 'No way can I leave here right now.'

Hearing the echo of his words, waiting for them to be deflected by satellite to the other side of the world, he'd been struck by the irony of the situation. Not this spring.

Not yet. But he was ill now and, all things considered, had expected to die years before Lawrie.

'No, no,' the solicitor said, 'I'm sure no one expects you to attend the funeral. Lawrence would have understood that.'

And the delayed reply, faint and hollow, had seemed to taunt him from the depths of eternity. Too right – Lawrie wouldn't have expected him to be at the funeral. On a personal level, Lawrie had expected nothing. It was he, Tillotson, who had made the demands – though after young Anthony Kenworthy died, Lawrie just hadn't been that interested in anyone or anything.

He put on his hat and considered his responsibilities to the widow. He would have to talk to her. Keep her abreast of what was happening here – and talking to her might not be so easy. He wondered what she was like, and how much she knew – about his friendship with Lawrie, as well as their business affairs.

Still, first things first, and he dropped his cigarette, ground it out with the heel of his boot and walked down the steps of the verandah. He had business to see to in Sydney, and while he was there an appointment at the clinic which, if the treatment zapped him as hard as it had the first time, would keep him in bed there for damned nigh a week.

I'll write to the widow, he thought as he walked out across the grass to the plane. *Tell her how sorry I am and suggest we meet when I'm over in November. The state she'll be in, that will be soon enough. Whatever else, I must talk to her about the future of the ranches.*

'Good night.'

Looking up from her desk Vivien saw Beth, wrapped in a long pale green bathrobe and flushed from her bath, standing in the doorway.

'Okay?'

'Fine.'

Yes, she really did seem to be. As calm and immaculate as always. Like most natural redheads her skin was always quite pale and she actually looked better for a bit of colour. So much for the weeping widow ...

The grapevine was working even better than she'd expected

36

and late as it now was, several people had phoned while Beth was in the bathroom. Amongst them had been Harding the vet who, devastated, had offered to look after the horse until its future was decided, and Mayhew, Beth's doctor. He'd heard the news when he'd stopped to fill up with petrol on his way home from a meeting, and had called to offer tranquillizers and sleeping pills and to say he'd drop by in the morning – though the way Beth was taking this, none of those things would be necessary.

'Good night, Beth. Sleep well. If you don't, give me a shake and I'll keep you company.'

She'll sleep. She'll be fine, Viv thought. *She doesn't really need me at all. I'll go over and see them at Luccombe, and as the funeral isn't until next week I might even go back to work for a couple of days. On the way I could spend a night with Robin. Beth is just fine.*

Except for her eyes ...

Which were brown, blank and staring.

Utterly dead.

My God, Vivien thought, realising it, *I'd better stay here then.*

Shock, she supposed, though she hoped Beth wasn't saving it all to freak out in the bank or somewhere.

Or worse still, at the funeral ...

Chapter Two

All Beth could feel was the pressure of her hands locked tightly together and pressed into the top of the pew in front of her. All she could see was the long beige box on its stools in the aisle.

In it was a body. Just a body. A lifeless male Caucasian dressed in a dark grey suit and cushioned by white satin quilting.

Above the box was the lectern; a vicious-looking carved wooden eagle, its head turned towards the congregation, its beak seemingly agape in an eternal, silent, and accusing scream.

But the body in the box had born little resemblance to Lawrence. And she'd be fine when this service was over. Nor could it last much longer.

In fact, even as she thought it, the vicar, clad in his pure white surplice, rose to his feet.

But turning to face the congregation, he looked directly at her – then opened his arms to form a human crucifix.

Anthea was glad she had refused to attend the funeral. From her vantage point at the edge of the wood on the hill behind the churchyard, she saw the six dark-suited pall bearers carry the coffin out into the sunlight. Watched the vicar and the family emerge behind them and start up the tarmac path; a sad tableau in black, white and grey, punctuated by the soft yellow-brown of the coffin, its wreath of red flowers, and the bitch's mane of bright carroty hair.

A stream of mourners left the church at a respectful distant behind and followed them up the path to walk between the headstones and gather around the cavern that had been prepared for him. The little church must have been packed, though Anthea wasn't surprised. There were his business colleagues and his acquaintances as well as his friends. Friends who, at one time, had been her friends as well. Divorce was so divisive. Affected loyalties way beyond the immediate family. Many of those people down there would have been in that same church on the day of her wedding. Had thrown the rice that had stung, so that, laughing, holding on to her arm, Lawrence had held out his top hat to shield her – and pretending that it hid them from the world, he had kissed her.

'You are,' he had said, holding her hand in the back of the car as they were driven home to Cloutsham for the reception in a marquee on the lawn, 'my saviour. My normality, my sanity, my lifeline.'

And until you walked out, Lawrie, I thought you were mine.

She watched the pall bearers lower him carefully into the ground, and the faint murmur of prayers drifted up to her on the warm afternoon air. Then, led by the family who took up a position by the lynchgate, the mourners began to file away from the graveside and, anxious to get on with their lives, were already leaving the churchyard and getting into their cars. No matter how long or how full a life a man had had, the disposal of his remains wasn't allowed to take long – less time in fact than it took each week for the council to empty the village dustbins. Concealed from general view by the church porch, two elderly grave diggers leaning on their shovels, were sharing a cigarette until the coast was clear and they too could finish for the afternoon and go home.

Kind, shy Graham Lang was waiting beside his beloved navy blue Daimler Dart parked by the churchyard wall. There'd been a time when she and his ex-wife Stella had been friends, and the four of them had gone to dances or to the cinema together. She hadn't seen Graham to speak to since the day Lawrie had remarried.

An indifferent June day, too bright too early – and Graham, trussed up in a dark blue suit too tight across the beer gut he'd developed since Stella had left him, had come up to the farm to collect the girls. Such a muddle. To have and to hold from this day forward until parted by death – but some people seemed to change partners as easily as the bands at those dances had changed tunes. And later, when she'd heard the church clock at Luccombe strike eleven, she had paused and let go of the sheep she'd been shearing, knowing that in the Registry Office in town he was repeating his broken promises to her to somebody else.

'The food was amazing,' Vivien had said later when Graham brought them home. 'Didn't you think it was good, Graham?'

'The food was good, yes,' he said, embarrassed.

Flushed with champagne, she was testing her eyes on her father's unmarried friend something wicked. She'd grown up very fast those past few months, had young Viv.

'She was all frothed up in a cream dress,' said Wanda, glaring at her sister. 'She looked like a meringue. That, or a Sindy doll.'

And Graham, embarrassed and hurting because he well knew how it felt to be dumped, had accepted a cup of tea as a matter of duty, drunk it quickly, and left.

By then Lawrence and the bitch were already on their way to Spain – and she had tried not to think of her own honeymoon in Wales. The miles tramped, often in companionable silence, the mountain scenery, the lush greens of the valleys. It would be hot in Spain, and she'd sincerely hoped that the sun would scorch the bitch's fair skin to a cinder.

Down in the road the last of the mourners were now walking away, and the family was getting into the long black limousine. Doors closed, the starter motor whined, and Anthea watched the car slide forward, come towards the school, and stop at the junction. In the few seconds before the limousine pulled out into St. George's Street and drove out of sight, she had a clear view of the bitch through the car's window; the face, white; the expression, haunted. A soul in torment ...

Perhaps she had murdered him.

Or perhaps it was merely that now she too knew how it felt to lose him.

'I need to talk to you,' he'd said, the February night, dark as pitch and raining stair rods, that he'd come home soaked to the skin from Cutcombe sheep sales. 'I'll pour us a whisky.'

He'd had a skinful already by the smell of him – and, seated opposite her beside the big log fire, he'd told her that the marriage was over, that he wanted a divorce, that he'd met someone else and wanted to marry her.

'You're drunk ...'

'I've had a few, but I know what I'm saying.'

It's the way that you're saying it, Lawrie, your voice harsh, your eyes too pale and hard as granite. This isn't you ...

'I know it's a shock,' he continued, 'And believe me it's in no way your fault. It's just one of those things. I'll see you right financially. Neither you nor the girls will go short. I just want a divorce.'

'Lawrie ...?'

'Please – for the sake of what we used to feel for each other, don't make me fight you.'

Used to feel? I still feel!

'Anthea, I have got to marry her.'

'Got to ...? You haven't slept with her. She's not pregnant ...?'

Him – with another woman? It wasn't possible. He wasn't that interested in women, and he'd never been that interested in that side of marriage any more than she had. Their marriage, based on friendship, went far deeper than sex.

'She's not pregnant,' he said.

'So you have slept with her,' she said, stunned.

'She's not pregnant,' he insisted, looking away. 'But I have to be with her. I need to be with her. She is everything I have ever wanted in a woman and with her I know I am truly a man.'

'I see.'

So I, then, am something less than a woman? What? A pair of shears that cut off your balls? Then suddenly, realising he meant every word he was saying, the bottom seemed to drop out of her world.

'Drink your whisky,' he said.

'What's her name?'

'You don't know her. She lives in London.'

'What's her name!'

'Beth. Elspeth. Elspeth Renolds.'

Elspeth Renolds – the woman who'd bewitched him. He did

41

look possessed ... Half demented. And then she remembered his visits to London when she'd assumed he was meeting Tillotson who had apparently stayed in England longer than usual. And since then, his restlessness and the sleepless nights when, innocent that she was, she'd thought he was worried about an increase in the mortgage rates he'd mentioned for the Barrington Heights ranch. Night after night she had got up in the cold and gone downstairs to make him cocoa. It had never occurred to her that it might be another woman. It was work, striking deals, making money, that turned his world.

'Where in London?'

'Oh, Anthea, really – does it matter where?'

'Yes!'

Of course it mattered! She'd wanted to know it all. Needed to know every minute, apparently useless fact, so that, somewhere amongst it all, she might identify something that would help her begin to understand how this had come about. Yet at the same time she couldn't bear to hear any of it, and when he began to tell her, forgetting that she was holding the glass of whisky, she covered her ears.

'I'm sorry,' he said, picking up the glass that had fallen on the hearth rug. 'But I have to be with her. It's a matter of my survival.'

She stared at him. A dream; it was a dream. In a minute she'd wake in a muck sweat and find herself in bed with him sleeping peacefully beside her.

'Have a sip of this,' he'd said gently, putting his glass in her hand.

She took a sip, and felt the liquid sting her throat. It wasn't a dream. Not even a nightmare. She felt sick, but had been far too shocked to cry.

'I'm sorry,' he said again.

'So am I. I don't think I can live without you.'

'Yes you can. You're stronger than you realise.'

You were right, she thought, looking down at the flower-covered oblong of turf in the now deserted churchyard. *I survived and you are dead – but nothing I achieved after you left was for me or the children. I did it to make you proud of me, and in that, at least, maybe I did succeed.*

The church clock chimed, and she looked across at the

tower. Glory ... Three-thirty. She'd left Gran on her own and any minute she'd wake from her nap and be wanting her tea.

I'll come and see you again, she told him silently, and wiping her eyes with her hands she turned away and jumped down the bank. She'd been right not to go to the funeral. Had known she would make a fool of herself in the church with the prayers and the music. She'd cried in that church at their wedding – and he had been mortified.

What happened to us Lawrie, she wondered yet again as she walked back through the woods to where she had parked her car out of sight in the lane. *That bitch – what was it she gave you that I couldn't?*

And, in the end, what did she do to you ...?

Could it have been murder ...?

Remembering the haunted expression on the face in the back of the limousine, she realised that it should have evoked the deepest sympathy for a human being so obviously in torment. Yet somehow it had made her feel angry and inexplicably aggressive.

As she drove home faster than was wise through the lanes, the aggression stayed with her, and the image of that white face seemed to have indelibly printed itself on her brain.

So this was a wake. To Wanda it had seemed more like a bloody cattle market. A crowd of people, supposedly Dad's friends, talking and laughing at the tops of their voices while pigging back sandwiches and pissing themselves out of their brains on his booze. If this was the way the human race demonstrated its grief for a friend she was ashamed to belong to it and, for most of the afternoon, had distanced herself by curling up on the window seat where, hugging her knees, she'd concentrated on the view down the valley to the distant strip of sea.

She'd passed much of her time doing just this when she'd been obliged to come to this house as a child. Because from here she could also see the roofs of Mum's farm at Luccombe, and it had made her feel closer to home and, somehow, less disloyal.

The room had gone quiet since most people had left, though at the far end, propped up against the fireplace, Viv's chap

43

Robin, and Graham Lang, were continuing to demolish a bottle of Bell's while still deep in conversation. And Beth, with a cup of tea, had come over to the window to stand behind her.

'I could never get tired of the view down that valley,' Wanda said without turning round.

'Umm. Wonderful.'

She hadn't enjoyed this shindig much either. Wanda could sense the misery and tension in her as surely as her nose would have picked up a strong perfume.

'Will you be all right living here on your own?'

'Yes. I'll be fine.'

'I'll come and see you sometimes if you like.'

'That would be nice.'

Would it? She turned to look up at Beth, but her expression was hard to read. *She doesn't believe I'll come anyway*, Wanda thought. *But I ought to. Better late than never ... She's like this house; a bit too controlled, too tidy, too perfect – and there's something about the way she is now that frightens me. But I must come.*

Beth had tried very hard to be kind when they were kids. She seemed to know how kids ticked; the things that made them feel good and where they liked to go, what they liked to eat, that sort of thing – and she always did her best to deliver. One exeat from school she'd made Dad take them to the zoo because Wanda had needed to go there for some project or other that she was working on – but because it was Beth who'd got Dad to agree, she had made herself sick. Had deliberately spewed up all over Beth's beautiful brown cashmere coat.

Shit – I was an awkward little git. I'm surprised she still talks to me.

I'll have to come and see her.

But for the moment Beth seemed tired and was probably quite ready for them to leave. As Viv came back into the room Wanda pulled her long skirt clear of her buttoned ankle boots and lowered her feet to the floor.

'All done,' Viv said, joining them by the window. 'I've just left you to turn on the dishwasher.'

'I could have cleared up after you'd gone, Vivien.'

44

'No worries. Now you can put your feet up.' Looking across at the men who had just refilled their glasses, Viv lowered her voice. 'My God, the Grey Ham is still talking ... Hasn't he got a home to go to? We mustn't be too long. Mum's expecting us for supper at seven.'

It was five to seven already, but Viv would say when to go. Albeit with less stridency than usual, Viv had arranged today's programme and had taken charge of everything for the entire week that she had been here.

'I'm telling you,' Graham was saying to Robin, 'cross one of those moor people and you might as well be dead. Butlin's sprawl has transformed the marshes behind Minehead seafront, and over the years you architect chappies have helped to put up a couple of trading estates and a fair amount of new housing – some that blend in with the local sandstone and the thatched cottages, some that don't. And the people are the same. Good people, and my God, they can endure, but you'll never change their thinking or the West Country character. Canny, proud – and faced with newcomers, there's always suspicion. An inborn wariness that some smart Alec from the city might get one over on them. Even these days some of them have never been as far as Taunton, and they never want to. Basically there are two entirely separate communities here – locals and newcomers – and there always will be.'

'S'truth,' Viv muttered. 'He is banging on a bit. And he's drunk most of that bottle on his own. If he doesn't go soon he won't be able to move.'

'How long have you lived in Porlock?' Robin asked.

'Over twenty years. It took me ten years to be accepted, and it was easier for me, my wife being a local. My ex-wife, that is ... They were all her clients to begin with.'

'I hadn't realised she was a solicitor too,' Robin said.

'She was indeed. Amongst other things,' said Graham, staring mournfully into his glass. 'We met at law school.'

'He never used to drink like this,' Viv muttered. 'I wish Robin wouldn't keep asking questions. Mum will be livid if we're late.'

Actually she wouldn't. Not tonight with Robin there. Mum hadn't met him, but she'd consider him a 'gentleman' and would rise to the occasion accordingly. Though she wouldn't be mad on his black corduroy suit ... He was thirty-one and his hair was beginning to recede a little but, sizing him up over lunch, Wanda had decided that he was okay, if a bit too serious and a mite boring. In fact, Viv's type exactly ...

'We must go, but we can't leave Beth here with Graham in that state,' said Viv, beginning to work herself into a fret.

'I'll be fine. I've dealt with worse drunks than him in casualty of a Saturday night I assure you.'

'Perhaps if we go he'll take the hint and leave with us. I can say you're tired if you like.'

'What sort of litigation?' Robin was asking Graham.

And suddenly, unable to contain herself any longer, Viv called across the room, 'Robin, it's late. We're leaving.'

The men stopped talking and looked at her in amazement. Robin opened his mouth, thought better of it, and drained his glass.

'See how obedient I am,' he said lightly, and put his glass down on the mantelpiece. 'And we're not even engaged.'

Graham laughed awkwardly. 'Anyway,' he said holding out his hand, 'good to have met you, Robin. See you again sometime I hope.'

Out in the low-beamed hall, Wanda collected her hat from the telephone table and the four of them went out into the evening sunshine.

'I'll call you,' Viv said to Beth. 'I'll keep in touch – and I'll certainly come to the inquest with you. In the meantime, you know where I am if you need me.'

'I'll come and see you too,' said Wanda. 'It's a bit difficult without transport, but I'll come and see you somehow,' she added, realising that misery now seemed to have closed around Beth like a dark cloak.

'Oh God,' said Viv, horrified, suddenly spotting Graham's ancient little Daimler. 'The state he's in, he can't drive! Rob, we'll have to give him a lift.'

'I'll drive him,' Beth said.

'Are you sure?' Robin asked.

'Quite sure.'

She was tired. Wanted them to go. And Robin was cross ...

'Get in, Vivien,' he said, opening the driver's door for her. 'God, I hope he doesn't drink like that when he's working.

46

Lawrence's estate is quite complicated. We don't need any cock-ups with the probate.'

'He's upset, Vivien, damn it. Your father was his friend,' Robin said, and slammed the car door harder than was necessary.

'Did you have to slam the door like that?' she said as he got into the passenger seat beside her. 'I don't know why you bothered to come if you're going to be difficult.'

'Oh – great ...!'

Viv, temporarily mellowed by Dad's death, was already calling him Lawrence again and generally snapping her way back to normal. The atmosphere in the car as she drove them through the lanes towards Luccombe was just awful. *What a day*, Wanda thought, miserably watching the hedges slide past the windows.

'Heavens,' said Viv with a chuckle, 'and to think I had a real crush on that Grey Ham when I was younger. I must have been mad.'

I this; I that – it's always I with Viv, thought Wanda – though Robin, still fuming, said not a word.

A foul day ... She couldn't wait for it to be over.

When Beth walked back into the sitting room, Graham, clearly in no hurry to go, was looking through an atlas he'd taken from the bookcase beside the fireplace.

'It's big world,' he said, closing the book.

'It is. I'll make you some coffee then I'm going to take you home.' Tonight she had neither the energy nor the inclination for a drunk's silly games.

'Sit down for a minute, will you?' he said. 'Would you mind?'

'I am quite tired.'

'I know you are. This won't take long.'

She sat on the sofa and, perching on the edge of the armchair, he swayed slightly and clasped his hands around one knee to balance himself.

'It's a big world, Beth, and if I may, I'd like to give you some advice. You'll have realised you aren't going to be short of money. Each member of the family has been well taken care of, and you've got a small income from Seligman and

Franks. Most important of all, you've inherited all the Australian interests.'

'I've told you, you can sell the Australian interests.'

'Unfortunately I've discovered that I can't. The London solicitors have informed me there's a time clause which was added as a codicil last November. Apparently they're producing some good breeding stock at Tarran Hills and Barrington Heights and they've started to export their horses to Europe and the Far East. There's a time clause with just over nine years left to run on it, which will allow the stock to make a name for itself. That way, when the ranches are eventually sold they will be more valuable.'

'Nine years ...?' she said, stunned.

'I'm afraid so. And in the meantime, whether you like it or not, I'm afraid you are Tillotson's business partner – though unless you want to, you won't have to be any more involved than Lawrence was. Just the one business meeting a year and your signature on the occasional document. That sort of thing. Tillotson will handle the day-to-day running of the ranches and keep you informed as he did Lawrence.'

Beth stared at him. He was speaking slowly and very precisely, though there was little sign of the whisky in his thinking. It was she who, thinking back to the day she'd seen Tillotson with Lawrence in London, felt punch-drunk. Tillotson's hand was all over this. A further premium, perhaps, for Lawrence's freedom and Tillotson's silence ...

'What if Tillotson dies?'

'Then the time clause is invalid and, as long as you agree, as Tillotson has no immediate family and has never married, everything can be sold and will pass to you or the beneficiaries of your estate. Yes,' he said, misreading her continued expression of horror, 'I admit, that surprised me too. After all, everything that's been achieved out there represents half of Lawrence's life's work. I'd have expected him to want to tie the interests for Vivien and Wanda, especially as it's obviously a growth set-up that they expect to appreciate with time.'

'He wouldn't want the girls involved with his life in Australia.'

'Oh ...? Oh well, no. Anthea's brother. Always a sore point. I'd forgotten.'

Beth suspected that, these days, it had every bit as much to do with Lawrence himself as with the brother-in-law, though she didn't say anything.

'And all this is legally binding, is it?'

'Absolutely.'

'And if I die?'

'The time clause remains valid, though Tillotson then has the option to sell and must in any case pay your share to your heirs.'

'That's odd isn't it?'

'Not really. As a going concern Lawrence has clearly tied things for you rather than for Vivien and Wanda.'

'I think you'd better make me a new will. As things are everything I have is willed to my godson, but whatever belonged to Lawrence should go to his girls.'

'Yes,' Graham agreed. 'I was going to ask you about that. Plenty of time. We can deal with that next time you come to the office. As to the rest of it, the details and the day-to-day running of the ranches and the stock, I understand from Mr. Tillotson that he'll be coming to London in a couple of months as usual and that he'll be contacting you to arrange a meeting, so he'll doubtless explain all that to you himself.'

He can try, Beth thought. *I'm not meeting that bastard. Not ever.*

'In the meantime ...' Graham said. 'Look, Beth – I didn't really intend to talk business today. That isn't why I stayed. I stayed to tell you that after the inquest, as soon as you can, I think you should take a holiday. I was going to suggest you might like to go out to Australia and take a look at those ranches.'

'That, I do assure you, will be the last place I'll go.'

'Pity ... It's spring out there – new pastures, new foals, new life. You do still have a life ahead of you, you know. A long one I hope – though it will be different.' He hesitated. 'It also occurs to me that, from the terms of the will and from something Lawrence said casually a few months ago – well, maybe he hoped you would take an interest in the business. That you and Tillotson would get to know each other. That you might like to go out there, at least for a holiday.'

She stared at him. 'You're wrong there, Graham. Right off the track, I do assure you.'

'Lawrence never mentioned it to you?'

'No, he did not.'

'I thought he said that you enjoyed your time in Australia?'

'So I did.'

He waited for her to continue, and when she didn't he said, 'Oh well – it's a big world,' and swinging wide his arm in a precariously expansive gesture which, for a second, almost caused him to lose his balance, he indicated the atlas. 'There are lots of places to choose from, and right now I do think it would help if you had something to look forward to. That is, after the inquest – which, I should warn you, will not be pleasant. They never are.' He was watching her, and suddenly he looked embarrassed. 'Look, Beth ... I do understand a little of what you're going through. When Stella buggered off ... Well, to be honest, it was bloody awful and I damned nigh cracked up. Though in a way, after all the rows and the bickering, losing Stella was almost a relief. Except that she took the kids with her ... But death is different. To lose someone you love, that must be hell. A sort of emotional amputation. I just wanted you to know that, well – I understand – and that I'll do whatever I can to help you. As Lawrence's friend, as well as your solicitor. He was bloody good to me when I was going through the hoop. But these things do get easier with time. It does get better ...'

His kindness increased the pain in her chest, and he too seemed close to tears. Or perhaps the accumulation of booze was at last beginning to have an effect. The better to judge she looked at his eyes, and noticed that they were tawny with flecks of brown that were as dark as his hair – which was quite curly with reddish lights through it. She wondered how he had come by the slight scar that ran up under his right cheek to the corner of his broad, square nose. A round, brown little man in a smart grey suit, but there was more detail to him than she had realised.

'Anyway,' he said, swaying a little as he stood up, 'I must go. I'm in court tomorrow. Things to prepare ...'

'I'll drive you home.'

50

'No, no. I've got Alouette.' Seeing she did not understand, he added, 'My car.'

'Oh ...' she said, and for the first time in a week she wanted to laugh.

He was slightly shorter than she was, though following him down the hall to the door she noticed that he appeared much less portly in a suit than he had in the sweater and brown knee britches he'd been wearing when she and Vivien had met him at his office. He could take his drink, too. The bottle of Bells was all but empty – though it really wasn't that obvious.

Until he went outside and the cold air hit him like a brick.

'Keysh ...' he said and, swaying, grabbed hold of the car while he searched his pockets. 'To drive a car one needs keysh.'

'One does,' she said, resigned. 'I have keys. I'll drive you in my car. You can fetch yours in the morning.'

'Dear lady – I wouldn't dream of it.'

'Graham, with respect,' she said, both tired and exasperated, 'I can't let you leave here in that car. At best if you're caught you'll be in trouble with the Law Society. At worst you might kill someone.'

'Ah ...' he said, and belched mournfully. 'Exchuse me ... Yesh.' He shook his head and wagged a cautioning finger. 'You are, of course, absooluthely right! That would not do.' He slammed the car door, staggered, drew himself up to as much height as he'd been blessed with, then walked towards her in a firmly disciplined perfectly straight if somewhat uncertain line. 'On any other occasion,' he said formally, taking her hand and bending to kiss it, 'I should be most honoured to be driven by such a woman as yourself. I believe you are a wonderful woman, and you are certainly divinely attractive. But I shall not allow you to drive me tonight. I would, however, be most grateful if you could ring for a taxi? I shall meet it at the end of the lane.' Turning, he walked away, and raising his hand in farewell, he called over his shoulder, 'I shall be in touch. I shall speak to you upon the telephone.'

He reminded her of a small friendly cartoon animal, and as she went back indoors she realised that she was smiling.

The hall smelt of stale cigar smoke and whisky.

51

And then suddenly the house seemed particularly empty and silent.

He marched along the lane, his head deliciously light in the chill evening air, his hands clasped firmly behind his back, the steel-tipped heels of his brogues smacking determinedly against the tarmac.

Nobody's fool, that widow, even under stress. God, she'd been brave today. And she was damned attractive ... A strange, compelling sort of attraction – if you liked that sort of thing. Lawrence had had it all; health, wealth and a happy marriage with a wonderful woman, and then the poor sod had upped and died.

I didn't tell her she was a wonderful woman though, did I ...? No, no, of course not. She is, though. And gutsy, as well as attractive ...

Damn – and it was a getting cold now the sun had gone and a sea mist had started to drift in up the valley. Pissed though he might be, it wasn't his eyes ...

The first mist of the autumn, that brought with it the promise of long winter evenings listening to music by the fire. This would be the tenth winter he'd had the fire to himself. The tenth winter he'd be free to listen to whatever music he wanted, and to eat for supper what, when and where he chose. In fact, since Stella had left and unless the kids were visiting, he could live like a pig in a sty.

Ten years ... It hardly seemed possible, though it was strange how the death of a friend or a member of the family caused one to count up the years and take stock. It always did. He'd noticed that quite often with his clients – and the chance remarks from bereaved relations could be touchingly revealing, particularly those made by widows and children. Unlike some, that nice little widow of Lawrence's wasn't going to be fazed by the paying of bills or the general running of the house and the garden. She was nobody's fool, that woman – though she might not find it so easy to live in that damned great house on her own. Some people never did hack that one.

Actually Graham quite enjoyed living alone, now that he was used to it – although there were of course times when he did get a bit lonely. He had Madeline, his secretary, to talk to on weekdays, and his clients, and there were always chaps in the pub of an evening – not to mention Christine, the amply stacked barmaid ... Though some nights – nights like this one – it would be nice to be going home to someone special. A sympathetic ear, a smile, a hot meal – a soft, welcoming body in a warm bed. Though he'd learnt from experience, it didn't do to dwell on that. Thoughts like that could drive you crazy.

In any case, with Stella, insatiable sexual athlete and – as he'd eventually discovered – nymphomaniac and general whore, it had been the other way round. The bed too hot by far, and the meals barely warm. If he was lucky and there was a meal. If she'd felt like cooking. If she was even at home. There'd been a hell of a lot of ifs in his life with Stella. More often than not it was he who'd done the cooking – and put the kids to bed.

Kids ... He'd often thought that he should perhaps have screwed up his courage and tried harder to meet some nice woman and marry again, if only so that he could go back to court for care and control of the kids. He did miss his kids. Still, it was getting a bit late for that now they were teenagers, and it wouldn't have been fair to a woman, marrying for that reason alone. He'd had a couple of brief encounters since Stella, though neither of them were women he could have faced waking up with every morning for the rest of his life. And anyway, financially, it was only recently that he'd been able to afford to think of marrying again. For the sake of the kids, rather foolishly perhaps, he'd allowed Stella to take far more than half her share of all they'd owned and worked to build together.

No-blame divorce, my arse, he thought as he marched on along the lane. *Give me the nights in Brighton hotels, the private eyes, and chambermaids employed for their ability to bear credible witness, any day.* There'd be a damned site fewer broken marriages jamming the courts, and a lot fewer maladjusted kids swamping the Health and Education services if the no-blame divorce laws had never been heard of. *And to think, I chose law as a career because I thought law was the same thing as justice. I soon leant different.*

Even so, Stella could have destroyed his sense of fair play and soured the whole human race for him in one fell swoop if he'd let her. Shit though, she'd have been good in a Brighton hotel room as a professional co-respondent. Very convincing, swinging from a chandelier in her frilly underwear. You could have fed a family of four for a month on what she spent on a set of underwear; pure silk, and invariably some shade of red. She might just as well have had WHORE tattooed all over her pert little buttocks. Even now all these years later, a glimpse of saucy underwear in a setting as innocent as a shop window or blowing in the breeze on the washing line of a total stranger had been known to reduce him to something damn close to terror. Give him clean white Marks and Spencer's cotton any day. You could tell a lot about a woman from her underwear, he was convinced of it.

A wimp, Stella had called him. It still cut him to remember that, so perhaps he was. Though she was quite definitely over-sexed – and it was sex that decided her on the law, he'd bet his life on it. A sense of voyeurism into other peoples mucky divorces. Other women shook hands when they met a man. Stella'd shake hands, and two seconds later she'd have her hand in the chap's flies. She could unzip a fly faster than a monkey at a banana. That was Stella ...

Oh, Stella ... And in his guts now, there was that old familiar churning from the loss, of what might, of what should have been. Christ ... And it only ever got him like this when he was very, very drunk.

Exactly how much whisky had he had back there ...?

Shit ... He vaguely remembered an almost empty bottle. And Beth's tired, tolerant smile.

He stopped walking and stared down at the grey tarmac surface of the lane. What the hell had he said to her?

No, surely not. He couldn't have ... On the day of Lawrence's funeral? Damn it, she wasn't even his sort of woman.

Well, she was. She was every man's sort of woman. He'd envied Lawrence the minute he'd set eyes on her at the wedding. What man hadn't? She was one of those women who had an almost magnetic effect on men. But he wasn't a complete fool. At least, not when he was sober. He'd known instantly that she was too much for him. Too sophisticated. Frilly silk underwear, for certain ...

54

His brain having been shocked into clarity now, slowly he walked on.

Lang – oh Lang, you can take yourself anywhere twice. Once, to apologise ...

What must she think of you?

And you, her solicitor?

Then, seeing the sidelights of the taxi waiting at the end of the lane, he looked up at the trees, let out a groan that was more like a howl, and started to run.

Christ ... He would have to apologise.

'No,' Robin said, 'I think everything went off very well.'

Like clockwork, the bit I saw, Anthea thought. 'As long as the vicar got his name right. You'd be surprised how often vicars get the names wrong at funerals.'

Having finished their meal, Wanda had taken Gran up to bed and Vivien had gone through to the dairy to see what she could find to take back for her larder. She wouldn't find clotted cream. The village shop had taken all Anthea had this week, though there was jam she'd made from Muriel's plums, and plenty of chicken's eggs collected this morning.

Left on her own to talk to Robin, the image of that woman's face still haunting her, Anthea saw her chance to ask a few questions without the girls realising how interested she was. She had rather taken to this unassuming young man, and he certainly seemed a good deal more genuine than the smooth, go-getting young men Viv had brought home in the past.

'Tell me, and how is Beth?'

'Vivien says she's being quite amazing, though from what I saw I'd say she's quite shocked.'

'Of course. Oh good,' Anthea said – and the young man could take that whichever way he liked. 'Poor Lawrence – though, being a nurse, I'm surprised she couldn't revive him?'

'Yes ... I imagine she must feel that too.'

She'd like us to believe she does, Anthea thought. *I have no doubt of that.*

'Has she had chance to make any plans, do you know? Will she stay around here, or will she go back to London?'

'I imagine its early days for her to know as yet.'

'Yes, I suppose it is,' she said, disappointed. The sooner that woman cleared out of this valley the better. 'They tell me its a lovely house inside as well as out. Beautifully decorated and furnished.'

'It's certainly a nice house. A quality renovation. I'd have been proud if it was one of mine.'

He began to talk about the house, mostly boring technical details about the materials and, somewhat ashamed of herself for trying to question him in the first place, she let him ramble while she tried to think what else she could ask that wouldn't be too obvious. Then Vivien opened the kitchen door – and Percy appeared at her heels.

'Percy! Don't let him in here, Vivien. Make him go back to his box.'

'Is he a house goose?' Robin asked, amused.

'No he's not – and he's not allowed in the living room,' Anthea said.

'Mum treats the kitchen like an extension of the farmyard,' said Vivien disapprovingly.

'Yes, well, that's how it goes on a farm,' Anthea said. 'His arthritis is very bad now autumn's coming.' There had been sick animals or birds in her kitchen for as long as she could remember, and she wasn't about to change her habits for her city-smart daughter.

'He's a very friendly goose,' Robin said. 'And very elegant.'

'Yes he is. He has two wives, and all three of them are almost human,' Anthea said gratefully.

'Mum!' Wanda called down the stairs. 'I can't get Gran into bed. She just won't budge. Can you come ...?'

'I'll go,' Viv said, and Anthea let her. Wanda would have undressed Gran and washed her, which was the bit that turned Viv's stomach. She only had to help Wanda persuade the old thing into bed.

'It must be hard work, farming, for a woman,' Robin said.

'It is sometimes. Oh, you get used to it,' she said, and although she had Robin to herself again the mood for questioning him about the bitch had passed.

He wanted to hear about the farm.

56

'Storm,' Gran said again as, in her white ankle-length flannelette nightie, her long white hair tied in a blue bow, she continued to stand by the window looking out at the night.

'There won't be a storm tonight, Gran, I've told you,' said Viv. 'It's too foggy.'

'Come on, Granny,' said Wanda, taking her arm, 'Now this really is it. Come away from that window and get into bed or you'll catch cold.'

'You'm a pickle with that lad.'

'What lad? Robin's Viv's friend, not mine. And look, Granny, I'm going away tonight. I've got to go back to work tomorrow. I'll come and see you again very soon – but you will be good for Mum, now won't you?'

'Cocoa,' the old lady demanded, allowing herself to be tucked into bed.

'Okay,' said Viv, 'we'll bring you some cocoa, but you promise to stay in that bed and be good.'

'Pickle ... It's you who's the pickle,' she chuckled, wagging her finger at Wanda.

'You're very lively tonight,' said Wanda, laughing with her. 'All this company seems to have done you good.'

They said their goodbyes to her, and out on the landing Viv said, 'S'truth, how does Mum put up with that day after day? It's like talking to a demented budgerigar.'

'No it's not. Not exactly. She seems to know what she's saying, so the problem's probably ours. We just don't hear it right.'

'You're as daft as she is, Wanda,' said Viv, not unkindly. 'And I tell you one thing – she looks more like a witch every time I see her. No wonder Dad used to call her the White Witch of Wookey.'

'It used to work, though didn't it. Her plants and her healing. Even you have to admit that,' said Wanda as she followed her sister downstairs.

Vivien, though, just snorted.

As Beth closed her bedroom window she noticed that the mist had thickened and begun to flow up the valley as a thick sea of fog. It had already obliterated the thatched, tall chimneyed cottages of her nearest neighbours across the field, and was now creeping on up the hill towards the house.

In bed, she switched off the light and lay listening to the silence. Her first night alone and the house seemed particularly silent, as if it too was listening.

She could hear the hiss of the fog as it caressed the sandstone, and rising up around the walls and the roof, oozed relentlessly on up through the woods to the moors.

She thought of Lawrence, and of the accident, and as she began to drift down into an uneasy sleep, it was as if the fog was beginning to suffocate her. She was also aware that this was part of a dream. That she had only to open her eyes or turn over in bed, and she would wake.

But somewhere out there, hidden in the fog, Lawrence was waiting for her in a small boat and it was right that she should join him.

He hadn't deserved to die ...

So she lay very still, waiting for the storm to break and release her.

'She thinks you're a nice young man.'

'I agree,' said Robin, mesmerised by the speed at which the car's red bonnet was swallowing the white lines and cats' eyes from the cold grey road. 'Slow down, Viv. This isn't a race.'

'I'm really worried about her. Heaven knows how she copes with Gran as she is,' she said, flexing the fingers of one hand as she often did when she was fussed. 'I'll have to find time to go down and see her much more than I have been. I must ...'

'Okay. I'll come with you. Slow down, love ...'

'It's not foggy here.'

'It might be round the next corner.'

You never did know what was around the next corner. Even though he'd never met old man Seligman, his death had brought that home to him like a message flashing in neon. That, and the uncomfortable fact that he'd have to drive his own life a great deal faster if he was to achieve a fraction of what Viv's father had in his time. Robin would be thirty-two next February, and so far, leaving Constable Makepeace to go it alone hadn't proved to be nearly as profitable as he'd hoped.

By the time old Seligman was thirty-two he'd had a mini empire in Australia, married, fathered Vivien, and was well on his way to making a name for himself in England.

Though judging by his wives, he might not have been quite so successful in his choice of women. One, the muscular, rather masculine wild-haired farmer, was a genuine, warm-hearted soul, yet even she hadn't been able to bury the hatchet sufficiently to turn up at his funeral. The other wife, all woman, looked like an angel and dressed like a model, but was dead-eyed and probably hard as granite. All Eastern promise and no delivery – though she did have marvellous hair ... Hair that somehow dared you to pull her down off her plinth and see if you could ruffle her cool. Some men would find that hair quite a challenge in itself – though Seligman's wives certainly seemed to disprove the theory that men who married more than once chose the same kind of female. They were both of medium height – but there the similarity quite definitely ended.

'Viv ...' he said, bracing himself as the car shot into a corner and the tyres squealed.

'Oh Robin, stop gibbering. If it's foggy in Porlock Vale it's always clear after Halsway hill, and I know this road like the back of my hand.'

As well, he thought looking at her profile in the light deflected back from the road, *as I know her body*. She had a lovely body, and he'd missed her. With the overtime she'd been working, he hadn't seen her for almost two weeks.

'I don't know why you didn't bring your own car if my driving bothers you that much.'

'Actually,' he said, aggrieved, 'I came down on the bus because I thought, tonight of all nights, you might like my support. I thought you'd be tired and might like me to drive home.'

'It's a company car. You're not insured.'

He hated it when she tried to be clever ...

'I don't see that insurance will make a great deal of difference when you've driven us up a tree and we're dead. Slow down a little – please?'

She did. A little – and although she drove fast, she drove well and there were few other cars on the road. She did

59

everything well. She already had a better job than a lot of men of her age. And some things she did better than others. When she was in the mood ... He looked at her again, loving her little frown of concentration. Her long fair hair, swept up and secured by a comb, looked like silk.

'I've missed you,' he said, resisting the urge to touch a curl that had escaped from its clip and tumbled down over her ear. She didn't like to be touched while she was driving. Hated to be kissed when she'd just put on lipstick. And tomorrow morning, in a hurry to get to work, she'd be as bad tempered as blazes. She was hell in the mornings. Luscious Viv ... Never mind, he'd take care of her tonight. She was staying with him in Taunton tonight.

'Well – have you missed me?'

'Of course.'

Of course. What sort of answer was that to give a passionate man who hadn't seen the object of his craving for what seemed like a lifetime?

'What – every empty, aching moment? You better had.'

'Oh Robin,' she said impatiently.

Oh Robin ... Oh Robin, don't paw me, oh Robin, not now, oh Robin, get your mind above your belt. Not now and not bloody ever, the hours she'd been working lately ... Never mind. She'd wrong-footed him several times today, but he wasn't going to make anything of it. Today there'd been mitigating circumstances, and before that she'd had one hell of a week. She'd been very attached to her father, or at least, very much under his influence. Probably too much so – and far more, he was sure, than she'd realised, even if the pair of them had scrapped like dogs in the process.

'A bad week,' he said. The speedometer was touching sixty again but, although the road was twisty and narrow, he tried to ignore it.

'It's Mum I'm worried about. I hadn't realised Gran had got quite so addled. She really ought to be in a home. And I'm really not going to have time to go down and see them in the foreseeable future.'

'Not if you're going to continue working weekends you're not, no.'

'Yes. And that will get worse before it gets better. Thane

60

wants me to go for the senior manager's job, so it's more than likely I'll get it.'

'Oh? I'm not sure you should even apply.'

'I've applied already.'

He looked at her. 'When?'

'I posted the application the day after Lawrence died.'

'My God ...' Good old Viv. Chin of steel. Leave the dead to bury their dead. 'You could have told me. You might have discussed it with me first.'

'I want that job, Robin.'

'So it seems. And where does that leave me? Will there be any time at all for me in your already overcrowded schedule?'

She glanced at him. 'You're jealous.'

'No – but I am fed up. I hardly see you as it is. And if you must drive like a bloody maniac, at least keep your eyes on the road.'

'I won't have to work so hard once the new staffing structure's sorted.'

'Maybe.'

'I won't, Rob. Once they've appointed the senior manager they'll reorganise the work load.'

The wing mirror narrowly missed a garden wall that butted on to the road and a large stone flew up and cracked against the car's undercarriage.

'Viv, for Christ's sake! I anticipate having a few years ahead of me yet – and I want every one of them.'

'There's no need to be sarcastic.'

'Okay, look – if you can't slow down, fucking stop and I'll thumb a lift.' He watched the needle on the speedometer gradually fall back to fifty, and with it his temper subsided. 'I'd like to know where I fit into your life, that's all. If I do fit into it. Because while you've been at Tivington, I've been thinking. I'd like us to get married.'

'Married ...?' Viv said. 'What – now?'

'Well, yes. Soon, anyway.' He hadn't meant to say it today, and he certainly hadn't meant it to be like this, but now he'd started he might as well say it all. 'And as marriage to me means children, within a year or two of us getting married I'd like us to try for a family. My father was over forty when I was born. It was too old.'

61

'Oh ...' she said. 'Well, I suppose we could. In a year or so anyway. My career will be better established by then, and we'll be able to afford a nanny.'

'A nanny?' he said, shocked. 'Why? How long do you want to go on working?'

'Well, I don't just want to be a housewife. I'd go spare at home all day with nothing to think about.'

'Okay. You can go back to work when the kids go to school.'

'What as? A clerk? I'll have lost too much seniority to be anything else.'

'Well then, start up a business from home or something. I don't want any kid of mine to have a nanny. Kids brought up by nannies are never your own, and from what I've seen, the mothers are crippled by guilt and the kids are smothered with the wrong kind of love that comes from it. They either grow up as spoilt, confused, drug-taking brats, or they leave home as soon as they can to get free. Either way – kids and parents – everybody loses out.'

'Robin – I've never heard anything so ridiculous! A lot of our parents' generation had nannies and they turned out all right. The aristocracy have had nannies for generations.'

'Yeah – and look at them. I'm not having a nanny for my kids, Viv. And that's final.'

'Listen, you guys,' said Wanda, 'I'd just as soon leg it from here if you're going to fight.'

Oh shit ... He'd forgotten the sister was sitting in the back.

'We're not going to fight,' he said, realising that they had passed the Crossed Keys junction and were driving into the outskirts of Taunton. 'I'm just telling her.'

'Oh right. Very masterful ...'

'Belt up, Wanda,' Viv said. And to him, 'You've got it all worked out, haven't you? Or you think you have. Why suddenly all this about marriage? You've never mentioned it before.'

'No, well, I've just realised that time's ticking on.'

'I don't know, Rob ... Anyway I can't marry you yet. Just now I've got a lot of commitments – and I won't get the job if Thane thinks I'm getting married. He practically told me that outright. Marriage means even more commitments.

Keeping house and shopping, as well as finding time for us. For you. With a new job, it's too much.'

'Oh good. So I am at least on your list of commitments. It's always good to know where you stand. Second fiddle to the company drum, and somewhere upstage of a sodding shopping trolley!' She laughed, and he said, 'I mean it, Viv. Every word.'

'We've got a lot to talk about.'

'We have.' But he'd already said far more than he'd intended to, and as he'd already swallowed a lot of aggro for the sake of peace, he could swallow a bit more. This would keep for a day or two.

It was foggy again in town and the soft halos of mist that had collected around the streetlamps gave off a strange light that had touched her hair with gold. And she was scowling, which meant she was confused, felt trapped. She could be very abrasive, but there were times when she looked so vulnerable, so lovely, that the sight of her almost paralysed his breathing. And in ten minutes, quarter of an hour at the most, they'd be at his flat with the whole night ahead of them. He wasn't about to let anything spoil that. He rested his hand on her thigh, and she let it stay there.

'We're both tired,' he said. 'We won't say any more about it tonight.'

'Is this Ashton Grove?'

'Second on the left,' said Wanda.

At least he was certain of tonight. As certain as one could be of anything with Vivien. She turned into Ashton Grove and, removing his hand, he turned to speak to Wanda. Lord, what a sight to scare a Christian. When he'd met her at lunchtime he'd found it hard to believe she was Viv's sister. 'Okay – Zebra?'

'What?'

'Are you all right?'

'Yes thanks.'

'Good ...'

She did look like a zebra – and slumped in the back seat, he couldn't tell her black make-up from the shadows. In the white face, her eyes were black holes. Dead eyes, like her stepmother's.

63

Viv had stopped the car in front of a row of slightly forbidding three-storied Victorian terraced houses with tiny front gardens separated from the pavement by a low wall, shrub hedges and painted wrought-iron gates.

'Just a minute, Wanda,' she said, her voice unpleasantly sharp as Wanda opened the door. 'Look – you could go home more often than you do. You're not nearly as busy as I am, and Mum can't go on as she is. Go down there next weekend and talk to her. She never gets out of an evening and pretty soon she won't even be able to leave Gran on her own while she's working. Tell her we want Gran to go into a home.'

'Gran isn't a piece of baggage, Viv.'

'Things can't go on as they are, Wanda. Surely even you can see that. Gran ought to be in a home. Go down there and talk to Mum about it.'

'We've talked already. She won't hear of it.'

'When ...? When did you talk to her?'

'This week.'

'So go down next weekend and talk to her again. She needs to see more of us anyway. She needs our support.'

'Viv, I've just been there for a week. And I was there for two weeks in the summer.'

'Oh yes – when you broke your arm. When it suited you to go home and dump on her. I'll have to work next weekend, and I'll have to work for the next few Saturdays. You've never been known to work a weekend in your life.'

'Actually, I can't go down next weekend. I've got other plans.'

'What's his name?' said Robin in an attempt to defuse the situation.

'My God!' said Viv. 'Whoever he is I hope he wears a condom. God knows what you might catch from the sort of bloke who'd go out with something that looks like she does.'

'Viv ...' he said.

'Well, I'm pig sick of her leaving everything to me. She spends her whole life hiding, backtracking and running away. You do, Wanda. Even those clothes you wear are camouflage. Gothic gear, my eye. You think about it!'

'I knew it couldn't last, all your sweetness and light,' said Wanda. 'But don't you try and dump on me because your conscience is stabbing you. I'll tell you something, Vivien –

all that's ever mattered in your life is you. So you think about that one!'

Then she flung open the door, jumped out, and slammed it behind her with more force than seemed possible from such a skinny scrap of a girl. Robin leapt out after her, but she had already slung the sack thing she used as a bag over her shoulder and was marching off up the street.

'Wanda!' She turned to glare at him. 'Your suitcase.'

He took it out of the boot and walked along the pavement towards her.

'No ... I'll carry it in for you.'

'You'd better not. She'll probably drive off without you. She has so little time.'

'She doesn't mean it.'

'Oh, doesn't she. Maybe I know her better than you do,' and in the light from a streetlamp somewhere behind him he could see that her eyes were bright with tears.

'Forget it, Zebra. It's been a long day for both of you. Have you got your key?'

'My name,' she said, 'is Wanda.'

The gate groaned on its hinges and he followed her up the path. A vast gleaming monster of a motorbike almost entirely filled the tiny front garden, and in the hall when she had opened the door, there were two bicycles.

'I'll carry it up for you – Wanda,' he said, as she again held out her hand for the case.

Two flights of dimly lit stairs covered with cracked linoleum, the walls peeling, the woodwork chipped and hungry for paint. Other than condemned properties it was a long time since he'd been in a place as seedy as this. What in the name of blazes was a girl like Wanda doing here?

Outside the only door on the top landing she turned and stood with her back to it like an animal defending its lair.

'It's home,' she said, as if reading his thoughts. 'Right now it's the best I can manage.'

'Sure.'

He nodded at her, smiled, and starting back down the stairs he thought what a family of strange and various females they were. And could be this one at the top of the stairs was the strangest of the lot.

65

'Robin ...'

He stopped, and holding on to the banister turned to look up at her.

'Thanks.'

'That's okay,' he said, and hesitated. She looked a real waif. A fierce yet bewildered puppy that he was leaving on a rubbish tip – and as far as he knew he was now the only male attached to her family.

'Look,' he said, 'my name's Robin Watson, and if ever you need it, my number's in the book. Flat One, The Old Manor, Trull.'

She put her case on the floor and sat down on the bed. How dare Viv say all that! And in front of Robin. He was nicer than she'd realised. Far too nice for Vivien ...

Oh God, what a bloody awful day.

The last time she'd been here in this room, Dad was alive. Nor was there any sense of his comforting presence here as there had been at Luccombe. All that was here was a crummy divan with her own duvet, a stained puke-yellow carpet, green curtains, a deal wardrobe and a chest of drawers – all crammed into a room eight foot by ten, which cost her fifty quid a week and permanently stank of cooking from the communal kitchen two floors below.

She lay back on the bed, and at last she was able to cry. Tears for Mum and for Gran and for Beth, as much as for herself. What a bloody awful life ... Dad was probably well out of it.

Crying wasn't constructive, but it was a release.

And from now on, she thought, *I'll have no shoulder to cry on. So from here on, it's all down to me.*

Right – well I'll show Vivien a thing or two.

Somehow ...

I'll see if I don't.

Chapter Three

The answerphone clicked into action and, standing at his office window, Graham looked down over the roofs of Porlock to the grey waters of the Bristol Channel. Listening to Lawrence's cheerful pre-recorded message, he felt his skin crawl. Beth couldn't hear it of course, but he wished to God that she'd rerecord the damned thing herself. He also wished that she would return his calls. He'd tried to contact her several times these past ten days since the funeral.

'Beth – Graham Lang again,' he said into the machine. 'We have a date for the inquest. Wednesday week – the first Wednesday in October. Two-thirty, at Minehead Magistrates' Court. I'll see you there, or if you prefer I can collect you and we can go together. Perhaps you can call me?'

He replaced the receiver and, picturing her house as it had looked when he'd gone back for his car the morning after the funeral, felt a twinge of unease. A large stone house, surrounded by fog, windows shut, curtains tightly closed, it had seemed bleak and forbidding – and because it was early, before nine o'clock, he'd left the bottle of whisky, a bunch of flowers and his note of apology on the doorstep and had been glad to drive away.

He supposed she was all right. Not lying dead in there ...

Widows quite often hankered to follow their husbands in the early months after a death, and he remembered the look of desperation on her face in the church and in one or two unguarded moments back at the house.

Turning away from the window, he looked at his desk. He had an appointment at ten-fifteen, and a brief to prepare for counsel.

He also had an overactive imagination. Beth had probably taken his advice and gone away for a few days. She'd have known he could contact her through Vivien if he really needed to do so.

Glancing through the unopened letters that had accumulated since Vivien's departure, Beth listened while he left his message, then listlessly replaced the letters on the pile.

During the week there had been an airmail from Tillotson which she'd torn up without reading.

There were so many letters. And so much she should be doing.

The garden in which she had so much enjoyed working with Lawrence was already looking untidy, but she hadn't the energy to do anything – indoors or out.

She wasn't sleeping well. The dream of the fog kept recurring – and she had never felt so utterly drained and exhausted.

At least now there was a date for the inquest. The pathologists wouldn't find anything they weren't expecting, but she'd be glad to get it behind her. Perhaps, then, she really would begin to feel better.

'Well – the pathology's not looking good.'

'You told me that in July,' Tillotson said. 'I need to know how long I've got.'

'If I knew that, Wayne, I'd tell you.'

'Well say something for fuck's sake.' Bloody doctors with their pristine white coats and carefully monitored sympathy. 'Have a guess, mate. I can't waste what time I have got lying around here in one of your beds. I've got a business to run.'

'Every case we've had so far has been different. You've responded well to both courses of treatment we've given you. You may go into remission and live a full life for years. Or it might be a matter of months. We've got drugs that will help, but the symptoms will become more frequent and more severe. This isn't going to go away. All we can do is help you come to terms with it.'

Marvellous, he thought – and said, 'I'm due to go to England next month.'

'Go – if you're well enough. You know our thinking. Go

everywhere you want to go, see everyone you want to see, and do all the things you always wanted to do and never got around to. Meantime, as and when you need us, we'll be here.'

Tillotson stood up and took a packet of cigarettes out of his pocket. 'I was thinking of kicking this habit. I don't reckon I'll bother.'

The doctor smiled. 'I didn't hear that.' He handed him the package containing his medication. 'Enjoy your trip to England. If you go on as you are I shan't need to see you again before then.'

I will have to go to England, Tillotson thought in the taxi as it took him to the airport to meet the plane from the Tarran Hills ranch. He'd talked his way out of the clinic, though now he was out he felt weak and sweaty. He damned well had to be fit enough to go to England and talk to that woman about selling the ranches.

'All this paper,' he'd said to Lawrie as they'd been going through the accounts in his hotel room the last time he'd been there. 'I reckon we should take a look at our wills. The business has grown beyond all expectations. Mate, these days we're a couple of Silver Tails, but time has taken her share of the profits as well. Neither of us can take a night on the town like we used to. You look crook. Bloody horrible.'

'Have you got any aspirins?'

'In my washbag. Help yourself – and bring a couple for me. Seriously, Lawrie, we're both getting to an age where things can start to go wrong.'

'Christ, you're happy this morning. When I drop off my perch you can do what you like with the ranches. I shan't give a damn when I'm six foot under, as long as Beth's provided for.'

'What about the men? We've got a couple of damned good foremen at Tarran and Barrington, and there's the rest of the blokes and their families. Australia isn't the land of milk and honey it used to be, and they've worked their guts out for us. Come to that, so have I. It may be nothing to you, but I'm proud of what we've achieved. If you chuck in your chips tomorrow I'd like to carry on a bit longer. See what more can come from our young horses in, say, another ten years. Pity you didn't produce a couple of sons. Aren't either of your daughters interested? And what about your wife? You said she enjoyed her time in Australia.'

'She isn't Rachel Evans,' he said, referring to his one-time fiancée from the neighbouring ranch a hundred miles away. 'And I don't want my kids anywhere near the place.'

'Will it matter when you're six foot under?' he asked slyly, feeding him his own propaganda. 'In any event, these days nobody out there knows you from a big black dog.'

Lawrie washed the aspirins down with the remains of a can of beer and shrugged. 'Have another ten years then. I can see the advantages. If I chuck in my chips, run the ranches for Beth.'

'Right on, then. Before I go back we'll thrash something out with the lawyers.'

He'd been pleased to get Lawrie to agree to do what he wanted, though at the time, of course, it had been merely hypothetical. It had never occurred to either of them that they hadn't got ten years left between them and, even now, most of the time he couldn't quite believe that the sand was running out. He'd been shattered when the doctor at the clinic had told him, but he did seem to be getting used to the idea now. Had felt well enough lately, perhaps, to be able to ignore it. Back home, in the peace of the country, that clinic and the bloody doctors seemed light years from reality, and although he'd just had another strong dose of the facts, the staff were, as always, cheerful, matter of fact and supportive. They almost made death seem like a promise; the inevitable meeting with an old friend. Perhaps it would be. One thing was for sure though, a trip to England wasn't going to be the same without Lawrie being there.

All very well for those white-coated freaks to hand out advice, he thought, resting his hands on the travel grip on his lap as he looked out of the taxi's window, but in the course of his work he'd already been to most countries he'd wanted to see, and in the course of his life he'd done pretty much all he'd wanted to do. He had no burning ambitions left to sustain him.

He liked to think that one day, amongst the new foals or the young horses in training, he'd find another animal of

70

the calibre of The Wild Chancer. But Chancer had been just that; a one-off genius of a stallion packed with intelligence, strength, stamina and a will to win. Every year he watched the new foals for that same package of genes. Damn good foals, most of them – but finding a horse like Chancer was the kind of luck most breeders never had, even once in a lifetime.

And right now his luck didn't seem to be running too high.

The only other thing he'd have liked to achieve was a family. Something to which he could feel he belonged. Being a kid who'd spent his earliest years in a Darwin orphanage until he was claimed by his spinster aunt who worked for Lawrie's mother at Tarran Hills, he'd have liked to have come from a big family. Grandparents, parents, aunts, uncles, cousins, brothers, sisters, nieces, nephews, wife, kids – the works. He'd have loved that. Especially kids ... But the nearest he'd come to any of that was Lawrie and his family. No one had known how close he'd come to topping himself when Lawrie, having taken off for England after Anthony's death, had written to say he was marrying the sister and would be staying there. Being given half the ranch at Tarran Hills had meant nothing in comparison, though Lawrie had never been able to understand that. For Lawrie it would have been more than enough ... Better, as he had pointed out, than giving him the whole thing, thereby severing ties completely. So the way Lawrie saw it, he'd given better even than his best.

Though none of it had mattered to Lawrie anyway. Not after Anthony. Young Anthony Kenworthy had arrived from England with a kitbag on his shoulder and a hat pulled low over his eyes, and as Lawrie had walked across the paddock to meet the plane load of new ranch hands, he'd spotted Anthony amongst them – and that had been it. Like love at first sight, it had been Anthony this, Anthony that, ever after. Nobody else got a look in. Every one of those new boys had been a jackaroo and green as spring grass, and as always, every one of them made mistakes. But in Lawrence's eyes – not Anthony. Perhaps the clean young man fresh from England reminded Lawrie of what he had once been, but whatever it was, Lawrie'd gone loco. Worked with him, covered for him and, if necessary, lied. Eventually he had

worn the lad down and won him over, and as a result he had
soured things for all of them. Rachel Evans – as near to being
a man as damn is to swearing, and the other half of the longest
engagement since England's Hundred Year War – had flown
over in her Daddy's biplane, landed Lawrie a vicious right
hook in the eye, and taken off for the city. In the bunkhouse
the jackaroos, driven to the end of their tether by the heat, the
dust and the lack of women, teased Anthony, then bullied him,
and finally beat him to within seconds of his life in a scene
that resembled the last day in Hitler's Berlin bunker.

Jeeze-us ... Poor little bastard ...

Things had seemed to settle down for a while after that.
Then, one morning in high summer, Anthony had packed his
gear in the truck and gone out to check the roo fence at the
furthest perimeter of the ranch, and somewhere along the way
he had flipped. When he got to the fence he just kept on
driving out into the desert. When the truck had run out of
petrol he'd ignored the spare cans in the back, got out and
kept walking. They'd found the truck two days later. And five
miles away they'd found Anthony, hatless and shirtless,
wearing just his boots and his shorts, so burnt by the sun he'd
been damned nigh skinless as well. There had also been
dingoes – so that the body they'd picked up had been hardly
recognisable as human.

Lawrie, half demented and tortured by guilt, had confined
himself to the house and taken to the booze, and a conspiracy
of guilt and of silence had descended over the entire ranch.
As, after a pack of crazed dogs had savaged a sheep, each
animal returned home and reverted to being the loving docile
pet of its owner, so were the men subdued and hard-working.
But not one living soul on that ranch had been entirely innocent, and every one of them had known it. Even Tillotson, had
known that, if nothing else, as soon as he'd seen what was
happening, he should have stood up to Lawrie and sacked the
lad.

But Lawrie, as confused by what had happened as any of
them, was not wicked or bad. In fact, in his guilt-stricken
grief, as far as Tillotson was concerned, the vulnerable Lawrie
was more loveable than he had ever been. He had understood
Lawrie's decision to go to England and visit the lad's family,

and had respected him for it. Though he had never stopped loving him, even after Lawrie had decided to stay there and marry the sister.

And although he had never understood quite why or how he had managed to marry Anthea, he otherwise knew Lawrie as well and perhaps better than anyone else had ever known him. The main thing about Lawrie was that he had always known when to quit, and his ability to set his sights and his energy on a new horizon and to pick up and move on had, throughout his life, been the key to his success.

And I, he thought, *am also quite well acquainted with myself. I'm made of a softer metal than Lawrie, and having been just about everywhere I'm going to, and having probably achieved as much as I can – what's left?*

He was, he supposed, quite looking forward to meeting the widow – Beth. He'd seen photographs of Anthony's sister and could understand what Lawrie might have seen in her. But that second wife must be quite some female to have hooked him. Lawrie had changed beyond all recognition since he'd been in England, and this past year he had begun to talk and write about her and his English family much more than he used to do. The letters, too, had become more frequent, and Tillotson had begun to wonder. It was almost as if Lawrie was trying to convince himself that he'd done the right thing. Because, maybe, after all these years, he had begun to miss what he had left behind in Australia.

Yeah – he was looking forward to his trip to England. Meeting and talking to that wife ...

'Thanks, mate,' he said cheerfully as he paid the taxi driver.

And walking towards the small terminal reserved for private aircraft and interstate airlines, he realised that there was a slight spring in his step.

There was something he wanted to do after all.

Chapter Four

Beth woke with a start and looked at the clock on the bedside table. Vivien was due around lunchtime to take her to the inquest. Past ten o'clock, but there was plenty of time – and judging by the light that was penetrating the patterned curtains, the day was overcast and probably raining.

The same sort of morning as that back in July when Lawrence had been up early to drive to meet Tillotson in London. Wrapped in his blue towelling dressing gown, he had come into her bedroom and, bending to pull the curtain aside, looked out of the window.

'How long will you be away this time?' she'd asked, watching him from the bed.

'A week at the most. I'll ring you.'

She'd allowed her eyes to run down the line of his back to take in the narrow hips and the backs of his strong, decidedly male legs. 'Lawrie,' she'd begged softly. She'd suppressed the memory of Morocco, all that it stood for. And he hadn't touched her in months.

'It's raining,' he said. Then, still looking out of the window, 'I love you, Beth. I will always love you. What ever happens, remember that.'

She remembered it as clearly as if he were there in the room and, caught unawares, the memory skewered her chest in a pain as excruciating as the sudden return of feeling to traumatised flesh.

As Graham had said – an emotional amputation ...

Push it down. Don't think about it.

Although, today, she was going to have to think about it –

and to shake off the pain she moved quickly; threw off the duvet, got out of bed and crossed the room to open the wardrobe.

Her clothes were hanging in a neat line, each garment waiting to be selected, examined, lived in – like memories.

Which and what should she wear to the inquest?

'It's not a trial,' Graham had said when she'd eventually called him. 'The coroner will only want to go through the statement you gave the police and ask a few questions to make sure that the death was an accident.'

Questions in the witness box, under oath.

Still, after what she had done to him, what did it matter if she told a few lies?

Robin selected several pencils from the pot beside his drawing board and began to feed them into the electric sharpener. He'd developed the habit of sharpening pencils to control his temper long ago, when he was still at school. 'You've signed on the dotted line then.'

'First thing this morning,' Vivien said, cradling her coffee mug in both hands.

'I thought we agreed to talk about it.'

'We did talk about it.'

'Briefly, last weekend. Though, as I recall, we didn't come to any decision.'

It had been, as so often with Vivien, a circular conversation that had got them nowhere. He wanted her to be his wife, and had set out his terms; she wanted her career, and had stubbornly stated hers. She was a very determined young woman, and he could see that, unless he was the one to back down, for the rest of their lives every single argument would end in this kind of deadlock. He was a peace-loving chap, but this time he was not going to back down. This one, long term, was too important. Scowling, he inspected the point on the pencil.

'Robin, a job like that – you didn't seriously expect me to refuse it?'

'It depends on what you want out of life. What you want now may not be what you're going to want in a few years' time, and by then it may be too late.'

'Too late for what? Ten years from now I'll still only be thirty-three.'

'And a director, pushing to be managing director, your clever little brain watching for signs that the chairman might be ailing.'

'You make it sound quite nasty.'

'It is. Career women can be. Hard-nosed, calculating and self-centred. Fat pay packets, nice houses, company cars, and a lover or two on the side. They think they're the chosen daughters of Abraham who've got the best of it all ways – until they click that their shelf-life's expired and the too much they thought they had to give up amounts, in reality, to damned bloody all.'

'Quite the little chauvinist porky at heart, aren't you? I can't see there's much I'll be past at thirty-three.'

'Try sixty. Climbing the ladder of success can be addictive. And when you're thirty-three, I'll be forty-one.'

'Now that is over the hill. You can even buy mugs that say so.'

She walked out of the small bedroom he had turned into an office and, throwing the pencil across the room, he got up to follow her. Shit ... She just would not see reason.

'Listen, Viv,' he said, keeping his voice steady, 'Forty is too old to be a father. It may not be for some men, but it will be for me.'

'Honestly, love – this room's in such a muddle ...'

He looked around. 'I'd hardly call one unwashed coffee mug and a crumpled sofa, a muddle. Anyway, I wasn't expecting you this morning.'

'I wanted you to be the first to know.'

'Yes,' he said as a sigh, 'and I'm pleased for you. Of course I am ...'

'Good. I think Lawrence would have been too – now it's happened.'

'Quite probably. And from what I can gather you're too damned like your father.'

'You didn't even know him,' she said, pumping up the cushions on the sofa.

'Look at you. Career woman? You're a real mother duck.'

'Only on my days off. Have a peck on the cheek.' She gave

him a kiss and took the coffee mugs through to the kitchen. 'Anyway, let's not talk about it any more just now. Not today. Beth's expecting me and if I don't go now I'll be late.'

Here we go again. Not today. When can I bloody talk to her? She always finds some excuse. He ran his hand through his hair. Bugger Lawrence ... Since his death he was sure she'd got more determined, more sure of herself. Their relationship seemed to have dived into a downward spiral the minute the breath left old man Seligman's body – and every time he tried to do something to stop it, he was blocked.

'All right, I'll see you this evening,' he said, for the moment, resigned. She picked up her shoulder bag and looked at him, blue eyes apologetic, yet defiant. 'You are staying here tonight?' he said.

'Actually ... I know I said I would, but it is a bit difficult tonight. I didn't really have chance to talk to Thane this morning so I said I'd meet him at six o'clock.'

'Perhaps you should marry Thane,' he said, lightly. 'Or is he already married to the bloody office, lock, stock, bed and barrel?

'I'll be down at the weekend, I promise.'

'We need to talk, Viv.'

'I know.'

He suspected that what they really needed was a bloody good screaming, brick-chucking row. He wasn't good at rows. He turned to sarcasm, and she fielded his tart comments neater than a West Indian cricketer.

'We'll work something out somehow. We'll talk all weekend if you like,' she said, putting her arms around his waist, pushing her hips against him. 'Well – almost all the weekend.'

'Bitch ...' he said gently, relaxing, laughing into the warmth of her neck. 'Don't start on me if I've got to wait until the weekend.'

She stepped back and hitched her bag back onto her shoulder. 'Graham seems to think today will be pretty much routine, though there will be a few gory details. Apparently they are also quite interested in knowing how he came by that drug he was using. Nobody's supposed to be able to get hold of it unless they're a qualified vet. However – that wouldn't have stopped Lawrence ... Come on, darling, smile. I promise I'll come for the weekend. I'll come down Friday evening, and this time I'll stay over till Monday.'

Death, love, work – it's all in a day's living to her, he thought as he opened the door for her. She met her dragons head on, slayed them no problem, and moved on to deal with the next.

His was the ground-floor flat, and together they walked across what had once been the grand entrance hall of the manor. Through the glass of the tall double-front doors he could see her car parked beside his on the gravelled circular forecourt. Right where he would have liked it to be for always ...

'Well, good luck,' he said. 'If that's appropriate for inquests. Give my regards to Beth. I hope she's looking better than she did at the funeral. Try to make sure she eats some lunch. She didn't eat a thing that Sunday we went down, and she was thin as a ghost even then.'

But it was the dead look in her eyes that had really got to him. She'd reminded him of a mechanical doll that responded only when spoken to, and replied automatically with any one of a selection of trite, pre-programmed phrases. Other than in body, most of the time she just hadn't been with them.

'She did look thin,' Viv said. 'Still, it's early days yet. Don't come out, darling – it's pouring. I'll call you tonight and let you know how it went. And I'll see you Friday.'

Depressed, he watched her run across the wet flagstones and on down the steps. Maybe he'd see her on Friday, and maybe, once again she'd have reason to change her mind. He did very much want her to marry him and share the rest of his life, but why, with her, did there always have to be so much hassle?

He watched until the car turned out through the stone gateposts into the road, then walked back to his flat. As always after she'd left, the flat seemed dull and rather shabby – and he'd believe in Friday when it happened. God, their relationship had become a high speed emotional switch-back. It wasn't at all the easy going sort arrangement he liked – or indeed needed in order to work well creatively. The trouble was, he loved her, so he supposed he was stuck with it.

Ah well, like she said, they'd work something out.

In the kitchen, waiting for the kettle to boil to make himself another mug of coffee, he helped himself to a liquorice stick from the jar he kept beside it and sniffed appreciatively at the aroma that was beginning to come from the cook pot on the corner of the worktop. If she wasn't going to be here this evening he might as well put that casserole in the fridge until the weekend and make himself his usual stand-by of cauliflower cheese.

Thinking about it Viv wasn't unlike a cook pot. A cook pot quietly doing its own thing with a load of meat and vegetables as, in her head, in her own good time, she worked things out in her own good way.

Lift the lid before she was good and ready, and you copped a face full of boiling hot steam.

Step on it, Viv ... She'd told Beth she'd be there at twelve-thirty, and at the beginning of the Bishops Lydeard bypass she changed down to overtake a line of cars tucked in like a string of dithering baby ducks behind an ancient steamroller.

My steamroller of a father may have wanted me to take over from him at Seligman and Franks, but he'd have been proud of me for landing the job at Thane's, I'm sure of it. So, this one can be for him. Director, when I get there, will be for me.

'You've got what you want, then – as usual,' she'd said to him once soon after he'd married Beth. 'You don't give a damn about Mum, how she feels, do you? God, you are selfish.'

'I prefer to think that I'm aware. It's a tough life, Vivien. A matter of survival. Don't think this has been easy for me, but sometimes, in order to do what you know you have to do, other people get hurt. Or think they do ... Your mother will be all right, I assure you.'

Am I so selfish, then, to want this job? Because, to be who I want to be, I do need it. If it was merely a want, that, I accept, would be selfish.

And saddened, braking to go into the corner under the railways bridge at Combe Florey, she thought about her and about Robin, and about their different expectations.

I am like my father ... But it was him who said I'd get everything I wanted if I wanted it enough. And I do want Robin. He's a good steady bloke, and I love him.

Ah, it'll work out ... As Lawrence used to say – she'll come right. And dismissing it from her mind, she put her foot down on the accelerator and began to think about the afternoon ahead.

After a morning spent shopping in Minehead, Anthea drove home via the back road to Dunster and parked her car by the lynchgate. It was still raining and the churchyard was deserted. The bitch would be well occupied elsewhere right now. Not that Anthea really gave a damn where she was. Let her come here. She'd welcome the opportunity to ask her a few questions.

One of the least contentious of these would be why she hadn't been here to tend his grave. The mound of uneven turf was covered in wreaths and sprays of cut flowers, the petals beaten and dead, the ribbons faded, and the cards attached to most of the tributes, illegible and soggy with rain.

She hadn't included a card on her circle of white roses, now brown and yellowed. What she had to say to him was between the two of them, not for churchyard stickybeaks – and she crouched to read the card on the large cross of scarlet roses she'd seen on the coffin, guessing it was from the bitch. It had been written in biro and was still reasonably clear.

All my love, darling ...

Yes, she thought, and as the image of the white face drifted through her memory she clenched her fists. *Well, we'll see what the Coroner thinks about that ...*

Beginning with the cross of battered red roses, she made the first of several trips to the bin by the corner of the church, and when the grave was clear she went back to the car to fetch the last of the summer's dahlias and the rosemary she'd brought from the garden.

He had planted that rosemary by the barn when Wanda was small. It had been a bright frosty day, and Wanda, wearing the tiny blue wellingtons of which she was so proud, had stamped her feet in excitement.

'Can I help you dig, Daddy? Can I ...?'

'No, Plum. It only needs one good dip with the trowel. It's only a little bush.'

'Lickle, lickle,' she said, jumping up and down. 'What's it for?'

'It's a herb.'

'Granny Kenversy uses herbs to mend people.'

'So she tells us ... And when it's grown a bit bigger, Mummy can use little bits of it for cooking. You know, in the old days, long long ago before even I was born, people used to put sprigs of rosemary in bunches of flowers as a token of remembrance. To say I won't forget you, or please don't forget me. There, see ... All done. One little bush all tucked in nice and comfy.'

'I won't forget you, Daddy. Never, never.'

'I won't forget you either, Plum,' he'd said, and laughing, he'd swept her up in his arms and lifted her on to his shoulders.

I remember it well, Anthea thought looking down at his grave. *But I'd forgotten you used to call her Plum. I miss you, Lawrie – though, Lord knows, you've caused me enough grief.* Grief for the loss of their marriage, and now the grief of his death and the loss of her hope.

I'll come and see you again soon. Keep you tidy. The bitch won't be here. She wouldn't risk dirtying her city hands. Heavens no – she might chip her nail varnish.

Pity really. Anthea would have quite liked to ask her a few questions. Given her a hard time.

Not just about the accident ...

That one she would leave to the coroner. For the present ...

Most of the light in the dark, wood-panelled courtroom was coming from three high narrow windows above the coroner's head. This wasn't a trial – though over the centuries, in imposing, claustrophobic rooms such as this, thousands of men, women and children had been tried and convicted, and not so many years ago many of them had been deported to Australia. For crimes as trivial as the theft of a loaf of bread.

Graham was sitting on Beth's right by the aisle; Vivien was sitting on her left. Including the usher in a black gown who had charge of the bible, there were about a dozen people sitting amongst the dark wooden benches. On the front bench across the well of the court sat a young shaggy-haired girl listening attentively to the pathologist's report –

81

probably a scandal scavenger from the local paper. Amongst the complicated medical terminology, such emotive words as blood, stomach contents, heart, lungs and liver, would make colourful copy for next week's edition.

'It amounts, then, to paralysis of the lungs and heart,' said the coroner, questioning the doctor. 'And, using a drug with such a high concentrate of etorphine hydrochloride, death would have occurred that quickly?'

'It would have been almost instantaneous.'

Beth looked up at the light coming through the windows, then, looking down into the darkness in the well of the court, she saw it again.

Lawrence lying in the long grass, looking up at her, clutching his thigh, the needle silver against his brown cord trousers.

'Quick' he whispered, his lips barely moving. 'The antidote. In the shelter. On the bale of straw.'

Yes, you bastard ... And it can stay there.

She hadn't thought it possible to hate anyone as much as she had hated him at that moment – but neither had she realised that the anaesthetic would act so quickly.

Later, they had loaded him into the cavernous mouth of the ambulance and taken him to the hospital. Had laid him on the slab in the morgue. Then in overalls, masks and thick rubber gloves had sliced into his beautiful inert body to take samples for analysis. Had butchered him like these bloody locals butchered the magnificent red deer that lived on their moors, and had thus divided him into the choice cuts that today were being offered for public consumption.

As the doctor stood down from the witness box, the girl with a full head of rats' tails continued her frenetic note-taking. Then, hearing the coroner call her name, Beth somehow managed to stand and walk down the steps to take the place the doctor had vacated.

Took the bible in her right hand ...

Swore to tell the truth; the whole truth; nothing but the truth ...

'You are Elspeth Anne Seligman, wife of the deceased, Lawrence Peter Seligman,' the coroner said. 'You are also a fully qualified nursing sister.'

'Yes.'

'Now, Mrs. Seligman, according to your statement, on the day of the accident your husband came home from his office at around one o'clock and told you he intended to geld the colt, Another Chancer. You asked him not to. Why was that?'

'I wanted him to phone his daughter during her lunch hour and ask her to stay for the weekend.'

'Phone Wanda now, Lawrence – please ... Ask her down here for the weekend.'

'Leave it, Beth.' He flung his jacket down and picked up the two hypodermics.

'Damn it, why won't you let me get to know your daughters? Even Wanda's old enough to have accepted the divorce by now.'

He was worried about Wanda; thought it was time she did more with her life than crashing cars, stacking shelves in Tescos or typing envelopes and selling paint to long haired artists – so she had suggested he asked her for the weekend. Asked her to the house, instead of meeting her on his own for their usual quick lunch or a drink in a pub.

'Ask her for the weekend, Lawrence. I'd like to get to know her, then perhaps I can help.' And suddenly, feeling even more shut out than usual, she was angry. 'All right – if you won't phone her, I will!'

'Leave it!' Eyes hard as rocks as only blue eyes can be, he snatched the receiver out of her hand. 'Damn you ... She's not your daughter.'

God, did he know where to hit so it hurt ...

'No ... I have no children. You made sure of that.'

'It was merely that you wanted him to phone his daughter,' the coroner said. 'It had nothing to do with the fact that you considered that gelding the horse might be dangerous?'

'No.'

It had been a row about nothing, really. It was what it had stood for; that he had continually refused to give her a child when he knew how much it meant to her. And when he had used his children as a weapon, all the hurt, all the disgust, had finally surged to the surface and boiled over in a fury of hate.

'So you discussed the proposed telephone call, and then your husband went out to the orchard and you followed soon after in order to pick apples. The horse was tied to the shelter and you saw your husband loading one of the syringes. Can you remember what happened next?'

'I'm leaving you.'

'Like hell you are. You had your chance to go in the spring.'

'I'm leaving, Lawrence. I can't go on living like this.'

He looked at her, the syringe in his left hand. 'You're not going anywhere.'

To her surprise he looked scared.

'I'm going,' she said, enjoying the sudden feeling of being the strongest.

Then, suddenly, he flew at her; grabbed her by the throat and was shaking her violently.

Struggling for breath, fighting him off, she fell against the horse's flank, and as it jumped sideways she heard it scream; saw it rear, and the flailing hooves towering above them; saw it plunge forward so that the rope attached to its headcollar jerked free from the metal ring tethering it to the shelter.

And as it swung round to gallop away up the orchard, it barged into them, knocking them both to the ground.

Lawrence had let go of her throat and, choking, coughing to get her breath, she rolled over on to her knees ...

Saw him lying in the grass beside her, the silver needle driven deep into his thigh.

'Quick ... The antidote!'

'Bastard,' she gasped, holding her neck, enjoying his discomfort.

Let him lie there. Let him stew!

'What happened then, Mrs. Seligman?' the coroner prompted gently.

Until now the questions had been relatively easy – and, until now, she had told the truth ...

'I was up the ladder ... I – I was at the top of the orchard picking apples. I heard him call. He called out, and ... Then the horse came galloping towards me and I realised – I realised it – it must have broken free, so I went back to see what had happened.'

'I see.' The coroner waited, then he said, 'And what did you find?'

Well, the next bit would also be true, and they knew most of it anyway ...

'He was lying on the ground. The needle was in his leg. There was another syringe on a bale of straw beside the shelter, and I realised it was the antidote. I injected it, and tried to resuscitate him. I worked on him for some time. Resuscitation can take longer than people realise. But it was too late. Even before I started.'

'Yes. From what Dr. Jones has told us, I imagine that it was,' the coroner said sympathetically. 'You did all you could, Mrs. Seligman. Far more, I'm sure, than any of us who are not medically trained could have done. I'm sorry, I do realise this is distressing for you. I have only one more question. Can you tell me, did your husband have any problems of any kind? Anything that might have been preying on his mind, be that professional, financial, or perhaps even personal?'

Looking again at the bright oblongs that were the windows, she allowed the light to blind her. 'No.' And in the long silence that seemed to follow, she lowered her eyes to meet the coroner's.

'Thank you, Mrs. Seligman. That's all. You may step down.'

Unsure who or what was controlling her legs, she walked back up the steps and waited while Graham stood up to allow her to get back to her seat.

'Well done. Well done,' he murmured and, limp with relief, her heart thudding in her ears, she sat down.

A mixture of truth, half-truths and lies, but now the coroner had called Tom Harding, the vet, and the questions being asked were merely technical. Her ordeal was over.

Graham was full of admiration. When she'd taken the oath she'd gone so white he'd feared she might be about to faint, but she'd done bloody well. He did like a woman with guts, and it had been bad enough sitting through that inquest as Lawrence's friend.

Now, standing outside the court with the afternoon sun in her hair, she looked bloody magnificent. Vivien had gone to fetch the car, and raising his voice to make himself heard above the traffic passing along Townsend Road, he said, 'You did well. I take it you're happy with a verdict of misadventure rather than accidental death?'

She turned and stared at him.

'You understood it, did you? You see, all the coroner had to do was to rule out ... To establish that Lawrence knew ... That is, well, as a thoroughbred, the horse isn't officially two years old until the first of January, so he was permitted by law to operate even though he wasn't actually qualified. Technically of course, using that particular drug was a bit ...' She was still staring at him and he realised that, relieved on her behalf to have the whole thing over with, he was yet again talking too much. Her husband was dead. What the hell did she care about the technicalities. 'Anyway – when I get back to the office I'll chase the chap at Newbury to get on and find a buyer for the horse. And now we have a death certificate I can start on the paperwork to wind up the estate.' There wasn't much he could do for the poor woman, short of getting on with the legal side, but it would be good to feel he was doing what he could. 'Meantime, if I were you I'd go home and have a large whisky. And think about that holiday ...'

'Maybe I will, now I know I'm not being deported.'

'I'm sorry ...?'

He frowned. Smiling, she waved his question away with her hand. Seemed, in fact, to be laughing at him. Women often did seem to laugh at him ... He never would understand them.

'Anyway,' he said, confused, 'I'll be in touch.'

In the car, as Vivien drove through Alcombe and turned out on to the Periton road towards Tivington, she held her own inquest on the inquest, and Beth remained silent, answering only when necessary. In any case, she wasn't really listening. The ordeal was over, the sun had come out since the rain, and people were walking along the damp-patched tarmac pavements. Mothers with children, running, laughing, stamping in puddles; pensioners in raincoats, carrying shopping baskets; an elderly man with a sack on one shoulder wobbling unsteadily on a bicycle; a small Jack Russell barking from inside a garden gate at a young girl who had stopped to talk to him; and a young woman in a shirt much too big for her was painting the front door of a house. People with full, purposeful lives.

And on the Porlock road, once they were clear of the built-up areas, she noticed that the woods were tinged with copper. Lawrence had been dead for four weeks and three days, and during that time, while she'd been living in a world of her own, late summer had turned into autumn and most of the fields had already been ploughed, exposing the dark red earth common to this part of Somerset ready for new life in the spring.

All around me, she thought, *there is so much life. And for me too there is now a future. One which, at last, that I can chose for myself. Life after Lawrence ...*

'What will you do?' Vivien asked. Have you made any plans?'

'Not really. I'll probably go back to nursing. I'd like to work in a children's hospital.'

'You'll be selling up here, then, and going back to London.'

'I think so, yes.'

She'd never felt she'd fitted into the West Somerset life. To some extent Lawrence had made sure of that. He'd seemed almost jealous of any friendships she had tried to nurture, as if he wanted her entirely to himself – and, of course, everyone knew Anthea and had heard how he'd left her to marry the scarlet woman from London.

Viv turned up the drive and stopped the car in the yard. Beth took the house key from under the stone flowerpot by the front door, and they went into the hall.

Even the house felt less oppressive.

'Two whiskies?' Vivien said, and while she fetched the glasses Beth took off her coat and went into the sitting room. She'd miss this view down the valley when she sold the house and went back to London. Vivien dealt with the drinks and sat down on the sofa.

'I was thinking – you must have had a good career going for you when Lawrence came along. Didn't you mind giving it up?'

'No. I never even thought about it.'

'Umm ... Well, I've got a problem.' She sipped her whisky.

87

'All of a sudden Robin wants us to get married. Here I am with this amazing new job, and he wants us to get married now and start a family within a couple of years. Nor will he hear of us having a nanny. Why he's got this marriage thing suddenly, I can't imagine. And – I'm not sure I can do it. I'd go round the bend being at home all day with a kid. I'm not even sure I want children. Or marriage, come to that ...'

'If that's how you feel, maybe you're not ready for it yet.'

'I'm not sure ...'

'No, well you do have to be sure.'

'I do love him.'

'Yes ... Well – maybe love in itself isn't always enough.' Viv looked at her. 'It isn't,' she continued. 'You have to want the same things out of life. Share the same goals.' *A lesson*, she thought, *that I learnt by bitter experience*. Though perhaps, in passing it on to her stepdaughter, the pain of learning wouldn't have been completely wasted. This must be how it felt to be a parent ... At least parents had the satisfaction of knowing that any lesson was worth learning if it could be passed on to prevent a child getting hurt as deeply. 'You do have to be sure,' she said again.

'Yes – and surely there's got to be more to life than marriage and kids?'

Beth smiled. 'Marriage and kids and a house in the country was all I ever wanted.'

Vivien laughed, shaking her head. 'Ah well ... Well, perhaps Robin isn't the right chap for me. How can I be sure?'

'You could try living with him for a while.'

'Mum would have a blue fit.'

'In this day and age?'

'You bet!' she said, flexing her hand. 'Pure aquamarine ... She's still living back in the forties.'

'Well, it's your life.'

'Yes it is. You're absolutely right! And Robin might settle for me living with him for a while. I need to be in Bristol for a month or two, but I could move down at Christmas. Brilliant ... Thanks, Beth. Thanks a lot. I couldn't talk to Mum like this.' She looked at her watch and finished her drink. 'Anyway, if I don't get going I might not have a job to worry about. You'll be all right?'

'Yes, fine.'

'I'm going to be really pushed for the next couple of months,' she said as she picked up her shoulder bag. 'So it won't only be you I'm neglecting. Do call, though, if you need me. Oh, and by the way – have you heard from Wanda since the funeral?'

'No. Should I have?'

'No,' Vivien said, her mouth tight. 'No ... Oh well, at least with Wanda no news is usually good news. She always calls when she wants something. Anyway, I'll come down and see you again as soon as I can.'

'You know,' she continued as Beth walked with her out to her car, 'I like having a stepmum I can talk to. I just wish it had happened sooner. It's such a pity you and Lawrence didn't have children. You'd have been a lovely mum – and I'd have loved a little half-brother or half-sister to spoil. I think it would have brought us all much closer together.'

Beth didn't reply, and Vivien rested her hand on the roof of the car.

'Could be I'd have enjoyed him or her more than I'll enjoy a child of my own. Still there – we are all different.'

Indeed we are, Beth thought – and returning to the sitting room, she suddenly realised that she didn't seem to know what she wanted any more than Vivien did.

The late afternoon sun, fierce yet fragile, had flooded the room with an uncanny orange light, and picking up her glass she went back to the window to watch the light shimmering on the wet trees and the fields in the valley.

If the 'misadventure' had not occurred, Lawrence would have been due home from the office about now, and she, having finished whatever she'd been doing, would be preparing a tray of tea to bring into the sitting room where they'd have sat together discussing the day and planning tomorrow.

Staring up at her from the grass, his blue eyes wide with horror ... And she, closing his eyes, had smoothed all expression from his face ...

He had not deserved to die – whatever the verdict.

Away down the valley the sun was shining on the wedge of blue sea that, beyond, merged with the Atlantic and all the other oceans that circled the world. And she was free now, her life full of possibilities.

Yet she doubted she had the energy to live it. Now that Vivien had left she sensed the depression closing in around her again – so, really, the inquest had changed nothing.

At that moment Wanda was walking home from work the long way that took her past Gliddon's garage and down Marshalsea Walk into French Weir. She quite often came this way on fine evenings to delay returning to the gloom of Ashton Grove, and because she liked to watch the river where it converged and poured down over the weir, brown water rising again into white froth as it raced away.

As time carries people, she thought, looking down from the bridge.

'Come out, Plum,' Dad had said from the river bank by the bridge in the oak wood below Cloutsham one day when they'd been out for a walk on their own and she'd insisted on stopping to paddle. 'Stone the lizards – it's March. The water's freezing.'

'You said you'd make me a fishing rod. I've got to see where the fish live.'

'If you fall in, we'll both be in trouble.'

'It's not cold when you're paddling, honest,' and knee deep in water, she'd watched him take his big pocket knife with the orange handle out of his shooting jacket and cut a stick from a nut tree. Then, while he was making the rod, she'd begun jumping from boulder to boulder. 'There's fish! Look ... I seen one!' and leaning forward to see better, she had slipped and sat down in water up to her waist.

'You were going to make me a fishing rod anyway, weren't you,' she'd said through chattering teeth as he'd dried her the best he could and wrapped her in his coat. 'You had all the things in your pocket.'

'I guess so,' he'd said and, resigned, he chuckled. 'And I guess you were bound to fall in. I should have brought a towel.'

Walking on, leaving the roar of the weir behind her, she realised she had never remembered things like that while he was alive. Only these past weeks had the memories come, poignant, stinging and strong. *He was lovely*, she thought, *especially when I was little* ... Remembering him now was like learning to love him over again, and perhaps rather better than she had when he was alive.

She walked along Staplegrove Road and, turning into Ashton Grove, she could hear the usual early-evening rumpus coming from number twelve. Pete playing his heavy metal compact discs at full volume with the windows wide open; Samantha and blonde Shirley screeching with mirth at something which in most people would hardly raise a smile. The neighbours would complain again soon. Poor devils ... Old Rogers cared little for his tenants beyond keeping his grubby little 'flats' free of divorcées, coloureds and queers – and for his neighbours he cared even less, though no one ever seemed to report him.

The communal kitchen was, as ever, cluttered with empty foil dishes and tonight the stale air reeked of takeaway curry. She took the bread she'd bought out of her sack bag and looked at the cooker. Shit – forget it. She'd cleaned that cooker a couple of weekends ago since no one else ever seemed to bother, and already it was filthy again. Even Mum had been horrified when she'd seen the place – and she'd only let Dad in because she'd had no option. The day she'd crashed the car, he'd come to fetch her from casualty and had brought her back here to pick up the clothes she'd needed for Luccombe.

'It might be best if you wait in the car,' she'd said.

'Why ... Shacked up with some lusty young lad, are you? Not that it's any of my business, I suppose. Unless he's not worthy of you.'

'It's the room. It's not up to much as yet. It needs painting, and new curtains and things, and I haven't had time.'

'Time – or the money?'

'Well, a bit of both.'

Immediately he reached into his jacket for his wallet.

'No, Daddy – don't. Thanks all the same, but it's my room and I can manage. I'm going to do it up soon.'

'On what?' And he'd insisted on giving her fifty pounds, 'To buy some paint. And a black rug and some white curtains or something. I suppose when you do it, it'll all have to be done in black and white.'

She'd put the money he'd given her towards the overdraft that she'd made sure he never knew about. *But I must do something about that room*, she thought, depressed. And she couldn't face that cooker tonight. She'd make do with the bread, a tin of sardines she'd bought at the same time, and a can of Coke which, wonder of all wonders, had been over-looked in the back of the fridge.

Upstairs in her room she put the food down on her bed and turned on the televideo he had given her last birthday. She remembered him watching her face as she'd torn off the bright green-and-red-striped paper.

'Oh, Daddy ...'

'Like it?'

'You bet I do!'

'I see you still haven't done anything to this room.'

'I will. I am going to.'

I must, she thought. *I must do it now, if for no better reason than that he wanted me to*. Watching some idiot bouncing around on the television screen, she thought about the inquest – and sud-denly his passing seemed absolutely, overwhelmingly final.

She needed to talk to someone. Not to Pete or to Sam or Shirley, although they were kind. She needed to talk to someone who was in this with her. And that had to be Viv. Forget the fighting – blood, as Mum always said, was thicker than water.

She took her purse out of her sack, ran down the stairs that were vibrating from the beat of Pete's music, and standing in front of the pay phone in the dingy narrow hall, she dialled Viv's number.

The phone rang for ages. Then, thinking that in her panic she might have dialled the wrong number, she replaced the receiver and tried again.

There was still no reply.

Damn it, no. Of course – she'd be with Robin. Whose number, so he'd said, was in the book ...

This is crazy! But she found the number, dialled, and waited again, listening to it ringing. Perhaps they'd gone out ...

And then he answered.

'Hi, Robin – it's Wanda. Viv's sister ... Is Viv there? Can I talk to her?'

'Hey, slow down. Hi, Wanda – Viv's sister. Oddly enough I was just thinking about you. Must be telepathy.'

'Can I speak to Viv?'

'She isn't here. Change of plan. She went straight back to Bristol.'

'Oh,' she said, disappointed.

'Why? What's up?'

'Nothing. I just felt ... It doesn't matter.'

'It sounds to me as if it might matter quite a lot. Do you want to come over?'

'You're busy.'

'No I'm not. Viv's going to call me about the inquest later on. Come over, and she can tell you at the same time.'

'If you're sure ...' She did need to talk.

'Of course I'm sure. Stay right where you are and I'll come and fetch you. By the way – do you like beef casserole?'

'Love it – but don't fetch me. I'll get the bus.'

'No you won't, Wanda. Not tonight. Stay right where you are. I'm on my way.'

Anthea retied the belt of the old thing's blue woollen dressing-gown, and having supported her weight while lowering her into her chair by the fire, began to pat dry the long white hair. Bath night and hair washing were always a bit of a performance ...

Pity I didn't inherit her hair. Or her skin, Anthea thought. *She has wonderful skin. At this rate it won't be long before I look older than she does. 'Struth, at my age she could do a day's work on the farm and still find the energy to spend half the night at her herbs and her healing.* And always, on midsummer nights, it was off to Glastonbury Tor. Amy never missed her annual reunion with her cronies and, as it nearly always rained, like as not she'd come home soaked to the skin.

How Anthony had teased her ...

'A healer you may be, Mother – but who's going to heal you when you go down with pneumonia? Now tell me that.'

In those days pneumonia wouldn't have dared. And look at the poor old thing now.

'Wanda will,' the old thing said suddenly.

93

'Wanda will what?' Anthea said distractedly, busy with the towel.

'She'm a right little pickle,' said the old thing, chuckling.

'Umm ... You know, Anthony had hair like yours. I don't know how I came by my wire wool thatch.'

Such a good-looking lad, Anthony. When they were little it was him who people had thought was the girl. Well, at least he and Lawrence wouldn't have to grow old and end up like the poor old lady, shrivelled in some places, bloated in others, and completely dependent.

Anthea too had begun to feel her age lately, if she let herself stop to think about it. Out in the weather all day, the creaking joints and the broken veins in her cheeks were a little more evident with every winter. She couldn't pretend that the money Lawrie had left her wouldn't help if she began to find the farm work too heavy and needed to employ a lad to help.

And if Gran really did have to go into a home – well, at least the extra money might help to pay her dues to one that didn't permanently reek of pee.

Such a nice letter Graham had written to tell her about the money.

He'd have been at the inquest this afternoon ... And yet again she wondered how it had gone – and about the verdict.

'What do you fancy for supper, Mum? Chicken, or a nice bit of fish?'

No response. Not a flicker. *Where are you now?* Anthea wondered. Pink face, healthily rounded; green eyes, bright and clear – but her thoughts could be anywhere.

I'm talking to myself again, she thought. *But she's alive and well in there somewhere ...*

It's not polite to watch a lady have her hair done, Amy said to the man sitting in the chair on the other side of the fire. Her scalp was sore from Anthea's rubbing. *She doesn't know her own strength, your wife.*

But in her head there were so many faces, so many voices ...

And suddenly the man was not watching her. He wasn't even there.

*

The late-evening weather forecast predicted storms – high winds, and more rain. Beth watched without interest, then turned off the television and went up to bed.

Lying in the darkness she listened to the silence. A silence which began to sound like the whine of a monitor in an intensive-care unit when a heart had stopped beating.

And as she fell asleep it settled inside her head as an endless, high-pitched scream that came with her into her dreams.

'It's got to be in here somewhere,' Wanda said, frantically scrabbling in her sack-bag. Then, triumphantly, she produced it. The door key!

'Sssh ... Give it to me. You'll wake the entire street.'

'Can you see? I've got a torch in here somewhere.' She began to scrabble again.

'What else have you got in there for God's sake?'

'Potions that will turn you into a pumpkin,' she said, giggling.

'Sssh, Wanda. Sssh ...!'

Robin realised that she *was* trying to whisper. It just wasn't working. She'd told him she usually drank cider, but he hadn't had any so he'd given her wine and, liking it rather well, she'd had a couple or three too many. 'By this time of night I'm half pumpkin already,' he said, and pushed open the door.

'Poor Robin ... Yes – you're so old.'

'I am. And elderly gentlemen need respect and a good night's sleep.'

The hall was lit dimly by some sort of pinkish night light, and suddenly serious she turned to face him.

'Thanks for tonight. I really am grateful. I'm sorry if I stopped you working.'

'You didn't. And you're welcome.'

He had laughed more than he'd laughed in weeks and felt a good deal better for it.

'I'm not going to ask you in.'

'I should think not, at this time of night. Every one bar you, me and the witch's cat was in bed hours ago.'

'Gran was a witch, I swear it. Well, that is, Dad called her a witch. Really, she was a healer. If Viv hasn't told you that, it's because she doesn't approve.'

That was more than likely. It didn't sound like Viv's scene at all. The witch's grandchild a senior manager at Hall, Thane and Daniels? Thane would love that. He could blame her for every bug in their computers and every consignment that disappeared in transit.

'What are you smiling about?' Wanda asked.

'Nothing.' He wasn't going to start Wanda up again. 'Just get your butt up those stairs, now there's a good Zebra.'

She looked at him hard, and in the mean light, the heavy black around her eyes looked like hideous purple bruises.

'If you don't like me calling you that, don't put that muck on your face,' he said. 'You're a nice-looking kid. You don't need any make-up at all.'

She pulled a face at him. 'I said you were masterful.' Then she blew him a kiss. 'Thanks anyway. Well ... See you around.'

'If you're passing The Winchester of a Saturday, look in and I'll buy you a cider. I'm usually there at lunchtime.'

He heard her close the door behind him, and as he walked down the path he noticed the moon shining on the petrol tank of the huge black motorbike parked in the tiny garden and, under his breath he began to whistle.

But driving back through the well-lit streets of Taunton to his flat, he glanced at the empty passenger seat, and when he thought of Viv the whistling stopped. God, she could be tricky – and to her sister, a right bitch.

'Wanda called. She wants to know about the inquest,' he'd said to her on the phone – and before he'd had chance to tell her the rest of it, she had jumped down his throat.

'Bloody Wanda is the bloody limit. She's been down to see Mum once and she hasn't been in touch with Beth at all. I've tried to call her twice this evening, so if she wants to know about the inquest she can now bloody well call me. I've got enough to do without phoning round half the county looking for her. Anyway, love, I'll see you on Friday.'

So it was him who had told Wanda the outcome of the inquest. She'd been upset at the start of the evening and she didn't need a rocket from Vivien.

And if he hadn't told Viv that Wanda was sitting there crossed-legged on his floor eating the beef casserole he'd intended for her – that was her fault and his business. She'd been so snappish and had rung off too fast.

Anyway, she only ever told him as much about anything as it suited her to tell him – if and when it suited her to tell him ... So it served her right.

What else hadn't she told him? Half-truths were as bad as lies. He hated lies – and now, damn it, she'd got him at it as well.

It was years since Anthea'd had a night as bad as this. She was usually so tired by the time she got to bed that she fell asleep instantly. Tonight she was restless, her body tense, her thoughts unreasonably angry and racing in circles.

Misadventure, Viv had said when she'd phoned.

Of course. What else had she honestly expected?

All the same, she'd like to give that bitch across the valley a good helping of misadventure for stealing Lawrence and dealing her seven years of misery. Seven years which, until his death had stirred up all the old hurt and the anger, she had thought she had pretty much accepted.

Instead, these weeks since his death, she had seemed to be living through it all over again – and eventually, just after two o'clock and as wide awake as ever she got up and went downstairs.

Percy was sleeping peacefully in his box by the Rayburn and, putting on her wellingtons and blue-quilted anorak over her pyjamas she went out into the garden.

It was a wonderful night. Clear and moonlit, yet warm, and she wandered down through the barn to the yard and looked into the shed where Gert and Petal were sleeping curled up in the deep straw, each in their opposite corners.

On hearing her approach, they raised their heads to stare first at her, and then, sleepily flexing their necks, they turned their attention on each other. They were becoming increasingly aggressive with each other since Percy had been spending so much time indoors, and before they could wake fully and start something, Anthea walked on to lean on the gate into the field where she'd put several lame sheep to graze near to home with the milking cows.

Concerned as to what she could do to prevent the geese

scrapping with each other if Percy needed to spend most of his time indoors during the coming winter, she looked out across the sleeping valley to the glimmer of the streetlights of Porlock.

A small town that was barely more than a village, but she began to wonder about the people who lived there. What they did with their days and their lives.

And this, I suppose, is my life. Up here on my own with Gran, my birds and my animals will be me now until I go wherever Lawrence has gone.

It wasn't a bad life. Most of the time she enjoyed it. It was just that there were times when she did feel somewhat isolated and, to be honest, quite lonely.

There were no lights in the house at Tivington. The bitch must be sleeping, her conscience untroubled. Anthea wondered what she did to be sufficiently tired to sleep; how she passed her time with nothing to think about bar that house and its garden.

What was the house like inside ...?

What was she like – the bitch? Not a murderess, apparently, though even now Anthea wasn't entirely convinced. In fact, she was becoming increasingly curious about that woman. Would like to meet her, and demand the answers to one or two extremely pertinent questions ...

Chapter Five

The end of October. He had been dead for seven weeks and four days. Beyond that, spending almost every day entirely alone, time had ceased to exist. Unable to concentrate on even the simplest of tasks, the growing pile of letters remained unanswered, the garden untended, and without Mrs. Westcott the house would have been thick with dust.

'My Stan, you know, he'd come up and see to that lawn for you,' Ma Westcott had said, watching her through pebble-lensed spectacles. 'Yays ... You only got to give him the say so.'

'I'll do it this afternoon.'

'And that coffee you spilt the other day has left a nasty mark on that there dressing-gown,' she said, unsure if she was overstepping the mark. 'I'll wash it for you, if you want. It'll dry lovely in this wind.'

Realising that it was almost midday, Beth turned to go upstairs to get dressed. Ma Westcott liked nothing better than a good gossip and, like so many of these locals, seemed to be related in one way or another to everyone in the district. Beth didn't need it to be spread about that she wasn't coping. Apart from any of Ma Westcott's other relationships, she had once let drop the titbit that she was first cousin to the girl who cleaned for Anthea. 'I don't like idle talk though, my dear, so you needn't bother yourself. No ... Me and my Stan, our loyalties are to you and Mr. Seligman.' All the same, Beth had been careful. Probably to the point where, compared to the other families for whom Mrs. Westcott cleaned, she found her stand-offish.

'Aren't you going to have any breakfast?'

'I'll have something when I come down,' Beth said, annoyed

'Yays,' said Mrs. Westcott anxiously, hitching up her glasses. 'Well I don't know what of then, my dear, because there's nothing in that there fridge.'

She meant well, of course. As did all the other people who had been kind; Dr. Mayhew and the vicar; Vivien and Robin who'd been down once for lunch, and Helen Franks who had called several times for a cup of tea and had repeatedly asked her for supper or Sunday lunch, all of which she had refused. Some of the kindest people were people she hardly knew; the milkman; one or two of Lawrence's clients, or those for whom he had gone out of his way to be helpful – and the lads at the police station had sent her a bouquet of flowers.

In response to all this she'd barely managed to be polite. She certainly had no energy for company – and with poor old Ma Westcott, the most consistently kind of them all, she seemed permanently on the verge of losing her temper.

If only Liz still lived here things might be different. She could have talked to Liz. But soon after Beth had moved down from London, the Common Market subsidies had finally put paid to Mike's attempts to farm sheep and he had found a job managing upwards of a thousand acres of grouse moor in the north of Scotland. As neither Beth nor Liz were letter writers, after a year or so their communications had dwindled to a few lines in Christmas and birthday cards.

Having seen the announcement of Lawrence's death in *The Daily Telegraph*, Liz had written immediately and, recognising the handwriting, it was the one letter that Beth had opened. A long letter full of news and undeserved kindness – and thus, even that letter Beth had been unable to answer.

She seemed to be existing now in some vast winter landscape of the mind. A cold grey marshland in which the path back was blocked, the way ahead obliterated by fog, and from which, the ground under her feet being so soft and uncertain, she had no energy to find her way out.

The days were the worst. And there was so much that she ought to be doing. Vivien had helped her to sort through his desk, but she still has his clothes to see to. And his car. She'd

100

have to clean that Range Rover and sell it. Ought not to leave it out there to rust in the barn ...

At least at night, with the help of Dr. Mayhew's pills, sleep did come eventually. And lying now in her bed waiting anxiously for a few hours of oblivion, she reached out for the bottle of tablets and took two more.

Relaxing into sleep, she could see the white Range Rover surrounded by tall blackened reeds in the barren marsh that she now inhabited, and as she watched, the reeds seemed to part and entice her in closer.

Scared but already deeply asleep, she eased further towards his side of the bed, and, holding on to his pillows, believing that it was him she was holding, the fog suddenly seemed to clear, and she saw it; the clearly defined path forward – and way out on the far side of the marsh, a cluster of bright welcoming lights.

'When, then?' Robin asked as they lay curled together, Viv's back against his chest like a two spoons in a drawer.

'Soon,' she said sleepily. 'New Year.'

'Forgive me if I don't put money on it.'

'Silly to move before.'

'Two weeks ago you said Christmas.'

'Things will be quieter by New Year.'

'Okay. So move in at New Year. Is that a promise?'

'Promise,' she muttered sleepily into her pillow, and pushed his hand away.

That was that then. *No oats for you tonight, Robin* – and although tomorrow was Saturday she'd be up at sparrow-fart to fly back to Bristol to keep the company warm. *We're like a long-married couple*, he thought. *Except the spark's gone out of us even before we've been through the ceremony.*

He eased away from her, turned on to his back, and pulled the duvet up under his chin. In a minute he'd have to get up in the cold for a pee, and thereafter it would take him ages to get to sleep. In future he'd do well to bear that in mind and go a bit easier on the beer.

'The rate I'm going, by the time we get married I'll be limping up the aisle with a bottle strapped to my trousers.'

She didn't answer. She was already asleep.

He lay looking at the glow of the streetlights on the ceiling and, comparing her with Wanda, wondered how two sisters could be so different.

Wanda was up and out of the house in Ashton Grove before any of the others stirred, and she returned from the Saturday market with some off-cuts of crimson carpet and a very jazzy pair of reasonably priced curtains just as Pete emerged, yawning, to polish his already pristine motorbike.

'You're up early. Had an expensive morning already by the look of it.'

'Twenty-five quid, the lot.' If you didn't count the cheek from the young male stallholder.

Pete grunted, and refolded the clean yellow duster. Wearing dirty trainers, old jeans torn at the knees and a shabby black leather jacket, he was, as always, far less well turned out than that motorbike which was the love of his life.

'Ere, by the way,' he said as she went up the path, 'Where's your Mum live? Down Porlock way, in'it? Only me and me mates is going to meet out over Exmoor tomorra' for a bit of dirt tracking. I could give you a lift if you want to go and see her.'

'Brilliant.'

'I don't want to be late getting back, mind. Clocks go back tomorra', and I'll have to clean the bike when I get home.'

'Of course,' she said with a grin. 'Okay, I'll phone Mum and tell her. Pete – you're a star.'

'Yeah ...' he said despondently, returning his attention to the mean black machine, 'You try telling that to Shirley.'

Wanda's room had always looked better in the mornings, especially when the sun was shining through the window, and since she'd set to work it was looking really quite homely. She hadn't realised that a coat of white paint and a few posters scrounged from a travel agent could make such a difference. Athens, Antibes, and Jamaica arranged on one wall, and on the other side of the room, Switzerland, Alaska and the Rockies in winter. You could turn one way or the other, depending on whether you wanted to be warmed up or cooled down. Free air conditioning, and or central heating.

She stepped off the chair and, standing back to assess the

overall effect with the new curtains and the carpet, decided that she was pleased. Couldn't think why she hadn't got around to it long ago. All she needed now was a duvet cover to match the curtains, and perhaps a few cushions. She hadn't been able to run to that, what with Christmas less than two months away.

Well chuffed with herself and her morning's work, she picked up her purse and ran downstairs to the phone.

'Hi, Mum. It's me. I thought you might be out in the yard ... Yes – lovely morning ... Yes, quite a frost earlier. What ...? Yes, I am. I'm feeling great. Look, Vivien isn't coming down tomorrow is she?'

'No dear, she phoned. She's working. She and Robin were down last Sunday.'

'Can I come home for lunch, then? Someone's offered me a lift.'

'Of course you can,' she said, pleased.

'Any chance of roast beef and apple pie? Oh, and Mum, you haven't got any cushions going spare, have you? And what about a nice colourful patchwork quilt or something, to go over my bed?'

'I may have some cushions. I'm not so sure about a patchwork quilt.'

Wanda replaced the phone and went back upstairs to admire her handiwork. She wouldn't even mind Robin seeing her room now. And she thought about her father.

'What ...? *Colours*? No black and white?' she seemed to hear him say.

In fact, in that room with its smell of new paint, his presence was suddenly quite strong, and she knew that he would have been pleased.

'Wanda ...! You up there ...?' Shirley yelled from the bottom of the stairs. Resenting the interruption, Wanda went out to look over the bannisters.

Shirley, looking up at her from the first landing, was dressed in a long red tee shirt, her hair was wrapped in a towel and her face – except for her mouth and her eyes – was solid and white with a face pack. 'Damn it,' she said through her teeth as she touched her cheeks. 'I've split me mask yelling ... I'm crumbling.'

103

Wanda laughed.

'Fancy coming out for a drink at lunchtime? End of the month. Me and Sam, we're feeling flush.'

'Naah ... Not today.' And then she had a thought. It was Saturday ... 'Which pub?'

'We thought we'd go out to Rumwell.'

'No, but if you're going through town I wouldn't say no to a lift as far as The Winchester.'

'Big quilt. Cloutsham. In the loft,' Gran said from her chair beside the fire. Anthea switched off the new-fangled mobile phone thing that Viv had brought her, set it down gingerly on the table and looked at her in amazement.

'So there is. Yours and Pop's from the big bed. It must be up there somewhere. Well I'm blessed ... Clever you!'

My, this morning's slight frost had sharpened up some members of the family no end. As for Wanda – the last time she'd been up early enough to see a frost she'd needed to have her nappy changed. And doing up her room? There was hope for the child yet.

'I'd better go up in the loft and see what I can find. She wants cushions as well. Have we got any cushions?'

'Yes,' Gran said, nodding solemnly. 'Oh yes ... Two and three farthings – and four ounces of sherbet.'

Ah well, Anthea thought, smiling. *I'll probably be like that one day.* Sooner than later, most like – though for the moment things were looking up. Viv and Robin last Sunday, Wanda this. She'd seen and heard more from both of her girls lately than she had in months.

It was hot in The Winchester and, thanks to a rabble of students strung out along the bar, horrendously noisy.

'You want to watch him, Wanda,' Keith shouted over the top of his pint. 'You know what they say about bald men.'

'Who's bald?' said Robin indignantly, smoothing the sides of his head with his hands.

'Receding, old chap. Definitely receding,' said Malcolm, laughing.

Wanda said, 'Yes well, I keep telling him – he's old.'

Keith gave him a friendly nudge. 'Nice sister-in-law you'll

have, chum. Stick from the family as well as your friends.'

'I have a hard life as it is, I'm telling you.' He slapped his knees. 'Well, my elderly ears have had enough of this racket. You lot aren't drinking, and I've had my lunchtime ration so I'm off. I've got work to do this afternoon. I'm going your way, Wanda, if you want a lift. I've got to go to the china shop in Richmond Road. I broke two more plates this morning.'

'What you need,' Malcolm said. 'Is a wife. They aren't as clumsy as we are, love 'em.'

'I'm trying, lad. Believe me, am I trying,' Robin said, squeezing past him to get out from behind the beer stained table.

'Bye, Wanda. Watch him,' Keith said.

'Oh, I reckon he's still got enough hair not to be too dangerous.'

'See you again,' Malcolm said with a grin.

She hoped so. She liked his friends. When she'd walked in and seen them with him strung out along the bench under the bookshelves at the corner table, she'd almost lost her nerve and backed out before he saw her. In brogues, cord trousers, expensive sweaters and tweed jackets, his friends had looked even older than he was, and fusty. They'd been surprised when he'd beckoned her to join them. Shocked, actually, until he'd explained who she was. And then she'd seen herself as they would be seeing her. A Zebra. All black and white ...

Now, as she left with Robin and waited inside the porch while he went to the Gents, she looked at her reflection in a mirror advertising Guinness. Staring back at her was a young girl with black spiky hair, white powdered face, black lips and eyes. The girl they had seen.

But what had they seen, exactly ... Some sort of freak demanding to be noticed? And she did look far more at home as part of an advertisement beside the tall glass of Guinness than she must have done with his friends in the bar.

'Right,' Robin said. 'Fit?' They walked across the road to the car park, and he continued 'You've seen my flat, Wanda. I've broken so many plates I could really do with six new of everything. I'm not much good at chosing things for the house. I suppose you wouldn't like to come with me?'

'If you want. Sure.'

'Thanks. Then I must go home and get down to some work.'

'You're lucky you've got work to do,' she said as they got into his well cool little black car. 'The property market's been dead since the autumn of eighty-nine and the bottom dropped out of the building trade around the same time.'

He put the key in the ignition and stared at her. 'How the hell do you know that? So precisely?'

'I just do,' she said, suddenly self-conscious. 'Around the same time there was a rise in bank rate, and that didn't help either.'

'You know, Wanda, you are full of surprises.'

'Robin – everybody knows about the recession. I'm not deaf and blind.'

'No, nor are you daft. All the same, I'm not having black and white crockery – I'm telling you.'

The Saturday traffic would be heavy in town, so he drove out along the Wellington Road and cut back through Bishops Hull and the trading estate. He parked in the compound of the large warehouse that sold china and glass seconds, and as soon as they were inside, he sort of went funny. 'I hate shopping.'

'Of course you do. You're a man.'

'Where do we start?' he said, looking round, stunned by the choice.

'Oh come on,' she said, laughing, and took hold of his sleeve. It wasn't even as if the place was crowded.

'I like plain plates with borders. You choose the colour.'

'But not black and white.'

'Definitely not, Zebra. No.'

To get her own back she teased him with one or two really grim, gaudy designs, but even then it took less than half an hour for her to find pottery plates with a multicoloured floral border that he liked. The assistant wrapped them up and he paid.

'That wasn't as bad as I thought it would be,' he said when they were back in the car. 'Viv would have wanted bone china, and she'd have been ferreting round in there for hours. Right then – it's a lovely sunny autumn afternoon, so what shall we do with it?'

A walk in a wood along paths thick with dry crunchy leaves, or across a beach somewhere; a game of tennis, or even a video in front of his fire ... She had plenty of ideas but she said nothing, because, in the warehouse, somewhere between the stacks of Minton and the Worcester, she'd suddenly had one idea that was wilder than all the others.

And he belonged to Viv.

'You've got work to do.'

'So I have,' he said. 'Yes ... So I have.'

Was it wishful thinking, or had he really sounded genuinely disappointed?

'Hello,' Martin said, stopping in the corridor outside Vivien's door. 'My, it must be tough at the top. I didn't expect to see you in on a Saturday afternoon.'

In a rainbow-striped sweatshirt, jeans and trainers he didn't look at all like the stiff, weekday Martin who wore dark suits and designer ties.

'Hi.'

'Started my Christmas shopping,' he said, holding up a fistful of carrier bags. 'I hope you're impressed by my efficiency out of the office as well as within it.'

'Go away.'

'Ah ... So *it is* tough at the top.'

'Not particularly.' She crossed out a section of the report she was writing and looked at him. 'However, if you stay any longer your sweatshirt will undoubtedly give me a headache.'

'Great, isn't it? My sister brought it back from America.'

'The Americans are famed for their appalling taste in clothes.'

'Oh ... I'm rather fond of it.'

'Yes ...' and laughing, she gave in, leant back in her chair. 'It's nice. I like it.'

'Do you really?' he said, pleased.

'Yes, I really do. Now – will you please go away?'

He raised the hand with the carrier bags in farewell, and smiling at his back she watched him walk away down the long antiseptic corridor to his office next to the one that had been hers. His trainers squeaked on the polished floor and he walked with a controlled spring, like a large predatory cat. He could be very pompous at times but she had always liked him. Fancied him, to be honest.

She rewrote the first paragraph of the report, and a while later heard his footsteps returning. 'Bye,' she called, without looking up. His shoes stopped squeaking and he didn't answer. She glanced up and saw him standing in the doorway holding a plastic cup of something from the drink dispenser and a snack-pack of biscuits. 'Martin ...'

'A little something to keep you going. I'm creeping of course, since you're now my boss.'

She rested her elbows on the desk and looked at him hard. 'That really bugs you, doesn't it?'

'As a matter of fact, no. Not at all. Though I admit I may have worn the joke a bit thin,' he said. Perching on a corner of her desk, he folded his arms and looked at her. 'I'm glad you got the job.'

'Kind.' She nodded at the tea and biscuits. 'But I don't believe you.'

'Try this then,' he said, his mouth twisting in a sardonic smile. 'You're the one who's working in Bristol on a Saturday afternoon. I'm the one who's just landed the new European Market Manager's job at Miller and Coots. You'll remember we discussed it a few months back when it was first advertised? The one based in Brussels, with a salary half as good again as yours?' He laughed at her. 'Vivien, my love, do something about your lower jaw or the flies will home in to hibernate.'

'You ... You jammy beggar. Well done!'

'You're madly jealous, but above all, astounded.'

'No,' she said. 'You deserve it, and I'm pleased.'

'Yes, well,' he said, opening the packet of biscuits and helping himself before he handed them to her. 'I just hope I'm up to it.'

'Of course you're up to it.' He was usually such a cocky sod ... 'To be honest,' she said, relenting, 'I thought this job was yours for certain, and I suspect I only got it because I'm a woman. Thane wanted a woman in senior management. Company image for the 90's – and all that.'

'You're certainly a woman,' he said, eyeing her appreciatively. 'Great for the company image – and the clever daughter of an able father – as our Mr Thane is well aware. As to your female attributes, I have recently begun to notice those myself. A little late in the day, perhaps, given the circumstances, but I have noticed.' He hesitated, and grinned at her. 'As a reward for her magnanimity in defeat, my new job being superior to hers, perhaps this attractive woman would allow me to buy her dinner tonight? A double celebration ...?'

'No thanks, Mart.' Smarmy beggar – though, despite what might have been a suggestion that she'd got the job because Thane had admired her father, she was tempted. She picked up her biro and looked down at the report.

'How about next Saturday then? A friend of mine's invited me plus a lady friend to go sailing.'

'At this time of year? You're mad.'

'Not the way Jonathan sails. It's a forty-foot yacht with heaters, showers and a television.'

'Lucky Jonathan. Sorry, Martin. Next Saturday I'll be in Taunton with Robin.'

'It's serious then, this thing with Robin.'

'We're getting married.'

'When?' he said, raising his eyebrows in exaggerated surprise.

'Sometime,' she said, again annoyed.

'Good Lord ...'

'People usually say congratulations.'

'Yes, I suppose they do. It's just that from what I've seen of Robin I wouldn't have thought you two had much in common.'

'Thanks ... Look, Martin, push off, will you? I really am busy.'

He got up from her desk and walked to the door. 'Maybe I'll ask you about dinner again when you've had time to think about it.'

'I'm not going to have dinner with you, Martin. Not tonight, or any other night.'

'Vivien,' he said lightly, 'in my opinion a woman like you will need a stronger man than Robin – but I am only asking you out to dinner. I'm not asking you to marry me.'

'Martin dear,' she said lightly, 'I wouldn't marry you if you were the last man on this earth.'

Because I'm going to marry Robin – one day. We have a

great deal in common, and he's worth ten of you.

'Would you not?' Martin said, and smiling easily, he bit into the biscuit, and walked away down the corridor.

Damn you, she thought, rattled beyond reason, her concentration blown. *You cocky bastard ...*

'Hi. It's me.'

'Hi, you,' Robin said, tucking the phone under his chin so that he could finish rubbing out a wall on the plan he was drawing. 'Busy?'

'Just finishing. Bloody Martin came in and distracted me. I do love you ...'

'I love you too,' he said, surprised and pleased. She wasn't usually so forthcoming with her affections, especially over the phone.

'I knew I'd feel better when I talked to you.'

'You'll be down this evening then, will you, if you've finished your report?'

'No love, my house is a tip. I'll clean up, have an early night and be with you first thing in the morning. Stay in bed ... I'll bring the newspapers and join you. We'll have the extra hour tomorrow.'

Now there was a promise for an October Sunday ... She took with one hand and gave with the other, but she wasn't often this yielding. His reward, perhaps, for doing the right thing. He hadn't expected her to phone but it was as well he hadn't given in to impulse and gone off with Wanda for the afternoon. He was intrigued by that little Zebra, and had begun to enjoy her company perhaps more than he ought to.

'What are you doing?'

'Working,' he said.

'And eating liquorice, I can tell.'

'Yes,' he said, taking the stick of it out of his mouth so that he could laugh. 'I am.'

'What will you do this evening? Go to the pub?'

'No, I'll probably watch the good old telly.'

Right now, if he had a halo, it would be glowing. Anyway he was past turning out to the pub more than once of a weekend. When he did go it was really only for the company.

*

'Okay, you aren't coming out,' Jerry said, fuming at the other end of the telephone. 'Why aren't you coming out?'

'Because I'm staying in,' Wanda said. 'I'm going to watch a video.'

'In other words, you'd rather stay in of a Saturday night and watch a video than come to a disco with me.'

'Yes, I would.'

'Great. That's it then, kid. Nobody does this to me. You won't get another chance.'

Big deal ... The line went dead and, making a face at the receiver, she replaced it on the pay phone. Jerry was a nice enough bloke – except for his hands – but they'd only been out together a few times and he'd started to act like he owned her. Ugh ... He had really creepy hands. White and puggy with short, fat, dub-topped fingers – and he bit his nails down to the quicks. The sort of hands you didn't want too near you ...

Robin, now – he had fantastic hands. Artist's hands, clean and slender with long bony fingers. In fact he was pretty special altogether. At nineteen (and as intact, unfortunately, as it was possible to be, having ridden horses since she could walk) Wanda knew she was hardly a world authority on men. But Robin sure as hell beat the lights out of those she'd known so far – Jerry, Tim the bassoon player from Tech, and Ginger, whose sole driving force was to earn enough bread to keep his slightly out-dated, four-inch, orange mohican in hair lacquer.

'Hi,' Shirley said, coming out of the kitchen with a plate of fish and chips. 'Want a chip?'

Wanda took one, and followed her upstairs. Pete was playing his stereo again, its volume belting the plaster and the floorboards.

'You in or out tonight?'

'In,' Wanda said.

'So am I.'

'I hired a video. Come up and watch it if you like.'

'What happened to Jerry?'

'I think he just exploded.'

Shirley let out a shriek of laughter. 'You're a one, you are, Wanda. Any rate, you shouldn't be going round with the likes of him.'

'What's wrong with him?' Apart from his hands ...

Stopping on the first landing, Shirley held out the plate to her again. 'Nothing's wrong with him, duck. Nothing's wrong with me, or Pete, or Sam either. It's just that you're different. Posh ... Been to a private school, and that. What's the video?'

'Death In Venice. Dirk Bogarde.'

Shirley pulled a face. 'Sounds cheerful. What's it about then?'

'Mahler yearning for a boy's youth and beauty while dying of cholera. It's a classic.'

'Great,' Shirley said doubtfully. 'I liked that Bogarde in the Carry On films, meself. See – you are different.' She shrugged. 'Okay. You put the film on, and I'll finish me chips and bring us up a couple of mugs of coffee.'

Wanda ran up the last flight of stairs to her room. Taking the video over to the television, she stopped in front of the mirror. She was certainly different. A Guinness girl ... A girl who dressed to catch attention? That wasn't really how she was at all. She was really very shy. The Gothic gear was fun, but for her it was also a protection – so Viv was probably right. A bit childish really ... And Robin hated it, which was hardly surprising. His friends were so tweedy; younger versions of Dad in a way. And although Robin wasn't as conservative a dresser as they were, his clothes – that black cord suit at the funeral and today's yellow ochre cord trousers and scarlet shirt under a navy blue Guernsey – weren't nearly as way out as hers. He was sort of halfway between the two.

So, since on the whole people are much as their clothes and make-up portray them, *who and what am I*, she asked her black and white reflection? More than a cardboard cut-out in an advertisement and, by birth, much closer to tweed than to art.

A prisoner, then, to all my family taught and made of me? But who and what do I want to be? That's the thing. Where will I fit in best and feel most comfortable?

'Find yourself,' Dad had said not so long ago. 'Then be yourself. That's growing up – but understand, we all have to bend a little, compromise, because we all do have to fit in somewhere.'

112

He'd been full of funny, preachy sayings, though the older she got the more she was finding that they were true. And in her case, compromise did seem to be about halfway between art and tweed. About, in fact, where Robin was ...

He belonged to Viv, but there would be other men like him out there somewhere and, frowning critically into the mirror, she pulled at a long spike of black hair. She was sick of it, to be honest. It was a mess. And putting on her face every morning took ages. Nor should it be too difficult or expensive to adapt her clothes. Fortunately the rich who sent their extravagant mistakes and nearly news to Oxfam didn't only wear black. There'd been a lovely red patterned skirt on the rail the last time she'd been in there for a look around.

'Can I come in? Can't knock, I got me 'ands full,' Shirley called.

Hands ... Robin's hands around the beer glass in the pub; turning over the plates at the warehouse; moving over the steering wheel as he'd driven her home. Hands she wouldn't mind touching her anywhere. The thought made her feel strange. And anyway, he was Viv's.

'Okay?' Shirley asked, beaming a scarlet smile.

'No. I think I'm having an identity crisis.'

'Oh, I'm always having those. Here you go – two coffees.'

'Brilliant.'

''Ere, I like your room ...'

'Thanks. Hey, Shirl, you're always dying your hair. D'you reckon I could dye mine back to its natural colour?'

'Which is what?' she asked, assessing it dubiously through narrowed eyes.

'Sort of light fair.'

'Gawd, no – don't touch it then. I wouldn't ... Grow it out. Cut it short, and keep cutting it.'

'I'll look like a piebald hedgehog,' she said, depressed.

'Better that than an artichoke, duck. Put dye on that black, and like as not you'll go green.'

Chapter Six

Towards the end of November, Ma Westcott, unable to watch chaos reign in Beth's garden any longer, had taken it upon herself to instruct her Stan to cut the lawns. But the rest of the garden, grown tall and untidy during days of unseasonably warm sunshine, the bedding plants scorched and blackened by the occasional night frost, now looked well on the way to reverting to the jungle it had been when they moved in.

Beth, still feeling exhausted, wondered how long it would take for the wisteria to cover the windows and black out the house as Lawrence's death seemed to have blacked out her mind.

She wondered if Vivien and Robin had noticed the deterioration, in her as well as in the garden, when they'd called in a few weekends ago – or Wanda, when she'd breezed in briefly on the back of a friend's motorbike one Sunday for tea.

Other than this and Ma Westcott's visits to clean, Beth, of choice, had continued to keep herself to herself, venturing only as far as the shop in the nearest village when absolutely necessary to keep herself supplied with the basics.

Nor did she need Ma Westcott's busybodying around her now. Had it in mind, after Christmas when her wages had helped Stan to pay for the kid's presents and the family turkey, to give her notice.

Tomorrow she had an appointment to see Graham. She could have done without the bother of that as well.

*

'Beth ...' he said, delighted, standing up to shake her hand as Madeline showed her into his office. 'How are you?'

'Fine.'

'Sit down – do. Please, make yourself comfortable.'

The poor woman looked worn out. Utterly defenceless. Rubbing his hands together to hide the confusing effect this had on him, he indicated the armchair beside the sofa under the bookshelves that lined one wall of the room.

'Will you be warm enough?'

He prided himself on his cosy, slightly shabby office in which, on less sunny days, he generally kept a coal fire burning. The people from whom he and Stella had bought the house had used this as a small sitting room, and as his clients were often battered by people or by life, he considered that a homely office helped put them at ease.

'Well – I've got all sorts of things to tell you,' he said, anxious to get on with it, knowing he'd feel easier with her once he was talking business. 'Another Chancer is shaping up in training since he's been gelded, and we have managed to sell him for two thousand guineas. They tell me that's a fair price in today's market for an untried two year old, even though he was sired by Deep Run.'

'Thank you.'

He crossed the word 'Equine' off the pad in front of him and, opening Lawrence's file, looked up to smile at her. He'd been phoning that trainer at Newbury two or three times a week to badger him to buy that colt. He'd done well for her, and he'd thought she'd be pleased. Instead, she seemed detached. 'I'm sorry ... I suppose all this is a bit like picking at scars.'

'It has to be done.'

'Yes, I'm afraid it has,' he said sympathetically. 'Still, it won't take long. If you could just endorse these cheques, and the transfer forms.'

He handed her his pen and watched as, bending forward, she signed her name. Her auburn hair was pulled back off her face and secured at the back of her head with a large tortoiseshell slide. She was wearing a navy and green tartan suit with a cream shirt buttoned into a high collar and secured with a cameo brooch. All laced in for protection, her face a deadpan mask of control – but the general effect made his heart considerably unsteady.

'Then there's this business with Tillotson,' he said gently as she handed back his pen. 'He'll have contacted you by now.'

'No.'

'What ...? Not even a letter?' he said, surprised.

'No.'

'But ... He was due to come to London this month. I was sure he'd have contacted you.'

'I haven't heard,' she said, looking past him at the window.

'I see,' he said, unsure why he didn't altogether believe her. 'I see. Well – perhaps he's had to change his plans.' And this was his trump card, the one piece of news which, although sad, would doubtless be a relief to her as she so clearly disliked the man. 'You see, I've spoken to the London solicitors again and apparently he's not well. In fact he's extremely ill. Terminally so, I believe. As it turns out I doubt that you will have to work with him after all. The ranches will have to be sold. He has cancer.'

She was still staring at him, and he realised that she'd had enough of death. Was drowning in it; her own blank eyes only just alive. Though in them he caught a flicker of something he took to be sympathy, and then she looked at her hands. 'What sort of cancer?'

'Well ... I didn't actually ask.'

Poor little woman. Living all alone in that great house. Lawrie'd been dead for three months, so about now his death would really be coming home to her. Although people made a fuss of you at first, they had their own lives to lead and could sometimes seem to have short memories. An outsider could be bloody lonely around here if their face didn't happen to fit. Yet whatever her reasons for disliking Tillotson, she could still feel compassion for him.

'Anyway, you'll be relieved that you won't have to work with him.'

Such a sad smile she gave him. Such sad, dead eyes. She truly did tear at his heart. And then, to his amazement, he heard himself say, 'Beth, if you're not busy, will you have lunch with me? Like me, you must get tired of eating alone. We could go down to The Ship at Porlock Weir.'

He was both nervous and surprisingly pleased that she accepted, and vaguely wondering about redundancy payments when the ranches were sold, he lead the way along the corridor and out through the kitchen to the garage. But if he'd had any serious doubts about asking her out for lunch, they disappeared as soon as she saw Alouette.

'That's quite a car you've got.'

'Yes, she's a beauty,' he said enthusiastically. 'She was a complete wreck when I bought her, but it was love at first sight. She has been known to be temperamental. Though not as temperamental as some females I could name,' he added as Stella marched across the back of his mind. He laid his hand affectionately on the car's bonnet. 'We've had some larks together – which is why I call her Alouette.' It sounded a bit fey now he said it, and he realised that making an ass of himself in front of Beth seemed to have become something of a disturbing habit. He expected her to laugh at him, and when she didn't he felt a rush of gratitude.

'Did you do her up yourself?'

'Every last valve and rivet – though Moody's garage did the paintwork,' he said, warming to her by the second as he helped her into the passenger seat.

'My father built a car once,' she said. 'Donkey's years ago, and nothing as smart as this. A "bitza" – largely from pieces he salvaged from rubbish dumps. But the engine was sweet as a nut, and it went like the wind. He used to take it on hill climbs.'

She was smiling and seemed to have come out of herself a little. Thank God for Alouette ...

'Well, how's this for sweet music,' he said, slipping the clutch and touching the accelerator as they drove down the road towards the turning for Porlock Weir.

'Positively Mozart.'

'You like Mozart?'

'I like most classical music – except Schostakovitch.'

'Air on a saucepan lid. I'm afraid I have to admit to more common tastes. I'm mad about Mantovani and The Beatles. Beyond that for me, it's the music of an engine.'

'Any engine, or just Alouette?'

'Oh, any engine will do in a crisis. Tractors, generators,

you name it and I'm there. I'd have been a mechanic if my father had let me.'

'That's a long way from being a solicitor, isn't it?'

'Not really. Law, like mechanics, is the application of basic components. Cogs within cogs, with the ultimate aim of harmony. Law is the basic machinery that holds civilised society together.'

'What about justice?'

'Ah ...' As they cleared the village he changed gear and put his foot down. 'No, I'm afraid justice is the human element, so there are occasions when justice can seem more like luck. A matter of whether the judge did or did not enjoy his breakfast. It can also depend on how well the lawyers present and manipulate the facts. Though the law is always the law.'

'Conscience comes into it too, surely. A murderer might walk free, but unless he's insane, he'll know what he's done. Have to live with it.'

'I suppose so. Though perhaps conscience is a kind of Divine intervention designed to run parallel to the legal railway lines. The element which should enable a human being to make the right choices.'

'Umm ...'

'Deep stuff,' he said, glancing at her as he laughed. 'I like trains too, incidentally.'

He noticed her smile, and was glad. Talking about the law seemed to have made her tense again, so he told her about the new carriage the enthusiasts were buying for the steam railway that ran from Minehead to Bishops Lydeard.

Over lunch and a carafe of house red in The Ship's cosy dining room, she seemed to relax completely – and so did he. It was a long time since he had lunched or dined with a woman and afterwards, as they walked back to the car park by the sea wall, he decided that, now he'd discovered it wasn't so bad, he might try it again. He was getting too used to his own company and food on his lap in front of the television.

'It must be high tide,' she said, as they stood by the wall and looked out over the tiny harbour, their hair ruttled by the breeze. 'I can never understand why people bother to keep boats on this coast. The tide goes out so far, they must be sitting on mud more than they're afloat.'

118

'I used to keep a boat here in the far off days before my divorce.'

'With an engine as sweet as a nut, no doubt,' she said, laughing.

'Of course. A diesel Yamaha.'

'Wouldn't know one if I fell over it. How long did it take you to rebuild the Daimler?'

'Three or four years.' Then, to his surprise he told her about the black dog on his conscience. The one he liked to pretend didn't exist. 'Could be that I spent more time rebuilding her than I did rebuilding my by then rocky marriage. I spent hours in the garage. I had always wanted to rebuild a car of that calibre, but coming when it did, it's possible that I used it as a form of escape.'

'Something practical. Something logical that responded as you expected. I can understand that.'

The breeze had blown her soft wavy hair across her face. A remarkable woman, he thought, returning her smile. Had she perhaps also sensed that he wasn't good with women? That he understood them even less than most men were supposed to ...?

'The kids were just babies when I started. I missed my kids. I still do.'

'I'm sure you do. I would have loved to have children.'

Watching a cargo boat in the distance, he thought about his children and counted his blessings. After Stella'd left, he'd have had nothing if it wasn't for Trish and Edward. It was looking forward to the occasional weekends with them that had kept his own personal keel clear of the mud. 'Are you beginning to get used to living alone?'

'It's the silence.'

Yes, he thought, and in that silence, one more raw recruit for life's emotionally battered army of Singles and Unattached will, just like the rest of us, doubtless think too much and too deeply. Being unable to stop that thinking was yet another short cut to the nut house.

'Perhaps that's why I'm always listening to music,' he said. 'So I don't have to hear myself think. He was a good man, your Lawrence. I don't think he'll have too many mistakes to report on Judgement Day. He made a lot of money, but he never forgot those less fortunate. Did you know, last year alone, he gave away over ten thousand pounds to various charities? Save The Children, Oxfam, Christian Aid, Salvation Army – Terrence Higgins Trust. You name it, he's given to them all at some time or other. Quietly ... He didn't make a thing about it.'

'He was good about giving to charities.'

'His death has shocked everyone who knew him, you know. Not just his friends – though poor old Len Franks was knocked sideways. I do hope you realise that you aren't alone in missing him.'

'You make him sound perfect.'

She had turned her head away and he watched her hair being tumbled by the breeze. Lawrence had indeed been a lucky man. One of those rare men who appeared to have got it all together. And yet there had always seemed to be a restlessness about him. An uneasiness within himself, as if at times, in his own estimation, everything he'd achieved counted for nothing, and The Big One, whatever that might have been, he had yet to conquer.

'No ... Nobody's perfect, but he was a damned good friend. And very human.'

Her face was still turned away from him and he had an uncomfortable feeling that he might have made her cry. He couldn't bear it when women cried. He was useless with weeping women. As Stella had known well – and had thus used tears as gangsters used guns. Unsure what to do, he checked his watch and saw it was later than he'd realised.

'Oh Lord – I've an appointment with a farmer about a boundary dispute at three.'

Damn ... If it wasn't for that farmer there was nothing on his desk that he couldn't have caught up on this evening. He'd have liked to suggest a walk along the path at the top of the beach. It was a shame to waste this weather – and he ought not to take her back to his office if she was crying.

'I ought to be getting back anyway,' she said. 'Things to do.'

He steeled himself, looked at her face. She wasn't crying but she'd retreated again.

'Yes, I expect you have. Plenty ...'

120

Unpleasant things like sorting through drawers, looking for papers, reading letters, finding old invitations – churning up memories, he thought as they walked over to the car. But the sorting did serve its purpose. Like cleaning a wound, it was part of the ritual that led on through pain to acceptance and healing, and it had to be lived through.

They got into the car, and he said, 'I hope you're not over-doing things.'

'I don't think I could. I haven't enough energy.'

'Good – because things seem to cave in on you if you get over tired.'

He remembered it well. She was making light of it, but he wanted to make her feel better. Hold her hand or something. Instead he started the engine – and wondered what she did on Sundays. In a society apparently geared to families and couples, Sundays on your own could be hell until you were used to it. One day soon perhaps he would ask her out again. For Sunday lunch ...

As she drove away from his office she watched him in the rearview mirror, a short, kind man in knee britches, waving from the porch. She waved in return, and pulled out into the road.

A compassionate man, who'd have understood about her soul darkness and the thing on her conscience, and who was easy to talk to. He understood a good many things and, as they'd talked about justice and later, about Lawrence, she had wanted to tell him. It would be so good to be able to tell someone.

And there was something else. In the car, almost subconsciously at first, she had noticed the smell of him. Beneath the light aftershave, there had been the unmistakeable meaty smell of a male that she'd never noticed while sharing the house with Lawrence, or previously, while working with men every day. A very basic smell; the essence, perhaps, of that which attracted the female to the male.

She wasn't attracted to Graham. He was merely a good friend and, in a relationship, was no doubt as big a bastard as all the others. She was finished with men.

But it was interesting to note how the male scent had effected her. Although existing in an emotional wasteland, her most basic primeval responses were obviously not as dead as she'd thought.

'Have you unpacked the hinged models, Wanda?' old Hodgson asked.

'Yes Mr. Hodgson – and they've sent us two horses.'

'Horses? We've got horses. I wanted men. Though possibly not as voraciously as your friend Adrian.' He bared his perfect set of false teeth in a crocodile smile. 'Is that the letter to Waddingtons?'

Pretending to look at the paper in the typewriter, he leant across her. Seeing his hand coming, she leant away.

'I want to see Adrian. Is it all right if I pop next door in my tea break?'

'Don't be long, then.'

'No – don't be long,' said Amelia meaningfully.

Neither of the girls liked to be left alone with old Hodgson.

Wanda winked, pulled a face, and having collected her coat, ran down the stairs and let herself out into the yard behind the shop.

In the yard next door Adrian was hanging towels on the line.

'Cheers, Wanda. Coming round for a cup of coffee? Oooh look – there's your friend at the window. Miserable old sod,' and miming an over exaggerated, 'Afternoon, Mr. Hodgson,' he raised a limp wristed hand and undulated his hips.

'You do wind him up,' Wanda said, giggling. 'He's convinced you're a poofter.'

'Silly old fart. Come inside, it's cold out here.'

In the cupboard of a kitchen the pungent cocktail of shampoo, hair spray, perm lotion and percolated coffee that wafted through from the cream-and-gold-plated unisex saloon tickled her nose and made her sneeze.

'Sorry, Adie – will you look at this regrowth again? I know you did your best, but it's really grim. Isn't there anything else you can do?'

'Yeah. For Christmas I'll buy you a hat.'

'I like the cut. It's my roots ... I feel such a mess.'

'You don't look it. Not since you've done away with that black gear you used to wear. Oooh – you wild, wilful thing, you ... I did warn you about the regrowth when you wanted to go all black and spiky in the first place.'

'I know you did.'

'Anyway, cheer up. Very short hair suits you. Makes you look like a mischievous elf. Oh, all right – come in after work. I'll trim it again and we'll try a rinse to disguise the colour. A semi-permanent that'll fade with washing. I won't charge you anything provided you come in on the dot of five.'

'You are good to me.'

'What's up, kiddo? It'is not like you to be looking so down. You in love or something?'

She laughed. 'I don't know,' she said, and added thoughtfully, 'Perhaps I am ...'

'Well,' he said handing her a cup of coffee. 'Roots or no roots – whoever he is, if he doesn't love you back he's got to be crazy.'

'Last minute orders,' Viv said, scowling at the print-out Martin handed her. It was always the same at this time of year. Everyone baying to have their consignments delivered before Christmas.

'How about Baltic Carriers? They had a ship in Oslo over the weekend.'

'They let us down last time we used them. Try Oulsen Lines.'

'It's your decision.'

'You don't agree,' she said, niggled, preparing to defend herself as she handed back the sheet of paper.

'I agree entirely. How about dinner tonight?'

'No thank you, Martin.'

'Dinner, Vivien. Just dinner.'

'No.' Her phone rang and she reached out, resting her hand on the receiver while she waited for him to leave.

'Eight o'clock. I'll pick you up at your place.'

'No, Martin. No!'

'I'll be there at eight,' he said. 'You've got to eat, so you might just as well eat with me as on your own.'

'Oh, all right,' she said, crossly. 'Just – go away.'

Grinning smugly he did so, and she picked up the phone.

'Viv? Hi. How are you doing?' It was Robin.

'Er ... Fine.'

'Busy?'

'Um ... No, not too bad.'

'Good. What time will you be finished?'

She realised, from the hollow clarity of the line, that he was phoning from his car. Oh Lord ...

'Where are you?'

'Exeter Services. I've been to Plymouth. Site meeting to decide final details before a topping-out ceremony. If I keep on up the M5 I can wait for you at your place and take you out to celebrate.'

'No, Robin,' she said, stricken with guilt. 'Not tonight, love ... How about tomorrow?'

For God's sake, she only had to buzz Martin and tell him no, once and for all.

'Okay,' Robin said, disappointed. 'Oh well, cauliflower cheese again then I guess. I'll see you tomorrow. About seven-thirty?'

'About seven-thirty.'

'And I'll stay the night.'

'Yes. Lovely ...'

Must he ...? Now, if it was Martin suggesting he'd stay the night ...

Oh Viv, she thought, dismayed – *what are you thinking? What the hell are you doing?*

I am entombed with him in the monument he built, Beth thought, as she stopped on the landing and looked at the closed door of what had been his dressing room.

It was also the room in which he had slept since their return from Morocco. In there were all his most personal belongings – and his clothes, like the sheets on the bed, would still hold the scent of him.

She hadn't been in there since she and Viv had chosen the grey suit in which he'd been buried. She hadn't even allowed Ma Westcott to go in there to clean.

Of all the tasks that she was going to have to deal with if she was to pick up the threads of her life, sorting through that room would require the greatest energy and courage of them all.

What it came down to was an inability to accept her right to live when she had allowed him to die.

But she did want to live. She knew that now. Had discovered it today, being with Graham.

Johnson's powder for babies and those who've come full circle, Anthea thought, as she put the tin of talc on the shelf and folded the seat that fitted into the bath. Bath seats, zimmer frames, incontinence pads, creams and potions – the elderly needed as much paraphernalia as babies. Other than the bond of love and the memory of how things used to be, she no longer thought of her as Mother. Just a body that eats and breathes, and occasionally leaks when it shouldn't. The fault today, no doubt, being the too sour stewed apple at lunchtime.

We have changed places, she and I. I, now, am the strong one who does the looking after and knows more of the answers. Though one day in the not too distant future, it will be me who's redundant. And so life goes on.

But she would do anything rather than put her in one of those homes which were little more than waiting-rooms where human beings await the dignity of death. There was a lot to be said for euthanasia, when the time came.

An option she might soon have to consider for Percy. His leg was much worse ...

But while she had no problem with any of the other livestock, when it came to Percy, someone else would have to do him the ultimate kindness of helping him on his way. And it would have to be someone who Anthea liked and trusted.

She finished tidying the bathroom, opened the window a little, and went downstairs.

The old thing, wrapped in her blue woollen dressing-gown was settled in her chair by the fire and didn't look unlike a large baby snug in its sleeping suit. Poor old lady ... It was years since she'd called her mother. She would like to be called Mum. To be reinstated ...

Anthea patted her shoulder. 'All right – Mum? Don't you worry about, it love. Accidents do happen.'

No answer. I should make time to be with her, talk to her to keep her mind in the present. Teach her to speak, as we did with Viv and Wanda, she thought. At times she can string a

125

few words together quite clearly. I'm sure she could learn again if only I had the time to spend with her.

Bicton Manor, about twenty miles north of Bristol somewhere in the Forest of Dean. One look at the place, floodlit and standing in its own well-kept grounds at the end of a long drive, had told Viv that this was to be no ordinary dinner. The dinning room was done out in colours of crushed strawberry and cream, with candlelit tables laid up to match. The napkins were cream monogrammed linen, the plates bone china, the glass Edinburgh crystal, and the cutlery good, tastefully plain silver plate. Around the walls, a number of oil paintings of local land and Welsh seascapes were lit individually, that and the candles on the tables being the only light necessary.

'You're pushing the boat out, Mart, aren't you?'

'Actually, I'm only too well aware that, for once in my life, and perhaps when it matters most, I might have just missed the boat. I told you, there are things about you I never noticed until a couple of months ago.'

'Some might say that indicated a lack of observation and foresight.' Two years they'd worked together, during which, while fancying him, she'd met and dropped Zac, spent several months unattached, then met and become so involved with Robin that a few weeks from now he expected her to move in with him. 'A distinct lack of observation, I'd say.'

Cross with him, she watched him slice neatly into his roast pheasant.

'Grow up, Vivien. We're not in the office now. This is life, not business administration. Chemistry, emotion, call it what you like – but it isn't something that can be planned or reasoned, and well you know it.'

'Perhaps you're a late starter,' she said, the angrier for knowing he was right. Unless people behaved as she expected them to, real life had always been so much more of a problem to her than anything she was likely to encounter in the course of her job. She'd been trained for her job. 'Or even, long-term, a loser ...?'

At that, knowing it to be unworthy of an answer, he simply laughed – and she knew he was breaking her down, eroding her arguments as easily as he was cutting that pheasant from its bones. What was worse, backed into a corner, he'd reduced her to being childish.

'What changed then, a couple of months ago?' she asked grudgingly.

'I don't know. Perhaps it was your promotion. Suddenly you were up and running. Highly motivated, and exceptionally alive. How's the trout ...?'

'Dead. Though not exceptionally so. It's very good.'

He laughed. 'Well, that's something.'

'How old are you, Mart?'

'Twenty-six.'

He looked older. Candlelight deepened the grooves on either side of his mouth, and had matured him. With his short dark hair he didn't look unlike a taller version of Lawrence.

'By middle age you'll be quite handsome,' she said, thinking aloud.

'Thank you. You find Robin handsome too, of course. Though do you honestly consider he's high flying enough to keep you interested for the rest of your life?'

'Are you?'

'Yes. And I'm stronger than you are. You'll end up despising a man who lets you be boss.'

Lawrence had said much the same, several times – and she wondered if that might be the real reason she'd never got around to introducing him to Robin.

'This was supposed to be an invitation to dinner – not an inquisition.'

'A chance to get to know each other better,' said Martin, refilling her glass. 'So are we going to spar right through the meal, or shall we call a truce and enjoy ourselves?'

'You sarky beggar.'

'You didn't have to come out to dinner with me. I didn't drag you here by your hair.' He laughed at her, and lowering his voice leant closer across the table. 'You are lovely when you scowl.'

She didn't really want to fight him ... She thought briefly about Robin eating his staple diet of cauliflower cheese, then pushed the picked-clean skeleton of the trout to the side of her plate and put down her knife and fork. Suddenly, noticing that

127

Martin really did have a wonderful long, straight nose, all the anger left her.

'How long is your contract in Brussels?'

'Two years initially,' he said, meeting her eyes.

'When do you start?'

'Mid February.'

She put her elbows on the table and rested her chin on the backs of her hands. 'I suppose there are planes and ferries.'

'Plenty. Does that mean you might be interested in catching them?'

But all this seemed a little too close too soon, and laying the fingers of one hand on the base of her wineglass she pushed it slowly in a circle.

'Well, I hope you enjoy Brussels anyway.'

'I'd say that was up to you, and the planes and the ferries. Don't move in with Robin just yet, will you?'

Slouched on the sofa in his office, Graham chewed the last mouthful of his ham sandwich and frowned at the sheaf of papers on his knees. His client, a delivery driver for a local butcher, hadn't been so far over the limit when he'd been breathalysed. An unexpected party followed by the same calculated risk that Graham himself had taken many times. The delivery driver was a quieter-living chap than most, but no matter how cleverly Graham twisted the facts in court tomorrow, the chap was doomed to lose his licence, his job, and his means of supporting his wife and four kids. As he'd said to Beth, justice was a tricky business – and in the long run the state yet again would be shooting itself in its own foot with this one, what with the unemployment benefit as well as its contributions to his client's Legal Aid.

'Good on you, cobber,' Lawrence had said to him once, slapping him on the back. 'Get to it, boy – someone's got to look after the little people.'

Extremely compassionate and, in addition to those less fortunate than himself, he was ever mindful of those who for one reason or another didn't quite fit or had fallen off society's sometimes somewhat rigid railway lines.

He'd probably be pleased to know someone was looking after his widow. Taking her out to lunch ...

It wouldn't be anything more than that. Ridiculous to even consider it. She was far too classy. One of the fancy underwear brigade, for sure. Though he'd enjoyed walking into that pub with her. Had pulled himself up to every inch of his five feet seven when those chaps at the bar had turned to eye her up and down.

Ah well ... He'd think about all that tomorrow, and as the file began to slip off his lap, he set it aside, clasped his hands behind his head and abandoned his senses to the delights of Mantovani. He'd recently treated himself to a very expensive stereo system and had wired loudspeakers to almost every room in the house so that he could indulge his tastes in music wherever and whenever he chose.

But how long ought he to go on indulging himself ...?

The kids, when they came for their occasional weekends, had already started to tease him about being set in his ways. At their age they knew it all, of course. Still – they had a point. If he didn't do something about it soon he'd be sitting here by the fire year after year with cobwebs and mould creeping up around him like some male Dickensian Haversham.

You're a lazy bastard, Lang, that's half your trouble, he thought, contemplating his big toe through a hole that had appeared at the end of one long olive-green knee sock. *You ought to do something about your life or it'll be too late. What will you say, then, to the Big judge in the sky when it's your turn to account for yourself?*

In mitigation, My Lord, you have before you here at The Pearly Gates, a man who is still, and to a larger degree than he cares to admit, suffering from the grief of his divorce. Nevertheless, I ask you to accept that he was a man – a mere human being – who, having come to accept that one cannot move forward satisfactorily without letting go of all hurts and mistakes of the past, thereafter, did do his best.

And incidentally, M'lud, he was indeed a man, not – as Mrs. Stella Edwina Lang was given to claim – a mouse.

So get off your arse, then Lang, and prove it.

The way he saw it, he had two options. One; screw up his courage and ask the widow out for Sunday lunch. Or two; go out more often with a view to finding someone more suitable to flirt with than the blonde barmaid at The Stag and Greyhound. Who, in any case, only made eyes at him for fun. A cat teasing the mouse ...

Christ, he'd be fifty-five next birthday. Well past half-way to his eternity, and even chaps like Lawrence Seligman didn't live for ever.

Furthermore, the kindest of barmaids was unlikely to flirt with a mouse when its hair and its teeth had fallen out ...

It looked like it had to be Option One then. And it was the option that appealed to him most.

Right – well tomorrow when he got back from court, he'd draft her new will for her, and when she came in to sign it he'd quite definitely ask her out for lunch. A nice little run in Alouette up to The Traveller's Rest, a big log fire and large plate of succulent roast beef.

After all, she was still mourning her husband – and even he, Graham, couldn't come to much harm over lunch in a Sunday-packed pub.

Chapter Seven

'Good morning,' said a deep male voice from the far end of the line when Beth answered the telephone on Lawrence's desk – and realising it was Graham, she remembered. He'd phoned, at least a week ago, to say he'd prepared her will and she'd completely forgotten the appointment she'd made to go in to sign it.

'Graham – I am so sorry!'

'No bones broken. How about tomorrow? Sometime in the afternoon. Around three?'

'Yes, fine. I'll be there.'

'By the way, there was a sizeable cheque from Australia in this morning's post. It's made out to Lawrence so it'll have to go through the estate. I imagine, with the dreaded Christmas only ten days away, you'd have preferred it to have been made out to you.'

'I'm all right for money. I don't seem to need much at the moment.'

'You've done all your Christmas shopping then? I wish I had. Okay, I'll drop Tillotson a line and tell him to get it right next time. I take it he still hasn't contacted you?'

'No.' There had been another airmail. The third since Lawrence had died. She hadn't read that one either, so no – he hadn't made contact with her.

'Strange,' Graham said. 'I really don't understand that at all. I thought he'd at least have written when Lawrence died, and the last I heard from Archibald, the chap in London, he was expecting to see him in November as usual. I suppose he wasn't well enough to travel. Anyway, the ranches are on the market and Archibald's promised to let me know as soon as there's any strong interest.'

'Thanks, Graham'.

'And, as Tillotson didn't make it to England in November, I doubt the poor chap will be bothering you now.' He paused. 'Well then, I'll see you tomorrow.'

'I'll be there. I promise.'

She replaced the receiver and looked through the letter she'd been trying to write to Liz. Since her lunch with Graham she had managed to find the energy to pay the household bills and had answered almost all of the letters, but she wasn't yet ready to write to Liz. Deciding that what she had written so far was stilted and nothing like the letter Liz would expect, she tore up the page and put the top firmly back on her pen.

She had, though, made a reasonably good start on the garden. But even on the outside work she couldn't seem to concentrate for long. Having forgotten her appointment with Graham, it also seemed that she was losing her memory. She knew that almost certainly she was clinically depressed but, getting up to go out to the kitchen to make coffee that she didn't really want, she began to wonder if all this might be the early stages of some more serious, permanent insanity.

Graham looked again at Tillotson's signature on the cheque. Lawrence had trusted him and the money did appear to be coming through. All the same, he'd feel a great deal easier if he could have persuaded Beth to go out there and be seen to be taking an interest in her inheritance. Pity she had such a block about the man.

Perhaps she doesn't like me either, Graham thought. When he'd phoned her last week she seemed to have enjoyed their lunch together as much as he had, but having forgotten her appointment, obviously his company was less memorable than that of a mouse.

She'd certainly have remembered that lunch if there'd been a mouse in the pub dining room.

Squirming with frustration, Amy tried to loosen the rug Anthea had tucked around her knees. She was far too hot with

132

that as well as the heat from the blazing fire – but she just could not shift it.

She wriggled one last time, and gave up. *Useless. I am useless*, she thought, sucking angrily at her cheeks. *No strength in my hands, my limbs, my whole body. Why can't I pass over ... I'm no use here. Not even to you*, she said to Lawrence in her mind.

Looking down at her hands it was hard to believe that those claws, mottled like blue cheese, were the same hands, young, firm-fleshed and strong, that had once achieved so much in the course of a day. The same hands that had held Arthur's hands. And tended the baby ... Anthony, the first-born Kenworthy grandson.

Arthur's family had disapproved of hers, dismissing them as moor folk and gypsies – until Anthony arrived. *One look at Anthony in his big basket perambulator, and your mother forgave me for everything*, she said to Arthur who seemed to be sitting beside her.

Anthony – the blond baby with big blue wondering eyes, who had grown into a tall handsome lad with a strong sense of honour and the disposition of an angel. Everyone had loved Anthony.

Oh my son ... And our love, our trust, our expectations, were what destroyed you. I did know how it was for you. How things were ...

To those born on the moor who lived close to nature, to sense such things was their birthright; a gift, the privileged payment for which was the pain of knowing what others did not. And the heat from this fire was nothing to the pain that her son had endured – at the last, his body black, blistered raw. She had known that too, though Lawrence had tried to spare her. Never did tell her ...

But someone was standing in front of Amy now. Intruding. Blocking communication and pulling her back to the physical confines of the room and her chair, so that the images of Anthony, Arthur, even that of Lawrence, also there with them and more densely defined, were fading.

Then suddenly there was something in her lap – and feeling the weight on her thighs, Amy looked down.

'No!'

'Steady, Mum. Careful!'

But Amy's legs were jerking in horror, and she felt the weight leave her. Heard the crash ... And looking down she saw them – the raw, blistered slices of Anthony scattered amongst the splinters of glass and the broken china on the rough stone hearth.

'No ...' This time the word left her as a moan – but Anthea was shouting.

Shouting and shouting. Hurting her ears.

Anthony had been so kind, so gentle, so patient – but Anthea, her face red and ugly with fury, was picking him up with the rest of the debris as if he too was rubbish.

And all the while Amy could smell the fire scorching the rug. Could feel it burning her leg. *I am sharing your pain, my son*, she thought – *and gladly*. The grief ached inside her and she wanted to weep for him, but she was too old, her body too dry – so that like him, she had no moisture, no tears left to give.

Cantankerous old woman – she'd done that purposely. And right now, when Burgess had roared down the telephone demanding that Anthea remove her sheep from his precious bloody garden hedge. What did they expect, these townies who moved to the country! After their removal he'd made it plain that he didn't care what happened to them – and Anthea was beginning to feel the same way. Len Pugsley had mended the dry-stone wall, but this was still the second time this week that those blighters had escaped.

Jaw set, she hacked off another two slices of ham and slapped them on a clean plate. She had a headache which was getting worse, the pain gathering in the tense, rigid muscles at the base of her neck.

Oh – sod it! Now the phone was ringing again.

Burgess probably, to say the sheep were through to his garden. If they were she'd cut her losses and sell every one of 'em.

The phone bell seemed to be directly wired to her nerves, each ring a jangle of pain that became worse as she scrabbled amongst the mess on the kitchen table to find the stupid cordless thing, gave up, and ran through the living room to answer it in the cubbyhole.

134

'Yes!'

'Mrs. Seligman?'

'Yes ...' she said, out of breath and relieved. It wasn't Burgess.

'My name's Tillotson. Wayne Tillotson. From Australia?'

With that accent, where else, but before she could reply, he said, 'You'll have been expecting my call.'

'No, Mr. Tillotson ...'

'I wrote to you,' he persisted. 'I know we've never met, but I hope to put that right within the next day or two.'

'Mr. Tillotson,' she said, her hand pressed on the back of her neck.

'I'm calling you from London as suggested in my letters. I have to return to Sydney on Monday as you know, so we'll have to meet this weekend, and time is getting short.'

That accent ... His voice slid up and down the scale like a strangled sheep trying to sing.

'I'm sorry, Mr. Tillotson, but I think you have the wrong ...'

'I have to meet you, Mrs. Seligman. It is important.'

'Mr. Tillotson ...'

'Wayne. Call me Wayne.'

Wayne, that rhymed with rain. The perfect name for a man with as much sensitivity as a tropical downpour. Did he ever draw breath?

'Wayne,' she said firmly and, screwing up her eyes against the thunder in her head, she summoned what remained of her strength. 'You have the wrong number. The wrong Mrs. Seligman. I am Anthea Seligman, Lawrence Seligman's first wife.'

Silence. The man was thinking. He was, then, capable of thought. Or perhaps he'd mesmerised himself watching the corks swinging from his hat.

'Then – you must be Anthony Kenworthy's sister?'

'Anthony was my brother, yes.'

'Starve the lizards,' he said, his voice softer. 'Anthony's sister. I'm so pleased to talk to you. After all these years ... That was another tragedy.'

'Yes ...' and anxious as she was to ring off, time seemed to spin backwards.

'They say that you're like him.'

'In some ways.'

His voice reminded her of Lawrie's when he'd first come to England. She quite liked the sound of this man after all.

'A female version, according to Lawrie. I'd like to meet you, Mrs. Seligman. Anthea ... Though I'm not sure I'll have time. Not this visit anyway.'

'Look Mr. Tillotson, you will have to forgive me. I'm afraid you've called at a bad moment. My sheep have escaped and are about to destroy my neighbour's garden.'

He chuckled. 'Now that really makes me feel at home. Sheep must be the same the world over. Give them a thousand acres of bush and they'll still find a fence to break through. Good to talk to you, Anthea. If I come down West, can I call you again?'

'You have the number.'

Smacking her hand on the phone and waiting for the tone so that she could dial Muriel's number, despite the pain in her head, she was smiling.

'Muriel? I'm desperate. The sheep are out and Gran's here on her own. Are you busy?'

'Be with you in a jiff.'

'You're maarvellous,' she said, and laughed because she'd picked up the accent.

Another favour I'll owe Mew, she thought as she hurried to give Gran her lunch. In this little corner of the world folk didn't live cheek by jowl with their friends and neighbours, and they learnt not to intrude but, when in need, there was always someone there to call on. Around here folk looked after each other. Presumably it must be very different in the vast impersonal expanses of the Australian bush.

Muriel's car pulled up in the yard. Running out to meet her, Anthea grabbed the ancient bicycle from the barn, unchained the sheepdog, and after peddling hard to get up the drive to the gate, it was freewheeling all the way down the tree-lined lane, past the turning to the village, and on down the hill to Burgess's neat cottage and immaculate garden.

The rush of cold air soothed her head, and she wondered about the problems of sheep farming in Australia. It would be good to meet Tillotson. In the early years, talking to Lawrie about Anthony and his life in Australia had helped her come to terms with his death. Perhaps now, talking to Tillotson would help her come to terms with Lawrie's.

Presumably Tillotson was here to talk to the bitch about the ranches. She was a part owner now. Perhaps, with luck and a following wind, she'd go out there and get bitten by something deadly.

Fancy him phoning her by mistake. People had done that quite often in the early years – and once, late on a Saturday afternoon, the butcher had delivered a large and expensive joint of beef to her instead of Tivington. She had taken a perverse, really quite spiteful delight in roasting it for the girls, hoping that Lawrie would be furious with the bitch for having nothing better than eggs for his Sunday lunch. Poor Lawrie, he had loved his Sunday lunch ...

But by now she had sped round the last corner in the lane, and what she saw ahead drove every other thought clean out of her mind. Outside Burgess's cottage there were two sheep in the lane, four more up the bank, and the rest were gambolling round the vegetable garden where the man himself was leaping up and down and waving his arms.

Even from that distance she could see that his face was a deep, ominous purple – and he'd already had one heart attack. Less than six months ago ...

As Beth pushed the wheelbarrow full of dead leaves across the yard to the bonfire on the rough ground behind the outhouses, she was followed by a blackbird which had begun to keep her company whenever she worked in the garden.

It flew ahead of her and pitched on the bumper of the Range Rover parked in the barn. Looking at the bird, she noticed that the car was splattered with bird droppings and covered in a thick layer of red dust in which there was a set of cat's paw prints. The dust made the car look as if it was already rusting.

'I really must sell that thing in the New Year.'

Apparently surprised that she had spoken to it, the bird cocked its head to one side and appeared to listen attentively.

Then, in the house, the phone began to ring. It had already rung once since the call from Graham but, working in the garden, she'd ignored it. These days, three calls in little

137

over an hour was something of a record. Actually, it was an intrusion.

'Don't need it, do we,' she said to the bird. 'You and me.'

And later, when she went back indoors, she switched on the answerphone.

'I'm sorry ... There's still no reply.'

'Right on, then – I'll try again later,' said Tillotson, his voice sounding unnaturally loud in the oversized hotel room.

Damn fool girl, first she'd got him the wrong number and now there was no reply from the right one. Where was the bloody second wife? When he'd written to say he couldn't make November he'd told her the dates he would be here, suggested they meet this weekend, and had said he'd call her today – Thursday – to confirm the venue. If he had to go down west tomorrow he'd need to find out about transport and book a hotel room for a couple of nights. He couldn't rush things like he used to, and he needed to know where and when he was going so that he could psych himself up to get there. Like some doddery old man ...

Shit, he thought, looking round. *I want to get this done and go home. I hate hotel rooms. Too damned impersonal ...* Just sitting there thinking how far he was from home, and he was starting to sweat. But he had to meet that woman. And he had to be back in Sydney for a meeting on Wednesday. As it was he'd be knackered after the flight and was cutting it fine. This sort of schedule was too tight for the old man he'd become.

But he did intend to talk to the woman about the ranches – even if it meant another long distance haul from Sydney to London and back in the New Year. And if he had to come back, he would make sure he met Anthea as well. Two of Lawrie's birds with one stone ...

It would have to be early in the New Year. He daren't leave it much longer. He'd never expected to be carted back to that clinic in November. Bloody disease. He'd had his bad days right from the start, but it had shocked him to realise he could no longer fight off even a cold.

Though what I'm really fighting, he thought, *is time. It's like gold dust to me now.* When he and Lawrie were kids, time

138

had been as plentiful as sand. Had never figured much beyond the next meal.

We came a long way together, you and me, mate. Youngsters, rounding up sheep on our ponies; that camp we made every summer by the billabong; the rabbits we used to catch for the cook. Jeeze – and that snake you caught, that grazed you. I thought you were a gonner. I buried you then, in my imagination. We couldn't have been more than six or seven, and all the way home with you hanging limp over my saddle I went through hell wondering what I was going to tell your old man. We were brothers, you and me ... You saved your love, the tenderness and the passion for Anthony.

He had often wondered about Lawrie and Anthony. Anthony had came out to Oz to look for the bloke he really was, and once Lawrie had helped him to find himself, young Anthony couldn't live with it. The sad thing was that after he died, his death then on Lawrie's conscience, Lawrie's spent the rest of his own life trying to play things straight. And until this past year, Tillotson had thought that he'd damned nigh made it. In every way, Lawrie was always more adaptable than anyone else Tillotson had ever known.

Lovely human being that Anthony was, it should have been Lawrie on his conscience, not the other way around. They couldn't have lived at the ranch, but if Anthony had been true to himself and to Lawrie, they could have moved some place else and lived happy ever after.

Some place where I could have come to visit you, Tillotson thought. *Because, damn it – I missed you ...*

Instead, after he'd left for England, Tillotson had wanted Lawrie to come visit him. What's more, given a little more time he had begun to think he would have. It was getting so that Lawrie did want to see the old place again; the stock, the white-fenced paddocks, the gallops, the new exercise pools. He'd sent Lawrie videos, but if he'd come out to Oz to take a look for himself he wouldn't have needed a bloody race horse in England.

The fact was that Lawrie was scared to return. Scared that he'd come face to face with what he'd spent twenty years trying to ignore – but as things turned out, it hadn't made a blind bit of difference.

I bloody do miss you, mate. And here in London I miss you even more.

For you it was Anthony, but for me, all I ever had that really counted was you and yours. I have to meet your women. And perhaps your daughters as well. It's my one remaining ambition. Meet them, before I meet my eternity.

That black silent nothingness, bigger even than Australia – the very thought of which, scared him utterly shitless ...

So maybe it wouldn't be so bad if he didn't meet Lawrie's family this visit ...

Funny how things turn out. He'd never have thought of meeting Anthony's sister if it hadn't been for that damned fool girl on the switchboard getting him the wrong number. Fate sure was dealing him an odd hand. *If I wasn't quite the full quid, I might start thinking you're up there on some cloud arranging it*, he thought.

But there were no clouds. Once you'd shot through you were gone – and aware of the traffic's roar below in Park Lane, Tillotson looked at the telephone. It was too soon to try ringing the widow again, but in one week from now he'd be sitting in a baby jet bound for the outback, so he sure as hell didn't have time to waste sitting around moping in a bloody hotel room. London was pounding with life, and there were plenty of bars where he could down a few beers in congenial company to help him forget.

Anyway, he thought, as he picked up his tan suede jacket and checked its pockets for his wallet, perhaps he should leave it to fate. He'd call the widow this evening, and if he couldn't raise her, he'd call tomorrow morning. If he didn't get her then, he'd let it ride.

Make damned sure he was fit enough to make the journey in the New Year – and go on having it to look forward to. Something left for which to fight.

He'd write one more letter to tell her he was coming, and then, if necessary, he'd just turn up on her doorstep.

Robin, seated at the drawing board in his office, screwed up the sketch he'd been working on, flung it at the wastepaper basket and grabbed the phone on its first ring.

'Hello, darling,' Viv said. 'You sound cross.'

140

'I am cross. Bloody cross. My floor space will not tie in with my minstrels' gallery and the planning authority will not allow me the one extra foot I need. One ruddy foot! This is the most interesting assignment I've had in months – or am likely to get for a while, the way things are – and short of a miracle, the finished thing is going to come out looking cramped and bloody poky. All for the sake of twelve inches.'

'People have been known to kill for just six.'

'Very funny.' For once he just wasn't in the mood. 'I'm going to have to rethink the whole design.'

'I'm having a bad day too. In fact, I've had a week of it. Darling, I'm not going to make this weekend. I thought I ought to warn you.'

'Oh? Fantastic. What is it this time? A campaign to raise the Titanic – or a march to prevent the Russians landing on Mars?'

'Partly work, and partly because I must finish my Christmas shopping,' she said calmly, thus infuriating him further. 'Darling – please don't be difficult. Everything will be so much easier once I've sold the house. Don't worry, everything will have resolved itself by the end of January – one way or another. Mid February at the latest. If the house isn't sold by then I'll find an agent to rent it out for me.'

What the hell had January or February got to do with that? If she'd rented the damned house out when he'd first suggested it, she'd have a tenant already and could be moving in here at Christmas as originally agreed.

'Oh well,' he said grudgingly, 'given tomorrow and Saturday and Sunday, I suppose it's just possible I might make something of my minstrels' gallery. I'll drive up and see you on Sunday evening then.'

'That'll be lovely,' she cooed, no doubt aware that yet again she'd got her own way. 'And next weekend it's practically Christmas. We'll have lots of time together then. Mum's really pleased you're coming for the holiday.

What about you, he thought, when she'd rung off. *Are you pleased? I wonder* ... No one else worked the hours she did, he was damned sure of it. So what else was she doing with her time? He rammed a pencil into the electric sharpener and clenched his teeth against the whine.

141

It had got dark while he was working and, getting up to draw the curtains, he noticed a stream of cars like a gigantic brightly lit snake winding its way up the hill from town. Cars driven by people going home to other people who were waiting. He was fed to the back teeth with Viv's excuses – and sick of being manipulated. If she loved him enough to eventually marry him, surely she'd have moved in with him weeks ago?

Maybe, just maybe, he was wasting his time with Viv ...

Oh, great – and they called this the season of goodwill.

Anthea heaved the adding machine on to the table and began to tap in figures from the farm account day book.

'Check on the cake,' her mother pleaded fretfully from her chair by the fire. 'Tiz burning, I can smell it is.' She'd been on about that mythical cake all evening, and when she was like this there was only one way to deal with it.

'All right,' Anthea said. Sighing, she got up, went through to the kitchen, paused, rattled a baking tin that was drying on the back of the Rayburn – and returned to the living room. 'There ... All done. I've taken it out of the oven.'

Amy stared at her, sucking her cheeks, and Anthea sat down, returning her attention to the figures on the adding machine.

'Taken what out of the oven?'

'Your cake,' Anthea said uncertainly, guessing what might well be coming next.

'Cake ...? I haven't baked a cake in years.'

Anthea rested her chin on her hand, closed her eyes, raised her eyebrows, and stretched her lips across her teeth in a sort of smile.

'And where's your Lawrence? That's what I'd like to know, because he bain't here,' Amy said, fixing Anthea with a clear, green-eyed glare as she waited for an answer there'd be no point in giving.

'Sssh, love ... I can't talk to you now. I must get these books done tonight.'

She hated the book work, and she was tired. She ought to make time for the accounts during the day – and rubbing a speck of dried mud off the face of her watch, she thought of Anthony. It had been his watch. Mum and Dad had given it to him on his twenty-first birthday, and thus it had already seen more of the world than she ever would.

It had been on his wrist the day he'd waved to them from the deck of the ship as it slid away from the dock at Southampton, though her eyes had been too full to make him out through the blur. And he'd been wearing it when he'd walked away from the truck to abandon time once and for all in the desert.

The watch, though, had kept on ticking, and she'd next seen it in her room at Cloutsham while unpacking a suitcase of his belongings that Lawrie had brought. Recognising the case in his hand as soon as he'd walked into the yard, she had initially taken far more notice of it than she had of the man who was carrying it. At the time she'd thought herself in love with Reg Pugsley. God forbid – but in those days it was Reg who escorted her to the hops in the village hall, crushed her against him as he stumbled and sweated through the waltzes and foxtrots, and breathed beer all over her as he pawed her in the truck parked in some gateway on the road home.

But when Lawrie had arrived on the scene Reg had sort of melted into the background of his own accord, because, invited to stay the night, Lawrie had stayed on for weeks helping Dad on the farm in return for his keep. Just a man who was a good worker, and to whom, at that time, she could talk about Anthony.

She already knew a good deal of his life in Australia from his letters, such as they were, but talking to Lawrie had made it come alive for her. He'd told her about the weekends off when the men flew to Sydney or, more often, to the nearest town two hundred miles away where it was his job and Anthony's to stock up on supplies before leaving the men to get drunk and enjoy the night life. He told her about the young stallion, a thoroughbred crossed with a wild brumbie that had jumped into the paddock, that he'd given Anthony as a present; about the times they had ridden out together or taken the truck to look at the stock and slept under the stars; about the heat and the flies; the shearing of thousands of sheep; the huge road trains that transported them; the crowds at race week in Birdsville where every cockie wanted to run a horse, would bet on anything that moved, and how the wooden trash troughs that ran the length of the street, although emptied every day, were overflowing with beer cans again every morning. He told her about the ranches: Tarran Hills and Barrington Heights; about the house where they lived; the beauty of Autumn; the green of the spring grass and the blossom; the snow on the mountains in winter, the dry cold, the log fires, and about the barbies in summer, and the kitchen where they cooked in winter after Anthony had moved in to live with him and Tillotson.

'Anthony – cooking? He couldn't boil an egg!'

'He was a damned good cook. What our housekeeper didn't teach him he worked out for himself. He always did the cooking when she had time off. It came so he was the only one she'd allow in her kitchen.'

It became clear that in the few years Anthony had been in Australia, he and Lawrie had grown as inseparable as Anthony and she had been, and every day as they talked and worked together Lawrence had gradually begun to fill the gap of Anthony's leaving.

Though she might never have realised she was in love with him if it hadn't been for the afternoon he'd discovered her way out over the moor.

A grey, windy, supposedly summer's afternoon, and needing time on her own she had gone for a long walk. As she trudged across a wild unprotected stretch of heather, the heavens had suddenly opened, so she had tucked herself under a thicket of tall gorse and had been sheltering from the driving rain for quite a while when she saw him riding Piper up the hill.

Wearing his wide-brimmed bush hat and a long brown waterproof that spread out behind him over the horse's back, he was cantering head down into the wind and rain, and although unaware of her presence he was coming directly towards her. He looked out of place in his Australian kit in the deserted uplands of an English moor; an exciting stranger from another time and place – and unwilling to spoil the tingle of illusion, she pressed deeper into the thicket hoping that he'd ride by without seeing her.

Some hope. He was checking the sheep, and she was hiding in just the sort of place where they would be sheltering.

144

'I suppose you're safe out here on your own,' he said, reining the horse in a short distance in front of her.

'Safer than you are. We call that hill up ahead the grave-yard.'

He raised his head to look in the direction she had nodded. 'Oh? How's that?'

'It's full of boulders hidden under the heather.'

'Maarvellous. So you were just going to sit there and watch me break my neck.'

She laughed. 'You're safe enough on Piper. You wouldn't have got him to go up there in a month of Sundays. He knows this moor better than any of us.'

'Any other hazards I should know about? Any chance of a flash flood, or perhaps a tornado?'

'You never know your luck. There's a nasty bog over there amongst those rushes.'

He touched Piper with his heels and came closer, and as he looked down at her the water streamed off his hat in a minia-ture waterfall. 'Want a ride home? I'm almost through for today, and Piper can manage the both of us.' Leaning down, he held out a hand slippery with rain to pull her up behind him.

Sitting so close to him, holding on round his waist, all she could see was his sodden shoulders, and as they rode on and Piper had to pick his way along a path around the side of the hill, it took all her concentration to anticipate his movements and keep her balance. The rain was behind them, driving against their necks and running down inside their clothes, so that when they had checked the sheep on the last hill, he urged Piper down to where a dry stone wall grown over by beech and oak saplings led into a wood that would give them more shelter.

He let her dismount, then jumped down beside her, and they walked down through the trees to the river. The path was steep and slippery in places. She went ahead, and as they neared the bottom of the track the drip of the rain from the trees was dulled by the rush of the river – and even now she could remember the light. It was a bright, almost fluorescent green.

'Tell me,' Lawrence'd said, as slipping Piper's reins over

145

his arm he removed his hat to shake of the water. 'Did Anthony ever tell you why he ran away to Australia?'

'He didn't run away,' she said indignantly.

'He didn't run away from you, that's for sure. He adored you.'

'Yes, well the feeling was mutual. And he wasn't running from anyone. He went out there to learn about managing sheep. Who said he was running?'

'Okay. Keep your wool on.'

'Why on earth should he be running?'

'Maybe we all run from something at some time in our lives.'

'I haven't.'

'No. You're a good woman. Though sometimes standing still and keeping your eyes shut is the same as running ... I've run away from Australia, that's for sure.'

'Have you?' Surely only cowards ran away, and he was the last man to strike her as a coward. 'Why ...?'

'It's done. All in the past. From now on, Anthea, I'd rather talk about the future.' They had been walking three abreast along the path by the river, Piper between them, and when Lawrie stopped again she turned to see why.

'Anthea, I've decided to stay in England. I'll set up a business, and then I reckon I'd better get married.

So he had a girl in England ... Aware of another loss, and the sick feeling of disappointment, she avoided his very blue eyes and watched Piper rub against his arm.

He pushed the horse's head away. 'Well – what do you think?'

'Well, yes ... If you love her.'

'I don't know much about love,' he said impatiently, 'but I do think it would be a good idea to marry you.'

She stared at him. 'Me?' Wetter than a drowned rat, and no oil painting even done up in her best. 'Me ...?'

'Who else did you think I meant? Don't laugh, damn it. I'm serious.'

'I'm not laughing at you. I'm laughing because I thought ... Because – I'm happy.'

'Right on, then,' he said, uncertainly. 'That is if your father agrees.'

146

'He'll agree.'

'I'm not so sure about your mother. She's never liked the look of me since I set foot on the farm.'

'She'll agree if Dad does. And I am twenty-seven.'

'Good, so it's settled then,' and leaning towards her he kissed her on the cheek, put on his hat, pulled the brim firmly down over his forehead and, placing himself between her and Piper so that he could hold her hand, they walked on down the path to the bridge.

Anointed with rain, she thought, remembering how the cold water from their sleeves had run down over their hands and there had been no further, warmer kisses to seal the agreement. Not for a while ... That day he had asked her to marry him neither of them had been so young, but each in their own way had been as green as that light through the leaves.

We grew up together, she thought. Learnt from each other. Discovered how to make love, and how to look after babies that grew into children; how to buy a farm and run it. Then somehow, without me noticing, we grew apart – and he met that bitch.

What went wrong ...?

She supposed, if she was honest, it might have been the sex. She'd never been that interested since Wanda'd arrived – and really, the lovemaking had never been anything like as good as it seemed to be for people in books or films or on television. Still, in real life, what was?

Actually, he'd never really seemed to fancy her that way. And if she was totally, brutally honest, the bitch was much smarter, much prettier, much sexier than she'd ever known how to be.

A log slipped in the fire, making her jump. Almost an hour had passed while she'd been dreaming, and she really couldn't be bothered to make up the books and write out the cheques tonight. Tomorrow was her shopping day. She could pay the bills when she was in Minehead – and while in the butchers she'd order the turkey.

This year Lawrie wouldn't be calling on Christmas Eve – but when she'd finished in town she'd come home via Dunster and put some flowers on his grave.

It was time she went to see him again.

147

Just after nine the next morning Beth was woken by the phone. Downstairs in the silence, she heard the answerphone click into action, and seconds later the clatter as the machine reset itself when the caller hung up.

Turning over in bed, she snuggled deeper into the duvet.

It was probably the same person who had been trying to talk to her yesterday, though it couldn't be important or they would have left a message.

Tillotson sat on the bed and replayed the widow's recorded voice in his head. She sounded a little wary – as if, unused to machines, recording the message had alarmed her. From the tone of the message he tried to imagine what she looked like and what sort of person she was. The voice was pretty much accentless, apart from the fact that she was obviously British and had what they called a good background. The British with so called good backgrounds never did quite manage to get those plums out of their mouths, no matter how far they travelled or how hard they tried. This woman was probably quite well travelled, and therefore probably fairly open-minded and easy to talk to. She sounded vulnerable, so she was also probably quite kind.

She intrigued him. He was very much looking forward to meeting her – but the sound of her voice would keep him going until he met her in the New Year. In fact, he'd call her a couple of times during the morning, and if she answered, he'd hang up. He just wanted to be sure he would remember the voice – and he intended to return to England in the New Year, even if it killed him.

For an hour during the morning Beth worked at the flower borders, the blackbird, as usual, sticking close in the hope of a few worms. When it began to rain she went indoors to take a shower and dress for her appointment with Graham.

She still had plenty of time, and as he had mentioned a headstone for Lawrence's grave, now seemed as good a time as any to go and take a look at those already in the churchyard. In any case, the phone had rung several times, and for some reason she had the uncomfortable feeling that whoever

148

it was might suddenly decide to turn up. If they did, she also somehow knew that she did not want to be there.

As she intended to visit the grave she supposed that she ought to take flowers, so she went out to the garden to cut a bunch of Michaelmas daisies. The blackbird was now pecking about under a rosemary bush – around which the wet, freshly dug, deep red earth suddenly reminded her of the flesh in a raw, new wound.

The emotional amputation again ...

The needle in Lawrence's thigh. His eyes ... Seeing it all, then looking through her as consciousness faded ...

The blackbird, too, had bright, all-seeing eyes. And she suddenly remembered what Mrs. Westcott had said once when she'd been telling her about local superstitions. That blackbirds which came close to the house after a death in the family were known as squatters and were considered to hold the souls of the restless departed ...

Later, when Beth walked out to her car, the bird was there again. This time watching her from the top bar of the orchard gate.

For a while she watched it in return – and then finally surrendered her sanity.

'I'm going to visit your grave,' she said. 'I wish to God you'd go and lie down in it.'

At the narrow junction by the new antique shop, Anthea waited for the cars to pass along the main road into Dunster, and thought of Percy. He was in a bad way this morning. Much as it pained her to think about it, when the worst came to the worst, she would bury him by the paddock wall beside his wives. The geese that were already buried there each had their own little headstone engraved with their name and the year they had died, and there was just enough room left for Percy, Gert and Petal. Then that would be that. No more geese. In any case, there could never be another gander as lovely as Percy.

'Starve the lizards,' Lawrence had said. 'Just half as much trouble with my headstone when I chuck in my chips, and I'll be delighted.'

As yet he had no headstone. The ground had settled and was ready – but it was no longer her business. Nor, she'd realised

149

as she stood by his grave, had she now any right to be buried beside him. The bitch had usurped her in death as surely as she had done so in life – and again the white face appeared at the back of her mind to taunt her.

Then suddenly, unbelievably, she was seeing the face for real. Bloody Carrothead in her blue Renault had just, at that moment, turned left into St. George's Street, passing wing mirror to wing mirror as she drove on up the lane towards the church.

Anthea checked on the retreating car in the rear-view mirror. It was her all right ... On her way to visit the grave which Anthea had just left – and burning with anger, she rammed the car into reverse, turned in a gateway and followed her.

The road was well below the top of the churchyard wall so the bitch couldn't see her – and the blue Renault was parked by the lynchgate. Anthea drove on up the hill, parked out of sight at the bottom of track, and walked quickly up through the dripping wood to the place where she had stood on the day of his funeral.

Below in the churchyard the woman, dressed to kill in tan leather boots and a beige raincoat, was putting flowers on his grave – just as she herself had done only minutes before.

Beth stared down at the tidy mound of grass and the pot of Michaelmas daisies and rosemary. The flowers Anthea had put there were identical to the bunch she was holding.

'No,' he'd said to her a long time ago, slipping his arm around her as they'd been working in the garden, 'much as I love you, I will not take out that rosemary. Rosemary is the shrub of remembrance, and as such, it's sacred. I'll trim it for you. Memories do have to be trimmed and controlled – but that bush was planted by people who lived here before us. I will not dig it up just to make the place look tidy.'

Had he, then, at some point in his marriage with Anthea, slipped an arm around her too and told her the same story while standing in front of a similar bush in the garden at Luccombe?

To him, was anything really sacred?

Was there anything he said to her that he hadn't said to Anthea already ...?

150

Was love, which should be so sacred, in reality so miserably unoriginal?

Oh Lawrie - you bastard ... I loved you so much at the beginning - and maybe she still loves you. No wonder she hates me! The hurt we must have caused ... And you told me the marriage was dead.

Well, you can rot. I shan't come here again.

Anthea watched the woman put the flowers on his grave. All done up, smart as paint - but she did care about him. She did come to see him.

Down there was a grieving widow. So what was Anthea, a supposedly well-adjusted middle-aged divorcée, doing up here spying on her successor through the trees in the pouring rain?

Ashamed of herself, she watched the woman go back to her car and when she had driven away, Anthea, drawn by a strange compulsion, picked her way down through the field behind the school, crossed the road, entered the churchyard, and walked over to his grave.

On it there were now two identical bunches of rosemary and Michaelmas daisies, side by side, but in different vases.

Identical offerings of love, but in different containers.

Was it also possible for a man to love two women equally, but in different ways for different reasons? Perhaps it was. And if death made all men equal, perhaps, after death, love too was equal.

What about the hurt ...?

'It's done. Let it go,' he'd have said.

She could almost hear him saying it. In fact he suddenly seemed very near. And if death was indeed just a passing into another invisible dimension as Gran has always insisted, did it really matter where the physical remains were laid to rest?

He seemed to agree with her. And he did love her. She had no idea how she knew, but looking at the flowers and soothed by the gentle, steady pattering of the rain, she just did.

'Whatever you put on the headstone,' Graham said, 'it'll be extremely permanent, and you can't go wrong with R.I.P.'

None too original, but for Lawrence, as an instruction, he

151

thought it might actually be quite appropriate, though he didn't say it.

'Rampaging In Perpetuity?' said Beth, accepting one of the biscuits he'd bought that morning in honour of her coming to tea.

'I was thinking,' he said, smiling, 'more along the conventional lines of Rest In Peace.'

'Yes ... Yes, of course you were.'

She was in an odd sort of mood this afternoon but they were getting on well enough. She was wearing long boots, a cream slim-cut skirt, and a soft olive polo-necked jumper which showed off her glorious hair to perfection. Having been to the grave, it was only natural that she seemed a bit strained.

'Anyway,' he said, steering the conversation back to a topic less tender, 'when you're ready to sell that Range Rover, let me know and I'll come to the garage with you if you like.'

'Would you?'

'Of course. I'd like to. You know me. Any excuse to get near a few engines.'

So many things to be done after a death before one could get on with the living, but bit by bit she was working it through. It did take time. After Stella left he'd slept with two unwashed pillowcases for weeks; one of Trish's and one of Edward's. Like a kid with a suck-suck, but the smell of his kids had been incredibly comforting. It was the sight of their toys and the clothes, theirs and Stella's that she hadn't bothered to take, which had been so painful. Even cooking with the pans that she'd used and hadn't washed properly had triggered angry memories which had turned to regret, and had hurt. The first time for everything had been a sort of milestone, the passing of which seemed to have shifted another piece of dirt from the wound, the better to allow it to heal – and Beth, doing all the things she ought to be, was making good progress.

'More tea?'

'If there's one in the pot. Don't make it specially.'

'Plenty.' He'd told Madeline to use the big brown pot. He'd thought this entire meeting out very carefully down to the last detail, and it seemed to be paying off. She certainly didn't seem to be in any hurry to go. She handed him her cup and leant forward to pick a leaf off the heel of her boot. As she flicked it into the fire and recrossed her legs, he heard the tantalizing, muted swish of something deliciously feminine and silky. 'No sugar.'

'No sugar.'

Her eyes are truly fascinating, he thought, smiling at her as he handed back her cup. Such a very dark brown – and eyes as dark as that rarely did show much expression. No need to rush her, but before she left his office he would quite definitely ask her out for Sunday lunch.

And in case his luck was in and Option One progressed as he had the temerity to hope it might, there was one vital question to which he must know the answer.

'I was in Minehead this morning. Christmas shopping. My kids have asked if it would be possible for them to have mountain bikes. Expensive little luxuries, kids. You can buy quite a good car for the price they charge for those mountain bikes.'

'So I believe.'

He drummed his fingers on the arm of his chair and smiled at her. After all, this wasn't so different from questioning a witness, and he'd done that thousands of times.

'All the same, a lot of you ladies seem to need children. Early days as yet, I know, but if you married again would you want a family?'

'Not now. I've come to terms with all that, and it wouldn't be fair to the child. I'm too old.'

Reaching over to put his cup on the desk, he breathed out slowly. Good ... Well, that was the first hurdle out of the way. He couldn't be doing with nappies and broken nights at his time of life – which was one reason, if he did marry again, it wouldn't be to a bimbo. He wanted a mature companion who'd sustained a knock or two and understood what life was all about.

'I did want a child very much,' she said, looking down at her cup. 'But Lawrence already had two and he considered that was enough.'

A bone of contention? Had Lawrence been selfish about something which even Graham knew could be so very important to a woman? Still, it was good to know she hadn't canonised him as did some bereaved partners. Much as he'd liked Lawrence, eulogies for breakfast, lunch and tea for the rest of his life would be depressing, and actually, quite rude and erosive to one's confidence.

'Will you see the girls at Christmas?' he asked, leading his witness gently on a roundabout route to the only other question that mattered for the moment.

'They'll be with their mother, but yes, Vivien said they would look in.'

'So really for you Christmas will be just another Sunday, then?' he said, nearing the jugular.

'I shall be quite happy with the television, a good book and a bottle of wine, Graham.'

'Yes,' he said. He wouldn't have minded spending it like that himself. 'My kids are coming to me this year, so it'll be a tree and all the trimmings.' He wondered about asking her to join them – but the kids would tease him something rotten. Anyway, it was far too soon for that. 'So ... What do you usually do on Sundays?'

'Wanda's coming down this Sunday. Her friend with the motorbike is giving her a lift.'

Damn ... Well go on, wimp. Keep going. Ask her. His mouth seemed dry, and he took a mouthful of tea. 'And next Sunday?' he said in a tone he hoped was suitably casual.

'Next Sunday is Christmas Eve.'

'Oh yes,' he said, deflated. 'So it is.'

It was dark by the time Beth got home. There were still no messages on the answerphone, but as she switched on the light and went into the kitchen she heard a fluttering noise in the utility room. The blackbird, although clearly scared of its achievement, had found its way in through a partly open window.

This was too close – for both of them. Huddled on the floor by the deep freeze, its dark eyes were blank with terror, and again remembering those other eyes, she backed into the kitchen and locked the door.

But the eyes haunted her all evening, triggering a succession of memories each of which she fought to suppress until, taut as a wire and trembling, even the house seemed alive, its ancient timbers and stones creaking in accusation and protest.

Just when she could have done with the support of a human voice, the telephone remained silent, and by the time it rang the next morning, having slept fitfully and now desperate for human contact, she grabbed the receiver.

'Yes,' she said, almost weeping with relief as Graham gave his reason for calling. 'Yes – lunch on New Year's Day would be lovely.'

Wanda walked up Castle Bow under the arch of The Castle Hotel and cut across the car park to the pub. *Please let him be there.* She'd taken to dropping into The Winchester quite often of a Saturday lunchtime, and sometimes he was there, sometimes he wasn't. Once he'd been there with Viv, but fortunately she'd managed to back out before they'd noticed. Another Saturday he'd been there with Malcolm and his wife Sally, and he hadn't immediately recognised her with short hair, hardly any make-up and her long black skirt revamped into a mini.

'Good Lord – Wanda! And you've got legs!'

She'd assumed it to be an exclamation of approval, though she wasn't too sure. Where Robin was concerned she was no longer sure about anything, other than that she seemed to be chasing him.

However, it was just too pathetic to keep sidling into The Winchester like some stray dog hoping for a smile and an affectionate pat that never came, so if nothing came of it today, that would quite definitely be the end of it. He did belong to Viv after all ...

She jumped over the low wall and walked between the tables stacked on the pub's tiny forecourt. In the porch she paused to check her reflection in the mirror. The Guinness girl had been replaced by a gypsy with a dark blue paisley scarf tied around her head. The scarf had been one of Dad's hand-kerchiefs, and knowing it seemed to give her courage. She took a deep breath and pushed open the door.

The heat, the cigarette smoke and the clamour of voices came at her like a great wave, and between the heads and shoulders and Christmas garlands suspended from the ceiling, she looked across to the table in the corner.

He was there – with Malcolm, Sally, and Keith.

So far things were looking good. Keeping an eye on the door in case Viv was there and had nipped out to the loo, she edged through the crowd and queued at the bar to order half a pint of cider. There was still no sign of Viv by the time she'd been served and, certain she was in the clear, she made her way back through the press of elbows and shoulders to join them.

'Hi, you guys.'

'Oh hi, Wanda – sit down,' Keith said, squashing up to make room for her on the bench.

'Hello, Robin.'

'Hi.'

He looked furious, and her heart sank.

'I like the scarf and the gold hoop earrings,' said Sally. 'They suit you. Make you like a gypsy. And am I glad you've arrived. These miserable devils are really getting to me. You're looking forward to Christmas aren't you? Please say you are.'

'Would I lie to you, Sally? I am really looking forward to Christmas.'

'Oh God ...'

'Of course she's not looking forward to Christmas,' Robin said morosely. 'It'll be the first without her father.'

'It's not so much that,' she said, trying not to look at him. 'It's just that every year you look forward to it for ages, then soon as it's here it's gone. Big anticlimax.' Not to mention the torture of divided loyalties – which, now Dad was gone and Beth would be on her own, would be even worse.

'I'll say one thing for it,' said Keith. 'It's a truly Christian festival. Not many of us get to spend it the way we want. Most of us spend it as someone else wants us to.'

Robin grunted and sipped at his pint. He was in a right mood about something, and now she'd turned up perhaps he was cross about that as well. Thought she was pushing in on his friends.

Malcolm said, 'I've never felt the same about Christmas since I found out about Santa Claus.'

'Aaah – diddums,' Sal said, grinning at him across the table.

'It's a big con, and it costs a fortune. It's not supposed to be like that. It really depresses me,' said Keith.

'What do you know about depression?' Malcolm picked up his glass and nodded at Robin. 'That's depression. If I look at that face much longer I'll burst into tears.'

'Okay,' said Sal suddenly. 'I've had enough of this. We'll have a party. Tonight, at our house.'

Malcolm groaned.

'Listen misery guts, it doesn't have to be a Christmas party. There's all those hedge cuttings and garden stuff you've been promising to burn, and it's not raining today. It's not even cold. We'll have a bonfire party.'

'You're mad,' said Malcolm.

'Of course. That's why you married me.'

'You'll come, won't you, Rob?' Sally said.

'Will I?'

'You're coming,' Malcolm said. 'All of you. I've got to be there so I don't see why you lot should get out of it.'

'You bring Janet and the kids, Keith. You're coming too, Wanda. Bring a bloke if you like.'

Robin glared at her, and as the others discussed who could take what in the way of food and drink, Wanda wondered who to take. None of the blokes she knew would fit in with this lot. She wasn't too sure she fitted in with them herself – and Robin, quite clearly, was livid. Did not want her here, let alone at their blasted party.

'Look, you guys – it's really kind of you, but I really don't think ...'

'You're coming, Wanda,' Malcolm said. 'Don't you dare rat on us. Come on your own if you'd rather.'

'The thing is ...'

'I'll bring Wanda,' Robin said.

She looked at him, and he met her eyes.

'I'll take you. That's if you'll come with me.'

The others were looking at him, looking at her, waiting for her answer, and the noise level in the bar seemed to have dropped. Staring at him she felt sick with pleasure and disbelief. God, she hoped he did want to take her, hadn't just asked her because he felt he ought to. But he had asked her ...

'Well – will you or won't you?'

'Yes.'

He gave a curt nod and picked up his beer. 'Good.'

'Right then,' Malcolm said, 'one more round, then Sal and I had better be off. I've got a bonfire to build.'

'It's my round,' said Wanda, and she took her purse out of her basket and got up to go to the bar.

He'd asked her out. It didn't matter how or why – and whatever she'd expected, hoped for when she'd walked in here, she'd never dared hoped for that. What in her whole life had she done that was so good, so right, to deserve this? What sorcery had brought it about? Perhaps Dad's scarf had brought her luck.

Elbows on the bar while she waited to be served, she looked at her reflection in a mirror between the bottles. In that scarf she looked like Gran had when she was younger. The very spit, in fact, although until now it hadn't occurred to her.

Then, at the far end of the bar someone roared with laughter, and she turned quickly to look between the heads and arms and glasses, expecting to see her father. For a second she could have sworn that was his laugh.

'Lassie ...?' the barman said – and from his expression and the grins of the lads around her, it wasn't the first time he'd asked.

'Oh sorry ... Um – three pints of Youngers, half of Strongbow and an orange and tonic.'

'Come to give you a hand,' Sal said, appearing at her side. 'Where's your sister again this weekend?'

'I'd be the last to know.'

'No, I suspect the last to know would be Robin. He's a nice bloke, Wanda. I'm glad it's you he's bringing to the party.'

'Why are you spending Christmas with him?' Martin persisted as he and Vivien walked back through Hyde Park to the car.

'We should have taken a taxi. These parcels are heavier than I thought.'

'You're turning me into a packhorse,' he said. They stopped so that he could take the parcels from her, and noticed an elegant elderly woman walking towards them with a spanking white poodle prancing at the end of green jewel-studded lead, he muttered, 'Though I'll make damned sure you don't turn me into a poodle.'

'I didn't ask you to come shopping with me, Martin. You insisted.'

'True. But why the hell are you spending Christmas with Robin?'

'Because my mother invited him.'

'That's no excuse, and well you know it,' he said, grabbing at a parcel that was slipping from under his arm. 'Regardless of what you might feel about me, you aren't in love with him, that's for sure.'

'I'm used to him.'

'Good God, Vivien ... You make him sound like a comfortable old coat. If that's the best you can manage, what the hell are you doing to him? Have you considered that?'

'I've considered all sorts of things.' Angry, she walked faster and gradually the silence between them became abrasive. 'It's never going to work for you and me, Mart, whatever you think. Listen to us. We'd drive each other mad.'

'It wouldn't be like this,' he said, and cursed the slippery parcels. 'Right now I'm fighting for what I know I want, and you're fencing because you can't make up your mind. Can't, or won't, I'm not sure which. You've had an extremely stressful few months one way and another, but you'd make it a hell of lot easier for yourself if you'd stopped fighting me and let us start pulling together for what we want as a couple. We'd make a formidable pair, you know. We could even go into business together. Set ourselves up as carrier consultants for road and air cargoes as well as shipping. You'd like being your own boss.'

She listened to the snappish clipping of her high heels on the path. 'How d'you feel about children?'

'I don't have any strong feelings either way.'

'And nannies?' she asked, glancing at him as they walked.

'Why not? Your career will be as important to me as my own. I wouldn't expect my wife to be tied to kids or a kitchen sink.'

'Conceived in Brussels, incubated in Bristol and born on a ferry in the middle of the English Channel.'

'Oh, I think we could work out something better than that.'

'Look, Martin, whatever it is that I feel for you, I'm not going to say anything to upset Robin this side of Christmas.'

159

'All right – after Christmas, then. I'll be at my sister's until the middle of January. When I come back I want a definite answer. I'm not letting you string me along forever, Viv. Before I leave for Brussels I need to know how to be thinking.'

'Pete,' Wanda said, stopping as they passed on the stairs. 'That big cream fisherman's sweater you've got ... I couldn't borrow it for this evening, could I? Please ...? I'll take great care of it.'

'I'm moving out of this place. You women are always after my clothes. Okay – but don't you dare bring it back honking of perfume.'

On her way home through town she had blown most of what remained in her bank account on a pair of light blue Levi's – and somewhere she had a quite presentable navy blue shirt that Dad had left at Luccombe.

'Where are we going?' Viv asked as they sat amongst the Christmas lights in a queue of traffic heading deeper into London.

'South of the river. We can park in the Festival Hall and walk back across the bridge. I want to walk along the Embankment. At dusk on a day like this at this time of the year it's the eighth wonder of the world.'

'Do you always get what you want, Martin?'

'Usually. I promised myself a house, a certain salary and a BMW by the time I was twenty-five. I achieved all three.'

Hearing him say it made the hairs on the back of her neck tingle. It was the sort of thing Lawrence would have said. And next on Martin's agenda was a wife. Like her, he was calculating, and not particularly passionate. They were both the sort of people who would always be more satisfied by a successful day's work at the office than by a romantic dinner or a night together in bed. Could be they deserved each other. A marriage made on a computer rather than in heaven – which in any case didn't exist.

Later, walking back across Waterloo Bridge, they stopped to watch the pale December sunset and the lights of the city reflecting in the river, and he took her hand.

'We'll remember today when I've gone to Brussels. We'll have dinner somewhere special, and take the evening nice and gently. Drive back when the traffic's easier.'

He states our plans like a string of orders, she thought, watching a boat cross the rippling black and silver river. And beneath the roar of the traffic she could hear the swirling of the water as it flowed on down through the city and away to the sea.

Five weeks from now Martin wanted her answer, and in less than two months he'd be gone. He did love her, but it wouldn't break his heart if she turned him down. Martin – sent to boarding school at seven, Charterhouse at thirteen, then Cambridge, and on to the pinstriped uniformed environment of the city for a couple of years Good Experience. No wonder he was good at suppressing his emotions and could deny the existance of personal pain. If she turned him down he'd simply move on and find someone else, no problem – much as further downstream the Thames would sustain other bigger and better boats. He functioned like a clockwork soldier; always holding a little of himself back even from her, and it was partly the challenge of that which attracted her to him. But for him, almost any other intelligent young career woman would do, as long as she didn't look too gruesome.

She thought about Lawrence who had loved her but had wanted to rule her life; and about Robin, who often made her dislike herself for being too strong – and who at that moment, blissfully unaware of where she was and who she was with, was doubtless working hard at his drawing board.

In her relationship with Martin, their strengths were about equal. He was a lot like Lawrence – and while he would never know how to be as affectionate as Robin, like it or not, he was probably much more the sort of man that she'd need as a husband.

Wanda, in the garage, helpless with laughter, holding her scarf on her head with both hands as she tried to bite into an apple suspended from a string. Wanda, in the kitchen surrounded by kids of all ages helping to turn onions and sausages into hot dogs and administering ketchup to the final, much in demand work of art. His nose accosted by the smell of frying, bonfires, beer; his ears bombarded by Springstein, laughter, people talking – but his eyes were only for Wanda who seemed to be everywhere.

'Well done, Robin,' said Keith, slapping him on the back. 'You're doing great with that bonfire. Grab another beer ...'

He'd drunk too much already, and he'd had two whiskies before he'd left home to get himself in a party mood, collect Wanda, and get here. Now, two hours into the festivities, he was still scared to enjoy himself, and everything was slightly hazy.

With the exception of Wanda, whom he could see with a clarity that was most disturbing ...

Wanda; touched by the glow of the bonfire, laughing, hitching up the too long sleeves of her huge cream jersey, clapping her hands, dodging, jumping, slim legs in blue jeans running – as the husky twelve year old from next door chased her in and out of the smoke drifting across the garden.

'There's some more hedge cuttings behind the garage,' Malcolm said, but Robin was watching Wanda and the boy. The boy who was almost a man, had caught her; had his arms around her, was trying to lift the young woman Robin had tried so hard to believe was a child.

And suddenly everything came into focus – and he wanted to grab the little bastard and choke him.

Christ, he thought, confused, as he walked over to the garage and pulled brushwood from the dead, tangled pile with a strength he hadn't known he possessed. *I'm jealous! Which sister do I want ...?*

'Jacket potatoes, bacon rolls ... Who wants another hot dog?' Sally called, coming round with goodies on a tray.

'I do. I'm in need of blotting paper.'

He was dragging a pile of brushwood half the size of a tree, and when Sally put the hot dog in his mouth, he dropped the wood and took it out.

'Christ, Sal, I'm pissed ... How the hell am I going to drive home?'

'I'll drive you,' said Wanda, suddenly beside him, her face flushed with firelight, a smudge of ash on her cheek.

162

'She'll drive me,' he said to Sally, and with a shrug of his shoulders he abandoned his worries. Holding on tightly to Wanda, he accepted another beer.

An extraordinarily warm night for December, he thought when he woke the next morning. They had ended the evening sitting in garden chairs singing Christmas carols around the dying fire. A bonfire party at the wrong time in the wrong season – and he had been with the wrong girl. Wanda, that blue scarf on her head, always laughing or smiling. Whereas Viv, these days, seemed permanently preoccupied and most of the time had a face like thunder.

His head hurt, his mouth was foul as a parrot's perch and, unwilling to face the day, he lay with his eyes as yet unopened and examined his emotions. Apparently they were no different now he was sober.

Groaning, he turned over, pressed his hands to his eyes. Then he opened them – and saw Wanda sitting up in bed beside him.

'Hello,' she said cheerfully.

Horrified, he blinked hard, his thoughts performing somersaults.

'Why are you wearing a scarf in bed?'

As if it bloody mattered what she wore in bed ... Why was she in his bed!

'I don't want you to see my roots.'

'Your ... What ...?'

'Never mind. Fancy a cup of tea?'

He looked around. This was not his bed. This wasn't even his room! Jesus Christ ... 'Wanda – where am I?'

'At my place,' she said brightly. 'You insisted on coming here. You wouldn't give me the key to your flat. I had a terrible time with you – on your doorstep, and back here. You behaved very badly.'

'How badly ...?'

She'd slept between him and the wall and was now climbing out of bed over the top of him. The scarf hid her roots all right, but as she was wearing nothing but a tee shirt and bikini pants he could see a good deal of the rest of her.

'How badly?' he asked weakly, closing his eyes.

Thank God, not that badly ... Under the bedclothes his hand

163

was reassuring him that his jeans were still on him, zipped up, and in tact.

'You might have to apologise to Pete about the motorbike. At two o'clock this morning you were sitting astride it out there in the garden honking the hooter and making vroom-vroom noises. You woke half the street.'

'Wanda ...'

'You were,' she said, grinning all over her pert little face.

Now she mentioned it, he did vaguely remember the motorbike.

'Actually, you were very funny.'

And you, he thought, watching her pull on a sweatshirt and a pair of floral leggings, *are downright beautiful. The things I couldn't do to you. Might do to you yet, if you don't get out of here in a hurry.*

'Oh, and by the way,' she said, 'You snore. Horrendously ...'

He watched the door close behind her, then closed his eyes. His head hurt like hell – but this thing he had about Wanda would pass. It had to.

He would not do this to Viv. He just could not.

Wanda, the only pillion rider amongst a group of huge black-leather-clad young men riding even larger snarling motorbikes, arrived on Beth's doorstep in a donkey jacket and blue jeans looking very small and exceedingly wet. Behind her the rain continued to lash horizontally across the yard.

'They're not going dirt tracking in this?'

'They are,' said Wanda, grinning with delight and streaming water on to the carpet. 'They go every Sunday all through the winter, and the more mud the better.'

'You'd better get out of those things and I'll dry them for you.'

Shivering as she laughed, she put down her motorcycle helmet and started to take off her clothes. 'I must say, this weather I really do miss my poor little car.'

'I'll get you a dressing-gown. You'd better have a hot bath ...?'

'No, no. I'll be fine when I'm dry.'

Smiling, radiating a happiness that was infectious, she looked very much all right as she was. In fact, having finally

164

abandoned her obsession for black and white, this was a whole new Wanda.

She was still smiling after lunch as, wrapped in her father's cashmere dressing-gown and curled up in a chair in front of the fire, they sat in companionable silence, she watching the Sunday afternoon film on television, and Beth half watching while glancing through a section of an over-stuffed Sunday newspaper.

'Umm ...' said Wanda, stretching appreciatively, 'This dressing-gown is really cosy.'

'You can have it if you like.'

'Can I? I like wearing Dad's things.'

'Oh well, when I get around to sorting out his clothes, I'll remember.'

'Yes – please. Sweaters, shirts, anything like that.'

'There's that long raincoat thing of his somewhere. You'd better take that as well or you'll get drenched again going home.'

Wanda looked across at the window. 'It's still chucking it down. You wouldn't believe two days of weather could be so different.'

But Wanda too was different. Her happiness seemed to have warmed the entire house, and over lunch she had talked excitedly about some party she'd been to the previous evening. Beth had a strong suspicion that there must also be a man involved in this somewhere – and remembering the feeling she envied Wanda her happiness, her youth and her unshattered faith in men. But being able to remember was enough. She was enjoying their day together. Lawrence's daughter had come home to share a winter Sunday, as any daughter of her own would have done.

'You mentioned cars, Wanda,' she said, looking up from the paper. 'It's just occurred to me ... I wonder if you'd like my Renault?'

Laughing at the film, Wanda looked at her, 'I'd love it, Beth, but I can't afford it. I doubt I could even afford to insure it.'

'I'll give you the car. I don't expect you to buy it from me, and I'll take care of the insurance as your father used to.'

Wanda forgot the film. 'I couldn't let you do that.'

165

'Why not? I'd like to. I'm going to sell the Range Rover in the New Year anyway, so I could quite easily trade it in for something else and give you the Renault.'

'What about Vivien?' Wanda said, her expression clouding.

'I'll take care of Vivien. She'd like your father's desk, I know. It's about the same, value for value.'

'Beth ...'

'You'd better clear it with your mother, I suppose. All I want in exchange is that you occasionally use the car to come and see me.'

'I'd come and see you anyway, with or without a car.'

'I know. But you might as well have the car if you'd like it. After all, your father bought it. It was his money, and I know he used to help you.'

'That's really, really kind of you,' she said, touched. 'I would like the car. Having a car again would make my life much easier.'

'You will have to clear it with your mother first.'

Wanda pulled a face. 'I suppose so. Okay ... Look, Beth, you've already given me so much, but there is one favour I would really like to ask you. I suppose I couldn't come here for Boxing Day could I? The house at Luccombe's quite small, and with Viv and Robin there for Christmas ... Well – it just might get a bit much, all of us together.'

'Of course you can,' she said, delighted. 'I would love to have you here.'

'Good day?'

'Great,' Pete said, as out in the yard Wanda adjusted her helmet and climbed up behind him.

'Plenty of mud I see.' He and the bike were plastered in the stuff.

'Yeah,' he said grinning happily under his visor. 'You have a good day too, did you?'

'Brilliant.'

He closed his visor over his broad friendly grin, and the bike shot forward with a roar. It had been, Wanda thought, clinging on tight to him as they sped away down the drive, a star of a day from the moment she'd woken up with Robin. She hadn't wanted to leave him, let alone turn out on a day like this to come down and spend it in that big barn of a place with Beth. But as Dad used to say – the more you put into things, the more you got back.

And apart from anything else, Beth had said that she could go there for Boxing Day. It was going to be hell, watching Robin with Vivien over Christmas now she herself knew exactly how she felt about him. Not that he and Viv would be sleeping together with Mum around, though there might be a few creaking floorboards ... And she did feel good about spending part of Christmas with Beth. Hadn't liked to think of her being on her own right through the holiday.

God, though, Beth had been so good to her. She did wish there was something that she could do in return.

The narrow street of tiny terraced houses was crammed with residents' cars and those of their Sunday-evening visitors. Only when a white Datsun pulled out did Robin find a place to park. He'd had the wipers on double speed all the way up the motorway from Taunton, and still the rain was hammering down. He reached for the umbrella on the back seat, got out, locked the car, and ran back up the street to Viv's house.

She'd switched on the outside light for him, and he let himself in.

'Hello ...? Anyone at home?' Even to him his greeting sounded too cheerful and false.

'In the kitchen!' And this evening she came out to meet him. 'Hello, darling. Here, let me take your umbrella.'

She was wearing the Garfield apron he'd bought her when they'd gone shopping in Bristol one Saturday back in the spring soon after they'd met. Both this house and his flat were scattered with little things they'd chosen together. And now, in his flat there was a set of plates he'd chosen with Wanda. How could he even be thinking about Wanda in the way he was when he and Viv had come so far?

'You're cooking. I was going to take you out.'

'I know you were, but it's such a foul night I thought you'd prefer to stay in. I'm cooking your favourite. Roast lamb. Here, kiss ...' She put his umbrella in the stand, and came back to put her arms around him, kissed him on the lips, then turned her face away to bury her head in his shoulder and gave him a long, fierce hug. Her hair, freshly washed, smelt of shampoo, and very slightly of cooking. 'And I've made you a chocolate mousse.'

Her thoughtfulness together with the unusually affectionate greeting increased his sense of guilt.

'I saw something I might buy you for Christmas yesterday.'

'What was that?' he asked.

'Aaah ... You'll have to wait and see.'

'I've no idea what to buy you. Any idea what you want?'

'Surprise me.'

She'd be surprised all right if ever she found out about Wanda. Wanda; in a dark blue gypsy head scarf, in bed beside him, wearing next to nothing else ...

'Okay, a surprise,' he said. Whatever he got her this year it would have to be something good. Something really expensive and special. Conscience money, but she didn't have to know that. He'd feel better if he gave her a decent present. Jewellery, perhaps – though it wouldn't be a ring.

'I've lit the fire,' she said, pushing open the sitting room door. 'There's beer in the cupboard, and you can read the paper while I finish off in the kitchen. I won't be long.'

She'd drawn the curtains, switched on the reading lamps on either side of the fire, and at the other end of the room she'd laid the table for two with her best mats and three new red candles in squat glass holders.

He did what he was told, and sat down in his usual corner of the sofa. Usually she liked him to come and talk to her while she cooked – and although the house and everything in it was so familiar, tonight he felt like a visitor.

'Did you finish all the rest of your Christmas shopping, then?' he asked, putting aside the *Sunday Telegraph* when she came back into the room.

'Yes, thank goodness. London was hell. So crowded you could hardly see what you were buying.'

'London? You didn't say you were going to London?'

'Didn't I? Anyway, it was a mistake. I shan't go to London on a Saturday so close to Christmas again, I assure you.'

She's a lovely girl, he thought, watching her walk towards him. *Surely I love her ...?*

168

'What did you do yesterday? Have you finished your minstrels' gallery?'

'I've done a couple more sketches.'

'Oh well, that's good. Anything special you want to watch on telly?'

'Not unless you do.'

'Tell you what,' she said, pointing the control at the screen, 'let's watch the nature thing you like on BBC Two, and by then the lamb will be ready.'

She was really going out of her way to be nice to him ... She hated watching television on Sunday evenings, much preferring to read the papers and listen to music. As they watched the nature programme, she held his hand, but for once the Sunday evening helping of animal eating animal, copulating, then dying, seemed miserably apt – and when she snuggled up to him, it was all he could do not to ease away.

Two pints of Special Brew and his half of the bottle of wine they had with dinner did help his inhibitions a little, but his guilt – not so much for what he had done, as for what he'd have liked to do, and might, given a chance, do in the future – had put an awkward chill on the whole evening.

'Are you staying the night?' she asked later, after they had washed the dishes and were curled up on the sofa.

Considering it, he turned the pages of the colour supplement. He could brave the deluging rain and drive back to Taunton, or stay here, share her bed, and behave like the animal she expected him to be. Tonight, with Wanda firing his imagination, he wasn't sure he could rise to it.

'Actually, I think I'll go home tonight if you don't mind. I've got a meeting quite early tomorrow morning.'

'Poor love, of course I don't mind.'

He did cuddle her then, as much to comfort himself as from anything he felt for her.

As for Wanda ... He had no idea what she might feel for him, if indeed she felt anything at all beyond sisterly affection – but somehow he'd already begun to view Viv as a 'nearly was' who, all passion spent, had become a good and loving friend.

All but overwhelmed by a wave of deep melancholy, he kissed her hair and concentrated on it's clean soapy smell that

169

he loved. He was trying ... He really was trying, but for the present at least, the magic had gone.

Feeling like this, God alone knew how he was going to get through Christmas.

Chapter Eight

A Christmas afternoon towards the end of her life. Amy knew that it had to be, for everything was changing, and she had woken in a different chair by a different fire in a different room. Anthea used the drawing room at Christmas, and through a chink in the rich velvet curtains, black branches were dissolving into the darkening sky as night fell on yet another Christmas Day even as she watched. Were it not for the flicker of firelight and the coloured lanterns on the tree, the room would now be in darkness.

In her life there had been so many Christmases. So many changes, both of people and of place – but this had been a good Christmas. They were all here, the people she loved. Anthony and Arthur in the shadows in the corners; Anthea asleep in a chair by the fire, her hands in the pockets of a full, red satin skirt. When asleep she looked younger, and resembled Vivien who was lying on the big brocade settle, a paper hat from a cracker in her hand. On the hat was a silver star, and in sleep she had turned, fallen away from Robin, whose hand on her hip was possessive and restraining, and although he too was sleeping, his expression was troubled. At his feet, nearer the fire, Wanda, her red paper hat askew, was curled up, her head on a gold velvet cushion.

All things in life were a pattern – and Amy began to see that the family cameo in that room hushed with Christmas was not as peaceful as it seemed.

Alive with their breathing the warm air, spiced with the scent of pine needles and brandy, was charged with their energy. Such energy that the coloured lights wound through the tree's glossy, tinselled branches, shone brighter than she had ever seen – each tiny lantern telling its own story, each perhaps signifying a Christmas in their lives to come.

My, but how they twisted and thumped at walls and dead-end pathways; how they fretted and grieved when, for each of them, as for everyone, the paths were already marked.

And for each of them in that room, that Lawrence, still with sufficient power to atone and see it come right, would continue to be with them in turn until it was done.

He was also showing her a little of the future ...

Soon, when the snow came to cover the moor, there would be one more player. A man with the sun on his skin ...

And as the Christmas star atop the tree had five gold points, so, within five months, would the storms have broken and passed; the pattern have finally changed and settled.

Next Christmas, that star and the coloured lights would shine for four adults – and there may already be a baby. Amy's great-grandson, blessed with the spirit of one who had lived on this moor and been of her family in a past generation. He would be born, she knew, at the latest within five years, and although his mother would never learn to use her powers to the full, he would see clearly and speak wisely and well. He would be born into this world. He must – for in his future he had a vocation to answer on another continent on the far side of the world.

I shall not meet him. Not on this earth, Amy thought. *For, by next Christmas, praise be to God, I shall not be here. Within the five months I shall grow stronger – but I see holly trees in blood-red berry, the garden in its autumn colours, and my wicker chair empty, danced about by a flurry of the first-fallen leaves.*

'Mum ...' Wanda said, sitting up slowly, 'something's the matter with Granny. She's all twitchy and her eyes are funny.'

Anthea roused herself, and stretching, looked at Amy as Amy looked back.

'Too much pudding – like the rest of us, I expect. A touch of indigestion. She seems all right now. She was probably dreaming.'

'I was not dreaming,' Amy said.

But they were all waking now. Moving around, and the pattern she had seen for the future had already faded into the past.

172

Chapter Nine

'Happy New Year,' Graham said, rubbing his hands together as he stepped into the hall. 'My word, and it's cold.' She looked every bit as good as she'd looked in the fantasies he'd allowed himself over the holiday – and the woollen dress she was wearing clung to her in all the most interesting places. 'Good Christmas?'

'Yes, fine. Did you?'

'Ate and drank too much as usual.'

'Would you like a drink here before we go?'

'Umm ...' he said, doubtfully. 'The table's booked for twelve.'

'Fine. I shan't be a minute. Go on through to the sitting room and I'll get my coat.'

He'd finally decided to take her to a comfortable well-run hotel at Exford, and had been anticipating this moment all over Christmas. Now that it was here, he was, to his annoyance, extremely nervous. The last time he'd been in this room he'd made a complete ass of himself ... This time, though, he was better prepared. Was determined to get it right – and when the shops had reopened after Christmas he'd taken Trish and Edward to Taunton. While they were rummaging through record shops intent on parting with the tokens and money they'd been given, he'd done the rounds of the book shops and had eventually found exactly what he wanted. A book entitled *Relationships The Second Time Around*, which he had since studied in detail.

Comforted by the knowledge that he was well prepared, he wandered over to the window. Looking at the breathtaking

173

view, he noticed a blackbird huddled on a corner of the outside sill. Then Beth entered the room behind him and he turned to look at her.

'You look ... Nice.' Not at all the word he needed. In a long black fur coat, she looked absolute magic. Like a soft and inviting Christmas parcel.

'It's fake, in case you're about to object.'

'In hunting country? If it's not a rare species I'm not sure I'd dare.'

'No ... Though the saboteurs do have a point.'

'Oh yes,' he said and, suddenly hungry, looking forward to his roast beef. 'You're not a vegetarian?'

'Heavens no.'

Fine. So far, so good. It seemed set to be a good day and, with luck, would be the first of many.

'No one at home,' Viv said as she got back into the car.

'I did suggest you phoned,' said Robin.

'Oh well, as long as she's enjoying herself.' He watched her flex her hand and examine her sheepskin glove. 'Where now? Luccombe?'

'We might as well, since we're down this way. Do you mind?'

'Not at all,' he said, and started the engine.

Anywhere, as long as she was happy. Christmas hadn't been easy for him with Wanda around, but he and Viv had been alone at his flat since the day after Boxing Day and, if anything, that had been worse. She'd be off back to Bristol early tomorrow. Meantime, the hours would pass more quickly in the company of others.

Damn it, why was he so pathetically obliging ... Ask Martin to drive aimlessly around the countryside on a cold grey afternoon and he'd have blown a fuse. Added to which, Martin would never have bought the tickets for last night's dinner dance if he hadn't wanted to go to it. She'd never have mentioned the stupid dinner if she'd realised Robin would go out and get tickets at the ridiculously expensive price they were asking. He couldn't afford those sort of luxuries at present, work in the building trade having been so bad for so long.

174

And now, today, another huge and expensive lunch, when she'd just as soon have stayed at home and slept off last night in front of the fire.

Preferably her own fire in Bristol – and on her own ...

Why the hell was Robin so generous, so patient, so thoroughly bloody NICE!

'Look, Robin,' she snapped, 'we don't have to go to Luccombe if you don't want to.'

'I want to,' he said, changing down a gear to pull out into the lane.

'No you don't.'

'I've said I do.'

'And I know you don't.'

'We're going,' he said calmly.

Damn him – he was so boring. He wouldn't even LET HER PICK A FIGHT!

He'd been patient, attentive and undemanding all through Christmas and the days they'd been together since. Because as long as he kept his cool, in time this thing he had about Wanda would pass and the rift between him and Viv would mend as if nothing had happened.

He drove through the lanes towards Luccombe in a state of self-controlled grace, and it was only when they had passed the village hall and the green and were driving along the main street between rows of thatched cottages with Christmas trees lit up in their windows, that it occurred to him that Wanda might have returned to spend New Year with her mother. Might be at the farm ... Driving up the lane under the avenue of trees, drawing level with the farm gate, turning down the drive, his stomach was alive with dread and nervous anticipation.

Down in the yard the dog rushed out on to the white-cold concrete, barking manically, straining at its chain – and the geese, whiter than the concrete in the gathering dusk, came sailing around the corner by the pond honking furiously, beaks pointing at the sky like three marauding pirate ships ahead of a high wind.

He stopped the car, wound down the window and smiled at Anthea who, in her working clothes, had emerged from the milking shed. 'Hello.'

'Hello, dears – what a lovely surprise! I'm almost finished out here. Go on in and put the kettle on. Wanda's indoors, reading to Gran.'

Wanda, squatting on the stool at her grandmother's feet, heard the door open and looked up.

'Hi,' he said, meeting her eyes. 'Happy New Year.'

Later, she wasn't even sure if she'd answered him, because, looking up, seeing him standing there, her heart, quite literally, seemed to have shot loose of its moorings and was thumping around in her chest. Above all else, she had suddenly realised that she wasn't wearing her headscarf, and that he'd see her roots. Utterly confused and blushing, she stared at the book in her lap, then glancing at Gran, she realised that she had been watching her and that about her lips there was a slight but approving smile. Somehow, then, Gran knew ... Must have sensed it – and for a second as Wanda's eyes met hers, she matched the smile, and recognised it as that of conspirators.

'I'll put the kettle on,' said Viv, her coat discarded and already on her way through to the kitchen. 'I must say, I didn't expect to see you here, Wanda. What's this, your New Year's resolution? Or would that be too much to hope for?'

'And how are you today, Mrs. Kenworthy?' Robin asked quickly.

Gran smiled up at him and, still conspiring, Wanda replied for her. 'Actually, she's very well. Very alert at the moment, aren't you Granny love?'

'What's Wanda reading to you?' he asked, looking at the cover of the book.

'*Homeopathic Remedies*. She still likes to hear about them,' Wanda said, still acutely aware of her hair. She could pretend she needed to go to the loo and nip upstairs – but if she came down with her scarf on it would be too obvious. Vivien would be bound to comment, and that would be even worse.

'You're all right, are you?' Robin asked softly, his expression as gentle as his voice.

'Never better.'

What did he feel for her? Was there anything in his eyes beyond friendship ...?

176

'Good,' he said.

'Have you made any resolutions, Wanda, as a matter of interest?' Vivien asked nastily as she came back into the room.

'Maybe.'

'I hope you have. You're here today at least – and I suppose you did spend Boxing Day with Beth. We called on her today but she was out.'

'Lucky Beth.'

'What's that supposed to mean?'

'I'm glad she's out. I hope she's having a nice time.'

'Oh ... Right, yes, I see. Yes, so am I.'

God, Viv was even touchier than usual. She'd soured the whole day the second she'd entered the room. And it was Viv to whom Robin belonged ... Though, actually, Wanda had made one New Year's resolution. Just a few seconds ago, and it was probably useless even to hope, but Gran, at least, seemed to be on her side – and as Dad used to say, when you see what you want, go for it.

'If you're looking for the Christmas cake it's in a tin in the drawing-room,' she said to Viv who had been searching the cupboards of the sideboard.

'Thanks ...'

No trouble. No trouble at all. It was the least she could do, considering her New Year's resolution.

'What did the manager say?' Graham asked, laughing.

'He wasn't too pleased, though I gather he was happier after Vivien had picked the tins up. And apparently that was the last time they allowed old Mrs. Kenworthy anywhere near a shop. Viv said she knew exactly what she was doing. Sheer mischief, I suppose, like a child.'

'I remember those cans stacked in pyramids when I was a kid. I used to get bored to death hanging around in the grocer's shop waiting for my mother to finish her seemingly endless conversations. Those precarious displays were very tempting. Perhaps, when I'm as old and disinhibited as Mrs. Kenworthy, I'll find the courage to do that sort of thing as well.'

Laughing, Beth leant forward to refill his tiny coffee cup. 'There has to be some advantage in getting older.'

177

'Oh yes,' he said, watching her. 'One way and another, I'm almost beginning to look forward to it.'

They had enjoyed an excellent lunch with a bottle of Burgundy and were comfortably settled with coffee and brandy beside a large open fire in the hotel lounge, at the other end of which four active elderlies were hogging another fire while discussing their pensions and their winter cruises. Retirement really wasn't such a formidable prospect if you had someone with whom to share it – and in his mind's eye he pictured them, all the Sundays for the rest of his life strung out ahead of him like warm, welcoming watering holes on the long straight road leading to his personal, inevitable sunset.

'And of course, when I'm completely disinhibited, I shall stand up in court and tell one or two of those cranky old judges exactly what I think about them and their pontifications as to law and justice. Yes, I am quite looking forward to it.'

Beth chuckled. He really liked the sound of her laugh. And then a waiter appeared in the doorway, hovered, and again retreated. They were the only people left other than the four pensioners were now obligingly getting to their feet.

'I suppose we ought to be going,' he said. 'Though it's very comfortable here. We can stay if you like. I'll order tea ...'

'Lord no. I couldn't. I'll make you a cup of tea when we get home.'

'We must come again, then,' and sighing with contentment, unable to remember a more promising start to a New Year, he patted the arms of his chair and stood up.

In the cramped, overheated powder room, Beth applied lipstick and brushed her hair. It had grown too long for a woman of her age, and needed a cut.

Lawrence, though, had liked her hair long ...

This time last year they'd been at the races. Had met up with that trainer from Newbury who had bought them lunch in the plush dining-room reserved for owners – one of whom had been thoroughly, if entertainingly drunk, and had kept apologising. Between talking business with the trainer Lawrie had won a lot of money on an accumulator and, later, had bought the champagne which had started a party that lasted well into the evening. A good day, and she'd enjoyed it – even though, if only as a shadow at the back of her mind, she had known for several weeks by then that she was probably sitting on an emotional time bomb.

That was last year – and returning firmly to the present, she dropped her hairbrush into her handbag and snapped it shut.

Graham was waiting for her by the reception desk. A shorter, plumper man than Lawrence, though for a moment, as she walked towards him, it was Lawrence that she saw; his familiar face and physique, transposed on to Graham's like the ghosted, badly focused negative of a photograph. The pain skewered her chest – but Graham was smiling.

Then he put his hand under her elbow – a solid, flesh and bone hand – and, together as a couple, they went out into the icy wind.

Unable to sleep, naked except for the towel around his waist, Tillotson sat by the open window and looked up through the fly screen at the stars. Yesterday, the first day of the year that might well be his last, the mercury in the thermometer on the coolest part of the verandah had risen to well over a hundred, and even now, in the small hours of the morning, the air was hot. This summer the heat was really getting to him.

He closed his eyes and, resting his head on the back of the tall cane chair, longed for England. The wet, bone-creaking cold of a British January ... And as, in his imagination, he savoured the thought of it, the cramp started again in his stomach.

He'd been struck down by a debilitating tiredness off and on since July, but the dose of radiation he'd had on his return from England in December had been the worst yet. He'd felt sick and giddy ever since. And the diarrhoea ... The pain and urgency were more like fucking dysentery. He was going to have to get to the dunny again. Fast.

When he came back he stood weakly by the window and, despite having had another cool shower, once more felt the sweat start to prickle his skin. He took the towel from around his waist and began to dry himself, noticing as he did so that on the far side of the paddock one of the men from the bunkhouse was leaning against the white railings having a smoke. He could see the red glow from the cigarette butt. One

179

of the jackaroos, probably. Both those new boys from
Tasmania were finding the heat trying. He just hoped the
young blighter would grind the butt out properly when he'd
done with it. Everything was tinder dry at this time of year,
and the risk of fire was a real problem.

Bloody fool ... He knew damned well that smoking was bad
for him ...

For others who knew that equally well, it was already
too late. And watching the lad whose name he'd just now
forgotten, he reached for his cigarettes on the table, lit up
and inhaled deeply.

The stinging fumes brought on a rasping spasm of coughing,
and when he got his breath he guessed that the lad had heard
him and was watching the house. The small light glowed
brighter as the boy took another drag, and Tillotson was suddenly filled with camaraderie and a deep sense of gratitude that
he was not, after all, passing the night entirely alone.

Jeeze, but it was airless ...

He balanced his cigarette in the ashtray and once again
patted his neck, his arms and his emaciated stomach with the
towel. It was a hot night, but sweating to this extent had, he
knew, more to do with the bloody disease that was devouring
him than the effects of the climate. And his guts were starting
again.

There was just no way he'd be fit to fly to London next
week.

But he was going to England at some point, and that was a
fact. Perhaps at the beginning of February ...

Tomorrow he'd get on the phone to the clinic and give them
hell. They were bloody well going to sort out his drug doses
and get his symptoms on hold – somehow. He had to talk to
that widow before he sold the ranches. And if he didn't get to
England at the beginning of February, the way things were
going, he wasn't likely to get there at all.

'Your tea,' Beth said curtly, to the blackbird, setting the
saucer of birdseed and raisins down on the deep freeze. Since
the weather had turned colder he had grown bolder. Had
moved into the house to roost every night on top of the
cupboard above the boiler in the utility room.

180

'I hope you're not feeding that bird,' Ma Westcott had said. 'It never does to encourage them squatters.'

'Want any help?' Graham called from the sitting room.

She shut the utility door. 'No ... The kettle's boiled. I shan't be long.'

The bird, of course, would not be able to get in if she closed the window – but whatever she had felt about Lawrence, she couldn't lock him out on a cold winter night.

Chapter Ten

Three weeks into a cold, clear January, during which Graham had often phoned Beth to talk and had taken her out for lunch or for dinner several times.

She, in her turn, despite Ma Westcott's warning, was still feeding the blackbird, which now came into the kitchen if she wasn't quick enough to prevent him, and always flew to her side the second she stepped out of doors.

Every day as she worked in the garden he was beside her, and as she and Lawrence had often worked in the garden together, she had begun to acknowledge that she was missing him more than she cared to accept.

He had also been with her in the barn when she had turned out the contents of his Range Rover, and again when she had washed it so that she and Graham could take it to the garage to be valued in part exchange for the Peugeot 205 he'd already helped her chose to replace her Renault.

As, this afternoon, she was to drive the Range Rover to the garage and leave it there, the blackbird would doubtless be in the yard to see her off.

'Come on then,' she said, resigned, as she opened the door into the utility to give him his breakfast.

But this morning he was not there. Not on the cupboard, or on the floor in the corner by the deep freeze.

'Oh, for heaven's sake ...' and angered by her own irrational belief as much as by the bird's absence, she opened the door and went out into the garden.

He was not there either, and having strolled around the lawn searching the shrub and flower borders, she walked around the side of the house to look in the yard and the barn.

'Lawrence ...?' she called softly, aware of the cold thread of fear in her stomach. *Where the hell are you? Sulking, because I'm selling your precious Range Rover? Or because, yet again, I'm meeting your friend?*

He wasn't in the barn or the garden, and looking across the yard at the orchard and the shelter, reluctantly, pressing down the memory, she began to walk towards the gate.

Oh God – no. Not again ...

But in the long frosted grass there was a flattened circle scattered with feathers and soft grey down.

'Beth ...' Already his lips were barely moving, and in his eyes staring up at her from the grass – anger, disbelief, horror, accusation, followed by acceptance and understanding – and finally, most unbearable of all, forgiveness.

She had stood by and allowed him to die and, understanding, he had forgiven her. Then he'd come back to keep her company, ease her days, stop her thinking – and, in the course of the night or early this morning, she had failed to protect him. Had, yet again, let him down ...

Desolate, remembering all too late the cat's paw prints on the Range Rover, she stared at the feathers and, kneeling in the grass, collected them carefully. Held them against her cheek.

It was sometime before she seemed to be able to move, and when she did, she was very cold and the pain in her chest was excruciating.

Oh, so you're back then, Amy said to him cheerfully. *And when's this weather going to turn to snow ...?*

Since Christmas she'd been feeling more alert in her mind as well as fitter in herself. With the aid of her thumbstick she could now walk as far as the kitchen again – and he was leaning against the Rayburn.

At least, he had been. A minute ago ...

Robin looked at the Aga sections which had been dumped in the hall to await assembly. He was not pleased. It had been a pleasant enough morning to drive down to Dorchester, but the site meeting with the builder he'd contracted to renovate what

183

had once been a lovely Victorian village school, was fast becoming a disaster. The school was to be a luxury private dwelling with swimming-pool and landscaped garden for a client who expected to move in on his return from Hong Kong in April. So far, boxes, wood and rubble all over the place, it looked more like a rubbish tip.

'Where did you get this timber?'

'Local supplier, like always.'

'Right, well it hasn't been stored where you say it has. The moisture content is way over the limit and as soon as it's fitted it'll buckle to hell. As for those doors, I specified four-panelled, not six. The whole lot will have to go back.'

The builder, a local man, looked morose. He was probably a friend of the chap at the builders' merchants, and like as not they'd fixed themselves a nice lucrative little deal on the side. He needed watching, this one. The workmanship of his plasterers wasn't up to much either.

'So, you'll arrange for another coat of plaster on those walls. And if you don't want to tell the builders' merchants to collect that load of tat, I will.'

Muttering something he wasn't meant to hear, the builder followed him upstairs. But Robin was in no mood to be messed with. He'd come down here to answer this beggar's moanings, and everyone of them had turned out to be the result of the man's own short cuts and shoddy workmanship.

The suite in the main bathroom had been installed; white porcelain and a good-quality bath finished with mahogany panelling and gold taps. This, at least, was looking okay, and he marched on along the landing to exchange a few complimentary words with the plumber who was now working in the en suite bathroom of the master bedroom. No problems there either, or with the downstairs plumbing. Thank God the plumber knew his stuff.

'You will be finished and out of here by the middle of February?' he said only half as a question to the builder as they went on down the back staircase.

The kitchen was almost finished. No dents or scratches on the stainless steel sink, and whoever had fitted the expensive dark oak units had finished them off with a clean and a polish. But given the builder's attitude, Robin had an uneasy feeling about the whole contract. He'd picked the wrong man for the job, and he was damned cross with himself.

'The decorators are due in on the nineteenth, and by then I want the place clean and the dust settled,' he said. Because the sooner this clown and his rubble were out of here the better. 'And forget the builders' merchants. I'll ring them about the timber,' he said decisively, as the builder accompanied him outside and across the mayhem that had once been a playground.

'Have it your way then, squire, if that's what you want.'

I'll have your guts on a plate as well before I'm done, Robin thought, disliking the sharp-featured little bugger intensely. In that greasy cap, he didn't look unlike a weasel. *If I'd clapped eyes on him before I'd signed him up*, he thought as he got into his car, *I might have thought twice about it.*

Looking up at the school before he drove away, he admired the arched stone windows, the Hamstone walls, the original bell steeple rising from the softly curved slate roof. These old unspoilt buildings were like gold dust and, in their original state, there weren't many of them left. No way he was about to have that weasel balls this up. He'd make damned sure he got a good landscape gardener to take on the final stage when the swimming-pool was done. Some woman who lived near Ilminster had sent him a file of her qualifications and experience. This job sounded right up her street, but he'd go and take a look at her first, and at one or two of her completed contracts. He wasn't having any weasel's wife messing about with the garden.

So far, he decided, as out on the main road he drove north towards Yeovil, this year had gone from bad to worse. Mainly because he hadn't seen or spoken to Viv for three weeks. Quite out of the blue on the way home from Luccombe on New Year's Day, she had suggested that they didn't see each other for a while. Had said that, at least until the end of January, she wanted some space. As he saw it, she'd already helped herself to plenty of that, and he wondered again if, on that one as well, he'd missed the wood for the trees.

'Is there anyone else?'

'Not at the moment.'

'But you want somebody else?'

'Robin, I'm tired, To be honest, I don't know who or what I want. Lawrence's death, and working myself into a new job, it seems to have taken more out of me than I'd realised. I need time to breathe. In the meantime, if there's someone else you want to ask out, I think you should feel free to do so.'

'Like who?' he said, risking a sideways glance at her.

'I don't know. Anyone you like,'

She couldn't know about Wanda. He'd taken great care not to even look in Wanda's direction when Viv was in the room. Had she sensed something over Christmas? Surely not. There wasn't much to sense. Anyway, Viv wasn't the sort to sense things. She had little or no nose for atmospheres, and no time at all for intuition. And Wanda ... As far as he knew she just liked him as a friend. A prospective brother-in-law.

'What have I done?' he'd said, looking ahead at the road.

'Nothing. Don't be silly ... It's just that it wouldn't be fair to expect you to hang around waiting for me to sort myself out.'

'I see. Well, thanks for telling me.'

'It isn't you, Rob, honestly. I do love you. It's just that right now I'm feeling very mixed up. I guess I miss Lawrence more than I thought I would, though God only knows why. Perhaps I've got to find out who I am, other than his daughter, and what *I* now really want for *me*. Until I get all that into some sort of perspective, I'm not sufficiently myself to team up with anyone.'

If I'd been less argumentative and duplicitous myself, perhaps I'd have seen it coming he thought, reaching across to feel for a liquorice wheel he knew was somewhere in the glove compartment. *I should have seen it coming* ... But whatever her reasons for setting him free, he'd had to admit he'd been somewhat relieved at first. The living with it hadn't been so easy – but it was giving him the chance to reassess his own situation.

Seligman's death had made him realise what he wanted. Now he had chance to think again about with whom. In February he'd be thirty-two – and sometime this year Wanda would be twenty. He'd never had a girlfriend that much younger than himself, and viewed in terms of a permanency and the future, he wasn't sure it was a sound idea.

186

Wanda, the woman-child, wearing a blue gypsy headscarf – playing games ...

Since he'd first met her she had changed beyond all recognition – though it was just possible that he'd been attracted to her right from the beginning. She'd drifted across his mind quite frequently long before that fateful party when they'd ended up in bed. Well, only in a manner of speaking – though since the party, she had also been plaguing his dreams.

Anyway, he loved Viv. And strident though she might be, she still loved him, so it was possible that she would want them to get back together once she'd had her bit of space.

Do I want us to, though? he wondered as he negotiated the roundabout on the outskirts of Yeovil. *Which sister do I want?* Not that he could afford to marry either of them at the moment, the way things were going – but it would be much easier if Viv and Wanda weren't sisters. If Wanda was anyone else's sister he'd probably pick up the car phone right this minute and ask her out without a second thought. After all, he would be able to make up his mind much more certainly if he had chance to get to know her better.

But it was Viv to whom, for the present, he still owed his loyalty, and as the speedometer touched ninety on the straight down to Ilchester it was Viv whom he continued to think about, wondering what she was doing, and with whom.

These past few weeks, every time the phone had rung he'd hoped it might be her to say she'd changed her mind. Still, he was coming to terms with that.

And his life had been a good deal more peaceful without her.

Perhaps he'd been in love with the woman he wanted her to be, rather than the woman that she was.

Perhaps it was over then, he thought as he turned out on to the A303 and again allowed the car to pick up speed. Perhaps they wouldn't get back together.

Well, one more week and it would be the end of January. By then, to be fair to them both, he would have to make up his own mind – regardless of what she wanted.

Viv heard the light tap on her door and looked up. It was Martin's first day back at work after his Christmas holiday

187

and an unexpected call to demand that he visit his new boss in Brussels. They'd kept in touch by phone but it was a month since she'd seen him, and all morning she'd been very aware that was once again, he was somewhere in the same building.

Silly to be nervous. Or perhaps, more than nerves, it was excitement.

'Hi.'

'Hello.' She sat back in her chair and smiled at him. He was tall; built like a wand. Amazing ...

'Well, I missed you, but it seems I've survived my sister's cooking. And an encounter with the Beast of Belgium.'

'That bad?'

'Well – he's going to be a stickler for detail.'

'I missed you too,' she said, the butterflies in her stomach beginning to land.

He pulled out a chair from under her desk and turned it round to sit astride it. 'And now I've come for my answer.'

It sounded so old-fashioned that she laughed.

'Well ...?'

'I haven't got an answer to give you.'

'We agreed – the middle of January,' he said, his expression suddenly serious, 'You've already had an extra week.'

'God,' she said, exasperated, 'you are so like my father, He had to have things all neatly taped in nice little boxes.'

'Sensible man.'

'Maybe, but I can't live like that Martin. This is a relationship, not a painting by numbers.'

'So ... Robin wins.'

'No – not at all. I'm not even seeing him at the moment.'

'Well, I guess that's a step in the right direction. What have you told him?'

'Nothing as yet. But I will, in due course. If necessary ...'

'We'll talk about it over lunch,' Martin said, dismounting from the chair. 'And tonight we'll go somewhere special to celebrate.'

'Celebrate ...?' Two minutes in his company and he was irritating her already. 'You really don't give up, do you?'

'Of course not. You'll probably give me the answer I want before this evening's over.'

188

'Oh, will I. You know, Mart – sometimes I think that I actually hate you.'

'Good. Hate is an extremely positive emotion. Come on – get your coat. We're going out for lunch.'

In Graham's profession it was easy at times to believe there were more bad people in the world than good. But some people were born carers. 'Leave it with me, Mrs. Seligman,' old Roberts had said. 'Full of memories are cars, and folk get attached to them – I know that as well as any. We'll send it on to our Barnstable branch. That way you won't have to worry too much about seeing someone else driving it around.'

Even so, as Graham was driving her back for tea at his office, she had started, very quietly, to weep. It couldn't be his fault this time, but he had no idea what to do about it; whether he ought to try and comfort her or leave her alone to cry in peace. He rather hoped she'd want to be left alone ...

'Shall I take you home?'

She shook her head, and his heart sank.

'Old Rogers will find it a kind owner.'

'It isn't that.'

Embarrassed, and paying far more attention to the road ahead than was necessary, he kept driving. She hadn't even taken much notice of the smart little red Peugeot GTi the garage was getting ready for her – a jolly neat little car, and a mighty nifty bit of engineering with fantastic acceleration and the road holding capabilities of a limpet.

She cried all the way back to Porlock, and when he'd turned into his drive and driven into the big double garage, he switched off Alouette's engine but left the lights on, hoping that she might yet change her mind and want him to take her back to Tivington. Lights on, it would be that much easier to make a quick getaway.

'Please don't cry ...' he said helplessly.

He'd never seen anyone cry like this. Silently, the tears just streaming down her face. He could see her in the lights reflecting back from the garage walls, and she reminded him of Trish when she was little.

Oh Christ ... Just remembering how Trish used to weep

189

when he returned them to Stella after a weekend made him feel as if he'd been shredded all over again.

Beth, slumped in the seat beside him, looked totally beaten – and he began to realise that this must be far more grief than that evoked by parting with Lawrence's car. Perhaps this was the first time she'd been able to cry since his death, and the car had been merely the trigger. This was grief in its most honest, purest form, and he was both fascinated and appalled. She was usually so proud, so controlled.

'Come on,' he said at last, and turned off the lights. 'I know what you need.'

In fact he hadn't a clue, but he knew he was going to have to do something – and in his office there was a bottle of brandy.

The fire was still just alive and he removed the guard and put on another shovel of coal. Then, unsure whether to be pleased or sorry that Madeline had already gone home, he gave Beth the box of tissues he kept in his drawer for colds and emotional clients, and found the brandy.

'Have a sip or two of this while I make us some tea.'

Having escaped to the kitchen with the large glass of brandy he'd poured for himself, he put on the kettle and began to curse *Relationships The Second Time Around* for not inlcuding a large section on how to handle leftover grief. The book was upstairs on the chair by his bed, but it would be a waste of time to go up for a second look. He already knew it so well that he could recite whole sections of it from memory.

Oh God ... She was still weeping when he took in the tea. Exuding drops of raw grief. He was beginning to feel quite frightened for her. He put the tray on his desk, poured out the tea and, crouching in front of her, nervously offered the cup and saucer.

'Hey ...' The word seemed to stick in his throat.

She couldn't speak either, so he rested his hand on hers and put her tea on the floor.

'Don't,' he said, and cradling her hand in his, lifted to his lips. 'It will get better, I promise ...'

Then, as that didn't seem to work either, taking both of her hands he stood up, and pulling her gently to her feet, he took her in his arms.

She leant against him for what seemed like an age, and after a while he slipped off her coat so that he could rub her back as he used to do for Trish.

But Beth's body, so warm against his, so female and, for him these days, so unusual – began to have a quite different, far more potent effect on him than his daughter's could ever have done. He held her closer and kissed her hair.

He had kissed her several times before. Just social pecks on the cheek when they'd met or he'd taken her out. Quite often he had wanted much more, and the book upstairs did state that 'a kiss of the type that gives rise to passion' was acceptable after three outings.

However, today, it just would not be right. Today she just needed to be cuddled.

Huskily, he said, 'Come over to the sofa.'

When Beth woke there was a half finished glass of brandy on the bedside table, the light was on, and Graham was asleep beside her.

They must have drunk a hell of a lot of brandy ... And she wasn't used to it.

She had no recollection of coming upstairs to his bed. Only that, desperate to fill the void and thaw the awful numbness that had been with her since Lawrence had died, she had encouraged Graham to kiss her – and she supposed it must have progressed rather too quickly from there. It had certainly been her who had taken the lead. Forced herself on him ...

Physically, the exercise had been a success – and she stole a look at his face on the pillow. He was as exhausted as she was and, satiated, was keeping his distance.

That suited her fine, because the more she had encouraged and excited him, the more he had repelled her.

Because, although Lawrence was dead, he still had a hold on her.

As, between the tangled sheets, she had screwed out her guilt and her grief with the plump unfamiliar body, she had suddenly glimpsed the picture of a blackbird on the front of a magazine on the bedside table – and, given the effect it had had on her, Lawrence might just as well have been standing there watching them.

They are all bastards in their way, she thought, looking at

Graham. *Every one of them* ... Sitting up slowly, she swung her legs out of bed and began to collect her underwear that was scattered around the floor.

Graham, awake now, was watching her from under his eyelids.

'Would you like me to take you back to Tivington?'

'If you wouldn't mind.'

Everything here was unfamiliar, not just his body – and she, empty, utterly drained and now horribly sober, just wanted to go home.

Christ, he'd thought as he'd lain there feigning sleep, *what have I done?*

How could I?

It had been fine the first time. Hadn't it ...?

But as she'd reached for him again she'd hesitated, laughed and pulled back to look into his eyes, and he'd just had time to register a certain something in hers – something alarming, almost predatory. And, in the second or so that it took for his body to slide into top gear and begin to cruise with hers at speed, he'd become aware of a technical malfunction. His body was doing all the things it ought to have been, but inside his head the main electrical circuit seemed to have gone dead.

'You're welcome to stay the night,' he said politely.

'Thanks all the same, but I'd rather get back.'

So much for the bloody book, he thought, checking to be sure it was well hidden under yesterday's shirt as he dragged himself out of bed and reached for his trousers. Introduce this one to Stella and together they could have rewritten the Kamasutra ...

Even her underwear reminded him of Stella's now that, passion spent, he had time to notice. Nauseously threatening frilly bits of nonsense in coffee coloured satin and cream lace. A female wolf in the fleece of a lamb. A red-headed vixen. A siren in a fake fur coat ...

And he'd rushed it. Got carried away – and blown his entire future.

Still – it was good to know that, ten years on, he could still cope with a Stella should the need arise. Twice in the course

of one not so long evening was quite good going at his age –
especially given that he was completely out of practice.

Neither of them spoke as he drove her home. It was trying to
snow, and as she took the key from under the flowerpot and
unlocked the front door, several flakes brushed her face like
frozen tears. He waited on the step until she'd turned on the
lights.

'Thanks ...'

'Not at all. I'll be in touch.'

Other than for matters legal, she knew that he wouldn't.
She'd ruined a damned good friendship.

Now the blackbird had gone there was no living thing but
her in the house – which felt cold and unwelcoming. But as
she went up to bed, she stopped to draw the landing curtains.

Through the bare winter woods at the edge of the moor
above Luccombe a light from Anthea's farm was shining out
across the valley through the darkness.

How strange ...

She had never noticed that light. Not in all the years that
she had lived here.

Chapter Eleven

Endless January – and yet another Sunday. In the past couple of days the wind had dropped and gone round to the south west, changing the threat of snow to a grey, persistent and depressing drizzle.

Sitting on the window seat watching the rain drift across the valley, Beth could see the farm at Luccombe quite clearly, the roofs of its outbuildings gleaming like soft silver pools. Smoke was rising from the farmhouse chimney and she pictured a welcoming fire in a large open fireplace. Sunday, the family day. If neither Vivien nor Wanda were visiting this afternoon, Anthea would at least have her mother for company – and down there in the valley, in other farms and cottages, other families, united against the world, were locked into their own self-contained Sunday lives. Grandparents visiting; mothers washing-up the lunch things; fathers spending time with their children. In the country the traditional family Sunday endured from generation to generation.

Beth knew she didn't fit in here. She never had. Even Graham had his children this weekend. Graham, who understood about newcomers in this closed community of locals. He was her one ally, the one person to whom she could talk – and she'd blown that too.

Not wanting to think about it, she thought back over other Sundays. Sunday afternoons in London when she been working for American Oil; Sundays with friends in Perth, sailing or in the park. Before that, in England, there'd been Sundays; on duty, rather than be alone while Ben went home to his wife. And, eons ago, Sundays with Liz while they were training at Bart's. Never had Sundays seemed so long or so empty as they did now.

Now, one day was very much like another. Her whole life was empty, and she felt too drained to do anything to make it otherwise.

It was during her time with Liz at Bart's that she had met Simon, a remarkably bright little boy of just seven who was suffering from a rare, untreatable form of leukaemia. Why, he had asked one night when, unable to sleep, he had asked her to stay and talk to him, did God tire himself out making everything else in the world before he made people, who were supposed to be the cleverest and the most important of all the species?

Speaking quietly, hugging his knees as he sat in bed and looked around the dimly lit ward at the other sick, sleeping children, he'd said, 'He should have made people and all the nice animals first, you know – before he made all the other things. Because I'm sure he got tired. My Dad gets tired sometimes. And, you see, if God had done it that way round, he might have come up with a formula for bodies that couldn't be born deformed, get sick, or wear out.' He grunted. 'And as for that nasty old serpent snake person, he must have been made last of all, after absolutely everything else, on the very, very last second of the very, very last day. Do you think God made people *meaning* them to suffer? I mean – is earth a sort of testing ground?'

'Perhaps. Honestly, Simon, I really don't know.'

'Well, that's the only way things would make any sense if you ask me. You do believe in a life after this one, and God, and all the things it says in the Bible, don't you?'

How could she tell this child that she didn't? 'Well ... There's also a book by a man called Darwin.'

'Yes, I know about that. I saw it on television. *The Origin of Species.*'

'That's the one.'

'But it's still possible, you know, if you think about it. Adam could have just been the first monkey capable of thinking like a man. God could have breathed that gift into him years and years and years after he'd caused the big bang that brought all the bits together to make the planet earth. He would have been a bit tired after that, I expect. Though I think maybe time as we know it could be sort of different, sort of much longer and wider than it pretends it is in the Bible. It could be, couldn't it? I mean, even for God it was quite a lot to do in one week. And perhaps, after He made Adam from a man monkey, he made Eve to keep him company from a lady one. I've thought about it a lot, and I think it is possible.'

'I think, actually, it's chimpanzees that are supposed to be closest to man, not monkeys.'

'You're missing the point,' he said dejectedly.

To be honest, she'd been completely lost. Had been stunned by the depth and extent of his thinking. But maybe Simon, with the uncluttered vision of a child, had been right. Perhaps there was a God, some sort of Grand Architect involved in it all. It was also possible, at least by Simon's reasoning, that God, exhausted and anxious for companionship, had made Man on the last day of the week in order to avoid being alone for one single day of rest ...

All manner of things could have been possible, according to Simon.

Brave and calmly accepting, he had died aged seven years, five months and two days. Knowing him had been a privilege, and caring for him in his final days had been a humbling lesson as to how easily a trusting human being could pass from life into death. Simon had never ceased to question his childish faith in a God whose track record, for him, had been dented since the Creation, nor was he sure about the existence of a better place he thought of as Heaven. But, tired of his pain and of a life restricted by illness, he was willing, even anxious, to move on to discover what might be an adventure – and had made death seem so easy. A simple matter, once you had tired of fighting and had accepted the inevitable, of no longer breathing.

Lawrence, now, had been dead for twenty Sundays. He had not deserved to die any more than had Simon and, having failed him a second time, Beth was, she realised as she watched the rain, too tired to continue living with her guilt. She too was ready to die.

Turning her back on the weather, she looked round the room. The house was tidy, all her affairs were in order and she had signed her new will. There was no one who needed or depended on her, and nothing left to be done that no one else couldn't do on her behalf.

Aware that her thinking might not be totally logical; that the dark side of her mind had made the decision; that the light side, like a faint dissenting pinprick at the end of a long tunnel, was waving to catch her attention to argue and fight on, she went out to the kitchen to fetch a glass of water.

It was almost half past four, beginning to get dark, and the drizzle had increased to a steady rain. She locked the doors, pulled all the curtains and took the water up to her bedroom. The brown bottle of pills Mayhew had prescribed was almost full. The other sleeping pills which she'd had for sometime were out of date. Even at their best they had been less potent than Mayhew's, but together it should be enough. She put on a clean nightdress and got into bed.

Gradually, as sleep began to claim her, she felt the bed begin to rock. It was extremely soothing ... The gentle rocking of a small boat as it pulls away from a jetty and sails out through the sheltered waters of a harbour. And Lawrie was with her. He was steering the boat, so she wasn't afraid.

But as they left the harbour and headed out into the open sea, the waves were larger, the sea quite rough. Vivien and Wanda, waving from the harbour wall, were getting smaller and smaller – and she began to see that this waving was urgent. That the girls were calling them back, but Lawrie, determined and pointing ahead, gestured for her to ignore them.

The sea was very rough now, and they were sailing through a storm, its strong wind lashing heavy rain across the decks. She didn't seem to be getting wet – but suddenly Lawrie was no longer with her and, alone in the boat, she was very afraid.

Then, between the white sea spray and the rise and fall of the bow as the boat climbed and dipped through the mountainous waves, she saw that beyond the storm, under a clear blue sky, there was an island of soft silver lakes, tall winter-bare trees, and a house where there were lights and which she knew would be safe.

It seemed a long way away and she wanted to turn back; wanted to return to the shelter of the harbour. Steadying herself, she reached out for the spiked wooden wheel, but although it turned through her hands, the boat, apparently steering itself, refused to respond.

So she knew then that she had no choice but to weather this storm and to get to the island.

Graham came out of the shoe shop in Park Street, head down, feeling decidedly Mondayish. The events of Friday evening painfully fresh in his mind, he'd been snappish with the kids over the weekend and, to cap it all, when Stella had collected them last evening on her way back to London with her latest fancy man, she'd had the damned gall to have a go at him about increasing her maintenance.

'Sorry ...' Now, two steps along the pavement, he'd bumped into some woman.

'Sorry.' A woman in a shabby navy-blue quilted jacket.

'Graham ...?'

'Anthea!' *Oh my God – another Mrs. Seligman*. Then he relaxed and laughed. It was only Anthea. 'Good Lord ...'

'Graham – I haven't seen you in ages!'

'It's been a year or so,' he agreed.

'Where've you been hiding? What are you doing in town of a Monday?'

'Pricing riding boots for Trish. Stella tells me the riding kit's my responsibility.'

'How is Stella?'

He rolled his eyes, and Anthea's face lit up as she laughed.

'She was always a bit flighty, your Stella, I must admit. Even when we were kids.'

'Now's a fine time to tell me,' he said, grinning. It was good to see this Mrs. Seligman. An untidy, good-natured, enduring sort of woman. He'd forgotten how much he'd liked her. 'It's good to see you, Anthea.'

'Your youngsters must be quite grown up by now.'

'They are. They've just been down for the weekend. I don't see them that often. Well, you know what it's like. It isn't easy. Neither is Stella.' Except in one way, and that of course, had been the main cause of the whole problem. That this had

198

crossed his mind while talking to such a wholesome little woman as Anthea made him feel quite flushed around the ears, but she didn't seem to notice.

'You'll have seen Viv and Wanda at the funeral,' she was saying. 'They're grown and gone really, though I have been seeing more of them again since Lawrie died. My old Mum is living with me now, of course.'

They were blocking the pavement and he put his hand on her arm to guide her closer to the shoe shop window.

'She must be quite an age. How is she?'

'Away with the fairies a lot of the time, but she's been a lot better since Christmas. That can be a problem too. She wanders a bit, in body now as well as mind.'

'Oh Lord ... I was so sorry about Lawrence. A bad business that. I miss him.'

'Yes ... I was only thinking the other day about that New Year's Eve the four of us went to that hunt ball over at Dulverton, and the Land Rover broke down in the snow on the way home. Do you remember?'

'How could I forget,' he said, chuckling. 'We trudged miles to the nearest farm to get help and the bloke thought we were four mad things in fancy dress who were trying to rob him. We might have been mad, but we had a lot of fun.' He looked at his watch. 'Blast ... I'd buy you a cup of coffee and we could have a nice stroll down memory lane, only I've got an appointment at eleven.'

'I can't stop either. I've got to fetch some antibiotics for my poor old gander. Anyway, it's lovely to see you.'

'Yes ... Oh, and give my regards to your mother if she remembers me.'

They turned to walk their separate ways, and then she called him back.

'I've just thought. What size boots are you wanting for Trish?'

'Six, so I'm told.'

'I'm not sure about sizes, but there's a trunk full of riding things up in my loft. Stuff that used to belong to the girls. Boots, coats, hats, everything, and some of it's almost new. Why don't you pop over and have a look? It's seems a shame to buy new when that lot's

199

just sitting there waiting for the moth.'

'Are you sure ...?'

'Of course. Come over anytime. I'm usually there.'

'You're on,' he said, and tapped her arm. 'I'll be in touch.'

Which was, he remembered uneasily as he strode off along the pavement, exactly what he had said to the other Mrs. Seligman on Friday evening. God, he'd hate Anthea to know he'd been consorting with her enemy. Still, she wasn't likely to hear about Friday evening ... She and Beth were famed for their lack of communication – but even if she did hear through the grapevine that he'd been seen out and about with Beth, he was her solicitor, so it could have been business.

No – on that one for certain he was in the clear.

'Hi, Robin. It's Wanda.' She hoped she didn't sound nervous. She'd been wanting to phone him for days. 'Everyone's out for lunch, so I thought I'd give you a bell and see how you're doing.'

'I'm okay. Quite busy.'

'Oh sorry, I didn't mean to interrupt you.'

'You aren't. Are you okay?' His voice, deep and resonant, made her feel sort of warm and fuzzy – and he had begun to sound a bit breathless.

'Yes, I'm okay.'

'You haven't been into The Winchester lately.'

'No ... The thing is, I rang Mum the other day and she seems to think you and Viv have split up. Have you ...?'

'I'm not sure. We have for the moment,' he said, his tone guarded.

'Oh.'

How long was a moment? Some moments – ones like this – seemed to last forever ...

'You're fed up then, I guess.' Taking a paperclip out of the tray she turned it through her fingers and ground it along a groove on the top of her old wooden desk. 'I wondered if you might fancy some company this evening.'

Silence again ... And this time the moment lasted an eternity.

Then he said, 'Actually, Wanda, I'm busy this evening.'

'Oh, right. Okay then,' she said, brightly, 'I'll see you around.'

200

'I've got a site meeting in Bournemouth this afternoon,' he added quickly. 'I'll probably be late getting back. I'm really not all that busy. In fact, once I've cleared what I'm doing now, the way things are looking I'll probably be on the dole.'

She couldn't think of anything to say to that and, after another eternal silence, he said, 'Anyway – thanks for calling.'

She replaced the receiver and proceeded to take her disappointment out on the desk and the paperclip.

'Destroying company property now, are we?' Hodgson said, coming out of his office.

Damn ... He must have come back from lunch early for once – before she'd phoned Robin. While she was in the loo ...

'And was that another private phone call?'

She glared, watching him walk over to her desk, and stiffened as he came to stand beside her. Then he bent over and put his arm around her shoulders.

'Never mind,' he said as, lightly, the tips of his fingers stroked her breast. 'You can have that one on me.'

She utterly froze. Then suddenly disappointment became anger, her thoughts cleared, and she put the paperclip down on the desk.

'And you, Mr. Hodgson,' she said, savouring the moment as slowly, very deliberately she lifted her hand and locked her fingers around his nose, 'can have this one on me.'

He let out a squawk of alarm, but she held on tightly, twisting his large gin-sodden proboscis as she squeezed.

'It'll get you into trouble, Mr. Hodgson – your nose. One of these days ... Not to mention your hands and the things they do to the female staff.'

Pulling away, he leapt backwards. 'You're mad! You're sacked!'

'That suits me just fine,' she said, standing up. 'You've got my address. You can send my money on to me,' and picking up the shoulder basket she now used as a bag, she marched across the office to fetch her coat.

'Just a minute ...' he said, his voice concerned.

'I think I've given you enough of my time. And when I ask for a reference make sure it's a good one, or you might hear a lot more about this.'

'You little ... I didn't know you had it in you.'

201

'Neither did I,' she said smugly, on a high as she buttoned her coat. 'But I find that I have. And I'll have plenty of witnesses. You're well known for your wandering hands in this street. Nasty hands they are too. Fingers like sausages.'

But as soon as she got outside, the bubble burst, and waiting around the corner to catch Amelia on her way back to the office, the cold breeze soothed her cheeks and she wasn't sure whether to laugh or to cry.

She had a good laugh with Amelia who, triumphant on her behalf, wished her well.

And walking home, she cried about Robin.

'Mrs. Seligman? Mrs. Seligman ...'

The voice filtered through to her consciousness and, opening her eyes to see someone bending over her, Beth slowly identified in Mrs. Westcott's pebble lenses, the reflection of her own face on the white pillow.

Then remembering, realising where she was and why, she turned her head away.

Did not want to be here ...

'I'm glad I looked in,' Mrs. Westcott said. 'I saw the curtains were drawn when I passed on my way home from Mrs. Combes's at dinner time. My word – you do look peaky.'

Beth groaned, closed her eyes again. Her mouth was dry, her head hurt and her whole body ached from a sleep too long and too deep. She heard Mrs. Westcott walk across the carpet, and light flooded the room as she opened the curtains.

'What's wrong, dear?' she said, coming back. 'Can I get you anything? A nice cup of tea ...? Would you like me to call Dr. Mayhew?'

God, no ... She didn't need any complications, but as she looked up at Ma Westcott she saw her looking at the empty bottles on the bedside table.

'No ...' Mrs. Westcott said, thoughtfully. 'I see you've been to the doctor already.'

The two brown bottles stood together like two small policemen, and could be that Ma Westcott had heard the evidence they were giving, loud and clear.

'Yes,' Beth said, more awake, forcing herself to sit up. 'Antibiotics.'

202

'Are they? What's wrong with you, then?' she asked suspiciously.

'Kidney infection.'

'Oh, right ...'

All the same, Beth wasn't sure that she'd convinced her, so she said, 'I'd love a nice cup of tea.'

'I'll bring it up to you then. Yays.'

'No, I'll come down for it. It'll do me good to move around a bit.'

If she couldn't convince Ma Westcott that all was well, in the blink of an eye this would be common knowledge throughout the valley – and she'd have blown this one as well. A repeat prescription for double the quantity, if she played the part of a nurse cleverly – and next time she'd remember not to draw the curtains.

Meantime, she must deal with Mrs. Westcott.

'I'll have a quick shower and come down,' she said, her head thumping as she pushed back the duvet. 'Honestly – I'm fine.'

But in the shower she suddenly felt dizzy, horribly sick – and had to sit down. It was difficult to focus her eyes, and later, as she went downstairs, each step seemed to rock and come up to meet her.

'I hope you're warm enough in that dressing-gown. You still look mighty peaky,' Ma Westcott said as Beth sat down at the kitchen table. 'Oh, and by the way, that telephone was ringing when I let myself in. I'm surprised it didn't wake you. Mr. Roberts from the garage says to tell you your new car will be ready for collection tomorrow afternoon.'

'Oh good,' she said pretending to be pleased.

She wouldn't be needing the car for long, and having answered a few questions about its make, size and colour, Ma Westcott, leaning against the sink and holding her mug of tea in both hands, told her about two other cars new to the village in the past year, then proceeded to delivered a few snippets of gossip about the people who owned them. For once Beth allowed her to prattle, aware that, had she felt able and willing to take part in this sort of gossip, she might never have come to feel so isolated.

Not that it mattered any longer.

'And of course, that stroke Mrs. Parsons had was much worse than old Mrs. Kenworthy's. Yays ... Though I don't know how Mrs. Seligman copes with Mrs. Kenworthy, I'm sure. She can be a very difficult old lady, can that one. If you ask me, what she needs is a companion. Someone who'd sit and talk to her. Mrs. Seligman hasn't got time with all she's got to do in a day. My though – that house is a terrible mess. But old people do like to have a natter. Mind you, some people are a bit afeared of Granny Kenworthy, her being a White Witch.'

'I think I'll go back to bed now,' Beth said, her head spinning.

'Yays, it won't do to have you getting cold. I'll come up and straighten your bed for you, shall I? Get it all nice to get into, I will.' She put her mug down on the draining board.

'No, no. I can manage.'

'Oh well, just as you like, but in the morning you stay in bed till I get here, my dear. Tomorrow's Tuesday, so you've no need to worry. I'll get here a bit early and bring you up a nice bit of breakfast.'

'I'll be fine by tomorrow I expect.'

'Yays ... Well, I'll keep an eye on you anyway,' Mrs. Westcott said. Then, still watching her shrewdly through the pebble lenses, 'You know – you need never feel you're alone in the world. Not while me and my Stan are around.'

Beth turned away quickly to hide the sudden tears. It wasn't even as if she'd treated Mrs. Westcott any too kindly, particularly over the past few months.

'I'll see you tomorrow then.'

'Yays, my dear, you will. And you know where I'll be afore then if you needs us. Just think now, if Granny Kenworthy was a bit younger we could have fetched you one of her potions.'

Pushing the chair back under the table, Beth smiled. 'Would it have worked?'

'Oh aye, it would have worked all right. The old lady knew her stuff.'

On her way upstairs Beth paused to look out of the landing window. It was still raining and across the valley the roofs of the farm at Luccombe were gleaming like tiny islands amongst the trees.

Somewhere in her memory, the picture seemed to strike a chord – but feeling too ill to identify it, she went back to bed and fell instantly asleep.

'Poor old Percy,' Anthea said, and when she'd poured boiling water into the shiny brown teapot, she replaced the kettle on the Rayburn and crouched to stroke him. 'Never mind ... Let's hope the medicine will make you better.'

Clattering his beak in a tired witter of affection, he lifted his neck listlessly and slowly shook his head.

'Yes ...' she said, still stroking him. 'That's nice isn't it ... Nice boy. Lovely ...'

Leaving the tea to brew, she picked up the bag of rubbish and took it out to the bin in the garden where, to her surprise, Petal was pecking about on the lawn a foot or so from the back door. Gertie, over by the barn wall, was hopefully inspecting the bald winter stems of a gooseberry bush. Neither of the girls usually came into the back garden, let alone anywhere near the house.

'Shoo, Petal,' Anthea said, but as she bent to push her away from the dustbins, Petal drew back her neck, then shot her head forward and landed a hefty peck on Anthea's hand. 'You beggar! Get out of the garden. Go on – out!' Anthea shouted.

Petal turned and ran, squawking, neck outstretched, making for Gert, and as Anthea chased behind her across the lawn, the two geese took off together, clearing the garden gate in a massive beating of wings.

'Nasty spiteful thing,' Anthea said to Percy when she went back indoors. 'Look what she's done – your vicious second wife.'

The gash was bleeding quite badly, and having run it under the tap she wrapped it firmly with a towel, poured two cups of tea, and took one, plus a slice of fruit cake, through to the living room.

'That blasted Petal's taken a chunk out of my hand,' she said, resigned to the fact that she'd be talking as much to herself as to the old lady. 'Here you are, dear. Now don't spill it, will you.'

Ignoring the tray Anthea had put down on the table beside her chair, Gran held out her hands, and, holding Anthea's hand gently, closed her eyes.

Lord, and the old thing was hot ... Anthea could feel the heat coming from her, flowing through her hand and seeping up her arm to her shoulder.

'Is it snowing?' Gran asked when she'd let go.

'Snowing?' Anthea said, surprised. 'Heavens no. It's too warm to snow. And you're warm as well.'

Though she wasn't ... Anthea had laid her palm on the old thing's forehead and she felt fine.

'T'will snow soon.'

'Yes dear, well it often does, coming into February.'

Poor old duck, she thought, unwrapping the towel from her hand as she went back to the kitchen. But, although the pressure of the towel had staunched the bleeding, she also realised that the wound was no longer even throbbing.

It will snow, Amy thought. *It's time for the storm. And, thereafter, gentle white flakes will cover the moor and the valley in a soft healing blanket.*

It will snow soon, I think.

Chapter Twelve

The car smelt new, particularly now that it was warm from its climb up the hill. The smaller steering-wheel, the shorter gear lever, the layout of the dashboard, everything about it seemed strange.

'You didn't have to call a taxi, Mrs. Seligman,' Roberts had said. 'I thought Mr. Lang would be bringing you in. I'd have brought the car out to you if you'd said.' He'd taken her through it's special features and explained the various switches as proudly as if he'd designed and built the thing himself. 'Going for a spin now, I expect,' and he'd watched her drive away from the forecourt like a father watching the departure of a favourite child.

She'd had no intention of going anywhere other than to the surgery to pick up the prescription she'd requested over the telephone, to the chemist in Dunster to have it dispensed, and home to Tivington. But leaving Dunster with the package on the seat beside her, she'd thought about Wanda. She intended, now, to give this new car to her, and would leave the keys in an envelope, together with sufficient cash to cover what would doubtless be a very heavy premium for the first year's insurance. Not having seen Wanda since Boxing Day, she wondered if she'd as yet cleared the gift of a car with her mother. Not that it mattered now. When she was gone they'd have to sort that out for themselves.

Though, for some reason, Anthea had been at the back of her mind all day. Lawrence had rarely mentioned her, but she'd begun to build up a picture of her from various things Vivien or Wanda had said. Was she really so naive, so

207

insular, so narrow? And what sort of life did she have at the farm, and how did she manage to run it with old Mrs. Kenworthy to look after?

Thinking about Anthea rather than concentrating on driving the car, she had somehow turned up the lane towards Luccombe instead of turning right for Tivington – and before she knew it, she'd been driving past the bottom of the lane that led up through the village to the farm. Then, suddenly realising where she was, alarmed in case Anthea should appear, and not daring to take time to turn the car in the lane, she'd driven on and turned up Chapel Steep on the road through the woods to the moor and Dunkery Beacon – so that, now, having pulled into the verge and switched off the engine, she was taking one last look at the view she loved best in, perhaps, the whole of England.

A view that had never ceased to catch at her breath. The weather had turned much colder today, and the clear air held the promise of frost. The cold winter sun had gone down behind the heather, and across the green stretch of water in the Bristol Channel she could see the lights of Cardiff and other smaller towns along the Welsh coast.

Below, to her right, in the darkened valley between Dunkery, North Hill and Porlock Bay, other lights were beginning to show in the hamlets and cottages amongst the patchwork browns and greens of the woods and fields, while, to her left, the moor sloped down to the deep wooded valley of Horner Water.

It was Liz who had first brought her here, shown her this glimpse of heaven, and since then she had passed along this road many times with Lawrence – although he, like all the other locals, knew the view so well that he had long since begun to take it for granted and had never noticed.

They were great watchers, though, the locals. Over the years she'd often sensed them watching her – the scarlet woman Lawrence had brought down from London – while appearing to be looking at something else.

And Anthea, too, was a local. Lived down there just out of sight below the slope of the hill in the one quiet corner of Porlock Vale which, being out of bounds to Beth, until today, she had never ventured near.

In fact, in the yellow after-light of sunset as she looked again at the view ahead, the entire valley seemed alien to her. A cold eerie silence had settled over the moor, and the dark clumps of heather and gorse closest to the car seemed to have grown; had assumed strange threatening shapes which, as she watched, seemed sometimes, almost imperceptibly to move, as if she was being watched in return.

No wonder the locals wouldn't come up here after dark. No wonder the moor people were known to be strange – and glancing at the chemist's white paper bag on the passenger seat, she felt for the ignition, started the car, and headed for home.

The security light came on as she drove into the yard, and having parked in the barn she walked across to the house. She hated arriving home to a house in darkness, though she had no idea why. Something, possibly, that had its roots in the murk of her long forgotten childhood.

Damn ... And the key wouldn't turn in the lock. She tried the door, and to her surprise it opened. For a moment she again experienced the uneasiness that she'd felt out over the moor. Nobody bothered to lock their doors out here once the tourist season had ended, but she was sure she had locked it ... And cautiously, she stepped into the hall and stopped to listen.

Absolute silence.

Nor was there any feeling of an intruder – and then white reason intercepted. Uncharacteristic though it was, she must have left the door unlocked. She had been forgetful since Lawrence had died. Snapping on the lights, she dumped her bag on the telephone table and took the chemist's parcel with her into the kitchen.

This time, everything would have to be done properly. Mrs. Westcott wasn't due to come in again until the end of the week – but you never knew with dear old Ma Westcott ...

She fetched a glass from the cupboard, then, as she opened the fridge to take out a bottle of mineral water, suddenly she froze; felt her skin crawl.

Someone was standing behind her.

Lawrence ...? Her thoughts in turmoil, slowly, she turned to face him.

'I let myself in. I hope you don't mind.'

209

What she was seeing didn't quite register – and stepping backwards she leant against the sink unit and held on tightly with both hands.

'Oh Lord, Beth – I'm sorry. I didn't mean to scare you,' said Wanda. *Wanda ... It was only Wanda!*

'I know where you hide the key so I let myself in.' She continued, 'I was waiting in the sitting room, and I fell asleep. Look, you'd better sit down. I am sorry ... I thought you'd have seen my suitcase.'

'Suitcase ...?' Beth could see it now. Out in the hall on the bottom step of the stairs. A huge case ... Staring at the case, then at Wanda, she gradually let go of her grip on the sink.

'I brought as much with me as I could. I hope you don't mind ... You see – I got the sack,' Wanda said apologetically. 'It took me ages to find that bloody job, so I daren't go home to Mum. She'll have a fit. The rent on my room's paid to the end of the week. I'll have to go back and collect the rest of my things, but I can't afford to stay in Taunton until Hodgson pays me what I'm owed. I wondered ... I thought ... I mean – that is – can I stay here for a bit? Would you mind ...?'

Bloody hell, Wanda ... Yes I do mind! In all the years you could have come here ... No – you can't stay! Not now!

'How did you get here?'

'I bussed to Dunster then I tried to hitch. In the end I had to walk.'

'What – all the way from Dunster with that huge case?' It was just about the biggest suitcase she had ever seen. She couldn't think how she'd failed to see the thing as soon as she'd come through the front door.

'The arm I broke is aching a bit. Look, do sit down. I really did scare you ... I am sorry.'

'You'd better sit down as well,' Beth said. Much as she resented this intrusion, it was going to be difficult to get rid of Wanda tonight. 'I expect you're hungry.' At her age they usually were and, reluctantly, she opened the fridge. 'How about eggs and bacon?'

'Oh Beth, that sounds brilliant. I'll do it.'

Still shocked, Beth got out the frying pan and, indicating that Wanda should go ahead, sat down at the table. 'How did you get the sack? What happened?'

'Hodgson. He's awful, and these last few months he's got worse.'

Wanda began to cook and Beth fetched a bottle of wine from the utility. If she was going to have to cope with this it would be easier if she didn't have to do it entirely sober.

And by the time Wanda had told her the whole story, given Wanda's sense of humour, the effect of the wine and the smell of cooking, even Beth was chuckling – and she too was hungry.

'Last time the dirty old sod put his hand right up my skirt,' Wanda concluded. 'Though I can't tell Mum any of that. She's such an innocent I'm not even sure she'd believe me. She'd accuse me of making it up.'

'Surely not ... Oh Wanda – come on.'

'She would. She's always been a bit odd about sex. God knows why, with a yard full of randy animals – but I certainly can't face telling her yet.'

'She isn't going to like the idea of you being here with me, you know.'

'Please, Beth ... If only for tonight? Everything's gone wrong since New Year. Absolutely everything ...' She looked tired, and suddenly she seemed close to tears. 'I really enjoyed that job, you know. Most of the time.'

'You'll find another job.'

'I'm not so sure. It's not that easy at the moment. I wish I'd worked harder when I was at school. Got some proper qualifications. Dad never stopped nagging Viv about working for her exams. Perhaps he should have nagged me as well. He probably didn't bother because he knew I hadn't got any brains anyway.'

'Of course you have, Wanda. And he knew it. He just thought it would be better to let you come round to it in your own time.'

'*Lawrence – phone Wanda. Ask her down here. Talk to her properly. All right – If you won't phone – I will!*'

'*Leave it – she's my daughter.*'

'*Yes – I have no children. You made sure of that when you sneaked off and had that bloody operation.*'

'Actually,' she said, 'We were talking about that on the day he died.'

211

'Oh, Beth, I'm sorry ...' About to sit down to her plate loaded with eggs and bacon, she paused. 'I'm being so selfish, banging on about me ... You must miss him so much.'

'Eat your supper before it gets cold.'

'Are you sure you don't want any?'

'It does smell good ... No ...' she said, getting up. 'You eat that. I'll have some cheese.'

'Beth – do you think I'm too old to start training to be a nurse?'

'A nurse? Good Lord no. I should think they'd be glad to have you.'

'Maybe ...'

'Cheer up, love. As your father used to say, at the end of one road there's always some sort of track that leads to another.'

'Did he?'

'Yes,' Beth said, and as the words hit home, she added thoughtfully, 'Actually – yes, he did.'

'I wish he was here. He'd know what I ought to do.'

'What makes you think you'd like to be a nurse?' she asked, sitting down with some cheese and biscuits and an apple.

'I don't know really. You said something about nursing at Christmas, and it's sort of been on my mind ever since.'

'Well then, perhaps you should run with it.'

'Yes, maybe I should. Oh, Beth, I'm so glad you're here. I was really depressed when I arrived and saw the house in darkness. I thought maybe you were away.'

I'm here – just about, she thought, realising that she didn't really want any food after all.

'By the way – about the car. Have you mentioned it to Anthea yet?'

'No – but I will. I'm sure she won't mind. What she will mind is me getting the sack again. Maybe I should look into this nursing thing, then at least when I tell her I was sacked I can tell her something positive as well. Perhaps if I could stay here for a day or two while I find out about it? You are good to me ... I hope you realise you've saved my life.'

Beth cut another slice from the apple and said nothing. It had been a couple of days since she had eaten and she was finding it difficult to swallow.

212

'Look, Wanda,' she said at last, 'you can stay here, but you will have to tell her where you are. She might ring you in Taunton, and worry. And you will have to talk to her about the car.'

Between mouthfuls she pulled a face. 'It's her jealousy that's the problem, isn't it? It always has been. It was understandable at first, but I really don't understand it now. She's done so well on her own – and Dad isn't even here any more for her to be jealous about. She didn't even come to his funeral. I thought that was really bad. It's as if she's sort of bogged down in a load of out of date emotions. What she needs now is a gentle push forward.'

She visits his grave, Beth thought. Lawrence had said that the marriage was dead, though it was clear to her now that Anthea hadn't thought so.

'Maybe it's not as simple as that.'

'Nothing's simple. Certainly not love,' Wanda said, sighing as she pushed her plate away. 'And that's another thing ... I think I'm in love. In fact, I know I am.'

Oh God, Beth thought, *and on top of everything else I'm to be the Agony Auntie.*

'I'm sure he feels the same as I do, but he's turned me down flat.'

'If you think he feels the same as you do, try again,' she said wearily, refilling their glasses. This was indeed going to be a long evening ...

'I don't know ... It's a bit complicated.'

'He's married.'

'No. In a way it's worse.'

There was only one thing worse than married and, of all things, Beth didn't want to talk about that. 'Of course, if you do want to apply for nursing, you don't have to train around here,' she said to change the subject. 'You can train anywhere. Exeter, Bristol, Plymouth, or you could go to London. It's very hard work though, and it's none too well paid. I hope you know what you're doing.'

'Yes, well perhaps I need something to get my teeth into. It's time I did something useful with my life – and since I'm not going to get the man I want, I might as well start something completely new that will help me forget him. No point in turning myself inside out yearning for something I can't have. I've got to find what I can have.'

'Try an apple.'

Wanda laughed. 'Thanks,' she said, helping herself from the bowl. 'How about you? Will you go back to nursing again?'

'I'm not sure.'

'You know, I was thinking the other day, this house would make a fantastic small country hotel. You could have hunting people in the winter – there's even stabling for their horses. And in summer you could specialise in fishermen. You're not far from the Exe. You'd meet some very interesting people. Men – and things.'

'Things – I have no doubt,' she said, smiling, and aware of how much the wine was helping, she again refilled their glasses.

'You don't fancy it, then. Pity ... You could convert one of the barns into bedrooms. Or perhaps you should start up a nursing home, and when I'm trained I'll come and work for you.'

'If I go back to nursing I'll be nursing children.'

'Run it as a children's home then,' she said, her eyes bright with the wine. 'Though it's a bit smart. Oh, forget it. The little devils would wreck the place. Forget it ... I'm very good at running other people's lives. It's mine I'm not so good at.'

Laughing, they finished the bottle, then Wanda hauled her case upstairs and had a bath. When Beth had finished clearing up in the kitchen, she followed her, and passing the sitting room door she went in to turn off the reading light.

Remembering what Wanda had said, she seemed to see the room anew. It, like much of the rest of the house, lacked identity. All the bits and pieces she had thought made a home, Lawrence had thought made a house look untidy. It would make a wonderful small hotel – but with the barns converted into additional accommodation, it could also be adapted to make an exceptionally good home for children. The whole place would be full of noise and laughter – and in her life there would be a new purpose with no time to dwell on problems of her own.

But as she went upstairs she thought about something else Wanda had said. There was, indeed, no point in turning yourself inside out over something you could not have ... So maybe, having accepted that it was too late to have children of her own, it was also time to stop trying to compensate by looking after children that belonged to other people.

Perhaps it was time to start something entirely new – and as the house could just as well be turned into a rest home for the elderly, she could use her nursing skills in an area where, these days, they were probably needed most of all.

And in any case, these days, although she had no children of her own, she did seem to have two stepchildren. On the landing, testifying to the presence of one of them, there were wet footprints on the carpet – and thin trails of steam still drifted from the bathroom. A wet towel had been abandoned on the bannisters and the air was thick with the scent of bath oil and the powder Wanda had spilt on the bathroom floor.

'I'll clean up in the morning, I promise,' she said, appearing in a large Snoopy tee shirt to stand in Beth's bedroom doorway.

'Okay.' Though Beth didn't mind. The house looked lived in at last.

'Can I come in and talk to you? I know you're tired ...'

'That's all right. You can come in and talk.'

'It's probably not fair to tell you, but I've got to talk to someone. You see, the chap I'm in love with ... It's Robin.'

'Oh Lord ...'

'I really do love him,' Wanda said. 'What am I going to do about it? What *can* I do about it?'

She did indeed have two stepdaughters, and it could be that, each in their own way, they needed her more than she had realised – because having slipped into bed beside her, snug under the duvet, she and Wanda talked until the early hours of the morning.

There were no easy answers. She'd known there wouldn't be. Not for Wanda, Robin or Vivien – or even for her now, despite the prescription she'd left downstairs in the kitchen.

Though maybe she could make things slightly better for Wanda if she had a word with Anthea ... Wanda had continued to talk about her as well, and there were things about which Anthea did seem to be very unreasonable.

*

215

Wanda woke early the next morning because her arm was aching. Switching on the light, she lay thinking about Robin and how hopeless was their situation.

After a while she lifted her arm to ease the ache – and began to study the blue lines and patterns of the veins on the inside of her wrist. In there, a little higher towards her elbow, out of sight beneath layers of skin and muscle, surrounded by nerves and blood vessels, the bone she'd broken had gradually grown back together until it was mended. The human body was truly fascinating. All the components that made up the whole, always at work, pumping, digesting, draining, building, demolishing. A flesh factory on constant twenty-four-hour duty.

Yet the bit that was You and occupied the office in the head, rarely considered what was going on amongst the workers downstairs until there was a malfunction. You took your body, its needs and its functions, for granted, almost as a matter of Faith. And Wanda now knew for certain that she wanted to find out how it worked. That she really did want to help bodies and the people who lived in them.

Perhaps, too, she should consider Faith more fully. It was a strange business ... On the night Dad had died – well, maybe he had spoken to her. A small voice inside her head had certainly reassured her. Promised she would know, when the time was right, what she wanted to do with her life. So perhaps he had spoken to her. Perhaps, in all sorts of small ways, he had been trying to guide her ever since she and Beth had talked about nursing at Christmas. There had been no great flash of revelation. Just a slow process of realisation, of understanding, and of accepting the facts, so that now, here in his house, it had suddenly all come together.

Nevertheless, it was a revelation of a kind – and to accept it as such was an example of Faith. In fact, thinking about it, and suddenly warm with the sheer joy of realising it, perhaps Dad had been with her, had been helping her quite a lot. So maybe, given time, if she and Robin were right for each other, he would help her with that as well.

He didn't seem, though, to have done much for Beth ... It was going on for five months since his death, and last night again, she'd seemed so alone. Once more, had seemed to be wrapped in that cloak of darkness.

216

Perhaps, she thought, *it's me who will have to help Beth Is it?*

God knows how ...

Though may be there was one thing she could do ... If she could find the courage to get it together. It was a hell of a gamble but, thinking the idea through, she realised there was much to be gained on both sides, and very little to be lost.

Other than her skin, of course ... Because Mum might well skin her alive.

'Beth' she said later when, having worked out a plan, she'd dressed and gone downstairs, 'I was wondering – are you going to be very busy today?'

'Umm ...?' Beth, sitting on the window seat, turned to look at her.

'Sorry,' Wanda said nervously. 'You were miles away.'

'Not really. Not as the crow flies. Your mother's having a bonfire.'

Wanda walked over to stand beside her at the window. 'So she is. She'll be burning the dung heap I expect.' Then she paused, screwed up her courage, and took a deep breath. Beth was never going to agree to this. Not in a million years. But it was time she and Mum met. 'I've been thinking about what you said last night. I think I ought to go over and stay with Mum for a bit so I can talk to her about this nursing thing. But I can't walk all that way with my case. Not again. My arm's still really sore. So – I was wondering. Do you think you could drive me?'

'Of course. D'you want to go now or after lunch?'

'After lunch will be fine,' said Wanda faintly, surprised at how easy it had been – and suddenly horrified by what she had started.

The lane deteriorated into a rough track, and where the trees met overhead to form a dark tunnel, it petered out into a foot-path that led on up through the wood. At one side of the track a five-bar gate stood open between huge, overgrown rhodo-dendron bushes. As Beth turned the car in through the gateway, the tyres squelching through the soft surface mud, she saw at the bottom of the steepish drive some chicken and a couple of geese near the white wall of a farmhouse.

217

'Even if Mum's at home, she isn't going to come charging at you with a pitchfork,' said Wanda, sounding none too certain. She'd hardly uttered a word since they'd left Tivington.

'Of course not,' Beth replied, though she too was nervous.

Perhaps Wanda had expected to be dropped at the gate, but she hadn't known the extent of Beth's curiosity, as to both about this farm, and the woman who ran it. There were also one or two things that she wanted to say to Anthea, and apart from anything else, she was tired of feeling that half Porlock Vale and its inhabitants who happened to be Anthea's friends or relations were, for her, no-go areas. She had as much right to be here as did Anthea, and it was time the woman grew up and accepted it. Wanda's request had been just the excuse she needed to make sure that she did.

At right angles to the house at the near end of a short high wall, there was a barn, the wide tall double doors of which were closed. And now that they had reached the yard she could see that the white walls of the house needed painting, the green front door was peeling, and that the window above it was broken and backed with a sheet of battered cardboard.

She turned the car by the pond at the end of the yard, and parked in front of a smaller sandstone barn and a row of low sandstone slate-roofed sheds on the opposite side of the yard from the house. In complete contrast to what she could see and had heard about the house, the farm and its buildings were well kept, the yard freshly swept and immaculate.

'Watch the geese,' said Wanda, her voice none too steady, as two large aggressive looking birds sailed towards them and, honking noisily, appeared to stand guard in front of the car. 'They can be a bit vicious ...'

Can't we all when driven to it ... Wanda had realised, then, that she intended to get out of the car – though for the moment Beth was more interested in the wild-haired woman in green wellingtons, who, pitchfork in one hand, had come out of what looked to be a milking shed.

'There's your pitchfork ...'

'Umm ...' Wanda said, her eyes fixed on it.

Her hands, resting on her knees, were clenched into white-knuckled fists – though Beth, determined to say her piece and with nothing to lose, had seldom felt calmer.

218

Ignoring the geese she got out of the car, watching in amusement as Anthea's expression changed from surprise through shock to purple hostility.

'Call off your geese, Anthea, can you? I want to talk to you.'

Help, Wanda thought ... *Oh God, I hope I've got this right. Wherever did I get the idea that Dad meant me to bring her here?*

What the hell have I done!

Well, she'd set it up so she guessed she'd have to handle it. She too got out of the car.

'Hi Mum ...'

Anthea, hearing a car, had assumed it was Reg come about mending the tractor. Then she'd seen the red hair – and for a second her brain had refused to believe what her eyes were showing her. Then her stomach cramped with fury and she felt the blood rush to her cheeks.

'What the hell are you doing here in the middle of a weekday afternoon, Wanda?'

'I'll come to that later.'

'Too right you will ...' *What the hell are you doing here with that bitch?*

'There's no need to take this out on Wanda.'

Anthea stared at her. Were her ears also lying? She felt invaded. Betrayed ...

And suddenly, sensing the mounting aggression, Petal attacked Gert. In retaliation, Gert turned on Petal and, with a mighty beating of wings, their necks still entangled, somehow they were suddenly airborne in one monstrous ball of angry feathers. When they landed, half flying, half running, wings outstretched, they made off towards the barn where they had another set-to before chasing each other around the corner.

'What's that all about?' asked Wanda.

Anthea, glaring at the bitch, didn't answer. She'd watched the geese building up for that fight for some weeks – though now that the scrap was over the yard seemed particularly quiet.

'Well ...?' she said to the woman.

219

'Mum, it's cold out here, and Beth did drive me over. You could at least ask her in for a cup of tea so you can talk in comfort.'

To give the bitch her due, even she looked taken aback.

'Oh, for God's sake,' said Wanda, exasperated. 'Can't you see how silly this is? I can almost hear Daddy laughing. Surely you can endure each other's company for the time it takes to drink a cup of tea?'

That wasn't the point – but suddenly it was all too much. The bitch was, as usual, done up like Fido's dinner; short camel jacket and a cream skirt, polished burgundy boots and matching handbag, hair caught up like a bronze halo, face plastered in make-up, long nails painted. In her workaday clothes, hair all over the place, and doubtless stinking of the cow shed, Anthea realised that she was totally outclassed. The only thing she had left was her dignity. But she would show the bitch she had dignity ...

'Wanda, go in and put on the kettle.'

'I do want to talk to you,' the woman said, the hint of an apology in her voice.

'I'll be in as soon as I've finished with the cows.'

The four-legged variety ...

Disconnecting the milking machines she wondered about slipping upstairs to change, and knew it was useless. She'd need to bath and wash her hair, and at her best she'd never been able to compete with that bandbox. There was only one way to play this one. Like a lady – albeit a lady farmer. There was, after all, no reason to be ashamed of being caught doing a decent day's work.

In the dairy, as she washed her hands, she could hear them talking in the kitchen. Wanda was explaining the reason for Percy being in a box by the Rayburn. She wished she'd had time to tidy the kitchen – and the living-room. Gran was asleep in the living-room, but they'd have to go through it to get to the drawing-room. The carrot-headed bitch would no doubt take in every detail, and she certainly wasn't having her drink tea in the kitchen.

Never mind ... Could be one day she'd play the same trick herself and turn up unannounced at Tivington. Take a look at the house that they all said was so perfect.

'We'll have tea in the drawing-room,' she said as she went into the kitchen, the look she shot Wanda daring her to comment. Anyway it would be cold in there, so the woman wouldn't want to stay long. 'Good,' she said to Wanda. 'You've made the tea.'

She had also found the best cups and some chocolate biscuits and laid it all out nicely on a tray. The silver teapot was pushing things a bit, but since they owned one they might as well flaunt it. She'd deal with Wanda before this day was out ... But first, she'd deal with the woman.

Gran was snoring gently as they went through to the drawing-room. At least it was tidy, though the air did strike cold, and the room smelt of soot. Too bad. She hadn't been expecting visitors. She advised the bitch to keep her coat on, switched on the electric fire, and Wanda put the tray on the low table.

'Go outside, Wanda, would you, and make sure those girls are behaving themselves?'

'Of course.'

'Shut Petal in the cow shed if you have to.'

'Anything else I can do while I'm out there?'

The request sounded genuine, but Anthea couldn't be sure. A mite too innocent perhaps, so this time the look she gave Wanda made her leave in a hurry.

As she fetched the Christmas issue of *Farmers' Weekly* from the pouffe under the window and spread it on the brocade chair to protect it from her working trousers before she sat down, she thought of the hours she'd spent going over the things that she'd wanted to say to the bitch, given the chance.

Now she was here; just the two of them, face to face on her own territory. She could say and ask any and everything she liked – but right at this moment she couldn't think of one single word.

'Go on then,' she said to the bitch. 'I'm listening.'

'Perhaps,' Beth said calmly, 'There's something you'd like to say to me?'

There were two deep vertical scowl lines between Anthea's dark-circled deep-set eyes, and her face was contorted with fury. Out in the yard Beth had been wary of her aggression, but as soon as Wanda had brought her into this chaotic little house furnished with good antique furniture, silver, china knick-knacks and family photographs, she had felt very much at home. Felt, in fact, protected. Nothing Anthea said would bother her now. Insults and accusations would bounce like arrows off a brick wall.

'Over the year's there've been a good many things I'd have liked to say, I assure you.'

'Go on.'

'Dear Lord, you've got some nerve, coming here.'

'Wanda needed a lift. I didn't intend to put you to any trouble.'

'You took my husband and turned my life upside down. Beside that, what trouble is a pot of tea?'

'Very little I imagine,' she said. 'Though to be honest, I don't think he'd have spared me a second look if your marriage had been as strong as you seemed to think it was.'

'How dare you!'

'It took two to make your marriage, Anthea, as it took two to make mine, so be fair. The break up of yours can't have been all my fault.'

'Are you saying it was mine?'

'Was it? You were his wife, the mother of his children, the woman he came home to every night. You had all the advantages. Held all the cards. I had none.'

'Don't expect me to cry for you. You bewitched him. I have never seen a man so besotted. He didn't stand a chance. No more did I, or his children.'

'Yes, I do feel guilty about the girls. I always have. I've got to know them much better since he died and I realise there are ...' She hesitated. 'Well – scars. But you did have the children, and you were the one who controlled the situation even after you'd agreed to the divorce. He stayed, didn't he, when you asked him to wait another two months so he could tell the children?'

'Asked him to stay? I didn't have to ask him. He wanted to stay.'

'I don't think so.'

'I don't give a damn what you think. I know. I could repeat that whole conversation to you word for word even now. He

222

asked if he could stay. He asked to stay until Easter so he could tell the girls he was leaving when they came home for the holidays. He loved his children ...'

'Yes he did.'

'He'd have liked more, but it didn't happen. And when he met you ... He told me there'd be no children with you. He made me a promise that I would be the only mother of his children.'

Her laugh cut Beth deeper than she could know. Nor was this at all the story Lawrence had told her.

'Such a favour he thought he was doing me, promising that,' Anthea continued. 'But I didn't give a damn. I had Vivien and Wanda. After that, for all I cared he could have fathered a tribe. It was him I wanted.'

Beth stared at her and, as the information sank in, she felt sick.

'I see ...' she muttered. 'Well that explains a great deal.'

'Anyway, now you know how it feels to lose him.'

Anthea had been shocked almost into silence when Beth had driven into the yard, but she was fighting now all right. Hitting below the belt, even if she didn't know where the belt was ...

'Yes – I know how it feels to lose him, but he had his faults,' she said, testing her, fighting back. 'He wasn't perfect.'

'He wasn't far off. He was a good husband to me until you got at him.'

'You're trying to tell me I was the first? That in all the years he was married to you there was never anyone other than me?' she asked, now unsure. If he had lied about the children, what else had he lied about?

'Of course there wasn't,' Anthea snarled. 'He wasn't that interested in women.'

'No ... He wasn't that interested in women,' she said, watching for Anthea's reaction. But if she knew how close to the edge they were standing she gave no sign of it, and Beth wasn't prepared to go any closer. Had she been standing in Anthea's corner when Wanda had suggested tea, she doubted she'd have carried if off as well as Anthea had, and was continuing to do. She admired her for that, and

223

for her directness, though she'd heard enough from the girls to know that Anthea was also vulnerable.

'Perhaps you came through a marriage with him better than I did,' she said lamely, backing off.

'I loved him if that's what you mean. I loved him, and I have never stopped loving him.'

Beth met her eyes, held the look. Then Anthea looked away.

'I didn't know that. If I had, things might have been different.'

'Huh!' Anthea said, dubiously, looking at her sideways.

'I loved him too,' said Beth.

In the beginning.

'Oh, so you didn't murder him, then?'

This was the other precipice ... The one she had not expected to have to approach with Anthea, and this time it was Anthea who had the advantage. Beth didn't have to answer, but she did need to tell the truth to someone.

'No, it was an accident, but I didn't react fast enough,' she said, her voice thick. 'We'd had a row and I was angry. I did all I could for him, but if I'd been faster there's a strong chance I could have saved him.'

Anthea was watching her, and when she spoke again her voice was less harsh. 'Is that easy to live with?'

'No it isn't.'

'What was the row about?'

'He was worried about Wanda. I wanted him to ask her down for the weekend to try and sort things out.'

'He wouldn't? No ... He never would confront Wanda.' She shook her head. 'With Vivien it was quite the opposite. He pushed her too hard because she was clever. He treated her like the son he never had.'

'Perhaps he felt guilty.'

'About the divorce? Yes, he did,' she said, though it wasn't an accusation. 'Afterwards. It wasn't like that before.'

'I'm sorry ... I loved him - but I thought ... I honestly believed your marriage was over. The things he said. The things he didn't say ... He was very loyal. He didn't really say very much about you at all. After that Christmas, that January, I didn't hear from him for weeks. I thought that was it. When he rang me, said you'd agreed to a divorce, I

224

assumed you'd discussed it and agreed, and that everything had been settled amicably.'

'Discussed it? He didn't give me the chance! Those months between Christmas and Easter ...' She looked away. 'He'd already made up his mind. Like I said, you bewitched him. Anyway ... So now you know.'

'Look – I'm sorry ... I really only came here to ... Well, I suppose mostly I really only wanted to tell you that I'm giving Wanda my old Renault.'

'Oh ...? Why would you want to do that?'

'Why not? But as you're her mother I thought you should know what I intend. Wanda seemed rather afraid that you'd object. Particularly as it was coming from me. I hope that you won't.'

'I'm not sure she deserves a car. Nor am I sure she's got the sense to handle it.'

'Don't be too hard on her. Things aren't too easy for her at the moment.'

'I suppose that's got something to do with her being here in the middle of the afternoon. She hasn't got the sack again, has she?'

'She's got a lot to tell you, Anthea. But as I'm giving her the car, I thought I'd give Vivien her father's desk. I know she'd like to have it.'

'He'd have liked that. I suppose Wanda might be all right with the car. She does seem to have simmered down a bit since she crashed the last one.'

'She needs a car.'

'Her father needs a headstone.'

'Yes I know. Why, have you got any ideas?'

'Have you?'

'I thought Cornish granite with dark script would be best in a country churchyard. Engraved with his name, the dates, and Rest In Peace.'

'We could surely manage In Loving Memory?'

'All right, if that's what you want.'

'I think so. Otherwise it's not much more than I put on the headstones for my geese.'

'You have headstones for the geese ...?'

'Every one of them.'

Beth looked down to hide her smile and when she looked up Anthea's face had relaxed. Her mouth was a thin line, but her eyes were almost smiling.

'I love my geese. They're pets, though, as a matter of fact, Lawrie couldn't abide them.'

'That one in the kitchen seems rather nice.'

'His wives are the fighters. I can't think what's got into them. They never used to be.'

Neither did we, Beth thought. *Probably because while Lawrence was around he never gave us the chance.* Looking at Anthea, she wondered if she was thinking the same. She also realised that as they had talked their aggression had subsided. That the barbs had turned to feathers – and while they were unlikely ever to become friends, things might be easier, especially for the girls, now Anthea appeared to realise that there was no need for them to be enemies.

'Well, I must go and let you get on,' she said. 'I'll see to the headstone. I'll go to the stonemason's tomorrow.'

'You know,' Anthea said, 'I'll tell you something. Row or no row, he shouldn't have been gelding a colt on his own.' Nor should he have been using etorphine hydrochloride.'

'Probably not – no.'

'Certainly not. And he'd have known it.'

Beth looked at her. 'Would he ...?'

'Oh yes, without a whisker of a doubt. Anyone who's ever had any thing to do with horses or cattle knows that one wrong move with that drug and it's lethal.'

'Thank you ...'

'He did what he wanted when he wanted, did Lawrie. I couldn't stop him. It seems you couldn't either.'

In the silence, somewhere in the house, Beth heard the telephone ring several times, and then stop.

Anthea said, 'Anyway – thank you for being so good to the girls.' They were standing now, and she looked down at the tea tray. 'Dear Lord – and I didn't give you any tea! It's just sat here stewing in the pot.'

'Never mind. I hadn't even noticed.'

'Stay,' Anthea said, flexing her hand. 'I'll make another pot.'

'No, no,' Beth said, 'I'm fine, really. So that's where Viv gets it from. She does that with her hands.'

'Does what? Oh yes, so she does.'

'Bring Wanda over to fetch the car,' she said, as Anthea opened the door and they went back into the living room. 'Tomorrow if you like.'

'Wait a minute ... I'll have a word with her before you go. If she's finished up in the yard for me she'll probably be in the dairy.'

Anthea went out to the kitchen and Beth looked at the photographs on the sideboard. There were so many photographs in this house, a good many of them in a variety of beautiful but heavily tarnished frames. The big chest of drawers in the drawing-room had been full of photographs, mostly of the girls in stages from their baby years to their early teens, but one quite small photograph on the sideboard stood out from the rest. Perhaps because its silver frame had been kept clean. It was a photograph of Lawrence. Younger than she'd known him and standing with a horse and another young man – who had to be Anthea's brother. His features were her features in a thinner face topped by shorter, fairer, less wild, wavy hair.

'Who are you?'

Beth turned to look across the room and smiled. 'Hello. You're awake.'

Sucking her cheeks, old Mrs. Kenworthy fixed her with an amazingly clear, green-eyed stare. Asleep she had looked like any other dear little old lady – but those eyes were something else. Beth could see why some of the locals were afraid of her.

'Don't mind Mother,' Anthea said, coming back into the room. 'She tends to stare at people. She doesn't mean to be rude. Wanda must still be out in the yard.'

'Goodbye Mrs. Kenworthy.'

'Is it snowing?'

'No, it's not snowing,' Anthea said crossly, and to Beth, 'She's obsessed with the idea of snow. I can't think what's got into her.'

The old lady was still staring at Beth. 'You'll be back, you will.'

Doubting it, rather regretting the fact, Beth smiled and followed Anthea over to the door.

227

But slowly, vehemently Mrs. Kenworth went on nodding her head. 'You'll be back.'

As Wanda came out of the telephone room, her mother came in through the front door. 'Oh, so that's where you were. She said to say goodbye. Seems we'll be seeing her tomorrow anyway. She said to fetch the car,' and she added grudgingly, 'You're looking mighty pleased with yourself.'

'I fetched you down some bales of hay, and I've fed the hens and the geese,' Wanda said as they went back through the house to the kitchen.

'I saw. Thanks.'

'Have you had a nice afternoon?'

'Don't push it, Wanda. Who was that on the phone?'

'My sister. Your daughter. Vivien. She rang to say she'll be down at the weekend.'

'Her, or Robin as well?'

'Just her. She's not seeing Robin at the moment, is she?'

'I gather not.'

'You like him, don't you?'

'I like him well enough, but I never thought he was right for Viv. Anyway, right now it's you I want to talk about. You can start by telling me what you're doing here.'

'Didn't Beth tell you?'

'No, she did not. We had more to talk about than you, young madam.'

Perched on the kitchen table Wanda told her the potted version, and for once in her life Mum listened without yelling at her. She even seemed quite impressed by her plans. So, all in all, it had been quite an afternoon of triumphs.

'What are you doing at home again?' Viv had demanded down the telephone.

'I'll tell you later. Mum can't talk to you right now either. She's in the drawing room having tea with Beth.'

'And I'm Madonna. Get Mum, Wanda – I'm busy.'

'So's Mum. I've told you – she's having tea with Beth.'

'What ...'

'Yes, well,' Wanda said, enjoying herself and taking advantage of Viv's stunned silence. 'I thought that feud had gone on long enough – and since Daddy's dead they've got nothing left

228

to fight about. You're so fond of telling me that I leave all the family horrors to you – so I thought I'd do something about it.'

She had never before known Viv to be speechless. It had been a great feeling!

'Well, go on then,' Mum was saying to her now. 'Don't stand there dreaming. Get Gran her tea.' About to go outside again, she was pulling on her wellies. 'I'll tell you one thing about that woman from Tivington. She's good to you and Vivien.'

'She'll be back,' Gran called gleefully from the living room.

'Over my dead body,' Anthea muttered, taking her jacket down from the hook behind the door.

All the same, she didn't sound too bothered about it.

'Dear Lord, it's a madhouse in here this afternoon. What did I do with my scarf?'

'She'll be back. Her'll be back,' Gran called. 'And it'll snow.'

'Oh, Wanda, for goodness sake make her some tea. Go and talk to her. Read to her or something. Anything – but for heaven's sake, quieten her down.'

Anthea heaved a fork full of soiled straw out of the cow shed and heaped it on to the wheelbarrow. The woman was a flesh and blood person to her now. A flesh and blood person who had stolen her man and wrecked her marriage. The facts hadn't changed, but she couldn't hate Beth the person as she'd hated the stereotype she'd carried round for so long in her mind. In fact, meeting her, talking to her, had been nothing short of a revelation on several fronts – and although she was reluctant to admit it, even to herself, she had actually rather liked the woman.

She'd guessed right about the marriage though. It obviously hadn't been that good.

But then, had her own honestly been as good as she liked to believe?

What mattered was that he had loved her.

Had perhaps loved them both ...

And, lost in thought, she continued to sort the clean straw from the dirty.

He had found a new woman, but perhaps what he was really looking for was a new self – the man he wanted to be, the man other people already thought he was. And if that was so, the flaws had been there right from the beginning, and all the agonizing, all the questions she'd asked herself since he'd left, had one simple if unpleasant answer – and it was likely that both marriages had failed for the same single reason.

'You deserve better than me,' he'd said to her that afternoon last August. 'One of these days you might realise you're well rid of me.'

And she remembered the woman's white, haunted face at his funeral.

The wheelbarrow was full to overflowing, and piling the clean straw against the back wall of the cow shed, she found herself wishing that she and the Carrothead could have talked for longer.

The barriers had been lowered on both sides, so perhaps they could talk again when she took Wanda to Tivington to fetch the car.

Though it was dangerous territory ... *A midden best left unopened perhaps*, she thought as she trundled the wheelbarrow across the yard, *or the stench might prove too much for us both*.

Some things it was better not to know for certain. And Beth had loved him. Was grieving. Had probably had enough shit in her life as it was.

I'll go to the stonemason's this afternoon, Beth thought the next morning as she drove into the village to buy fresh ground coffee. Go to the stonemason's and get it done. Because, feeling more alive than she had in months, suddenly nothing was too much trouble.

'I've arranged the insurance on the car,' she'd said when Wanda had phoned. 'They're sending the cover note.'

'Mum says it'll be expensive and she'd like to pay.'

'No, this one's on me.'

'I don't know what you said to her but she's being really great. She even says she'll help with my living expenses while I'm training – and she's going into Minehead to get some cash to lend me so I can go straight back to Taunton and find out

230

where to start. I'll have to find another job, of course, because even when I've been accepted for training they're not likely to want me to start immediately.'

'*When* you're accepted ...?'

'Oh yes, Beth. There are no ifs in this one. I've got a good feeling about it. I'll tell you about that sometime – though you'll probably think I'm mad.'

Beth doubted that. After all, following years of bitching and unpleasantness, yesterday she'd had tea with Anthea Seligman, and today she was coming for coffee.

'I'll take really good care of it, Beth, I promise,' Wanda called across the yard as she got into the Renault.

'Just don't kill yourself,' said Anthea, standing with Beth on the doorstep.

'Go in,' Wanda called again. 'This wind is really bitter.'

'Rush, hurry, bustle,' Anthea said. 'She gets more like Vivien every day. However, I can't tell you how glad I was to see the end of the black and white era.' They laughed and, waving as her daughter drove away, Anthea continued, 'All her life she's been given to flights of fancy. I hope she'll go for this nursing thing and stick with it. Somehow I think, this time, she might.'

'I think she will too,' said Beth as she closed the door and they returned to the warmth of the kitchen. 'And if you'll let me, I'd like to pay for her training, or at least give her an allowance.'

'No, no – it was more than generous of you to give her the car.'

'It was her father's money, Anthea. It's no more than he'd have done for her, and I've got more than enough money for myself.'

'Well – if you're sure,' said Anthea, considering it. 'Since you put it that way – and I can't pretend it wouldn't help.'

'No problem. More coffee? Have you got time?'

'A quick one, then,' Anthea said, taking a closer look round the kitchen now Wanda wasn't here to notice. 'Then I must get on into town.'

She still couldn't quite believe she was here – and Tivington Heights was, as she'd often heard, a show house. The sort of

231

house you saw in glossy magazines. The white fitted kitchen complete with split-level cooker and built-in machinery, had every modern gadget imaginable – and apart from a selection of coordinated storage jars, every surface was clear and wiped clean. You could perform open-heart surgery in here without suffering one single infected stitch. Every mod con ever invented, Anthea thought, watching Beth refill the smart green and gold mugs from a glass jug. At Luccombe she boiled up coffee in an old enamel saucepan. And in this kitchen, it was warm even without a Rayburn.

'We'll have this wind for a day or so yet according to the farming forecast,' she said. 'Then it'll go round to the north west and bring snow.'

'Mrs. Kenworthy will be pleased.'

'Yes,' Anthea laughed. 'Lord knows what goes on in her poor old head, because I'm sure I don't.'

'It must be difficult for you farmers when it snows.'

'It is if you let it catch you unawares, but we've rounded up the sheep and brought them down from the moor. You don't want them stuck up there in the snow.'

'How on earth do you manage to find them?'

'We meet at Webber's Post – men, dogs, trucks, ponies. Then we ride out over, round them up and herd them down to the pens. It's easy enough to sort them according to their markings once they're penned. Well, it is with help from the dogs. It's a long hard day on horseback though, and sheep get themselves into some mighty daft places.'

'You round them up on horseback?'

'It's the only way to get at them in some of those gulleys. Anyway, mine are down in the home paddocks now, and by the end of the month they'll be lambing.'

'I couldn't spend a day on a horse to save my life.'

Anthea chuckled, and conceded, 'Well, I'm not cut out to be a nurse. I'd rather deal with animals any day. Some of the things I have to do for my mother ... She hates me having to do for her – though lately she's been a bit too spritely for comfort. The other day I caught her trying to make tea. Staggering about the kitchen with a kettle full of boiling water ...'

'How will you manage when you're lambing?'

232

'This time, heaven knows. I'll have to arrange something. I do like your kitchen.' *So spacious, so bright, so new. And so incredibly tidy ...*

'Lawrence chose the kitchen. Would you like to see the rest of the house?'

Lawrence – chosing kitchens ...? He'd never given a damn where his food was cooked as long as it was, and appeared on his plate. 'Yes I would,' Anthea said, surprised.

How much she had wanted this, how long she had waited – and how easily it seemed to have come about now the time was obviously right.

It was easier to talk to Beth, too, without Wanda there. In fact, she and Beth were getting on quite well, though she suspected that however often they might meet in the future their attitude to each other would always maintain its strong undercurrent of respect and its awareness of boundaries that must never be crossed. Like Gert and Petal, who circled each other stiff-legged and respectful after their too-close encounters ...

'It's a lovely house ... Really lovely,' she said as, having taken her on a tour of the ground floor rooms, she followed Beth up the open backed polished pine staircase.

Upstairs was every bit as perfect. The thick cream carpet throughout; bedrooms for each of the girls, a double spare room overlooking the yard and the orchard, an exquisitely equipped modern bathroom – and a second bathroom just as plush attached to the main bedroom, both windows of which looked out over the moor and on down the valley to the sea.

The bedroom was too feminine and far too frilly for Anthea's taste – though it was dominated by the largest double bed that she had ever seen. Recovering from the impact of its size, she imagined Lawrie lying there with Beth – and to her surprise, she realised that not only did it no longer hurt, but that suddenly, inside herself, she somehow felt free.

'And that was his dressing-room,' said Beth, as out on the landing again she indicated the only door that was closed. 'I haven't sorted through his things as yet ...'

'I'd heard it was a lovely house,' she said, wondering if there might be more feeling of him in his dressing-room.

233

She'd have liked to see that room. But the moment had passed, and she was following Beth into the room that was Vivien's.

'I'm sure you've heard quite a lot about all sorts of things over the years,' Beth said, turning to smile at her. 'Though as far as the house goes, you've probably noticed that everything is far more to Lawrie's taste than to mine. I prefer a house that looks and feels lived in.'

Anthea looked at her. His taste ...? There was absolutely nothing here that she could identify with Lawrence in any way at all. None of the genuine old furniture he favoured, none of the china vases he used to bring home so proudly from auctions, no Indian rugs, no heavy oil paintings in thick goldleaf frames. All the pictures here were modern reproductions.

Did she even know the man who had lived here?

Or was it the man who had lived with her that she hadn't known ...?

To disguise her confusion, she wandered over to Vivien's desk and looked at the photograph on the wall. A photograph of Lawrence taken in Australia a long time ago ... With his hair cut much shorter he looked completely different.

'He looked like this when he first came to England,' she said, and turning to Beth, 'it's almost as if you and I married two completely different men.'

'Yes ...' But Beth was thinking about a different photograph. That of him with Anthea's brother on the sideboard at Luccombe.

'When he married you, perhaps he changed,' Anthea continued. 'He must have. Look at us – you and me. Our homes, our lives, our clothes. We are so different.'

'He didn't change,' she said, because as Anthea had turned towards her, the light from the window had caught her face and she so strongly resembled her brother that suddenly Beth understood exactly how it must have been. Understood the whole story. 'He didn't change – though he did try to.'

She also knew, now, why he had left Australia, turned over the ranches to Tillotson, refused to go back even to visit. 'He told me once that he didn't like the man he was in Australia.'

'Perhaps he didn't,' Anthea said. 'He ran away from Australia, he told me that.'

'After your brother died.'

'Yes ...' And the way Anthea was looking at her, she realised that they both knew what they were saying. And that, to all this, the brother was the key.

'Anyway,' Beth said, backing away from the danger zone. 'It was all a long time ago.'

'Yes,' Anthea said gratefully.

So ... It was all very clear to Beth now. After the brother had died in an accident Lawrence had thought was his fault, he had come to England to see the family, and had fallen for the lookalike sister. He'd seen the chance of a new start and, being Lawrence, he'd grabbed it. It wasn't the sister's fault that the marriage had failed. A homely, sturdily built little female farmer with a soft heart ... There was nothing wrong with Anthea and, until he'd caught sight of a different kind of woman, he'd doubtless been very happy with her.

But he had said to Beth – with you I know I'm a man.

Yes, she thought, *but even so, in the end I wasn't woman enough to subjugate your true nature any more than Anthony's sister could.*

'Perhaps he shouldn't have married either of us,' she said.

'No,' Anthea said, 'I don't think he should have.'

Beth could even guess, now, at the brother's reasons for going to Australia. A man of his persuasions wouldn't have been welcome in this narrow community, so he'd had the good sense to get the hell out of it – for his sake as well as for that of his family. The saddest fact of all was that, even on a continent as vast as Australia, he'd ended up in another community that was every bit as too small for him; the microcosm of an outback ranch.

She knew from the girls that Anthea had adored her brother. She'd have liked to say something to make her feel better, but she knew she couldn't. Not now, and probably not ever.

'Anyway,' Anthea said, 'I must be going. I've got to go into Minehead and my help wants to leave at lunchtime. I daren't leave my mother too long on her own.'

They had come downstairs and were standing in the hall. She picked up her smart tweed jacket. 'Thanks for the coffee.'

235

'You're welcome. And look, Anthea, if it helps, I could look after your mother while you're lambing. That is, if you like. If you can't find anyone else.'

'Heavens, no. I wouldn't dream of it. Thanks all the same, but she can be that awkward.'

'I've worked on geriatric wards. I'm quite used to awkward elderly ladies. I'd be glad to help you out.'

Anthea put on her jacket, and Beth opened the door and walked with her across the yard. In the back of Anthea's car, something moved. Something white in a large cardboard box that was partly covered by a blanket.

'Is that Percy?'

'Yes, I'm taking him to the vet. I only hope I'll be bringing him home again. He hasn't been well since the autumn, and now he just seems to be fading. I just hope the vet will come up with some answers.'

Hugging herself against the cold Beth bent to look in the window. Percy eyed her suspiciously.

'His eyes are blue,' she said, surprised.

'He's part China. Chinas have blue eyes, those rich orange knobs above their beaks and the long orange legs.'

'He doesn't much like the look of me this morning.'

'Don't let it bother you – that's his blind eye.'

'Poor Percy. Though maybe there are times when it's good to be blind in one eye,' she said, wriggling her shoulders to keep warm. 'In fact, when it comes to human beings, it might even be that partial sight is a pre-requisite for survival.'

'Lawrence said that. Nor does being blind in one eye prevent this one from being a very loveable gander.'

'No it doesn't,' Beth agreed, understanding Anthea's meaning.

'Beth, the things we've said this morning, don't pass any of it on to the girls. They've no idea. It's best that way.'

Beth nodded. 'In any case, for a good part of the time he was as happy as he could ever have been with us both.'

'Yes. I can agree with that.'

'Good ...' Beth said. 'Well, I hope the vet can do something for Percy. And call in any time, if you're passing.'

Anthea managed a smile. 'Go in, Beth. You're frozen.'

*

236

Go in – you're frozen. Anthea'd heard that before as well. *I must have said it scores of times to Anthony,* she thought as she drove away. Scores of times in scores of places; on the beach; beside the old outdoor swimming-pool at Minehead; on the bank by the deep pool in the river at Landacre.

But blue from the feet up, Anthony would stand there shaking like a jelly in an earthquake, refusing to give up and get dressed before any of the other boys did. He hated swimming because the one thing he was scared of was water, and to make matters worse he felt the cold. But he'd have died rather than quit and have them call him a sissy.

But so what if you were, Ant ...? It's not as if you were a child molester or a rapist, or even a thief. Is what you were such a terrible thing? To be honest, Anthea had always known he was different. More different than just being special because he was her brother, and nothing to do with him being better looking than most – girls included, and her especially. *I was the smudged carbon copy, but I never minded, even when people remarked on it – because I loved you.*

I loved you more than I loved myself, right from the beginning – from the days when I was still in my pram and you used to walk beside me holding my hand. That soft bit of hair that kept falling into his eyes; kind eyes, with long lashes – and, later, she had realised that he had a body as good as any on this earth. She used to look at naked boys in the art books at school and Anthony was more beautifully put together than any of them.

He was ... A young god. Though it wasn't just physically that he was beautiful. At junior school, how he was petted and given extra sweets by the nuns – who loved him for his kindness and gentle manner, regardless of the fact that the Kenworthy family weren't Catholics. And it was always Anthony who looked after the other boys who scraped their knees in the playground; led them upstairs to Sister Sick for iodine and a plaster; who rescued the younger boys from bullies and dried their tears.

And I was the one who fought for you; on the school bus, walloped the boys with my satchel, bloodied their noses. I must have sent that Roger Weston home bleeding and crying to his mother a dozen times ... She thought to herself.

But not you, Ant. You were the peacemaker, the mender. He had been every bit as strong as any of the other lads, and could put up his fists to defend himself if he had to. It was just that most of the time he preferred to shrug his shoulders and walk away.

As he got older and the other boys hung around the village or congregated in Minehead of a Saturday leering at girls, Anthony had preferred to ride out over the moor with Anthea, at one with nature, enjoying its tranquillity, appreciating it in every mood, every season and every kind of weather.

You were better than all of them lumped together – but you just didn't fit in, love, did you ... You must have known why, but it was the one secret you couldn't bring yourself to share. Not even with me. I'm not sure exactly how or when I realised why you were so desperate to get away. But I knew – eventually.

No wonder Lawrie had never liked to look at her naked. But they had loved each other, she and Lawrie. *Though, I wonder – did we love each other for ourselves? Or, brought together by the grief of losing you, when he looked at me and I looked at him, half blind, was it really you that we were seeing ...?*

And did it even matter? She and Lawrie had loved each other, whatever the reason.

So what if Anthony had been a little too kind, a little too pretty, a little too gentle ...? It didn't change anything. He was as he was – the brother she had adored. And he always would be.

Half blind, Beth thought, because all these months she'd been too frightened to see or to let herself feel any emotion.

If I could just find the courage to look, it might start to get better, she thought. *Like the first incision in an operation ...* Anthea had seen. Had faced it. She wasn't bleeding to death.

And now it was her turn.

Go back to the beginning. Pick up the scalpel and cut.

You must start at the beginning ...

Over a year ago in November. A Thursday. Lawrence had gone to London to meet Tillotson, and for once she'd gone with him to do some shopping. He'd dropped her in Knightsbridge and she'd looked around Harrods, but by lunchtime her back had been aching and, tired of shopping, she'd hailed another taxi to take her to Shaftesbury Avenue. As she wasn't meeting Lawrence until seven, she'd queued for a matinee ticket for one of the shows.

God knows how many millions of people lived in London or how many thousands more poured in to work every day, never mind the tourists or those up for the day like herself. Arrange to meet someone at a given time in a given place, and even then if you didn't keep your eyes skinned you could miss them in the crowd. So it had been one of life's unkinder coincidences that coming out of the theatre's side entrance just after five, she had happened to look across the street and had seen Lawrence and a tall man in a short, well-cut suede jacket coming out of a bar. The were talking earnestly, their heads close together, and for a second they stopped and Tillotson looked back up the street. In the blaze of light from the bar she saw his face clearly; long, with deep set eyes and a long narrow nose. Then Lawrence said something, Tillotson touched his face and, hugging each other, they had walked on down Greek Street and turned the corner.

She had known what she was seeing. She just hadn't wanted to believe it.

'Good meeting?' she asked when at seven he'd picked her up outside Harrods.

'Tall poppy. Fair dinkum.' He was the pastoralist again, the big Aussie land owner, though he was somewhat subdued and preoccupied, so that if she hadn't known better she might have thought he was concentrating on driving in the heavy traffic.

'I went to the matinee of *Les Miserables*.'

'Good on you. Did you enjoy it?'

'I cried.' Benign tears. Nothing like the unshed tears of hurt and disgust she'd held inside her since this last spring and Morocco. 'It's on at The Palace, Shaftesbury Avenue,' she'd added, and waited for the information to hit home.

It didn't appear to do so.

'It's all right for some,' he said. 'I've been stuck in a stuffy hotel room all bloody day with Tillotson and my accountant.'

'Didn't you even go out for a drink?'

'Nope. We've been there all day. Had lunch sent up to us.'

Oh Lawrie, she'd thought. *And to cap it all, you are lying.*

239

Come on then, she told herself now. *Be brave. You've started – so just keep going ...*

She and Vivien had sorted through the papers in his desk before the funeral. She'd been numb then, so it hadn't been difficult. Clothes were much more personal. She'd been dreading the thought of having to sort through his clothes – but when she had washed up the coffee mugs, she dried her hands and went upstairs.

The key to his dressing-room was in the drawer of her bedside table.

'Umm ...' Tom Harding removed the stethoscope from his ears. 'Well, his heart's coping and his breathing's clear. The antibiotics seemed to have worked. To be truthful, I'm foxed. Kept in the right conditions with the right feeding, geese are probably the healthiest of all domestic farm stock, so I don't get to treat many. How old did you say he was?'

'Not that old as geese go. Twenty-one, twenty-two.'

Tom stroked the long white neck. 'All the same, he's no gosling. Nor is he a happy chappie. I'll give you something different for the arthritis and if he doesn't respond to that ... I'll give you some Pentobarbitone. About three times the dose I'd use as an ordinary anaesthetic, and it'll just quietly put the old fellow to sleep. You'll know when the time comes to use it.' He stroked Percy's neck and went over to the drug cupboard.

'Tom ...'

'I know ... This wouldn't be a large dose for a human, but be careful. You're my favourite farmer. We don't need another accident.'

It wasn't that. It was the thought of putting Percy to sleep. The final kindness to an old friend. She couldn't do it – but neither could she tell that to Tom. She might be his favourite farmer, but he also considered her to be as sensible and practical as they come.

He gave her a small bottle and a disposable syringe packed in cellophane, and noted it down on the card. 'Okay, if you open the back door and I'll carry him out for you. He's a big lad ... My, he's a weight.'

She'd left the car in the gravelled yard by the loose boxes

240

where he had kept the race horse after Lawrie's accident. She had thought that was a black day ... All in all, this one was as bad.

'When you're ready to worm the sheep let me know and I'll put up the powder for you,' Tom said, as he ducked under the car's tailgate to tuck Percy in with the blanket and replace the hot water bottle in the cardboard box. 'Poor old chap. You've had him a long time, but I'm telling you – in the end, let it be quality. He's had the quantity.'

He's been with us for twenty-two years, she thought as she drove off along Tregonwell Road and headed for home. *I can't do this to him*. He'd been just a few weeks old when Pop had dropped him by as a present on his way back to Cloutsham one market day. The flock he had joined was quite large – and Viv had been just a tiny baby. She, Wanda and Percy had grown up together, and over the years he had been sweetest, the tamest, the most friendly of all her geese.

When Viv, aged about two, had taken to wandering off, she'd usually be found curled up with Percy under a hedge or in the straw at the back of the barn. And later, after she'd transferred her affections to a Shetland pony, Percy had mothered Wanda, following her round like a nervous under-sized nanny. Wanda, in shiny red plastic mackintosh and tiny blue wellingtons trotting along beside the tall, stately, broad chested gander ... The commotion he'd made that day she'd fallen in the pond had been loud enough to bring half the neighbourhood running.

How fast time does go ... At that point Anthony would have been dead barely five years. Lawrence, now, had been dead for five months. And the girls were grown up. When Percy died it would be the end of an era.

Suddenly she was crying for them all. Couldn't see to drive properly, and the box of tissues she kept in the car was empty. She had to keep using her sleeve.

On the landing, Beth looked down at the key in her hand. Behind that locked door there were all sorts of memories, every one of them likely to be painful.

Nevertheless – it had to be done. The room couldn't remain sealed off from the rest of the house for ever.

241

She put the key in the lock and turned the handle. Then, taking a deep breath, she pushed open the door.

'Mum – what on earth are you doing?' Anthea said. 'What's that terrible smell?'

'Oh, Mrs. Seligman ...' said Mary, scuttling through from the living room as Anthea struggled to set the goose and its box down by the Rayburn. 'Thank goodness you'm back. She's been that awkward this morning.'

'Yes, but cooking? She shouldn't be cooking! That's enough now, Mother, you'll scald yourself. Come and sit down.'

Amy shook off Anthea's hand and, steadying herself against the stove, continued to stir the pan of brackish liquid.

'Mother – come and sit down. What's in that pan anyway?'

'All sorts of things,' Mary said ominously. 'I caught her wandering around out in the yard. Collecting things, she was. This weather, mark you – and no coat on. And all she had on her feet were them slippers.'

Amy snorted. She was a mop head, that Mary. Mazed as they come, and lazy with it. Hand her a duster and she went into a trance.

'Mother – what's in the pan?' Anthea asked suspiciously.

'Chestnut,' Amy said, ignoring mazed Mary and peering closer at the thickening liquid. Sweet chestnuts, bark, crushed leaves – and it was almost done.

'Chestnuts ...?'

'Chestnut.'

'You shouldn't be cooking anything,' said Anthea, leaning across to push the pan further on to the hotplate. 'You should have stopped her, Mary. Why didn't you stop her?'

Half smiling Amy narrowed her eyes and looked at Mary who nervously eyed the thumbstick resting against the Rayburn.

'I tried. You ask her ... She waved that there stick at me again. I'll come in and clean for you Mrs. Seligman, like I always have, and since she's here, she's here – but don't you ask me to be responsible for her. She ought to be put away.'

'Toad,' Amy muttered under her breath and, seeing Mary flinch, she chuckled.

242

'Mother ...' Anthea said, vexed.

'What did that vet tell you about your gander?'

'He just said that he's old. Come on now, Mum. It's time you sat down. Sit down, or you'll fall down and likely pull that pan over on top of you.'

Amy was ready to be helped back to her chair. To be truthful her morning's exertions had all but exhausted her, and the mixture in the pan had turned to a deep amber. When it had cooled it would clear. She lifted the wooden spoon to point to the colander hanging on the wall. Drips from the spoon sizzled on the hotplate and glaring at Mary she allowed Anthea to take hold of her arm.

'Strain, cool 'en, mix it with his food.'

She might still be able to heal a goose, but she could no more have turned that daft affrighted Mary into a toad than could she make the snow fall before its time was good and ready.

'You be careful, Mrs. Seligman. If I was you I should throw it away,' said daft Mary as Amy took hold of her thumbstick. 'A lot else went into that pan besides chestnuts. She were gathering all sorts of things from that yard.'

Mazed, Amy thought, sucking her cheeks. Daft, doubting and faithless, the lot of them. That Lawrence may have had to pass from this life before he learned better – but the times after he'd left this house that she'd dosed Anthea's food with a potion of chestnut to cure her dejection and brighten her outlook ... If it were poisonous she'd have been dead long ago.

'Oh ...' Mary said, trailing behind them as Anthea helped her through to the living room, 'And a Mr. Lang phoned. He wants to know if he can come over sometime tomorrow. Some'at about some clothes. He said could you ring him.'

The room smelt musty and a thin layer of dust covered the chest of drawers and the trouser press.

So much to sort through ...

His underwear and his sweaters in the chest of drawers, and the big white wardrobe built in along the width of the wall was full of his shirts, trousers, jackets, his suits and his shoes.

Wondering where to start, she went over to the chest of

drawers and looked at the bits and pieces Vivien had taken from his pockets when the hospital had returned his clothes. Cuff links, a few coins, a safety pin and a receipt from the cleaners. Beside the tray his tortoise-shell-backed hairbrushes lay locked together as he had left them on the morning of the accident.

Parting them, she saw the strands of his dark hair wound through the rich beige bristles – and she picked up his comb. Ran it through the brushes, and looked down at the soft tangle of hair in her hand. Wondered what to do with it.

All that remained of him ...

She rolled the hair into a ball and slipped it into her pocket, then went over to the windowsill to pick out the roses that had been left to die in a vase.

He'd been fond of that vase. Had bought it one holiday in Portugal ...

A little after ten in the morning, the air already hot and smelling of freshly caught fish on sale in the market. A covered market that sold every kind of food as well as fish and, having shopped, she'd been waiting for him outside in a shady garden of hibiscus and palms beside the river.

'Ah, there you are,' he said. 'Come with me ...'

He'd taken her across the road and up a cool narrow alley between tall white buildings in need of repair, but at the top of the hill there'd been a new, air-conditioned shop done out in green marble and clean, sparkling glass.

'See that,' he said, pointing out the vase on a shelf at the back. 'The colours, the shape – isn't it lovely?'

'Is it?'

'Don't you like it?'

'No I don't. It reminds me of those urns the Greeks used to pickle viscera. Heart, liver, lungs ... Yuk ... Byron's probably spent time in that vase.'

'Oh. I think it's nice,' he said, disappointed. 'I was going to buy it for you.'

'Thank you, my darling, but I'd really rather you didn't. How about that one? The white with the gold rim.'

He bought her the white vase – but on the last day of the holiday he'd been waiting for her when she came out of the fish market, a parcel under his arm.

'Stone a crow, you aren't taking fish home in the car? It'll smell to high heaven,' he said.

'Only a half a dozen sardines and a kilo of squid. It'll be fine in the cool bag.'

'Maarvellous ...'

'What's in your parcel,' she asked suspiciously.

'Er, well ... Byron?'

'I knew you wouldn't be able to resist it,' she said, laughing as they walked away arm in arm through the little garden. 'Fine ... Okay – but you keep him in your dressing-room.'

Everything in this room had a memory. Each item of clothing; everything she would touch. Some memories would be more vivid, more painful than others, but she was ready for them now.

It was a matter of deciding where to begin.

Munching the last of the three liquorice strips that had substituted for lunch, Robin screwed up the bag and dropped it in the bin beside his drawing board. Then he sharpened several crayons. He'd made a good start on the plans for the main building. It was the buildings that surrounded the courtyard that had stumped him. He'd sat here all week fussing with them and the lines of the link bridges, and had made little or no progress. He just couldn't seem to see it in his mind. And there was a deadline on this one, so he'd have to keep at it. He'd been lucky to get the job at all ... An exclusive private nursing home for the elderly. One of the few growth areas in the building trade at present, it seemed.

But all he could see in his mind was Wanda. Wanda at that damned party; Wanda in bed in tee shirt and scarf; Wanda at Christmas, laughing at him as he tried to catch the house cows for milking; Wanda at New Year, reading to the grandmother – who pretty soon might need to be in a home like this one that he couldn't seem to get right.

Wanda, Wanda ... And when she'd phoned, suggested he might like some company, he'd stonewalled and put her off.

He hadn't heard from Vivien in weeks. He could take Wanda out now if he chose to – surely ...? He looked at the phone. He only had to pick it up and press out her numbers.

*

The Careers Office had given her an address to write to, and on her way to the hospital she'd posted the letter requesting an application form for training. 'Why do you want to be a nurse?' the man had asked her. 'My father died ...' she'd said, and the words had sort of tailed away. She'd have to do better for the selection board, but basically, that was the reason. And now that she knew what she wanted, she was going to do it properly.

Meantime, they had recommended she find herself a job as a nursing auxiliary for experience, and to be sure that it was what she wanted, and could take the work load.

It was, without a doubt, what she wanted, and she returned to Ashton Grove well pleased with herself. For once her room, reinstated with all her belongings and a thousand times nicer since the alterations, actually felt warm and seemed to welcome her.

Daddy was pleased ...

Though how much longer she'd be calling this home ... Because if Musgrove Park didn't want her, she'd try the private nursing homes. By this time tomorrow she'd have found herself some sort of job in a hospital, even if it meant moving as far as Bristol, Exeter or Plymouth.

This is all thanks to Dad, she thought. *But I've had plenty of help from Beth and from Mum to get started. I shan't let let them down.*

And I'll show Viv that in my own way, I'm as good as she is - before I'm done.

Martin said, 'I got you a white wine and soda.'

'Thanks.' She hung her coat on the stand and sat down beside him at their favourite table in the alcove.

'I began to think you weren't coming.'

'Right at the last minute Thane wanted an estimate of the January figures.' She took a sip from the glass. 'Umm ... I need this, I really do.'

'Shall I get you something stronger?'

'No thanks, love, this is fine.'

'Well, and was Thane pleased?'

'Is he ever? In the best of years January's figures are never good, and since the recession they've been awful.'

'The lovers aren't in tonight either.'

She laughed. All through the autumn and every evening since his return from Brussels she and Martin had met here for a drink after work before going on somewhere to dinner, and almost always, sitting at the small table under the clock, there was a couple in their fifties who held hands surreptitiously and looked up nervously every time the street door opened to admit a new customer.

'Is love in recession too, d'you think?'

'Far from it,' he said, squeezing her hand. 'I was thinking that perhaps they've been rumbled.'

'Well, don't sound so pleased about it.'

'If they're cheating it serves them right.'

'Perhaps her husband beats her. Perhaps his wife is already cheating with someone else,' she said, wondering how Robin would feel if he walked in and saw her sitting here holding hands with Martin.

'You're lecturing me again,' he said, amused.

Sardonic bastard ... She took her hand away and drank from her glass. Put the glass back on the table.

'Anyway, we've nothing to hide. And I've got a surprise for you. We shan't be in here tomorrow evening either. One of the Beast's henchmen phoned this afternoon. I'm required in Brussels again. They want me for a meeting on Saturday, and to inspect the flat they've laid on for me.'

'You must be costing them a small fortune in air fares.'

'This time they'll be paying for two. I've booked two seats on the seven-ten flight from Heathrow tomorrow evening, returning Sunday late afternoon. You're coming with me.'

'Mart, I can't! I've told Mum to expect me this weekend.'

'Okay, so cancel it. Love, this is business – and I want you to see the flat and generally get the feel of the place. After all, if I decide to stay on in Brussels at the end of two years, it shouldn't be too hard to find you a job in the same set up.'

'I don't want to work in Brussels, I told you that.'

'Don't go sulky on me, Viv. I've fixed the tickets. When I'm working out there you can see your mother any time you like.'

'Okay ... But I wish you'd asked me before you arranged it.'

'Oh, by the way, I bought you these,' he said, and reaching under the table he produced a box of chocolates.

'Oh, Mart ...'

She did love him. Most of the time ... He could be so considerate, so giving. She just wished he'd stop manipulating her. Was this what she'd done to Robin ...? Was this how he had felt? Poor Robin ...

And whenever Robin had bought her chocolate, it had been Bendick's dark coffee creams – because he'd taken the trouble to find out that they were what she liked best.

As Beth took the green-checked shirt off its hanger behind the wardrobe door, her courage almost deserted her. A shirt he'd worn for a few hours ... But pressing it against her cheek, she breathed in and closed her eyes – and suddenly he felt very near, almost as if he was comforting her.

She laid the shirt over the dressing stool, and went over to the chest of drawers. She'd keep his gold watch and his cuff links until his girls married and perhaps had a son.

Or may be Anthea should keep them ... It would be a nice gesture to give them to Anthea. She put them in the drawer and began to sort through his handkerchiefs.

Handkerchiefs, socks, underwear ... What she needed here was a system. Garden sacks; one for rubbish, one for Oxfam, one for Wanda. She wondered about Anthea. She might be glad of one or two shirts and sweaters for work. His chunky Icelandic sweater would look a lot better to work in than the awful Air Force blue cardigan she'd been wearing yesterday, though she'd have to be careful how she offered it. In complete contrast, this morning Anthea had looked rather smart. Had obviously dressed for coffee rather than for taking Percy to the vet ... She'd keep his navy-blue V-neck for herself – and the brown Kashmir. Wanda might like the red, and his green Guernsey.

The chest of drawers was relatively easy, and by tea time she had cleared it.

Tomorrow, when she returned from the stonemason's and had ordered his headstone, she would start on the wardrobe. To her surprise, now she'd faced it, made a start, she was rather looking forward to it. She had turned on the radiator so

248

that the little room was beginning to feel quite snug – and the memories that had come to her as she worked, rather than painful, were poignant and bitter sweet.

She picked up the pale blue cotton sweater she'd put on the pile for Oxfam, and reconsidered it. She'd bought that sweater for him one pouring wet summer's day when they'd been in Exeter. He'd liked it at the time – and running from the shop in South Street to the bar of The Ship in Cathedral Close, they'd got drenched. 'You don't think that colour makes me look a bit aged, do you?' he'd said as they'd sat at the bar.

Vain creature ...

'No I don't. Not at all. It looks very good on you.'

But that sweater must be at least four years old, and at most he'd worn it three or four times. It could go to Oxfam – and she put it back on the pile.

The trouble is, she thought, *the last strained, unhappy months of our marriage smothered the years that were good.* She had forgotten how good – and reliving each memory was like getting to know him again; the Lawrence she had married, the man she had tried to convince herself that she could no longer love.

Latterly, knowing what he was, learning to live with it, had made her life hell.

Though in this room as she sorted through his clothes, she had felt closer to him than she had in months. Fourteen months ...

In fact, as she switched off the light and closed the door to go downstairs and make a cup of tea, she almost wished him a goodnight.

Amy, dozing by the fire, woke to see Anthea dump a pile of riding clothes on the sofa. Someone was coming to look at them, and Anthea was covered in cobwebs. Had been in the loft. Was it snowing? Amy daren't ask. Anthea, tired of her asking, would be cross.

Nor yet were the storms over in this family – but Lawrence was stretched out in his favourite armchair, and my, he looked tired. He'd had a busy couple of days and she sensed he'd not long returned from Tivington. Exhausted ... His aura was much less distinct than it had been, and greyish. Wait much

249

longer and in this state, on his own, he wouldn't have the power to pass over.

Where was the snow? And the wild card, the man with the sun in his hair?

Tillotson woke with the dawn and got out of bed to sit by the window to watch the sun rise. This summer, watching the sunrise had become an important ritual; something continual and certain in a life that he had now accepted was transitory. As he watched the sun gradually emerge from behind the grey distant hills across the rolling plane to burn away the pink and navy clouds in a constantly lightening sky, it proved to him that he had survived one more day.

Each sunrise was the same, yet was also different; the greens of the meadows, the density and position of the clouds, their precise colouring, the fractionally altered angle of the sun itself. And every one of them was now intensely precious to him. He'd felt a good deal better these past couple of weeks, but he was past trying to kid himself.

Nor, for some reason, was he nearly so scared as he had been. Watching the sun rise over the silent bunkhouses and the sleeping fields gave him an enormous sense of resignation and of peace. A feeling that he might not be so alone after all; that someone, something, perhaps a god of some sort – might just be sharing this beauty with him.

So perhaps there was a God. And another life after this ...

Watching the sunrise was also a good time to think. That rich cockie Mattheson from Brisbane looked about ready to go firm on his final offer for the ranches. A bloody good offer. Knowing he could afford it, Tillotson had pushed him several grand beyond current market value, and had demanded a guarantee on the two manager's jobs and that of the trainer at Barrington into the bargain. Every day there were phone calls, more questions, but they were only minor details. It was the way Mattheson operated, and basically, mad keen to buy, he'd agreed to every condition and all that remained was for the bastard to pick up a pen and sign the God damned contract.

Tillotson knew he wouldn't be getting another offer to match this one, and for Lawrie's sake, and his widow in England, he wanted the very best deal he could get.

But he also knew Mattheson. He was an impetuous bastard who had to be handled carefully. He'd sign that contract at the exact moment he was good and ready – and when that time came Tillotson would need to be there or the deal would be off.

He dare not let Mattheson go cold ... And today was Friday. Next Wednesday, he had a flight booked out of Sydney for London Heathrow. A flight which, this time, he really could not afford to postpone.

Going out to fetch a cardboard box from the barn the next morning, Beth noticed that the bitter wind had dropped, but that it was still very cold and the sky was leaden and yellow with the promise of snow. Then, having made a large mug of coffee, she took it and the box up to the dressing-room to start on the wardrobe.

Jackets and trousers to the right, shirts in the middle, suits on the left, all rigidly at attention like a row of empty soldiers. The floor was dotted with sacks and piles of clothes and, as soon as she'd come into the room, she'd noticed an unusually strong smell of his fresh citrus-based cologne.

She pushed the hangers along the rail to look at his suits, and glanced down at his shoes stored neatly in pairs. Inside a new pair of brown brogues, a clear footprint had partly obliterated the gold lettering. She had never realised that shoes were so very personal – and the citrus scent of him was overwhelming. She wanted to cry.

'Come on ...' he seemed to say to her. 'Chin up. Best foot forward.'

She put the brogues to the back of the cupboard, divided the rest of his shoes between Oxfam and the dustbin, and started on his shirts.

Vyella-checked and plain; cotton or silk; white, cream, plain, striped; brightly coloured short-sleeved sports shirts – and three, hideously and variously patterned with parrots, palm trees, skyscrapers and crocodiles, all of which had been bought while on holidays abroad, and probably while under the influence of the alcohol of the particular country.

Some would do for Wanda, one or two for Anthea, most for Oxfam. The elaborate, expensive dress shirts? Robin was too

251

slight – and Graham too short. In any case she couldn't offer them to Graham. Having had the dead man's wife, he wouldn't want his shirts.

As for the parrots and crocodiles – they could go to the dustbin.

'*Beth* ...' he said reproachfully.

No, Lawrie, they're awful, she replied in her mind. *I told you that when you bought them.*

Oh, all right then ... I suppose, on the remotest chance that somebody somewhere might just have the same awful taste for holiday wear as you did – they might as well go to Oxfam.'

Robin sketched in the rough outline of a man under the entrance archway of the courtyard. The design for the main entrance had come to him in a flash of inspiration, but the rate he was progressing, by the time he finished the rest of this complex that was to be a nursing home and flats for the elderly, he'd be about ready to move into the place himself. If he could afford it, which he doubted. Another couple of months, and judging by the bank statement that had arrived in this morning's post, his financial future looked pretty bleak. Nothing left over to offer to a woman, that was for certain. And his thoughts strayed back once again to Wanda.

For God's sake man, at your age you should have been able to get all that into perspective long ago.

Wanda who was nineteen, rising twenty ...

The man he'd drawn in under the archway looked a bit like old man Seligman in one of the photographs at Luccombe. And beside him, he sketched in a young girl.

Wanda ... Then, because this was a nursing home complex, he added a nurse's cape and hat.

The digital clock on his computer screen showed eleven-thirty and, sighing, he put down his pencil. Perhaps it would improve his concentration if he took a break and went for a walk.

On his way home he could call in at the Spar and buy some more liquorice. He was eating too damned much liquorice, and for some reason too much liquorice always gave him spots on his bum. Still, no one was going to be seeing them there.

Unfortunately.

'I'm sorry if I seem to be rushing you,' Graham said, raising his voice to compete with the honking of the two geese that had met him at the car and were following him through the semi-darkness of the barn that opened on to Anthea's back garden. 'Only Friday's my afternoon off and Stella's calling in tomorrow on her way to Cornwall. This man she's haunting has a house down there and a horse he wants Trish to hunt. He sounds quite well heeled.'

'He'd have to be to suit Stella. Shut up you two!' Anthea said, turning on the geese and clapping her hands. 'Shoo ... Push off!'

Graham laughed. 'Yes, you're right. I wish he'd marry her. What a joy to be let off the hook!'

She laughed with him, and as they walked across the lawn to the house he caught a glimpse of the younger, carefree Anthea he remembered from a long time ago. She had always been good to him, had Anthea. Quite often after Stella had left he'd come over here and talked to her rather than to Lawrence. Had talked and talked, trying to understand in order to come to terms with it. He'd probably driven her crazy, but she'd known him a long time, and it had been easier to talk to her than to a man. Chaps had to put on brave faces for each other.

'It's been a while since I've been in this garden.'

She stopped on the path so that he could look around. 'It's a bit overgrown. I'm afraid I'm not much of a gardener.'

'Show me a farmer that is.'

A light, isolated flurry of snowflakes floated down from the glowering sky and he was glad when they went indoors.

The kitchen hadn't changed at all and it still smelt of wood smoke, and of warm, freshly made bread. There had often been some bird or animal in a box by the Rayburn. Today it was a rather limp-looking goose. 'I always liked your kitchen.'

'Yes, well it's a working kitchen, so you'll have to excuse the mess.'

253

'Oh, I like organised chaos.'

'Beer?'

'Lovely,' he said, rubbing his hands together. 'Look, Anthea, don't go to any trouble. You didn't have to ask me to lunch.'

'It's only a snack. Soup, bread and cheese. We have our main meal in the evening. And we'll eat in here. Mother's in the living room.'

'Is she? I'll go through and say hello.'

'She might not remember who you are, but go in and have a look at the clothes anyway. They're on the sofa.'

She opened the door and standing on the step he glanced round the room. Nothing had changed in this house since the day he'd first seen it – except that the old lady was watching him from her armchair by the big log fire.

'This is Graham Lang, Mum,' Anthea said. 'Our solicitor. Remember? I told you he was coming.'

'Is it snowing?'

'A few flakes, Mrs. Kenworthy. But I doubt it'll come to much. And how have you been keeping?'

The old lady fixed him with a narrow-eyed stare, then, grunting, she seemed to lose interest.

'Sorry,' Anthea said, touching his sleeve. 'I did warn you. Have a look at the clothes while I lay the table. The boots are sevens and the black hunting coat's a fourteen. I'm not sure about the rest of it, you'll just have to guess.'

She went back into the kitchen, and sorting through the clothes he glanced at the old lady and tried again. He was rather fond of old people. 'Don't you like snow, Mrs. Kenworthy?'

She didn't answer. In fact, dear old thing, other than in body, she didn't really seem to be there. Didn't even seem to have heard him. 'Mrs. Kenworthy ...?'

'Graham Lang,' she muttered, apparently addressing the fire. 'Married to Stella Newcombe that was. Divorced. He'll marry again ...' And suddenly she turned to look at him and her face lit up. 'Oh yays, young man, you'll marry again.'

'Now what's she saying?' Anthea said, coming through to join them. 'She seems to have a lot more to say for herself these days but it doesn't always make sense.' She set a tray of bread and soup down on a table and moved it in front of the old lady, then came over to join him by the sofa. 'Anything any good?'

'Difficult to tell,' he said. Frowning at the clothes, he suddenly felt sorry for the old lady. Anthea was a bit dismissive. Still, living alone with her couldn't be easy. In fact, when she'd looked at him and muttered about him remarrying, she'd made the hairs stand up on the back of his neck.

'Take it all then, and let Trish try them on,' Anthea said as she secured a clean white napkin around the old lady's neck.

Mrs. Kenworthy busied herself with her food, and he followed Anthea back to the kitchen. 'Will she be all right in there on her own?'

'She's used to being on her own. She spends too much time on her own really, but it's easier for us to eat in here today. We'll go and sit with her a bit when we've finished.'

'It must be hell to be old. I'm dreading it,' he said watching her ladle out soup from a stockpot as he sat down at one of the places she'd laid on the cleared half of the scrubbed pine table.

'This poor chap isn't enjoying it much either,' she said of the goose in the box on the floor beside her. 'Are you, poor Percy ...'

The goose looked up at her, then with an elegant twist of its neck, rested its bright orange beak along the line of its back.

'That's something else I remember about this kitchen,' Graham said, 'the livestock.' She put a large bowl of soup down in front of him and he sniffed appreciatively. 'Smells wonderful. What is it?'

'Homemade vegetable.'

'I haven't smelt soup as good as this in a long time. And you've made bread. How ever do you find the time?'

'Oh, most things seem to get done eventually if you keep going. Help yourself ...' She pushed the bread and the jug of beer across the table and sat down opposite him.

'We've had a few drinks at this kitchen table, the four of us.'

'Like four green bottles – hanging on the wall. And now we're down to two,' she said, smiling.

255

'Here's to us then,' he said, lifting his glass. 'To you and me, the survivors. And to Lawrence.'

She drank with him. 'I'll tell you something, Graham. One old friend to another ... It's something I've only very recently discovered myself, but you wouldn't want Stella back, and neither, now, would I want Lawrence.'

'But I thought ...'

'Yes, I know,' she said, cutting him short. 'I love him. I suppose I always did and I always will. But times change and people move on. The man I really do still miss is my brother.'

'Yes ... He went off to Australia soon after I came here, but I remember him. Nice chap. Good-looking, too.'

'Yes, he was. More bread?'

'I will, thanks ... I'd forgotten you were such a good cook.'

There was quite a lot he'd forgotten about her. Her directness, her sense of humour, her ability to cope ... Talking to her, it was all coming back to him. He always had admired Anthea.

'Well, I wouldn't have Stella back if she paid me – as well you know. A bad business, divorce. The things people say to each other in the process of pulling apart. They scythe each other back to nothing and it can take years for one's self-confidence to build up again.'

'Yes ...' Anthea said thoughtfully, understanding.

'You'd be appalled at the things I often hear in the course of a working day. Sometimes I'm so saturated with other people's hurt by an evening that I feel like putting my head in the gas oven.'

'It doesn't work any more.'

'What ...?'

'The gas oven. North Sea gas, or whatever it is now – it doesn't work.'

'Oh right,' he said, laughing with her. 'Anyway, I don't think I'll try it.'

'Is that why you've never married again? Other people's hurt? Or are you still sore at Stella?'

'Lord, no. Neither. I'd quite like to marry again,' and remembering what Mrs. Kenworthy had said to him, he laughed. 'No, I would like to marry again, though I don't think it's very likely. Actually, well – you see ... To be honest, I'm not really much good with women. In fact, to tell you the absolute truth, Anthea, I'm really rather scared of them. And as for the wooing and winning ... It's been so long now, I'm not sure I'd know how to start.'

'You would if the right woman came along. Of course you would. And we'd do better next time, both of us. Older, and hopefully a bit wiser, we'd pick more carefully.'

'Would you like to marry again?'

'If the right chap came along, yes I would. Not that I'm likely to get the chance.'

'Why ever not? You're a nice-looking woman. And a good cook.'

Laughing, she tucked in her chin and looked at him. 'You should have been a diplomat.'

'No – you're a good-looking woman.' Actually, he thought, meeting her eyes – not only does she look good, but she looks comfortable. As opposed to Beth who was gorgeous, and downright terrifying. 'Anyway, what are looks? Only the packaging. And,' he said, controlling his urge to shudder as he remembered the stunning brown-eyed redhead with her creamy skin and her fancy underwear, 'speaking as a man, one can get badly tangled up in the pretty paper and string.' How the hell he'd ever got involved with Beth he never would know ...

'I would like to have someone to share my life with again,' Anthea said. 'A friend, a companion, someone to care for. It can get lonely up here sometimes – but let's be honest, who'd want to marry a middle-aged farmer and a yard full of animals, not to mention a senile old grandmother, dear old thing that she is.'

'There must be plenty of nice men who would, but if you do think of marrying again, be careful. You've worked damned hard at this farm. If it goes wrong, you don't need to lose half of what you've worked for to a charlatan.'

'If I do meet someone, I'll get you to give him the once over,' and laughing, she got up to make coffee.

The goose in the box by the Rayburn lifted it's head to watch her and, once she'd put the kettle on, she crouched to stroke his neck. The goose went quite weak with delight, wagging its head and quietly clacking its beak in response.

257

Anthea had a lot of affection to give. Damn shame, really, to waste it on a goose ...

'Is he ill, then, What's-his-name? Percy? Or just old?' he asked as she stood up to go over to the sink and the goose struggled half-heartedly to get out of its box and follow her.

'I'm not sure. No, Percy, stay there ... He seems a bit better today.' They watched Percy twist and turn his neck as he settled down to groom his feathers, and self-consciously she chuckled. 'Actually, Gran made up one of her potions for him. I was going to throw it away, but I put some in his drinking water. He's definitely a bit better – and I haven't started on the stuff the vet gave me.'

'That's a turn up for the books,' he said, grinning. 'You never used to believe in any of that.'

'I know. Well, would you?'

'Probably not,' he said, watching her push back her hair. Actually, she was very handsome-looking woman. And as she'd reached up to rearrange her hair, he couldn't help but notice that she was rounded in all the right places.

'Poor old Percy, he's only one of my problems. Lord knows what I'm going to do about Gran when we start lambing.'

He stirred sugar into his coffee. 'When do you start lambing?'

'End of February, beginning of March.'

She could do with a break before then. Perhaps a night out ... What was more, he had a legal dinner thing coming up next Friday and he really couldn't face going to it yet again on his own.

'Anthea, one old friend to another – will you do me a favour?'

'If I can.' Then, 'I'd love to Graham,' she said when he'd asked her, 'But how can I?'

'Isn't there anyone who'd come in and sit with your mother for an evening?'

'Well,' she said doubtfully, 'it's difficult ... You see, she's so rude to the people who sit with her. The woman who helps me in the house is scared to death of her. I could ask Viv or Wanda. They lead such busy lives, but I could ask.'

'Yes,' he said. 'Do ask. Do try. It would do you good to

258

get out. And you're never going to meet any nice prospective male companions if you don't go anywhere.'

Kind, shy Graham, she thought, watching him drive away up the lane bordered by the tall rhododendron bushes. There'd been a time, until Lawrence came along, that she'd quite envied Stella. In middle age he was carrying a bit too much weight, and in knee britches with his close cut curly hair, he reminded her of a dear little bear.

Paddington ...

Why did he wear those awful knees britches? He looked much less of a bear in a suit. And he had always looked good in a dinner jacket.

Oh God, she thought suddenly, *and what the blue blazes am I going to wear to a dinner dance?*

Three forty-five, and craving for yet more liquorice. This must stop ... Angered by his continued lack of concentration, Robin threw his pencil across the room and got up to put on his duffle coat. Any excuse to get up from the drawing board.

There had been a light fall of snow since lunch, but the path through the Manor's grounds to the shop on the other side of the main road had been dried white grey by the wind. As he walked his knees felt stiff. A sign there was more snow to come – or the approach of old age? Reserve a room on the first floor of the nursing home looking south over the land-scaped garden ... He must phone the lady from Ilminster about the landscaping. He liked her, and he liked what he'd seen of the plans she was preparing for the house in Dorset. Then he thought about old Seligman in the frozen earth, and wondered about worms and the process of decay. This nursing-home job was depressing him ...

The shop was bright and warm and, surprisingly at this time of day, there was only one other customer. A girl of about Wanda's age in a cheerful red coat. She didn't look unlike Wanda ... The same sort of haircut. He picked up several sticks of liquorice, a packet of chocolate biscuits, a tin of spaghetti, a cauliflower, and an evening paper. The motherly middle-aged woman behind the till had a friendly smile and a

259

large round face like a rosy apple, surrounded by a bush of white hair.

'It'll give you spots, all this sweet stuff you're eating.'

'I'm too old for spots. Unfortunately. Well, mostly,' he said remembering his bum.

'Get on with you,' she said. 'You can't be a day over twenty-five.'

He put his head on one side and looked at her. 'How about thirty-two?'

'If you like. Does it matter? I always says you're as young as you feel.'

'Tell me,' he said suddenly, and glanced at the door to make sure the girl had gone. 'Have you got any daughters?'

'Four. Twenty, nineteen, eighteen and seventeen. I've led a busy life, and I'll tell you, my lover, they girls don't get any easier.'

Then, on impulse, before he could stop himself, he said, 'How would you feel if the nineteen year old went out with a man of my age?'

'Oh, so that's it. Yez, I thought you looked a bit down.'

'How would you feel about it?'

'Listen, my love, if you loves each other, you get on with it, that's what I do say.'

'Thanks,' he said, backing away.

'Here ... You've forgotten your change.'

'Put it in the Barnado's box,' he said, grinning.

'There now, a man like you I'd have for a son-in-law any day.'

He held the door open for a young mother with a baby wrapped up like an Eskimo in a pushchair, and two little kids in school uniform that were tagging on behind.

'You'd better know what you're in for,' the woman called after him, nodding at the kids – and, laughing, he stepped out into the street.

His feet were inches above the pavement – and he simply could not bear it any longer. Wanda finished work at five-thirty. She'd be home by six. Whatever she felt about him, he loved her madly and he had to tell her so. Had to see her – tonight.

The next hour and three quarters crawled. He ate the

260

liquorice, half the packet of biscuits, felt sick, drank tea, read the paper, watched the evening news – and with great self-control forced himself to wait until six-thirty. After all, he'd been short with her when she'd phoned on Monday. Maybe she wouldn't want to speak to him. Maybe she didn't fancy him at all ... Maybe it was all in his imagination and she'd never fancied him but was just sorry for him and being kind ...

'Hello? Can I speak to Wanda?'

''Ang about, I'll give her a yell.'

Thank God – she was there. Any second she'd speak to him.

'Wanda?'

'Robin ...?'

'Wanda, I've got to see you.'

'Why? What's wrong?'

'Nothing.' Silence ... And then he said it. 'It's just that I love you.' Another silence. Longer this time. *Oh God* ... 'Wanda? Are you still there ...? Look, I'm sorry – I just ...'

'I love you too,' she said.

'Do you? Oh, Wanda ... Thank God!'

'Steady on,' she said, laughing. 'Are you at home? I love you very much, and I'm coming to see you. I'm on my way. So much has happened. I've got so much to tell you!'

Tucked at the back of the wardrobe as Beth sorted through his jackets, she found his ghastly yellow corduroy jeans and remembered having hidden them there. They were so awful that she used to hide them quite often.

'Beth ...?' he'd called down the stairs. 'Where are my trousers? The nice fir green ones.'

She stopped stirring the saucepan of milk on the cooker. 'Which fir green ones? You haven't got any fir green ones.'

'The cords. The ones you mended.'

'You mean those awful faded yellow things?'

He came halfway down the stairs and leant over the bannister. He was wearing the blue denim shirt she'd just now put aside for Wanda, and the white boxer shorts with red hearts on them. When she looked at him she could see the panic in his eyes.

261

'They aren't faded. Darling, those are my favourite trousers. What have you done with them?'

'I gave them to the jumble,' she said, stirring the milk that was to become a white sauce.

'What ...?' He shot down the stairs and into the kitchen. 'When!'

'Saturday. They'll have gone with the collection last Monday.'

'Beth ...!' He looked so indignant, so bereft, so very funny, standing there in his pants. His legs were tanned and covered in dark hair, but wearing trousers rubbed the hair off his knees so that they were white and bald. 'You didn't?' he said – and she started to laugh.

'No,' she said, relenting. 'Give me a kiss and I'll tell you where they are.'

'Tell me first.'

'No kiss, no tell.'

'All right. What colour knickers are you wearing?'

'I don't know. I can't remember.'

'Black?'

'Maybe.'

'Black, or the coffee and cream set I bought you?'

He'd been good at buying her presents. Liked chosing clothes for her. Had often bought her fancy underwear. 'I don't know,' she said, laughing. 'I was barely awake. Black probably. I can't remember.'

'Too bad, then. You lose. Blue's the colour for today.'

'That's cheating!'

'Where are my trousers?' he said, leering. 'I warn you, I'm going to get mean. I'm going to get passionate!'

'Promises, promises ...' she said, laughing, fighting him off as he tried to lift up her skirt. 'Stop it ... Stop! The milk's burning! Your lovely old trousers are in the sitting room!'

'Since when? What for?' he said, and pulling back to look at her, he kept hold of her bottom. 'Are you sure?'

'Positive.'

'Show me.'

Giggling, they jostled some more as he pulled her out into the hall.

262

'Look – there! By my sewing box, waiting to be mended. They need mending again.'

'So they are. I'm still going to have to deal with you though. Get up those stairs ...!'

'Turn off the cooker, then,' she said, as she ducked out from under his arm. She took the stairs three at a time, and he started after her. 'Turn off the cooker!'

'Stone the lizards ...' He turned, and she stopped to watch him run back down to the hall. 'You won't be able to treat me like this when I'm old, you know,' he called as he disappeared into the kitchen. 'When I'm old it'll be damn the milk and right on, right then, or never.'

Oh Lawrie, she thought, smiling at the memory. *When was that? Three, four years ago? I loved you then. How I loved you ... In those days I had no idea what you were, what was to come, how it would end.*

But I do love you ... Even now.

Holding on to his trousers, she sat down on the divan. She could hardly see the carpet for cardboard boxes, bulging grey sacks and neat piles of clothes. As they obscured the carpet, so had the last bad months of the marriage obscured the good.

But she did still love him. Every bit as much as she had ever loved him. Despite it all.

They had hugged each other so tight for so long that in the end Wanda could hardly breathe. Suddenly, in a matter of days, everything, absolutely everything, had fallen into place – and now they were sitting together on Robin's sofa in front of his fire, and he was holding her hand as though he never meant to let go of it. He didn't, from the things that he'd said. It was all so good that she could hardly believe it.

'You're going to be a nurse, Wanda. It think it's a fantastic idea. In fact, you've got to be a nurse. I drew you as a nurse on some plans only this morning. I'll show you later.'

'There is one problem though. You want babies. Within the next two years. I heard you telling Viv.'

'That was with Viv. It was different with Viv. You're younger. You need to be trained at something, and as long as I've got you I don't give a damn about babies. We can think

263

about all that three years from now when you're through the preliminaries.'

When he woke in the night she was curled in beside him, her body smooth and cool like a lithe young animal. It had been years since he'd been the first with a girl. Not that Wanda had needed any teaching. She was warmer by nature than her sister – and she lacked the stubborn selfishness and the cutting tongue.

He nuzzled his cheek against her shoulder, and stirring in her sleep she pressed closer to him. Smiling, he covered her with the duvet. He would have to tell Viv. And God only knew what his future mother-in-law would think ... Still, he'd face that when the time came. The main thing was he'd got the right sister, and he'd never felt so complete, so happy, or so contented.

She woke in a strange room, and remembering, she smiled and turned to look at him. His side of the bed was empty. Then from the bathroom she heard the rush of water as he flushed the loo.

'Where are you going?' she said, sitting up as he came back into the room. He was dressed in jeans and a polo-necked jersey.

'To the shop to get rolls for breakfast. And we're out of milk. Stay where you are. I won't be long. How are you this morning?'

'Battered. Damaged for life.' She wriggled, screwed up her face and gave him a big, smug smile.

'I do hope so,' he said, coming over to hug her. 'I did my best.'

'Where's my scarf.'

'Darling, you don't need it. Really you don't. Your hair looks fine.'

'I'll put the kettle on.'

'No, no. I'll do that. You have a nice soak in the bath and when I get back I'll bring you breakfast in bed.'

She felt far too lively to stay in bed, and when the front door had slammed behind him she leapt out, grabbed his dressing-gown and looked at herself in the mirror. Her hair didn't look that bad, it was true. It had grown well these past few months and, with Adrian continually cutting it, the black had almost gone.

She was looking at the real Wanda. She pulled a face at herself, and on the way to the bathroom she started to sing.

'You look a lot happier this morning,' the woman said as she took his empty basket and tossed it on the stack by the till.

'I am,' he said, grinning.

'There you are then, my lover,' she said, and gave him his change. 'No extra charge for advice to my regulars. No liquorice this morning?'

'No thanks,' he said. 'Not this morning. Oh well, perhaps I will ... Just a couple of wheels.'

When he got back to the flat Wanda was still in the bath. He made a cup of tea and took it into her. 'Scrub your back?'

'Umm ... Lovely. Perfect, except ...'

'What?' He bent over the bath and she lifted her hand to put bubbles on his nose.

'What about Viv?'

'Yes ...' he said. 'We'll tell Viv. Well, I will.'

'She and I never did get on too well. I guess this'll be the final straw. She'll be well gutted.'

'Does that worry you?'

'Not particularly. Sad, but that's just how it is.'

'She never really wanted me, you know.'

'I want you,' she said, splashing him with bath water.

'I know you do.' He hesitated. 'What ... Again?'

'Again.' She stood up, bubbles and water streaming off her smooth young skin.

'Are you sure you're all right?'

'Try me,' she said, teasing, leaning against him as he wrapped her in a towel.

He'd definitely got the right sister. Viv had never been like this.

'What time is it?'

'Two o'clock.'

'Is it really? Ought we to get up?'

'Probably. I'll get up.' He was lying on his back, his arm

over his eyes, and he made no attempt to move. A gorgeous long, well-muscled forearm – which he moved from his eyes in order to look at her. 'There's a bit of cheese in the fridge. I didn't think this morning, but we'll need more than that for the weekend.'

'I ought to go home and pick up some clothes.'

'All right,' he said, and dragged himself up on to the pillows. 'You go back and pack a suitcase, and I'll go to Sainsbury's. Set us up for a seige.'

'How big a suitcase?'

'As big as they come. Wanda, I want you here with me.'

He gave her a key, and they left the flat together. It was cold outside but the wind had thinned the cloud and above the tops of the tall cedars that bordered the grounds, there was a hint of sunlight. She followed his car along the drive, out into the road, and drove behind him down the hill towards town. As he turned up Shire Hill he tooted and, already missing him, she drove on unescorted through the Saturday traffic.

When she reached Ashton Grove, Pete was polishing his motorbike in the patch of front garden, and Shirley, as usual on a Saturday afternoon, was doing her hair.

''Ere, Wanda – what time of day is this to come in? We were startin' to get really worried about you,' she said, leaning over the bannisters, her hair in curlers.

'I'll make some coffee and come up and tell you. I can't stay long ...'

She hung her basket bag on the newel post at the bottom of the stairs and went into the kitchen. Clearing a space amongst the piles of unwashed plates and mugs, she was suddenly aware of an impending loss. She was moving on – and much as she loved Robin, wanted to be with him, she'd done a lot of growing up in this dump. She would miss it, and its people.

'A new year, a new life,' Shirley said.

'Seems like it. Yes. I'll be back to see you.'

'Oh, Wanda, I'm ever so pleased for you.'

'I'll leave you the phone number. Just don't let my sister know where I am. Not that she's likely to call ... Oh Lord, and don't tell my mother either. You can say what you like to my stepmother. In fact, I'll give her a ring from here before I leave.'

266

'You'd better leave a list of instructions by the phone,' Shirley said doubtfully. 'You know what this madhouse is like. We're bound to cock it up somehow.'

A while later, in her room on her own before Shirley came up to help her to pack, she thought back to the night Robin had come in with her on the night of the funeral – and silently, she thanked her father. This was his doing, she was perfectly sure of it.

'Oh, Wanda,' Beth said, 'I'm so glad, really I am.'

'Anyway, I wanted you to be the first to know. And for the next few months, I'll be working as a domestic at a private nursing home. I got the job yesterday. I start on Monday. It'll be a while before I know if the college has accepted me.'

'I expect they will. So absolutely everything has worked out right – I am so pleased for you.'

'Anyway, we'll see you soon. And meantime, not a word to Mum or Viv.'

'No, of course not. You will tell Anthea soon though ...'

'Yes, yes. It's a matter of when.'

'Fine,' Beth said. 'But do tell her as soon as you can.'

Beth hadn't any plans to see either Vivien or Anthea, but now that the contact with Anthea had been made, it was possible that they would meet again. It was also possible, now, that if Anthea gave Wanda a hard time, she might be able to put in a word on her behalf.

She replaced the receiver and, going back across the landing from her bedroom to his dressing-room, she thought back over the years and remembered how it had felt to be in love. When Lawrie had phoned her in London to ask her to marry him, she'd been so happy she'd thought she would burst. You never forgot that feeling, that supreme high, that sense of soaring and the devil take tomorrow. The devil usually did, of course – but you never forgot the feeling, no matter what came afterwards.

In his dressing-room her work was almost done. All the good memories had been faced, then packed into sacks and boxes. All that remained in the wardrobe were the few clothes that she intended to keep; the puke yellow trousers and the brown brogues; the safari suit he'd worn the day

267

she'd first met him; the dark grey-double-breasted he'd worn on the day they were married; and the tweed suit he'd worn to go to the Gold Cup meeting at Cheltenham a year past November when, for some reason, he'd first started to take an interest in racing again.

'What d'you want for Christmas?' he'd asked on the way home.

'How much did you win?'

'Just say what you want for Christmas and it's yours.'

'Lawrie just how much did you put on that animal?' She'd been wide-eyed with alarm.

'Enough to buy a very nice present for the woman I love,' he'd said, grinning. 'What more do you need to know?'

Nothing ... Absolutely nothing, she thought, looking at the suit.

Because I loved you then, and that was after I saw you with that bastard in London. What was more, she had loved him all through Christmas too, and all through that boring New Year which they had seen in with the Franks, and all through the spring. All through that bloody holiday in Morocco, and right on through the summer when he'd moved in to this room and refused to come near her, she'd loved him. And every day, as she watched him torturing himself, twisting inside as he tried to come to terms with the man he was – she loved him.

As much as you loved me, she thought.

He did love her. She had seen it in his eyes as he died. And at that moment, both of them knowing that his fight to conform was finally over, perhaps she had loved him more than she had ever loved him.

Her senses seeming to fill with the memory of him, she reached for the safari suit, and hugging it, relived the feel of his arms around her.

'*I still love you,*' she seemed to hear him say. '*Nothing has changed.*'

Everything has changed, Lawrie ...

Because she loved him even despite his promise to Anthea that only she would be the mother of his children. A promise which had denied Beth what she thought she wanted above all else. But she could love him for keeping that promise, even though he lied and had never explained.

And absolutely everything has changed, she thought, *because, now I've accepted just how much I love you, how can I live without you?*

Still hugging the safari suit, she realised that she was looking at the suitcase full of the papers which she and Vivien had moved from his desk – and somehow she felt that she ought to open it.

Sitting on the floor beside it, she began to sift through the contents; personal papers, his address book and diary, their marriage certificate, old cheque books and bank statements ... Much of it could be dumped. She'd go through it properly sometime but, now that she'd gone through his clothes, there was no hurry. There was nothing in there of any importance. Just the remains of the last seven years of his life. His life with her ...

Then, gradually, as she continued to look through the case, his neat, familiar handwriting seemed to draw her back to his life before she had known him. Right back into his childhood ...

She imagined him, a small boy in the Australian homestead, picking up a crayon, puzzling over its feel in his hand; his fascination at the resulting scrawl that appeared on some wall or on paper. And later, being taught by his mother to form numbers and the letters of the alphabet; later still, in a board school fifty miles nearer the Blue Mountains, coping with joined words in pen and ink. And afterwards, learning to read in whole sentences; gradually, as he grew older, learning arithmetic, scripture, history, the map of the world; learning to identify countries – amongst them, England where unbeknown to him at the time, he would eventually settle and live out the last half of his life.

She wondered about the house where he'd been born and to which he returned during the holiday; his parents, his teachers, his friends – Tillotson indulged. Even the dog and the pony he'd mentioned. Everything that had made Lawrence the boy into Lawrence the man.

My God, she thought, sitting back on her heels. How much a human being has to learn in the course of a lifetime. How much luggage the average adult is carrying in the form of knowledge, personal experience and responsibilities by the day of their death.

There was damage too of course – of different sorts, in every life. But how much that is positive and good dies with a person, and is wasted.

Damn it ... And there were no photographs ...

So what did it look like, the ranch where he'd been born and grown up? There was so much about him that she didn't know. Because so much of his life, so much that was him, had been left in Australia.

Chapter Thirteen

'Hello, love. It's Mum. Did you have a nice time in Brussels?'

'It was interesting.'

An exchange of cross words with Martin at the airport on the way out had set the tone for the whole weekend. She had taken an instant, gut-reaction dislike to his boss; the flat they'd allocated him was more like a twenty-first century cage from which to view the city, and her rusty classroom German had fallen far short of the necessary.

'You sound worn out. I hope you're eating properly.'

'Mum ...' she said reproachfully.

But she *was* tired. Worn down, really – and ever since their return Martin, clearing his desk at Thanes and packing up his flat in Bristol, had been snappish and self-absorbed.

'I was just wondering,' Mum said, 'If you were thinking of coming down this weekend?'

'Not this weekend, no.'

It would be Martin's last in England, and although she'd begun to realise that he'd be hellish to live with, and therefore, long term, was probably a dead horse, he would nevertheless expect her to flog him to the end.

'I thought I'd come next weekend. Why ...? Does it matter?'

'No, no. Not really. I just need someone to sit in with Gran on Friday evening.'

'Why don't you ask Wanda. I don't suppose she's doing much.'

'Yes ... I'll ask Wanda.'

*

'Mum ...? I got a message to phone you.'

'Hello, Wanda, love. How's the job going?'

'Brilliant. Today I did the morning shift, and I tell you – I put a shine on a bedpan second to none.'

Anthea laughed. It really did seem that Wanda had at last found something at which she'd decided it was worth working.

'Listen pet, I need a sitter for Gran. I wondered if you could help me out.'

'Wow!' said Wanda, delighted when she'd told her about the dance. 'Well, we were going to a party, but if you've got a man I'd better come down.'

'Oh, Wanda, don't be so stupid. He's just a friend. I've known him for years.'

'Who ...?'

'A friend, Wanda. Just a friend.'

'It's never old Reg is it?'

'No it's not,' said Anthea crossly.

'This is getting better by the minute. I'll definitely come down and Granny-sit.'

'No you won't. Forget it.' She pictured Wanda grinning all over her face. And grinning at Graham when he arrived to pick her up ... She was making far too much mileage out of this, and it would get worse. 'Forget it,' she said again. 'You go to your party. There are plenty of other people I can ask.'

There weren't, but it was only an innocent invitation from a very old friend and it really didn't matter to Anthea if she went or if she didn't. She might have known Wanda would bite, and gnaw it to death like a bone.

'Hello ...! Anyone home?'

'Hello, Mew,' she said, going back to the kitchen in time to see Muriel take off her woollen headscarf.

'My word, it's raw out there. I wish it would snow and be done with it.'

'The hens don't like it either,' she said, putting on the kettle. 'They're hardly laying at all, but I kept you a dozen brown.'

'Bless you. Umm ...' she said appreciatively, looking at a batch of scones cooling on the table. 'And you've been baking.'

'I've made another batch of the marmalade Merv likes too.

272

I suppose I'd better put back a few pots for Viv and Wanda – though I must say, I could happily throttle Wanda.'

'What's she done now?'

But by the time Anthea had given her the gist of her conversation with her daughter, Muriel's eyes were also shining, and all too late, Anthea realised that she was going to have every bit as much trouble with her.

'I'll Granny-sit for you. Of course I will!'

'No you won't. You know how rude she is to you. She's got worse lately. She actually prodded Mary with her thumb-stick the other day. And anyway, Merv likes you to spend the evenings with him.'

'Rubbish. I spend every evening with him. He won't mind at all,' said Muriel, her eyes adance with delight. Romance, long overdue in Mew's opinion – and eventually marriage – were already a foregone conclusion.

'Mew, Graham's a friend,' she said firmly. 'A very old family friend.'

But now that both Mew and Wanda were making so much of it, she was beginning to be a little nervous. Was beginning, herself, to consider this innocent little outing in a completely different, rather more serious light ...

'I've known him for years, Mew, and well you know it,' she said.

'I do,' Muriel said, gleefully, 'I do ... And what are you going to wear?'

'I haven't a clue,' she said, suddenly hating the whole idea.

'I suggest you borrow my long aubergine two-piece. We're much of a size.'

'I'll look like a cart horse.'

'Anthea, my dear – not when I've finished with you.'

Her heart sank – and remained in her boots all week as she clumped about the yard. Muriel went with her to Minehead, insisting on supervising the purchase of suitable shoes, and that Anthea booked a hairdo and a manicure for Friday afternoon.

'I feel,' said Anthea miserably, 'as if I'm being prepared for slaughter.'

'Even if you are, dear,' said Muriel, determinedly, 'I expect you'll enjoy it.'

273

But, as a matter of fact, she didn't look at all bad in the two-piece, and by Friday afternoon when Muriel arrived to sit with Gran while she went to the hairdressers, though increasingly nervous, she was quite looking forward to her night out.

'Hello, dear ...'

'Mew – you look like death!'

'Streaming cold. I'll keep away from the old lady. Sit in the kitchen. I'll be all right.'

Anthea wasn't so sure. She dashed into Minehead, fretted while the girls in the hairdressers poured, brushed and painted, and dashed home again.

'You look wonderful,' Muriel said. 'You really do! Let me see your nails. Lovely ...'

Pale pink. Working hands, but with the gloves and the handcream she'd been using all week, they were quite transformed. She'd kept looking at them on the steering-wheel as she'd driven home, and had been reminded of Beth.

'Mew – you're never going to last until midnight. You go home right now, dose yourself with aspirin and put yourself to bed.'

'I'm not going to let you down at the last minute. And what about your man? You can't let him down.'

'I shan't. And Graham is not my man ... He's just a friend. Now, bless you, Mew, but go home to bed. I'll ring Mary.'

And plead ... This late in the day she really couldn't let Graham down.

Muriel left, protesting to the last, and Anthea picked up the telephone. There was no answer from Mary, so in desperation she tried Wanda's number at Ashton Grove. No answer there either. It was four o'clock. They'd all be at work and she hadn't thought to ask Wanda for her number at the nursing home. Perhaps Wanda was working the afternoon shift that finished at seven. In which case it would be hopeless ...

Fending off the panic, she went to fetch her gloves to go and milk the house cows. She'd give it half an hour, then ring Mary again. Never again would she accept an invitation like this. Never ... It just wasn't worth the hassle. She'd put on her boots and grabbed the gloves when the phone rang. Oh

274

glory ... Glancing at her watch, she ran back through the house to answer it.

'Have I caught you at a bad moment?'

'You have rather, Beth, yes.'

And then it occurred to her that this just might be the best moment at which she could have ever hoped to be caught. She sat down, and thought fast. Either she sacrificed her pride and asked Beth, or she'd have to let Graham down. Graham, an old friend, was more important than her pride ...

'I won't keep you,' Beth said. 'It's just that I've been sorting through Lawrence's things. There's some cuff links and a gold watch you might like to keep for your grandchildren. I was wondering if you'd like to call in sometime when you're passing and collect them?'

'Yes. Thank you. I would. That's kind of you.' She crossed her fingers. 'Look Beth, please say no if you feel this is a liberty – but you did offer to look after my mother during the lambing. That'll be a week or so yet, and right now it's tonight I'm worried about. I'm supposed to be going to a dinner dance, and my Granny sitter's ill.'

I should never have said I'd go in the first place, she thought. *All this is way out of my league ...*

But Beth was asking sensible questions about what time she wanted her there, and would she like her to stay overnight, and suddenly Anthea went limp with gratitude and relief.

Well I'm damned, Beth thought. *So there is life in the sticks. Anthea does have a social life. I wonder who with ...?*

Graham put on his black overcoat and took a final look at himself in the mirror. Pulled at his scarlet satin bow tie. He was hardly a male model, but he'd do. After all, Anthea'd known him for years, so she wasn't expecting Sean Connery. He checked his flies – and his pockets for money, tickets and a handkerchief. Sneezes apart, you could never be sure that these women weren't going to burst into tears. Though, of course, there'd be none of that nonsense with Anthea. There'd be no fancy silk stuff under her evening dress either. White M and S cotton, he'd bet his frilly-fronted shirt on it.

He walked jauntily on down the passage to the kitchen,

275

locked the back door and got into the car. He was really looking forward to this evening. The tingle he felt was anticipation of a good evening in pleasant and familiar company. He wasn't at all nervous as he would have been if he'd been about to collect any other woman but Anthea.

Beth was clearly amazed when Anthea opened the door to her.

'You look wonderful ...'

One to me, Anthea thought. *Beth had only really ever seen her in her working togs.*

'All borrowed, except the shoes and the jewellery,' she said cheerfully. 'It is good of you to come – and at the last minute.'

'No problem. Is that your engagement ring?'

'It was, yes.'

Beth smiled wryly, and placed her hand beside Anthea's. Both rings were made up of large oval sapphires surrounded by diamonds. Both appeared to be exactly the same colour and size.

'Oh well,' Anthea said. 'A ring is a ring. He was never very original.' Nor, yet again, did it hurt. Where Lawrence was concerned, she really did seem to have mended. And anyway she had other things on her mind. Walking back down the hall she said, 'Gran's in her chair, but she's ready for bed and she's had her supper.'

'Hello Mrs. Kenworthy.'

Gran looked at her, and said nothing.

'I do hope she won't play you up, Beth. I warn you, she might.'

Would, for certain ... She had that look in her eye.

'Don't worry. I'll cope.'

'Help yourself to anything you want,' Anthea said, showing her around the kitchen.

'Oh, and there's a packet of photographs on the table you might like to look through. I found them last week while I was rummaging around in the loft. I'll show you your room.'

Help yourself to anything, she thought gratefully as they went upstairs. *Perhaps a sadness shared is indeed a sadness halved – though I certainly never thought to see a time I'd be pleased to have you sleeping under my roof.*

Then, as she crossed the little room to draw the curtains, she saw the lights of Graham's car coming down the drive.

Graham recognised the new red Peugeot parked by the pond and his heart all but stopped. What the bloody hell ...? Those two women had never been known even to speak to each other ...!

Dear God – he was right in the shit now.

Remembering the coffee-coloured silk underwear, the heavy cream lace, her naked body in his bed, his courage all but deserted him and it was all he could do not to turn the car round and put his foot down hard.

But he was a man, not a mouse ...

And a man of his word. So whatever storm was about to break when he rang Anthea's door bell, he was just going to have to stand there and weather it.

He looked very smart tonight, the solicitor. He'd come for her daughter, Amy knew that – though when the woman from Tivington came through the door at the bottom of the stairs, there'd been vibrations coming from the pair of them fit to shake the pictures off the walls.

'You know each other, I think,' Anthea said.

Know each other ...? Anthea my child, Amy thought – *you don't know the half of it.*

'I didn't realise you knew Beth that well,' he said, feeling decidedly shaky as he opened the car door for her.

'I didn't. It happened very fast.'

Yes, he could believe that. When Beth was involved things did tend to happen fast.

'I had no idea,' he said.

'I'm very grateful to her, Graham. My Granny-sitter had to let me down at the last minute, and if Beth hadn't rung up exactly when she did to offer me some things of Lawrence's, I wouldn't be here with you now.'

He negotiated the gateway at the end of the drive and turned down the lane to the village.

'You don't like her,' Anthea said. 'That's obvious ...'

'She's not one of my favourite clients,' he said and, opting for caution, 'Nor is she one of the most emotionally stable just now, I think.'

No thanks to you, Lang ...

'After all she's been through, I'm not surprised.'

Oh Lord, he thought miserably – but how can any man be expected to understand women? They don't speak to each other for years, and the next thing you know they're doing each other favours.

'You won't drive too fast in this machine of yours, will you?' she said. 'I'm not very good at driving or being driven at night. I'm not used to it.'

'Not a tick over sixty, I promise,' he said, and pushed Beth to the back of his mind. 'By the way, I meant to say how nice you look.'

He could think about the Beth thing later ...

'So do you. You always did look good in a dinner jacket.'

'I don't think I've ever seen you looking so nice. Maturity suits you.'

'Is that a back-handed compliment or what?' she said, laughing.

'No,' he said, confused. 'It's the truth.'

She did look nice. He'd told her that the other day, but done up in her glad rags she was a damned sight better looking than he'd realised was possible.

'Very nice ... Tell me, do you find you're more nervous about things than you used to be?'

'Do I ... This year I even got scared bringing in the sheep. The mist came down quite suddenly, as it can up on the moor, and I lost all sense of direction. I was wet through, and frozen, and then my horse went lame. I thought I knew that moor like the back of my hand, and I knew they'd find me – but I just seemed to panic.'

'Panic attacks. Loss of confidence,' he said, his own confidence soaring at the knowledge that she suffered from them as well. 'I'm certainly more nervous about some things than I used to be.'

Thank God, attractive though she was, underneath all her finery, she was still only Anthea.

*

278

Beth pushed a large log to the back of the fire and replaced the guard. So – Anthea was going out with Graham. How long had that been going on? And in what way? They'd known each other for years, so perhaps it was just a friendship. Not that Beth was interested in Graham. It was her contact with Anthea that concerned her. She loved being in this house, and she sincerely hoped Graham wouldn't say anything that would prevent her from coming here again. Or, indeed, anything that would put up new and permanent boundaries in place of those which had started to crumble so recently and so well.

'Well then ...' she said dusting off her hands as she turned to the old lady. 'Anthea says you like to watch the television. Or perhaps you'd like me to read to you?'

'Bath.'

'I'll give you a bath if you want one,' Beth said, sitting down on the edge of the sofa. 'A nice soak in warm water will do you good.'

'Bath. Out Glastonbury way. That's where they're going.'

'Oh, I thought they were going to Taunton.'

Mrs. Kenworthy stared at her. 'It'll be Bath next time, then. Any case, you couldn't lift me.'

'Oh, you'd be surprised. I've lifted people a lot heavier than you in my time.'

'Anthea baths me, not you. Cocoa.'

'With sugar?' She didn't attempt to get up. The old thing was testing her, playing her like a fish, and would now change her mind.

'Yays.' The clear green eyes were watching her. 'At bedtime.'

'Anthea told me. She's left it ready.'

Viv had said the old lady was senile, but Beth suspected she was too canny for that. As for living in a world of her own, if she did, it was probably because she was bored.

'I'll give you a bath if you like. I do know how to bath people. I used to be a nurse. I won't let you fall.'

The old lady snorted disdainfully, and turned away to look at the fire.

'All right then, you don't want a bath, and if you don't want to watch television or want me to read to you, I guess we'll just have to talk to each other. It seems a shame to waste a

279

whole evening just sitting here in silence, and it must be quite lonely for you here all day with no one to talk to while Anthea's working.'

Mrs. Kenworthy looked at her suspiciously. 'The others don't talk to me. Mazed Mary and that mop head Muriel.'

Beth laughed. 'Don't they? Why not? It's good for you to talk. If you don't talk you'll forget how to.'

'Can't talk. Had a stroke.'

'I know, but I'd say it was only a mild one.' Her speech was only a little slurred, and the movement in one side of her body, only slightly impaired. 'Actually, I'd say you were really quite fit for your age.'

The old lady narrowed her eyes and looked at her hard.

'And right now,' Beth continued, 'I think what's mostly the matter with you is that you're cross because Anthea's gone out. She does need to get out with her friends.'

The old lady looked away.

'You used to go out a lot too,' Beth said. 'I know you did. Long walks out over the moor, gathering herbs. The girls have told me. Vivien and Wanda, your granddaughters ...'

'I know who they'm are.'

'Yes, I'm sure you do. Though I think there are times when it might suit you to let people think that you don't.'

The old lady looked at her with new interest.

'What did you say you were called?'

'Beth.'

'Yays ...' and nodding the old lady watched her thoughtfully. 'You were married to Lawrence.'

'Do you want to talk about that?'

'Not unless you do. I never liked him much. Make me a cup of tea.'

'I'll make you a cup of tea if you say please. You can perfectly well say please. In fact it seems to me that you can speak quite clearly when it suits you.'

'You've got a lot of lip for a youngen.'

'You don't do so badly for an old one.'

And suddenly Mrs. Kenworthy chuckled.

'All right,' Beth said, laughing with her and patting her arm. 'I'll make you some tea.'

Grateful for an excuse to escape, she went into the kitchen.

Communicating with Mrs. Kenworthy was hard work, but it might get easier now that they seemed to have reached some sort of truce.

The goose was sleeping in its box, and the kettle, already full, had been standing on the Rayburn so that the water was quite warm. She moved it on to the hotplate and, waiting for it to come up to the boil, found a tray and set it with two of Anthea's pink willow-patterned cups and saucers.

It didn't take long to make the tea, but when she took it through to the living room Mrs. Kenworthy, hands folded in her lap and her head dropped forward, was asleep. She was a fascinating old lady, and still quite a force to be reckoned with when she chose. Yet, dressed for bed, her long white hair secured with a black velvet ribbon looked soft as silk, and although her hands were wizened, her face was as smooth, as full and unwrinkled as a child's. If you didn't know she was old it might be difficult to put an age on her, for in Granny Kenworthy, age and youth seemed to have settled on a timeless compromise.

Beth put the tray down on the small table beside her and, looking across at the photograph of Lawrence on the sideboard, she again realised how very much at home she felt in this house where he had lived, after all, for much longer than he had lived with her at Tivington.

'You've been going through his clothes,' said Mrs. Kenworthy, quietly, her voice distant. 'And he was with you.'

Stiffening, Beth turned to look at her – and meeting the gaze of the large, clear green eyes that, wide awake, seemed to be looking right through her, she suddenly felt her whole body begin to tingle.

'You can know these things for yourself, young woman. You too are a healer, but, like Wanda, you must learn how to see and how to listen. How to recognise the signs. How to trust your own judgment.'

Beth stared at her, and only when the old lady shifted her gaze to look at the photograph was she able to look away.

'That's him. Lawrence ... With my son. And there are more photographs. You must look at the photographs. He says they will be important.'

Who says ...? He says ...? Who's HE ...?

But looking at the packet Anthea had left on the table, Beth's body now seemed to be charged with energy, every hair standing on end.

'Yes – those,' the old lady said. 'They will show you what you need to know.'

'Need to know ...?'

But Mrs. Kenworthy was looking at the teapot. She looked tired and much older – and, somehow, the atmosphere in the room seemed, suddenly, to have totally changed.

'Tea,' she said, querulously, 'Is that tea?'

My God, Beth thought ... And shaken to the core, unsure what she had or had not felt or heard the old lady say, she picked up the teapot and, her hands decidedly unsteady, poured two cups of tea.

'Pah ...' said the old lady, dribbling. 'That's not cocoa!'

'No – you asked for tea.'

'I want cocoa,' she whined. 'Cocoa in a mug with violets on it.'

Even her voice had changed, and whereas before she had spoken clearly, even eloquently, her words were running into each other again.

'I want to go to bed. I want cocoa when I'm in my bed,' she said petulantly, her trembling hands slopping tea into the saucer.

I'm going mad, Beth thought, taking the cup from her – and, every bit as confused as the old lady, half lifting, half pushing, she helped her up the narrow enclosed stairs to her room above the kitchen.

'That man Anthea's with,' Mrs. Kenworthy said when Beth had helped her off with her dressing-gown and into the high mahogany bed, 'he's not for you, you know. He's going to marry Anthea.'

'Oh dear ...,' said Beth, her head spinning with the implications of that now as well.

Am I mad, she wondered – or is she ...? Or perhaps Anthea knows about Graham and me – and has told her?

But then, revived and as perky as before, Mrs. Kenworthy said, 'And who's the little boy? A happy, healthy child with fair hair. Playing with a monkey ...'

'I've no idea.'

282

'You'm do. He says his name is Simon. He says you nursed him.'

Beth was so shocked that she could only stare.

'There's no need to be scared,' the old lady said matter-of
-factly as she settled down amongst the pillows. 'Things are
as they are. Just accept it, my dear. And you can call me
Amy. I quite like you.'

If she is mad, Beth thought, as she started back down the
stairs, *then I too am quite certainly raving. Because there was
just no way that the old lady could have known about Simon.*

Yet when, minutes later, Beth returned with the mug of
cocoa, Mrs Kenworthy, seemingly diminished and looking
like any other old lady, was again fast asleep.

Beth was not at all sure what to believe – but later, sitting
by the fire, she accepted that, regardless of what white reason
decreed, she'd experienced enough in this house this evening
to know that she had to believe something. It was possible that
Lawrence had been with her when she had cleared his dressing-room. It was also possible that she sensed him with her
now as she opened the packet of photographs – but having
accepted that these things might be possible, and that his
intentions were to help, not to harm, she wasn't in any way
alarmed or frightened.

The photographs were mostly old black and white snapshots
of him as a child in Australia. The sort of snapshots that had
been missing from the suitcase in his dressing-room. While
interested and pleased to have seen them, she had no idea why
Amy – or Lawrence – should have considered them important.

Though Amy's kind of thinking seemed to have got to her,
and therefore, having replaced the photographs in the packet
and put them back on the table, she accepted that it might
simply be that the time was not yet right for her to know.

'Tired?' Graham asked. They were through Dunster. Almost
home.

'A bit. I'm usually in bed by ten,' she said, trying not to
yawn as she laughed. 'Oh sorry, Graham ... It was a lovely
evening.'

'I enjoyed it too,' he said, concentrating on the road ahead.
The rain that had started soon after they'd left Taunton had

turned to snow and was beginning to collect in soggy transparent patterns at the sides of the windscreen where the wipers couldn't reach.

But he had enjoyed the evening even more than he'd thought he would, and he'd enjoyed dancing with her – as had the other men at their table. She was as supple now as she'd been as a girl, and if she moved like that on the dance floor ... Well, he'd often heard it said that women who had good rhythm on the dance floor were good in bed, and watching her dance with that puffed-up ass of a solicitor from Bath, he'd felt a tingle of jealousy reminiscent of the days when he'd had to watch Stella dancing with other men.

Stella; legs all over the place, on or off the dance floor.

But somehow it no longer seemed to matter.

And Anthea – she was quite different. You'd know where you were with Anthea. No acrobatics or silly underwear. Just gentle companionship, give and take – and a friendly, round little body.

'You've gone very quiet,' she said. 'Don't go to sleep.'

'No, I'm all right,' he said, glancing at her to smile. 'Just thinking.'

Thinking, in fact, that being with her had had the strangest effect on him. Christ, though – what about Beth ... If Anthea found out, it would really mess up his chances of any more outings like this. Perhaps he should tell her, and wipe the slate clean. Or maybe he should keep quiet and ask Beth to do the same ... Neither option was particularly appealing. He needed time to think about this one. And if he decided to have a word with Beth, probate was through on Lawrence's estate so he would have to meet her again soon in any case.

Anthea, however, would be seeing her at breakfast tomorrow morning ...

'You'll have company for breakfast tomorrow, then,' he said, keeping his eyes on the road.

'I shan't,' said Anthea. 'I'll have to be out milking the house cows. I've got a lot to do tomorrow morning.'

Well, that was something. They wouldn't have much time to talk, so he'd just have to hope, then make sure he talked to Beth before she did. God though – with women you could never be sure about anything.

284

And now they were almost home. When they got to the farm he'd quite like to kiss Anthea goodnight. Just a light kiss to say thank you for a nice evening – but he couldn't kiss her with Beth there.

'We'll time it about right by the look of it,' Anthea said. 'I do believe this snow is starting to pitch.'

'Yes ...' Large flakes of it were scattering past the beams of Alouette's headlights and in places the hedges and the road were already quite white.

Then, seeing a gateway ahead, he checked his rear view mirror and slowed down. He'd stop for a second and give her a quick kiss in the gateway.

'Yes,' he said as he pulled in, 'and this time it looks like it could be for real.'

'G'day boss. Christ, and it's gonna be a warm one. The wife asked me to call on my way back for breakfast. See if you've got any early orders.'

'Nothing that can't wait.' Tillotson checked the list beside him on the table. 'You can take these letters and make sure they leave with Bern on this morning's plane. Oh, and when your missus gets in, I'll have her confirm my flight to London.'

'You're going then,' Sam said, picking up the post.

'Yup. And this time it's for certain.'

'Reckon you're fit enough?'

Tillotson pushed the rest of his scrambled eggs to the side of his plate. He used to like fried eggs and steak for breakfast. It was one of his housekeeper's specialities, but it was some months since he'd been able to stomach that.

'I'll have to be, Sam. I've got things to do in England. People to see.'

'What if Mattheson comes back while you're away?'

'He won't. The bastard's gone cold on us. I reckon there's every chance we can warm him up again, but if he doesn't contact us this week I'll work on him when I get back.'

'Fair dinkum. You're the boss. Even so, Big Maisie'll be after you, leaving those eggs.'

'Big Maisie can go to hell.'

Sam grinned and put on his hat. 'You're a brave bastard,

you are. In your shoes I'd be damned nigh as frightened of Maisie as I'd be about that bloody disease that's eating you.'

'Yeah ... Well, when your missus gets in she'd better confirm that flight and I'd better catch it while I've still got the strength to get up the steps of the plane.'

'It'll be cooler in England.'

'Too right. Do me a favour ... As you go out, turn on the fan?'

'I'm glad you slept well,' Anthea said, waving the knife distractedly as she looked around for the bread. 'That's Viv's room and she's always complaining the mattress is lumpy. Bread ... Where did I put the bread?'

'Behind you, on the fridge,' said Beth seated at the kitchen table.

'So it is. Look, do help yourself ... Sorry – did you say tea or coffee?'

She was in a real tizzy this morning and had slept hardly at all despite the time at which she'd got to bed. And now she realised, when she'd come in from the yard, that she'd forgotten to take off her boots. All round the kitchen where she'd walked there were puddles of brown melting slush. There was a good four inches of snow out there today, its blueish white light reflecting back into the kitchen – and according to the weatherman there'd be more in the coming week. After breakfast she must break out some bales of hay for the sheep in the bottom paddock ...

She sliced the bread into what turned out to be doorsteps and, muttering about it, squashed the slices in the wire griddle, opened the Rayburn's hotplate and left them to toast. 'I don't think there's too much snow in the lanes. All the same, it might be best if you wait here until the council come through with the snowplough. Where's the teapot ...? And, I still can't remember if you said tea of coffee?'

'Coffee. Anthea, I could be getting the breakfast. You've got enough to do.'

'You can take up Mum's tray if you like. I looked in on her earlier. She seems very pleased with herself this morning. I hope she was good.'

'Yes – she was fine.'

'She certainly seems to have enjoyed you being here. She says you'll be living here while I'm lambing.'

'Does she ...? Well, I will if you like.'

Anthea made the coffee, sat down, then remembering the toast, leapt up again to turn the griddle.

'Actually Beth, to be honest, that might be the answer to a maiden's prayer. I don't know who else I can ask ... She seems to think she is going to teach you about her sort of healing. Anyway, you can soon put a stop to that.'

'No, I'd be interested to learn.'

Anthea sat down again and looked at her. She wasn't feeling up to any of this. Not this morning ...

It wasn't so much a busy early morning after a late, sleepless night, as that Graham had kissed her. She was middle-aged, grey-haired and a lot plumper that she used to be, so the dear Lord alone knew what he saw in her – but in the lane, in a snowstorm, he had pulled into a gateway and had given her a kiss.

It was years since she'd been kissed. What was more, she wasn't sure she had ever been kissed quite like that. Not with so much feeling ...

Beth helped the old lady to stand so that she could pull up her thick woollen stockings for her.

'She enjoyed herself then,' Amy said.

'She said she did. That's it – hold on to the bed.'

'Ah, well ... You'm cassen keep the snow from falling.'

I don't doubt it, Beth thought, *though I must have a quiet word with Graham.* He's just the sort of gentle innocent who bears his soul and confesses all. This one, he must keep to himself, because Anthea wouldn't be able to take it. In many ways she was as defenceless as one of her newly hatched geese – and it just would not do for her to hear that the woman who'd taken her husband had already had a go at what was probably her first man friend in years.

'Keep still, love. I can't find your suspenders. That's a nasty old bruise you've got on your thigh.'

'Took a tumble. Needs arnica to draw it. And you could do with wild oat. Wild oat help you find your new life's path. I'll teach you the herbs, and a lot more besides. Then, when I'm gone, when the time comes, you can pass it on to Wanda. She'll be interested one day, and the knowledge shouldn't be wasted. I'll show you the plants I brought from my medicine garden at Cloutsham – and I'll teach 'ee the wild ones. Where to find 'en ... Arnica from the meadows below the moor, or in the sandy ground behind Bossington, and wild oats from the fields in the valley. A few drops of tincture of arnica in cold water used as a cold compress works wonders on bruises. Or you can make 'en up as an ointment. Tiz toxic, so you never uses it on skin that's broken ... You must get a notebook. Write these things down.'

I will talk to Graham, Beth thought. *I must. For my sake as well as Anthea's. I need access to this house, and I need this friendship with Amy. I want to learn the things she has to teach.*

'There you are. Now, let's straighten your petticoat so you're comfy and I'll help you downstairs. Pity the weather isn't better or I could have helped you take a stroll in the garden. You need to keep your legs moving. Does anyone ever massage them for you?'

'No. You can. Yays ... I'll teach you all the herbs and plants. Everything I knows – but I want you to get me some of those new-fangled stockings like the young ones wear. I cannot abide these pinching suspenders any longer.'

'You mean you want tights?'

'If that's what they're called, then that's what I want. You get them for me, and I'll pay you. I've got my pension.'

Martin stopped to watch a flock of squabbling gulls that were dipping and weaving, swooping in to threaten attack on other gulls that were paddling along the edge of the tide.

Vivien, hands deep in the pockets of her long green Loden, tucked her nose deeper into her scarf and kept walking. Why Martin had demanded that they walk along Weston-Super-Mare beach on a day like this, she couldn't imagine. The flat sea, a lighter brown than the sand, was the colour of weak, greasy coffee – and she felt slightly queasy this morning as it was.

And, God, it was cold. The strong breeze was blowing straight in from the north, and apart from themselves and the gulls there was no other living thing crazy enough to be anywhere near the beach or the promenade.

Beside a large grey pebble in its own pool of water, she stopped and turned to look back at him; a solitary, dark-haired figure in a dark grey overcoat way back down the beach. Even at that distance he looked what he was; an executive from the city. He could be from any city in the western world – and although, last night, she'd again shared his bed, he was just any man to her now.

Feeling precisely nothing, she watched him start to walk across the expanse of sand towards her. There was no longer any tingle of anticipation at his approach, nor any smile on her lips waiting to greet him. Everything she had to say to him had been said, and tomorrow he'd be leaving for Brussels.

She looked down at her boots and, waiting for him to catch up, kicked a deep empty hole in the sand.

'We might as well go back, then,' he said.

And walking apart from him, she watched her feet retrace her own footsteps that led back across the beach to the slipway from which they had started.

The snowplough had cleared the lanes by midday, and Beth drove back to Tivington. As she got out of the car she heard the phone ringing in the house and ran through the fresh snow in the yard to unlock the front door.

'Graham! I'm so glad you phoned. I need to talk to you.'

'And I you. I've received the letters of probate and everything is in the process of being transferred to the beneficiaries, though I do need a couple of signatures. Do you think you could spare me half an hour this afternoon if I come over?'

'Well, yes ... Fine. I didn't think you worked on Saturday afternoons.'

'I don't usually. However,' he said, sounding strained, 'this isn't only about work – as you've probably guessed. I'd rather not say any more over the telephone.'

'Fine,' she said. 'I'll see you later. Any time you like. I'm not planning to go anywhere in this weather.'

A good coating of snow still lay over the hedges and fields as Graham drove along the main Minehead road, and it looked quite thick out over Dunkery Beacon and on North Hill behind Selworthy. It was a far more wintry day than the first time he'd driven this road to see her at New Year. And today he was far more nervous. He'd never got himself into anything like this situation before – and to make matters worse, that kiss he'd given Anthea had turned into something considerably more than friendly.

He groaned out loud, and, turning up the drive to Tivington Heights, hoped that Beth wouldn't keep him standing on the doorstep. Once, when he was a kid, standing on a dentist's doorstep, he'd been so nervous that he'd wet his pants. He remembered it well – and walking across the yard to the door, he remembered how he'd felt at school when, once or twice, he'd been summoned to see the headmaster.

'Come in,' Beth said. 'What's the main road like?'

'Clear. It'll be fine unless it freezes tonight.'

He tucked his briefcase under his arm, and rubbing his hands together stepped into the hall. Noticed her fake fur coat hanging on the rack of hooks under the stairs by the cloak-room door; remembered how it had held the warm, tantalizingly musky smell of her perfume.

'Come into the sitting-room.'

'How's the car going?'

He'd have quite liked a pee, but he'd look such a wimp if he asked.

'Fine. I'm really pleased with it.'

He followed her down the hall, making a determined effort not to look at her bottom. She was wearing what was almost certainly a rather expensive pair of well-cut brown-striped trousers. Talk about ferrets fighting in a bag, though rather than fighting, her ferrets appeared to be mingling affectionately.

In the sitting-room he sat down on the sofa and put his briefcase on the coffee table. Anxious to get started, he took out the papers and undid his fountain pen.

'One or two papers to sign, that's all.'

She knelt on the carpet, and he watched her abundance of hair fall around her face as she leant forward to write her name. Elspeth Seligman. For him there was still a certain music to it. And when she stood up, moved across the room to sit by the hissing gas coals, lay back in the chair, slid one leg elegantly across the other ... He was alarmed to realise how strongly he was still attracted to her – and suddenly the room seemed rather warm.

'Fine ...' she said, watching as he ran his finger around the inside of his collar. 'Well, now that's out of the way, you can tell me the real reason you're here.'

'Ah ... Well, it's just that I think perhaps I owe you an apology. Or at least some sort of explanation ...'

'Do you? I can't imagine why.'

Oh God, she was going to enjoy this. She'd squeeze his balls, laugh as he squealed, then she'd probably burst into tears.

'You know damned well why,' he said, his nervousness flaring into anger. 'I didn't expect to see you at Luccombe last night, and well you know it.'

'You're my solicitor, Graham, but I didn't think I had to account to you for my every move – any more than I expect you to account to me for yours.'

'Oh for Christ's sake ... You know what I mean.'

'No, I'm afraid I don't.'

'Whatever you may think, I am not in the habit of dining out with half the women in the West Country. I would not have had you walk into that room to find me done up like a penguin. About to take another woman out for the evening ... Not any woman, let alone Anthea. If I'd known, if I'd even suspected you'd be there, I'd have at least had the courtesy to warn you.'

'Only half the women in the West Country ...?'

Yet again, she was laughing at him.

'I was going to say,' he said, gritting his teeth, 'that I've known Anthea for ever. That she's a friend. That until I bumped into her in Minehead a couple of weeks back, I haven't seen her for years. But having met her in Minehead she gave me some riding clothes for my daughter. As a form of payment for the clothes I asked her to come to that dinner dance with me. I also thought she needed a night out.'

'Graham,' she said, patiently, 'you don't have to justify yourself to me. We went to bed together. It was wonderful

291

while it lasted, but I think we both knew that to make more of it than that would have been a mistake.'

Wonderful while it lasted ...? Was it? Oh, good ... Yes, indeed it had been. Bloody marvellous ...

'You're right,' he said firmly, recovering his wits. He hadn't come here to dwell on past pleasures. He was here to make sure he could forget them. 'It was. But it would have been. A mistake – that is ...'

'I enjoyed it,' she said, smiling.

It really was very warm in here ...

'Thank you ...' And suddenly, shyly, he laughed and met her huge, lovely brown eyes. 'Yes. So did I.'

'All the same, I think it might be best if we could forget it happened.'

'Yes,' he said, relieved. 'Yes, I agree.'

'Please don't mention it to Anthea.'

'Good God, no. In fact, that's why I'm here. To ask you the same thing. She's a friend. A long-standing family friend. It could be very embarrassing for both of us – for you and for me.'

'She won't be hearing it from me I assure you, because, strange as it might sound, I value her friendship. I need her friendship, for all sorts of reasons.'

'Look Beth, what I told you is true. Before Lawrence met you I used to see a lot of both him and Anthea, but since then, until I bumped into her the other day I honestly hadn't spoken to her since the day of your wedding.'

'And now it's you who's getting married.'

'No, no.' Then, suddenly, he realised what she was thinking. Realised that she had completely misunderstood him. 'Anthea ...? Good Lord, no. Heavens, no!'

'Why not?'

This woman was unbelievable. 'Well – we're friends,' he said. 'Just friends. We have been for ages.'

'Well it does help if you like the person you marry, and you're ideally suited.'

She'd cornered him, damn it ... What exactly did he want from Anthea?

'Well ... I suppose it's just possible that at some time in the future it may become ... Well ... A relationship.'

'Tell me something, Graham – are we still friends, you and me?'

'Yes of course.'

'Fine. So, as your friend, I'll tell you. With Anthea, I suspect it will be marriage or nothing.'

Actually, she was probably right. And he would like to get married again – to the right woman.

'There'd be no marriage if she knew about us,' she said. 'In fact, if she ever got to hear about you and me, I very much doubt that you would even keep her friendship.'

'I see that. Anyway, she doesn't need to know. She's been through enough.'

'Perhaps more than you realise.'

Oh ...? Oh well, there may well be things that Anthea as yet had to tell him, but whatever they were, it wouldn't make any difference. He'd known her too long and too well.

'And I need to keep her friendship as much as you do,' Beth said. 'I feel far more at home in this community since I've met Anthea, and suddenly I can even think about the future.'

'You'll be staying around here I hope,' he said, all animosity gone.

'For the foreseeable future, anyway.'

And now it was his turn to tease her.

'What, not even a holiday? Not even a couple of months in Australia?'

She laughed. 'No way. But when the weather picks up I would like to visit some friends in Scotland.' She nodded at his briefcase. 'Anyway, now things are settled, you'd better send me a bill.'

'I'm afraid so. Oh, rates for mates. It won't be so bad.'

He stood up, and as she walked with him to the door and on down the hall, he decided that he would ask her the question she'd put in his mind.

'If I did ask Anthea to marry me, do you think there's any chance she might accept?'

'Well – she'd be a fool to refuse you.'

'Do you really think so?' he asked, surprised.

'Of course. You're lovely.'

'Oh ...'

An image of her clad in that coffee-and-cream silky underwear flashed through his mind – then, looking away, he banished it forever. Placing his hand on her arm he gave it an affectionate squeeze. She was absolutely terrifying. Far too hot, too brazen, too smart for him to handle – but all the same, she was a wonderful woman, and he was extremely flattered.

'Thank you,' he said. 'For everything ... Thank you very much.'

When he had gone she sat down at Lawrie's desk to write a letter to Liz. A long-overdue letter full of news and questions about the family. She was ready to write to Liz now. And she was ready to travel to Scotland. Seeing Liz, talking to her, would be, she sensed, the next necessary step on the road forward. In order to move forward to a life she now both wanted and needed, she did seem to have this need to go back over the years and relive them; to decide what to keep and what to leave behind her. She had discovered the benefits of this regression therapy – if that's what it was – while sorting through his dressing-room.

Also, she needed to talk. And Liz was an old, unshockable friend who already knew so much about her. It would be good to see Liz again – and to get to know young Danny, her Godson, who was only a matter of months younger than her own child would have been.

Her child – and Ben's ... Though that too, was a wound which had now healed – and she had reached the far side of the grey marsh, and was reading, following the signposts. So strongly could she sense her life opening up that the feeling was actually physical. Once more the world was full of colour, full of sensations to be savoured.

And out in the yard the next morning, clearing a path from the porch to the barn, this occurred to her again as she relished the extreme white and the cold of the thin covering of snow, the grain of the wood on the barn door, the feel of the shovel in her hands, the biting wind on her cheeks, the feel of sweat as it trickled down between her breasts. Even the ache in her back from the unaccustomed hard physical work was a pleasure.

That Wanda and Robin arrived as she was finishing was an added bonus. Unexpected visitors, like phone calls were no longer an intrusion. She welcomed the contact.

'Well now,' she called, laughing as she leant on the shovel and watched them get out of the car. 'Isn't that just fine? How did you two great husky young things manage to time it so well?'

'Husky?' Wanda said. 'Robin? He's all ribs.'

'That,' Robin said, 'is because I'm an artist.'

'Balls,' said Wanda. 'You're a merely a talented draughts person.'

'With balls,' he insisted.

'Oh, certainly with balls,' she agreed.

Laughing, Beth put an arm around each of them.

'Come in and have some coffee. I was just about to make some.'

Arm in arm and positively glowing, they leant against the worktop by the toaster.

'We're on our way to see Wanda's mother,' Robin said. 'To tell her Wanda's moving in with me, and that we're going to get married.'

'She'll be gutted about the moving in bit,' said Wanda, 'but that's just too bad.'

'Oh I don't know,' Beth said. 'You might be surprised.'

'Why? Oh yes ... There's a man, isn't there! What's she up to? Who is he – do you know?'

'Yes – but that's for her to tell you.'

'Oh come on, Beth ... Don't be a mean ...! Is he nice? Is it serious?'

'Wanda, I am not going to tell you. I didn't tell her your secrets, and I'm not telling you hers. Anyway – there are times when we old ladies must stick together. And by the way, have you two said anything to Vivien about your arrangements yet?'

'No,' Robin said. 'But I must. I do intend to.'

They are so strong, so easy, so open with their love, the young, she thought, and watching them together, she did feel a little sorry for Vivien. Still, Vivien was nothing if not resilient ...

Remembering Lawrie she felt a wave of nostalgia – but for Wanda and Robin she was delighted. She'd had her love. A love that had lasted for seven short years, but it had been stronger and more meaningful than many people experienced

295

in a lifetime – and warmed by the knowledge, she felt wise, experienced, and was suddenly aware of being older.

'If you want sugar, there's a new packet in the utility,' she said.

They were so damned young. So energetic. If they wanted sugar, they could fetch it.

There must be, Viv thought as she drove slowly back into Bristol in a queue of traffic, very few more depressing errands in life than having to drop a failed love at an airport on a cold, dark winter Sunday evening, and then return home to an empty house.

'My God, Viv you're a hard wall to climb,' Martin had said as they'd said goodbye. 'Anyway – you've got my phone number.'

She wouldn't be using it. He knew that as well as she did. But he'd get over this, and so would she. For both of them the sensation of emptiness would only be temporary.

Anyway, her bedroom and the kitchen could do with redecorating, and what with that and her job and her friends and her family, she had plenty to fill her life.

Chapter Fourteen

That he should talk to Vivien niggled at the back of Robin's conscience all through the following week. After what they had meant to each other – or at least, she to him; he had never been quite sure what he had meant to her – it wouldn't be right to tell her about Wanda on the telephone or in a letter.

The rest of Wanda's family had taken the news surprisingly well, but for all their sake's, he must find an evening and arrange to meet Vivien soon. He'd written Wanda's shifts at the nursing home in his desk diary; mornings this week, afternoons next. It would be easier to see Vivien the week after when Wanda was down to work evenings.

He liked Wanda working the morning shift best. He got out of bed at six-thirty when she did, so that he was sitting at his desk by half past seven and was able to get in a good hour and a half of uninterrupted work before the damned telephone was likely to start ringing. The plans for his nursing home would be completed by the deadline, no problem. Content and settled in himself, he was working well.

His office suddenly seemed darker, and closing the diary he glanced up at the window. It had started to snow, and seriously. Big smoky flakes of the stuff were falling steadily against the lighter yellowish grey of the sky.

'Where've you come from then, guv? Somewhere sunny by the look of it,' the cabby said as they queued with other traffic to go down into the underpass leaving Heathrow, the windscreen wipers thumping back and forth, dealing with the snow.

'Australia,' Tillotson replied, not wanting to talk. He felt damned ill and the flight had exhausted him. He just wanted to get to an hotel and crash into bed.

The widow still wasn't answering his letters and as Archibald had said that she knew the ranches were up for sale, she'd probably given him up for dead. Which, practically, he was. He certainly needed to rest up in London over the weekend. Couldn't possibly face travelling down to the West Country before Monday.

'Too bad you didn't bring the weather with you,' said the driver. 'They're saying we're in for a few days of this white stuff before we see any sun.'

At lunchtime, Graham phoned. 'Are you all right out there in the snow?'

'It's a nuisance, but yes, we're managing,' Anthea said. 'The wind's getting up and the lights are flickering. I'm just hoping we shan't have a power cut or this afternoon I'll be doing the milking by hand. Mother, of course, is over the moon. She's been going on about this for weeks.'

Graham laughed. 'Are you managing to feed the animals?'

'Yes, Graham,' she said, patiently, smiling to herself. She was touched by his concern, but hill-country farmers knew about animals and snow and how to survive in it. The feed bins in the barns and the cupboards in the kitchen had been well stocked since before Christmas, and all the sheep were in the fields closest to the farm.

'I keep thinking about you up there on your own. I thought I might come over and give you a hand.'

'No, Graham. You won't get here. The snow's already a foot thick in the lanes. And it's drifting.'

'They'll have the snowploughs out in the morning. I can leave the car in the village and walk up the hill.'

The man's mad, she thought. He'd already been over one afternoon during the week to return the clothes Trish couldn't use, and had stayed on all evening. But it was rather nice to know he was concerned.

'All right,' she said. 'We'll decide in the morning. Give me a ring, and if necessary I'll drive over and collect you in the four-track.'

*

298

It was at lunchtimes that Vivien missed Martin most. Having worked alone in her office all morning she had enjoyed getting out to meet him for lunch.

Her secretary was out, and watching the falling snow from her window high above the white roofs and brown-slushed streets of the city, she finished the carton of apple and cottage cheese that she'd bought from the sandwich boy who came round every morning with a basket, and dropped the carton in the bin.

Then she sat down at her desk to patch up her lipstick. Coral ... It was a little too red and it dried her lips. She could go out in the snow and buy a new one – but she couldn't be bothered. The waistband of her skirt was starting to cut into her too – and she'd paid a fortune for this suit ... And she was still hungry. Why was she so restless ...?

The weather, probably. She hated snow. Had hated it even as a child when, some winters, they'd been snowed in at the farm for days on end, unable to get down even as far as the village.

She did miss Martin. And, in a way, she also missed Robin. Though, mostly, for both of them, it was a good miss. The miss of a too tight waistband when you'd taken off the skirt.

Well, at least with Martin gone there wouldn't be any more regular lunches and dinners. She'd soon lose the weight from her middle.

Robin heard the front door open. 'Is that you ...?'

'No, it's the bogey lady. How many other women have got keys to this flat?'

Viv had ... But fortunately it was Wanda, muffled in a donkey jacket and scarlet scarf, who appeared in his office doorway. 'You're home nice and early.'

'I'm going out again in a minute. Shopping. It's your birthday on Sunday, or had you forgotten?'

'I'm trying.'

She laughed. 'No, don't get up. I only came back for my cheque book.'

'Listen, Wanda, don't you go wasting your money on me,' he said, holding on to her hand as, having gone behind his chair to

299

hug him, she pressed her cold cheek against his. 'Just because you inherited some money from your father ... You save it.'

'It's nice to have some money, but I do miss him. I'd much rather have him than the money. But – I am going to get you a birthday present.' She hugged him tightly and stood straight. 'And I'm getting my hair cut.'

'Again?'

'The last of the black, then if you like, I'll start growing it.'

'No, don't. Don't, Zebra – I like your hair as it is.'

He had loved Viv's long fair hair. In retrospect, it was probably the best thing about her. But Wanda was different. Very different, and that was the way he liked it. He loved every bit of Wanda exactly as she was.

'Oh, and I almost forgot. I've got a surprise for you. I've got two days off. We can stay in bed all weekend. That is, if you're up to it – you poor old thing.' She'd started to walk away but he grabbed at her coat. Laughing, she pulled away. 'I'll be back by five at the latest.'

It also seemed strange to be going straight home after work instead of meeting Martin in the wine bar – though it was wonderful to know that she had the whole evening ahead of her to do whatever she wanted.

Cooking herself a simple meal of scrambled eggs, she eased her thumb around inside her waistband and thought about Robin and his staple diet of cauliflower cheese. He didn't carry an ounce of surplus flesh, any more than had Martin. Though neither did Martin have Robin's liking for chocolate biscuits and liquorice wheels.

She did feel a bit guilty about Robin ... She'd asked only for some space, but it had been weeks and she hadn't even bothered to call him. And on Sunday it was his birthday ...

This time last year they hadn't long been going round together and he'd taken her to Cornwall for a winter weekend away. The weather had been warm and sunny, and he'd made her take off her tights and join him for a paddle in the sea. The water was freezing. She'd yelled, and he'd laughed at her. Then he'd made her sit on the warm rocks while he dried her feet with his hankie. Quite biblical, really ... She'd realised then that he was in love with her and, as best she

300

could, had allowed herself to love him in return. She was very fond of him, even now.

While she ate the scrambled eggs she glanced through the evening paper. There was nothing going on in Bristol worth going out for and nothing much on television, so she might as well get on with decorating her bedroom. She'd begun to take a real interest in the house again now that she knew she'd be staying here. And now that she had some time to herself, she'd renew her subscription at the leisure centre. Would go swimming some evenings, play squash, go back to aerobics. The possibilities were limitless. It was so good to be free!

However, surely she and Robin could at least continue to be friends ...?

On her way to bed Beth went into his dressing-room. Stood in the middle of the room, lost in thought. Outside the wind was howling, whipping up the snow into drifts around the house and the barns, but this was a snug little room, and being directly above the boiler in the utility it was one of the warmest in the house. If she bought a fitted cover and some cushions for the divan, and perhaps a small coloured television, it would make a perfect sitting room for her, especially in winter. She felt particularly close to him in this room. And there would also be space for a small desk. She would need to buy herself a desk when Viv had taken his. A desk on which to make plans for her old people's rest home – in the event of which she could keep this as her private sitting room and office. Of course, Robin was the chap to talk to about converting this house and the outbuildings – and she'd have to talk to the local Health Services.

If she was serious about running a rest home ...

The more she thought about it, the more it seemed that she very well might be ...

'How are you doing?' Graham asked.

'Okay. It was a bit wild up here last night. We lost the phones and our electric, but we had the hurricane lamps. There are some spectacular drifts in the yard.'

'I'm coming over.'

301

'No, Graham – you won't get here. I can't even get the truck out of the shed.'

'I'll walk.'

'Graham – it's miles.'

'It's not that far across the fields.'

He had some snow shoes in the garage. Strange things like wood and string tennis racquets which they'd inherited from the previous owners of the house and, having wrapped up well, he collected them, a thumbstick, a thermos of sweetened coffee and a compass. Then he locked the house, and set off down the back garden, over the fence and across the field – making, as far as he could, a direct line over Doverhay for the camp site just south of West Luccombe. He'd calculated that it should be a tramp of about a mile, and that if, thereafter, he continued on a south easterly course, skirted Horner, made for the centre of Luccombe village, then cut up through the pine woods behind Wychanger, it should only be another two miles at most.

The sky was overcast and it was hard going through the snow, but he enjoyed a good walk – and today he was a man with a mission. A knight on the way to rescue a lady friend. Not that Anthea was in need of rescue, but he hadn't anything else to do with his Saturday, and on a farm, this weather, she'd be glad of an extra pair of hands to help with the animals.

It was only when, three hours after setting out, he came out of the woods above Wychanger and, leaning on his thumbstick, wiped the sweat from his forehead and looked down at the farm, that he began to doubt he was now actually fit to feed anything, himself included. Sitting all day every day at a desk, he hadn't realised he'd become so unfit. He ached all over, his socks were wet with melted snow and he was fairly sure that his heels were blistered. Right now, what he really wanted was a large whisky, a whacking great sandwich followed by a hot bath and a long sleep on a nice soft sofa in front of a fire.

And down in the yard he could see Anthea hard at work shovelling snow away from the outhouses ... Puffing out his cheeks, he eased his aching back and started down across the fields. He'd come to help – so help he would have to.

302

'Lord,' she said as he all but collapsed against the stable door. 'You look all in. You'd best come indoors and sit down for a bit. Anyway, it's lunchtime. I've made a stew.'

What a woman ... In the kitchen he unzipped his waxed cotton jacket, pulled out a chair from under the table and, allowing his legs to give under him, could not prevent the groan that escaped from what felt like his entire body as he sat down.

'I see Percy's indoors again. Didn't your mother's potion work?'

'I think it helped, but I'm on to the stuff the vet gave me now. Poor old Perce – and it's much too cold for you out there at the moment, isn't it ... What you need just now,' she said, crouching beside the gander and stroking his neck, 'is a warm bed and some tender loving care.'

Don't we all, Graham thought enviously.

Dear God, man – but what now? Is the mouse jealous of a goose?

The stew smelt wonderful, and he was famished. Couldn't remember when anything had tasted quite so good. After lunch he sat by the fire for a while and talked to the old lady. She seemed in fine fettle, and as she slurred her words some, having to listen carefully kept him awake. Full of fresh air and good food, it would have been so easy to sit there and nod off ...

It would also have been decidedly wimpish – because Anthea was full of beans, and as soon as she had washed up, she put on her boots and her coat and was once more ready for the off. Gallantly he insisted on dragging himself out of the chair and went out with her.

All afternoon they worked, shovelling snow away from the shed doors, mucking out cow sheds, feeding chickens, ducks, geese, cats and the collie dog that lived in a straw igloo in the barn. Finally, while she milked the two house cows, he collected eggs, and together, around tea time as it was beginning to get dark, they loaded the truck with hay and he drove it slowly around the home paddocks while she stood in the back and broke open the bales for the sheep.

'Tea?' she asked, as they went back indoors.

'Got any whisky?' He was so exhausted he hardly knew

how to get himself as far as the kitchen – and only now did it occur to him that, somehow, as yet, he still had to get himself home.

'I'll drive you in the truck after supper,' Anthea said. 'They'll have snowploughed the lanes by now, but the way you've worked, you can't go home on an empty stomach.'

God only knew how he'd kept going as long as he had ... And to his shame, while she prepared the supper, he fell dead asleep.

Later, much later, after supper when Anthea had put the old lady to bed, she too at last sat down. Sank into her mother's chair, sighed, rolled her eyes, and laughed.

'You must be exhausted,' he said, though since his sleep and the whisky he felt rather better. 'I don't know how you do it.'

'I'm used to it.'

'Have another whisky.'

'If I do, I shan't be driving you home.' She looked longingly at the bottle. 'Would you mind staying the night?'

'No, not at all. I can help you again tomorrow.' He reached for the bottle and splashed whisky into her glass. He seemed to have been reaching for that bottle all evening ... He must buy her some more. A couple of bottles of good malt. As he'd once had to do for the other wife – her successor.

'You are naughty ... Gran likes a nip of whisky now and again, but you got her quite tiddly,' Anthea said, chuckling.

'Never mind, it'll do her good. This is whisky weather.'

'I suppose it is,' she said, and yawning, she slipped off her house shoes and wriggled deeper into the chair. 'Oh Graham, you couldn't put another log on the fire, could you?'

It was an honour to be asked to tend the family fire in this neck of the woods. He stood up and stepped over Percy, the collie dog and a tabby cat, all of which in one way or another had wheedled their way indoors and curled up happily together were taking up most of the hearth.

'They shouldn't really be in here,' she said, not stirring herself to evict them any more than she had to evict him. And for what remained of the evening they all snoozed together in front of the television.

He slept in Vivien's room, went out cold the second his head touched the lavender scented pillow. When he woke the next morning the tabby cat had crept upstairs and was curled into a ball by his feet. He wondered if Anthea'd be able to lend him a razor – and if so, whether it would have belonged to Lawrence.

It was still early, and he thought of her asleep in the room along the landing. Wearing pyjamas ... Or perhaps a long cotton nightie. Whatever she wore in bed it would be world's away from the awful silk nothings that some women favoured – and he remembered what Beth had said. That with Anthea it would be marriage or nothing.

No point in creeping along the landing, then ...

Marriage though ... That was a hell of a big step ...

There had been no snow since Friday afternoon and by Sunday morning the main roads out of Bristol were clear and running with muddy water. Having joined the M5 on the westbound carriage way, Viv put her foot down, and just after ten o'clock, exceeding the motorway speed limit by just over twenty miles an hour, she noticed the cloud begin to thin as, gradually, the sun appeared.

A day of thaw – and of reconciliation. She glanced at the birthday cake and the neatly wrapped present on the seat beside her and, smiling to herself, she reached up to open the sun roof. It was good to be getting out of the city for a day. And it would have been churlish to ignore his birthday.

'You're beautiful,' Robin said, watching her breasts move under her tee shirt as she brushed her hair. 'Your hair is beautiful too. Stop brushing it and come back to bed.'

Wanda put the brush down, and sprang at him. Landed half on top of him.

'Ouch ...!'

Then she was rummaging about under the duvet and, rolling around in a bundle, laughing, they were pretending to fight. 'You're a brazen hussy, you are,' he said, drawing up his knees to defend himself. 'What are you ...!'

'A brazen hussy.'

'You are. Thank God – you are,' he said as she stopped

struggling, and holding her down he pulled the duvet up over their heads.

She came off the motorway at the Taunton junction, crawled through the numerous sets of traffic lights – all of which, infuriatingly, seemed to turn red as she approached – drove up through the town, and on up the hill towards Trull. Now, on a road she'd driven so often with him, she realised that her heart was beating a little faster. She was really looking forward to seeing him.

She turned down the lane to the Manor, and well before she turned into its grounds, through the snow-topped leafless hedges, she could see his car parked in its usual place on the forecourt below the snow-topped stone balustrade.

Dear Rob ... Such a creature of habit. He really did love her – and she had treated him so badly. Perhaps, this morning, she could make up for some of that.

Wondering if he was still in bed, she parked her car beside his, collected the cake and the present, and ran up the steps. The big double doors were unlocked, so she let herself in, marched across the high spacious entrance hall, rang the bell of his flat – and waited.

He was still in bed ... She rang the bell again – and as she waited she looked at the bunch of keys hooked on her finger. She still had his door key ... There was a chance, of course, that he was out. Had gone for a walk, or to buy a newspaper and his weekend supply of liquorice. In which case she might as well let herself in and wait for him.

She slid the key into the Yale, turned it, and as she stepped into the hall – some female shuffled sleepily out of his bedroom.

Wanda ...?

Shit – it was too ...!

Wanda – bare-legged, short hair on end, and wrapped in his striped towelling dressing-gown ... They stared at each other, both seemingly rooted to the floor.

'Rob!' Wanda called, recovering faster than Viv did, and sinking her hands defensively into the dressing-gown's pockets. 'You'd better get up. It's Viv ...'

'Jesus Christ ... Bloody hell!'

306

And as she and Wanda continued to stare at each other, he appeared, wound up in the duvet.

'I see you still expect your women to answer the door for you.' She held up the key. 'Sorry ...'

'Viv – I'm sorry. I was going to tell you.'

'Sure ...' she said, watching him put a protective arm around Wanda. 'And who are you going to fuck next? My mother? Or perhaps you'd rather fuck Beth?'

Wanda looked as if she was about to burst into tears – of course. And suddenly Viv felt exceedingly sick.

'I was going to tell you,' he said, his eyes hard. 'I wanted to meet you.'

'That's nice. Well – it seems that I've saved you a phone call. My God, Wanda, you didn't waste much time. I never knew you could move so fast. In fact, I seem to have under-estimated you in all sorts of ways.'

'You'd better come in,' Robin said firmly, taking control of the situation, and leaving Wanda he walked towards her. 'Come in, and let me explain.'

'Forget it,' she said, and remembering that she was holding the cake and his present, she thrust it at him and struggled with the key ring to remove his key. 'Here, little sister, you've got his cock and the rest of him – have his key.' She tossed the key at her, turned on her heel and walked out, slamming the door behind her.

'You'd better go after her,' Wanda said, looking at him.

'And say what? It's her own bloody fault for walking in here.'

'Even so ...'

'It's no good going after her in that state. I'll talk to her when she's cooled down.' He looked at the cake. 'Oh God ...'

'I love you,' said Wanda, scared.

'I love you too,' he said, and put the cake and the present on hall table so that he could take her in his arms. 'I love you very much. I'm so sorry – it's absolutely my fault. I should have talked to her long before now.'

Walking back across the entrance hall seemed to take forever. At every step she expected, dreaded the sound of the door opening as he chased after her. What a fool she had looked! The shame of it ... And the terrible things she had said!

Driving away through the grounds she could hardly see for tears. Tears of anger and shame, rather than disappointment. God, she had made such a fool of herself. And supposing he pulled on some trousers, jumped into his car, tried to follow her ... She flexed her hand, thought fast, kept checking her rear-view mirror – and at the bottom of Trull hill she turned left on to the Wellington road instead of right, which would have taken her back through town. He'd expect her to go back through town ...

After about a mile, she forked right and joined a lane from where, having crossed the railway lines at the Silk Mills crossing, she could double back to the motorway. She was crying in earnest now – and she realised that it was the first time she had cried properly since Lawrence had died.

Thinking about him, rather than about herself, Robin or Wanda, somewhere out in the country between the railway crossing and the housing estate at the edge of town, she pulled up on the snow-covered verge, turned off the engine, and allowed herself to howl.

After a while, when she had calmed down, she began to think about her other relationships – those with Robin and with Wanda, which, although for different reasons, had been every bit as unsuccessful as that with her father. She and Wanda were sisters – yet strangers. And Wanda and Robin were quite clearly very much an item already.

To be honest – she'd never felt like that with him or with Martin.

Perhaps she wasn't capable of that sort of love. She'd never go to pieces about any man the way Wanda would if he dumped her. Or the way Mum has over Dad ...

Nor had any man ever broken her own heart the way Dad did. Perhaps no other man ever would. Anyway, love was a pain. A trial when you'd got it, and when you lost it, it hurt like hell. *So – who needs it ...?* There was always so much else to think about, so much else on offer – and men were a bit like buses. Another one came along soon enough – if you could be bothered to catch it.

Then, looking at the clock on the dashboard, she thought about how Dad had dumped Mum, and about Beth, also having to live without him. Mum, of course, was well over it now ...

But the sun was shining on the snow, she had the whole of Sunday ahead of her, was already halfway to Tivington – and she hadn't spoken to Beth in ages.

In addition to which, since that week she'd spent with Beth after Dad died, she'd discovered that her stepmother was a good and a wise listener.

She blew her nose, and checking the rear-view mirror, she started the engine and pulled back on to the road to drive to a phone box. This time, no way was she going to arrive unannounced. She'd had enough shocks for one morning.

'Darling, how could I have told you?' Beth said.

'Sorry, no. I know you couldn't. I'm not blaming you. I made a right ass of myself and I'm thrashing about to try and make me feel better. Actually, I suppose they're rather well suited. And I really did say some terrible things.'

'They'll forgive you. Given time. People in love are always magnanimous.'

Viv groaned. 'I even asked Robin if he fancied you – though I didn't put it as politely as that.'

'Forget it, Viv,' Beth said, and remembering her encounter with Graham. 'We all make fools of ourselves at times, believe me ...'

'Thank God I've got you to talk to. Who do you tell your troubles to these days?' And smiling, looking at her sideways, 'Mum ...? Lord ... So much has changed since Dad died. For all of us.'

They watched the Sunday lunchtime weather forecast, and as it predicted frost, Vivien left to drive back to Bristol in mid-afternoon. Further snow was promised for Monday, and when Beth drew back her bedroom curtains the next morning it was snowing hard.

'You country postmen never cease to amaze me. You get here whatever the weather,' she said when he arrived in his red van barely an hour later than usual.

'Ah well, tiz like this – we like to look after our friends. You all right, are you? Got everything you need?'

The letter he brought was from Liz. A long letter in reply to hers, and full of news about the family and their corner of Scotland. As Beth had anticipated, delighted that contact had been renewed, Liz suggested that she should visit for as long as she liked, and as soon as possible.

Bloody weather, bloody journey ... The points were frozen, it was snowing again, and the train had been late leaving Paddington. Tillotson would happily have paid through the nose to travel down to Somerset by taxi but none of the drivers he'd spoken to had been prepared to risk the roads, particularly over somewhere they called Salisbury Plain. He surveyed the blank, shut-down expressions of his fellow passengers scattered through the carriage, and resigned himself to another hour of stuffy, window-steamed incarceration.

Although England was tiny, the West Country was further from London than he'd considered, and when he reached Taunton, so they'd told him, he'd still have another hour's travel by road. This Exmoor place where Lawrie had lived seemed about as far from civilisation as the Australian outback.

Anyway, he was glad to be here and to have got this far. Several times these past few months he'd doubted he'd make it. Nor was he particularly worried that the woman wasn't expecting him. He'd realised by now that if she'd known he was coming she'd probably have avoided the meeting. It wasn't going to be easy ... But if she wasn't at home, he'd visit the other wife and they could yarn about Anthony. Whatever happened, he'd see Lawrie's house and the places he'd talked about.

So – this was England. As much as he could see of it – which was pretty much sod all even though he kept wiping clear a patch of the misted window. It was the first time he'd ventured west of Bayswater, and all he could see beyond the steamy window were railway embankments and a blizzard of snow.

Where was the England of the picture books that people

310

kept on their coffee tables – the lush green fields, the thatched cottages, the ancient churches, the country villages, the scaled down to child-size landscapes?

It seemed strange to be at these Monday morning meetings without Martin seated amongst the others at the table.

'Why were we late with the Nor Val consignment, Vivien?'

'The ship had engine trouble and arrived a day late, Mr. Hall. We couldn't get the papers from customs over the New Year holiday.'

'Oh yes, of course.'

She'd told him that weeks ago, the old fool ... She'd begun to hate this chewing of fat at Monday meetings. What had started as meetings to plan ahead, seemed increasingly to have become post mortems to point fingers and air grievances, of which, amongst the senior managerial staff, now she'd come to know them better, there seemed to be too damned many. Was there one of these disgruntled, post-menopausal men who was happy in his job? She had been so pleased to be promoted ... Now she'd begun to wonder what the hell it was about. Every one of them seemed bitter and twisted about something. No wonder Thane had wanted some young blood to dilute this regular dose of Monday gall.

They were a prime example of the archetypal committee that set out to design the horse and came up with the camel. And suddenly, looking at the dusty files strewn across the table, the fusty men in their seats, she knew that she was fed up with files, men in business suits, ships that arrived late or were delayed on one side of the world when she needed them to be somewhere else. And she was fed up with the ships that did get to the ports where she needed them, then being further hassled by dockers enjoying an extended holiday, or a tea break that amounted to a sit-in. Strikes, engine trouble, oil leakages, damaged propellers, containers shifting about the decks in high seas, holds filled with rotting grain about to burst into flames – she'd heard it all. And she was tired of tapping information into computers and shuffling papers that sent containers full of goodies to Montreal, Cairo and Timbuctoo. She wanted to touch the goodies, see the ships, smell the ports.

311

What she supposed she must need was a holiday – quite literally in order to re-create and freshen her outlook. Perhaps she'd go skiing. Get some clean mountain air. Or get right away to somewhere completely different, like the Philippines or Hong Kong. She had some money from Dad, and she was due for at least four weeks leave.

After the meeting she'd talk to Thane about it. If the meeting ever ended ... If the yellow-toothed whingers in grey suits were ever going to shut up long enough to allow it to do so.

The station was damned nigh as deserted as the outback when the train arrived at Taunton. He'd wondered if this was how England always was beyond London, or whether the bloody poms always shut up shop and went home when it snowed. The man in the ticket office told him, in a slow soft drawl that sounded as if he was talking in his sleep, that there were no taxis or drivers to be had this morning – though eventually he'd found three of the rare species holed up in the parcels' office sharing a thermos of soup. He'd asked to go to Tivington, and they'd looked at him as if there were kangaroos loose in his top paddock.

An hour later, seated in the back of a taxi as it headed west along roads no wider than lanes and bordered in places by high curling drifts, he began to see why. In desperation he'd doubled the fare they'd quoted, and the youngest of them, Terry, whose wife had just given up work to have their first baby, had phoned the police for a road report, and had agreed to take him. It had stopped snowing now, but the sky was still dark and threatening, and although Tillotson was becoming aware that the countryside he was travelling through was, with its wooded hills, gentle white valleys and the occasional glimpse of the grey Bristol Channel, as beautiful as any he'd ever seen anywhere, he would have liked to think that there was a warm house and a friendly face waiting at the end of the journey. Getting down here was beginning to seem every bit as exhausting as the long flight from Sydney.

'Nearly there, squire. This is Dunster,' Terry said, pointing. 'See the castle?'

Beneath the glowering sky, across a flat stretch of snow-

312

covered meadow, he saw bare-leafed woods and, amongst the snow covered trees, the turreted sandstone castle perched on the edge of a hill.

'The Indians used to come and play polo on that flat ground. That's Dunster polo lawns, that is.'

Dunster polo lawns, where Lawrie had said he'd met Beth at a summer show ...

'I've heard of it,' Tillotson said, aware of a tingle of anticipation.

'My Granddad remembers the Indians – Maharajahs, flunkies, ponies, the lot. Thick with history round here, it is,' said Terry. 'Looks like one of those snow scenes in those globes kids play with, dunnit? A fairy castle in a book. Do kids read fairy stories in Australia?'

'Yes,' Tillotson said gruffly.

Kids read fairy stories – and damned fool men dreamed dreams ... All this would have seemed magical to him even without its gilding of snow, because here was where lived the people who were the closest to family that he was ever likely to know.

But, driving through the snow, they'd hardly seen a car since they'd left the town of Taunton, and that too had added to the magic and the feeling of unreality. They seemed to be driving along a track which led to the end of the world, so that this, his last ambition, would be fulfilled in a Never Never of pure, ethereal white.

Having turned off the main road they were now driving down the wide main street of Dunster, past a snow-covered medieval yarn market. The deserted street was bordered on both sides by ancient tiny picturesque shops and houses, and on the hill directly ahead, much closer now so that it seemed to overpower the village, was the fairy castle, apparently carved from ice. Its gates, its drive and its walls that faced the village were white with snow – while below in the village the snow in the road was brown, rutted and dirty.

Contaminated ... And he was feeling bloody crook again ...

In a village such as this many of the residents would have surnames known here for hundreds of years. He thought about them, their lives, their passions – and acutely aware of the disease he was carrying, and of the havoc it could wreak in

313

such a small community, he began to feel increasingly light-headed, as if he might faint.

And he thought about the widow.

Wondered how much Lawrie had told her about his illness ...

'Norman, that castle,' said Terry, swinging right at the end of the street into a much narrower road where the houses were smaller and even older. 'On your right there's a Norman church – and see the stocks, there in the wall, where they used to stone the bad guys ... Beats me, though. I mean, they pelted 'em with bad eggs and rotten tomatoes, so why build stocks into the wall? Why give 'em shelter? If they've done something anti-social, I say leave the buggers out in all weathers and let 'em suffer as much as possible.'

Tillotson closed his eyes, unsure whether he was merely about to faint, or whether, this time, he was actually dying. Bloody ignominious, to chuck in your chips in the back of a taxi. Was this how it felt to die ...?. He was so God damned tired. Throbbing with exhaustion – and past caring ...

How innocent, upright young Terry would cheer if he knew. How surely he would aim his rotten eggs ...

'There's an ancient pack horse bridge down there,' Terry said, continuing to relish his role as tour guide. 'I'd take you down and show you if it weren't for the snow.'

Thank God for the snow ...

'And just you wait ... If we can get along this lane to the right, I'll show you a real sight for sore eyes. Yes ... Good, the ploughs have done this one, and tiz tucked in under the hill and the woods. I didn't think it would be too bad.'

He seemed to remember that they drove through another strung out village, and that under their covering of snow, some of the cottage roofs were thatched. Just after the village there was a pub. At that moment he'd have gladly given both the ranches away in exchange for a large brandy. He'd broken into a cold sweat, and once again his guts were giving him hell. Then he might even have blacked out for a bit, because when he came to Terry was saying, 'There ... Now didn't I promise you a treat? That's Porlock Vale. What d'you think of that for a view, then?'

A wide flat valley stretched out below them, on either side

314

of which were snow-covered hills broken by woods. The valley hamlets looked like lumpy icing, and in the distance, the white plane rolled away to a flat silver sea.

'Right ...' Tillotson agreed. He hadn't the strength to muster any of the enthusiasm the view deserved or the lad expected, and he knew he had disappointed him.

'How long are you going to be? D'you want me to wait for you?' Terry asked, addressing him via the driver's mirror.

'I'll tell you when we get there.'

If the widow was in, he just hoped he'd be able to summon the strength to talk to her.

'Are you okay, squire?' the lad asked anxiously, again looking into the mirror.

'Dinkum.' He knew damned well he didn't look it. Not only was he sweating like a pig, he was probably white as an albino roo.

'We're here,' Terry said. 'If I can get up the drive I'll take you to the door.'

The car, a big heavy Volvo with chains on the tyres, got up the drive, no worries. On two sides of the yard there were barns – and as, in one of them, there was a small car and there were no tyre prints in the fresh snow, he guessed that the widow was at home.

'What d'you reckon, then? D'you want me to wait?' Terry asked, turning to him.

'No, you get on lad. Get home to your missus in case it starts to snow again.'

'Watch it, then,' Terry said, concerned. 'And keep an eye on the weather if you want to get out of here.'

'Right on ...'

But there were barns. If the worst came to the worst he could always kip down in the barn. He'd slept in worse places, and if he was going to chuck in his chips ... He felt too crook now to care where he did it.

'Are you sure you're all right ...? I can wait back in the village for an hour or two.'

Tillotson shook his head. 'You get back to your missus in case she starts with the kid.'

'It isn't due till April,' said Terry, looking worried. He was barely more than a kid himself.

'Good on ya. Well that's all right then,' said Tillotson, taking out his wallet to pay him.

He wanted young Terry gone. The widow was more likely to let him in, hear what he had to say if he'd cut off his line of retreat. He just hoped he was up to taking a fair crack at saying it.

He'd bloody well have to be ...

'Thanks, squire.'

'No, lad, thank you. No other fucker would drive me. And here ...' He took out another fifty quid note. 'Give that to your missus for the kid.'

The new, clean life inside her ... Sired by a strong innocent lad ... He was a nice-looking lad. It would be a good-looking foal.

'Hey, man – are you sure?'

Certain. Terry had done well for him this morning. He was doing his bit to colour the planet, was Terry – and compared to him, Tillotson felt profaned and inadequate. A passenger on the planet now, in more ways than one – and he hadn't even been much of a passenger for the youth who, having seen a strange Australian fall off the train in a snowstorm, had probably been hoping for some interesting conversation and some tales of adventure.

April, he thought as he struggled out of the car with his hat and his flight bag. *I might see this April, but I shan't see another.*

He stood in the snow, steadied himself against the car and, turning up the collar of his sheepskin coat, he looked at the house. The house where Lawrie had lived ... Months of planning, months of imagining, and at last he was here.

Then, in the process of devouring every detail, at one of the upstairs window's, his eyes met those of a red-haired woman.

She recognised the wide brimmed hat, the long cadaverous face, immediately – but just could not believe what her eyes were showing her. The taxi turned, drove away, and when the doorbell rang, she automatically went down to answer it. She was so shocked that only much later, thinking back, did it occur to her that she could have ignored it. Could have pretended to be out, and left him standing there in the snow.

316

'How dare you come here!'

'Well, that's a start. You obviously know who I am.'

Then his knees seemed to give under him and he leant heavily against the doorpost. He looked half dead ... His face was so haggard, so thin, that the skin, an unhealthy yellow beneath the tan, was clinging to its bones. And his eyes ... She saw the lids droop – then too much of the whites that were also too yellow.

He was still on his feet, hadn't quite passed out cold, but she was going to have to get him indoors or he might well die on her doorstep. From the look of him the cancer had probably got to his liver and she doubted he had long. Burning with anger but remembering Lawrie, this time she allowed the nurse in her, the training, to win. Even so, she could not bring herself to touch him, and without a word she stood aside and pointed down the hall.

'Thanks ...' he said.

He tackled the doorstep with difficulty, dropped his luggage, and somehow got himself as far as the sitting room where he collapsed into an armchair. As he undid his bulky full-length sheepskin and stretched out his legs she saw just how much weight he had lost since she'd seen him in London. He was little more than a walking skeleton.

'Sorry ...' he said, producing a hip flask and some tablets from his pocket. 'It's all right. I'll try not to die on you.'

'Why the hell are you here? You shouldn't be travelling in that state.'

'I wanted to see you. Drink ...?' He offered the flask.

'No thank you.'

'Wise sheila.'

'You can't take tablets with that,' she said grudgingly. 'I'll get you some water.'

'No thanks. Fishes fuck in water,' and putting the tablets in his mouth, he took a good swig from the flask and swallowed. Watching his scrawny neck, the sliding Adam's apple, she wanted to put her hands around it, and squeeze. Then he let out his breath, bared his teeth and wiped his mouth with the back of his hand.

She could do with a drink herself. Feeling trapped, invaded, and experiencing a confusion of hatred, revulsion and pity for

317

the living skeleton slumped in the chair, aware that she seemed to be standing in the eye of a storm about which she could do nothing but live through, she went over to the table and poured herself a brandy. Replacing the decanter on the tray, she glanced at him. The colour was returning to his cheeks.

'Why the hell have you come here?'

'Ah, come on, lady. You can't be that surprised to see me. I wrote you enough letters.'

'You don't think I bothered to read them ...?'

Though she'd never dreamt he'd come here to her house ...

'It wasn't too bright if you didn't – since, in a manner of speaking, I pay your wages.' He looked round the room. 'Like it or not, lady – I helped to pay for some of this.'

'Tillotson,' she said, her voice shaking with fury, 'I don't give a damn about the ranches or what you do with them as long as this is the first and the last time I have to meet you.'

'It probably will be. And I haven't just come about the ranches. I wanted to meet you. Lawrie's wife. And I wanted to see where he lived.'

She had lifted her glass to drink from it, but her hand stopped in midair and she stared at him.

'Are you crazy?'

'Probably. A little,' he said, wiping his forehead with a large spotted handkerchief.

'All right – you want to talk business. We'll talk business. I believe we may have a buyer for the ranches, but before anyone signs anything I wanted to talk to you. Those ranches pay you a damned good premium – but more important than that, Lawrie grew up on one of them. Lived there for half of his life. He cared about them and the business – and he went on caring even after he'd come to England. Whatever you may think, what we now have out there represents a lifetime of his work as well as mine, and I personally feel it's a great pity that everything we achieved is about to be sold.' And suddenly he too was angry. 'Christ – Lawrie had two wives and two daughters. Isn't one of you sufficiently interested in something that meant so much to him even to bother yourselves to at least come out for a visit and take a look? I'll pay the bloody air fares!'

318

'He didn't want us near Australia. He was a different man in Australia.'

'Ah, so that's it. So he did tell you. Good.'

'No, he didn't tell me. He didn't need to. I saw you together in London. Your so-called business meeting in November the year before last.' He looked confused now, as well as ill, so she said, 'I saw you coming out of some dive in Duke Street. You were all over each other. I pieced it all together from there. God – you disgust me.'

'So that's how you knew who I was.'

She snorted. 'It wouldn't have been too difficult. Not too many pedlars turn up around here carrying Quantas flight bags.'

She was far too angry to intend this to be funny – but he laughed.

'What did he tell you, as a matter of interest? How much do you know?'

'I understand from my solicitor that according to the terms of Lawrie's will you'll have to sell the ranches. The stock – everything,' she said, wanting to keep this to business.

'Unfortunately, yes. Unless you're going to come over and learn how to run the set-up. But I wasn't referring to the business.' He got up to take off his coat, coughed and patted his pockets. 'D'you mind if I smoke?'

With a cough like that? But for all she cared he could burst into flames. She nodded at the ashtray on the mantlepiece.

'He didn't want us anywhere near Australia, and certainly not the ranches. He definitely didn't want his daughters anywhere near you. He made that very obvious in the will.'

'The will was partly my idea.'

'I thought it might be, but no matter whose idea it was, he signed the thing.'

'He did, and gladly. But those girls are adults now,' he said, exhaling a cloud of smoke as he snapped shut the silver storm lighter. 'They know the facts of life.'

'There are facts, Tillotson – and there are facts. Your facts are different. Those girls don't need to know what their father was.'

'So who's going to tell them? Not me – and there's no one left out there who'd know what Lawrie was, or what we were

319

to each other. You could come out, any one of you. If nothing else, at least come for a holiday and let me show you the ranches before it's too late.'

'Did he come out? Like hell he did!'

'No, but he did suggest you might come for a holiday if he died before I did.'

'Oh did he.'

'Yes, lady, he did.'

'Don't talk rubbish, Tillotson,' she said, less certain, remembering what Graham had said a long time ago.

'It's as true as I'm sitting here. And if he didn't come back to visit, it was because he was scared. You'll have heard of Anthony Kenworthy? His death shook Lawrie to the core. He blamed himself. Hated himself. Other than with Anthony he'd always felt himself to be something of a misfit, so when he came over here to see the family he saw his last chance to get himself straight. He married Anthony's sister, and years later when that hadn't sorted him out, he married you. I can see why. You're all woman – and a right little fire cracker ... Just the type to make him all man the way men are supposed to be. But you can't change nature. You can't change the instincts you're born with. He tried. God, how he tried. That's why he stayed away from Australia. He was scared to come back, scared he might want to stay on, be himself again, instead of the man he'd worked so hard to become.'

'Because of you,' she said, less venomously, realising how much the talking was exhausting him. And although she didn't want to hear any of it, she knew that what he was saying was true.

'No – because of Anthea and the daughters. And later he wouldn't come back because of you. He loved you. Truly loved you ... Believe me, he felt more for you than he ever felt for any of us. That was quite hard for me to take – but I accepted it. I had no choice. But he lived the last few years of his life at a crossroads fighting his nature, not able to go on, not wanting to turn back.'

'Yes. And the real reason he never came back to Australia was that you were there. But you couldn't leave it at that. You came here, got at him in London instead.'

'I loved him. As you did. I can't help what I am.'

'You revolt me,' she said again, turning away.

'Do I? You surprise me. You, a woman of the world, a nurse?'

'Yes, me, a woman of the world. I also am as I am, and the things you men do to each other ... How could you get at him again when he'd tried so hard to be normal?'

'What's normal? All we're arguing about is that your normal happens to be different from mine. And,' he added quietly, 'it takes two. The only difference between Lawrie and I was that, for me, there was never anyone else but him. After he left Australia, there were others of course, eventually. But they didn't mean anything. They were just an outlet for loneliness. You could close your eyes and pretend they were who you wanted them to be. In your whole God damned life, can you honestly say you have you never done that?'

She thought of Graham ... And beginning, though much against her will, to identify with what Tillotson was saying, she got up and went over to the window.

'There were others for Lawrie. After that November. After you ... You might have been the first, but there were others afterwards,' she said, to hurt him. 'Men – not just women.'

It was starting to snow again, but across the valley she could see the roofs of Anthea's farm – and in a way, this meeting with Tillotson wasn't so unlike her first meeting with Anthea.

'I don't doubt it,' Tillotson said. 'He couldn't deny his nature for ever, and since he never loved me as I loved him, to put it bluntly, Australia would be a fair way to come for a fuck.'

'My God, you're a crude bastard, Tillotson ... And knowing all this, you still seriously want me, want his daughters to visit the ranches?' she said, turning to look at him.

'Why not? I'm proud of what we achieved out there – and so was he. Hell, lady, and there's nobody working there now who knows about him, other than that he's the other half of the money. The boss from England. They don't even know about me. All that was over twenty years ago – and subsequently, I saw the havoc it caused with Anthony Kenworthy. The lads on the ranch think I'm dying of cancer.'

321

'Well ... Aren't you ...?'

'Of a sort.' He watched her face. 'Didn't he tell you? No ... Obviously not. Lady, amongst other complications, I have Kaposi's Sarcoma. I am dying of AIDS.'

She sat down on the window seat and, staring at him, felt her face turn to stone. Maybe at the back of her mind, she had wondered – though she had never considered it seriously.

'I thought he would have told you.'

He too seemed shocked.

'Well he didn't'

'I see,' he said, reaching for another cigarette. 'Well, that is what I've got. D'you want one of these?'

She realised she was staring at his cigarette. 'No. Yes ...' She got up to fetch it. She hadn't smoked a cigarette in ten years. He lit it for her, and she went over to refill her glass. 'What's in the flask? Brandy?' Because like it or not, suddenly she was in this with him.

'Whisky.'

'Neat?'

He nodded. She half filled a tumbler from a bottle on the tray. Took it across to him. Both of them were thinking fast, playing for time. AIDS had been little more than a scare, a frightening rumour at the time she'd given up nursing to marry Lawrie. She'd read about it of course, but she'd never knowingly looked it in the eyes. This – Wayne Tillotson – was what it looked like.

And it was possible that she too was infected. To distance herself from him, she went back to sit on the window seat. Sweet Jesus – and what about Graham? Who was probably, by now, sleeping with Anthea ...?

'I thought you knew,' he said. 'I thought he'd have told you. Is there any chance that you ...?'

'Probably.'

'Right on, then. Well, I'd better tell you as much as I know. I had a routine blood test in December a year ago, and it was negative. In the summer, around January and February, I started to feel bloody awful. I didn't make too much of it. I thought it was the heat. But things didn't improve, and since none of us get younger, when I came over to see Lawrie in what was your spring, we discussed what should be done with

322

the business if it ever got to the point where I wanted to retire or couldn't carry on. Soon after I got back to Australia I heard that several people I knew in Sydney had tested positive for HIV and that one of them had already developed the full-blown thing. By early June he was dead. By then I'd noticed some dark marks on my legs, so I went back to the clinic. It was the real thing for me too – and I came to London to tell Lawrie. That was the beginning of July. You can work it back from there.'

She continued to stare at him.

'I am sorry ... I did think he'd have told you.'

'Sorry ...! Sorry?' But gradually the details he'd given her were sinking in – and having worked back over the dates, she checked them again to be certain. 'Did you sleep with him in July?'

'No, of course not. By then I knew I was infected.'

'Are you sure? For God's sake, tell me if you did.'

'No I didn't, I swear it.'

'Then he was clear. Absolutely.' Even if Lawrie had slept with him in April, before Morocco. Even if Lawrie had picked up something in Morocco ... 'He had a full medical in July. He said it was for some insurance thing. They tested him for just about everything, HIV included. He told me that.' Had made a joke of it. 'He was negative.'

'Good. Lucky Lawrie. But since then? You said there were others.'

'Not around here. He promised he wouldn't. Anyway, around here everyone thought he was the man he tried to be. He wouldn't have risked blowing the illusion.'

The cigarette tasted filthy. She didn't need it now, and she opened the window to throw it away.

'What about you? This bloody disease is everywhere. Did he go away anywhere after his test in July?'

'No. Anyway, it wouldn't change things for me if he had.'

'Why not?'

'It wouldn't.' And then, perhaps because Tillotson too had been hurt by Lawrie, perhaps because despite how she felt about this man, he was dying and she was in the clear, she said, 'He hadn't touched me for months. Not since a holiday we had in May.' The pretty boys by the swimming pool ...

She closed her eyes against the memory. God, no wonder this pernicious disease spread ... 'It seems he preferred your kind of love to mine in the end,' she said, looking out of the window.

'Perhaps he was just making sure you were safe. You, above all of us – because you were the one person with whom he so nearly achieved what he wanted.'

'He was my husband. He shouldn't have needed any of you.'

'Lady,' he said gently, 'he was born needing us. It wasn't any shortcoming of yours.'

'I loved him,' she said, staring into her glass. 'I really loved him.'

'Yeah ... So did I. So did Anthony Kenworthy. Lawrie was a loveable sort of bastard.'

'Anyway ...'

'What about blood? I'm sorry, but I have to ask you. It's unlikely, but if you had an open wound and he was infected, bled on you.'

'No,' she said, thinking back. He was a baby about cutting himself, seeing his own blood. If he'd cut himself anywhere near her, she'd have remembered. 'No.'

Tillotson nodded. 'It's sad that you won't come to Australia. It did mean a lot to him, particularly when he was a young man. I thought I might manage to persuade you.'

Her mouth was furred with the aftertaste of nicotine and she took a drink of her brandy and let it stay in her mouth. It was snowing hard now, and the farm at Luccombe had been obliterated by a white mist.

'Tell me about Anthony.'

'Beautiful – but tortured. He topped himself, there was no doubt about that, regardless of what they put on the death certificate. His contract with us was almost up and his old man expected him home to run the farm here in England. Anthony couldn't face that. Nor could he face staying in Oz. What he really couldn't face, of course, was himself.'

She looked down at her glass. Remembered the young smiling face in the photograph. A face full of life, full of fun.

'It was what you did to him out there that he couldn't face.'

'He was his own man, Anthony. Most of us can accept that

we're different. Some actively revel in it, of course, which does the rest of us a great disservice, particularly since this AIDS thing started. But it was worse back in the sixties. I've seen blokes stripped, beaten and strung up by their feet. That's what they did to Anthony ... And coming here, driving down this morning I began to understand how it must have been here as well. In Anthony's day, there can't have been much room for a black sheep in this little outback either.'

'There still isn't.'

'Lawrie and Anto – they were in love, you know. It was a love just as strong as that between a man and a woman. Perhaps it was stronger – because all the odds were against them, so it had to be. If Anthony had lived, if they had moved into the city ... I think it would have worked. You would never have met him. Perhaps you'd have preferred it that way?'

'No,' she said looking at him.

'Good. I'm glad. So tell me, is it so much worse for a woman if her husband goes off with a man instead of another woman?'

'Of course it is.'

'Why? Surely it exonerates you completely? It isn't just you he's abandoned, it's the entire female sex – simply because it's impossible to abandon one's own nature. Or perhaps, more than hurt or disgusted – you're ashamed. Why? A lot more men than most people realise are bisexual at some point in their lives. So what *are* you ashamed of?'

'The same thing he was, I suppose. The same thing Anthony was ashamed of. Shame itself. The shame of being involved in something different. Aren't you ashamed?'

'No. I know what I am, and I accept it. If other people judge me by standards that are different, that's their problem. Beyond that, I don't need to shout my sexuality from the roof tops any more than you shout about yours. And I loathe guys who do. You don't have to be a wowser to want to keep that private.'

'A wowser?'

'A prude. Sex is the strongest instinct of nature because it's directly connected to survival. And in order to survive most of us also need companionship, love and a certain amount of privacy. But it's the love that's important. He did love you, you know.'

Yes ... But, in his way, he had also cared for Tillotson. So, like it or not, she probably had as much in common with this man as she had with Anthea. Like it or not, despite what she felt about him, there was a bond between them.

'Lawrie did tell me he had a medical in July,' he said. 'I knew he was clear then, though I did wonder about the accident. And after Anthony ... He didn't seem the sort who'd top himself either, so I wasn't sure. I suppose it was an accident ...?'

'It was an accident,' she said. 'The horse spooked and he was using some lethal drug you use in Australia.'

Even if he was ill; had, by the remotest chance been infected by someone else since July, his death had definitely been an accident. That was the one thing in all this of which she could be certain.

'Which drug?'

'Etorphine hydrochloride.'

'Jesus bloody Christ ... We haven't used that in years, it's far too dangerous for the lads to mess about with. Jesus ... There are far better sedatives to use for horses now. Drugs that are kinder to their nervous systems. If he'd come out to Australia occasionally, he'd have known that. And why did he want a race horse in England? There's no money in racing here. Where did he get the damned thing from anyway? What was its breeding?'

'I've no idea. He seemed to think it was something special. All I know is that it came from Ireland. I gave all its papers to my solicitor.'

'If he wanted a race horse that much he could have had one of ours. I flew a couple over to an owner in France only last week. Lovely animals – Roosville and Sarah's Son, two of our best. They'll be racing next season, so if you hear they're running, put a few quid on them.'

'I don't bet. Life itself is enough of a gamble for me.'

He laughed. 'Ah, come on lady. You've got it all ahead of you yet.'

Maybe she had. She was healthy. Because Lawrie hadn't touched her ... Now she understood why – and being so fit,

326

looking at Tillotson, she actually felt guilty.

'It's snowing hard again. Is the taxi coming back for you?'

'I'll call one if I can use your phone. I've got a room booked at a hotel in Minehead. It can't be far. If I can I'd like to meet Anthea Seligman before I go back to London. And may be Lawrie's daughters. D'you think that'll be possible?'

'Perhaps.'

He was now so exhausted that he could hardly speak, and he was sweating. Would die soon, perhaps in a matter of weeks ... She, though, was going to live. And he had loved Lawrie, whom she also had loved. A tumultuous triad that she would never understand, but which, nevertheless, was a fact that could not be changed.

'You'd better stay here tonight,' she said. 'You won't get a taxi to come out for you in this weather.'

He closed his eyes and seemed to crumple into the chair. 'Thank you ... I'll move to the hotel tomorrow.'

She had rarely seen anyone look so sick, even on wards in hospices for the dying.

'Look, Tillotson – God knows why I'm doing this, but I'll look after you for as long as necessary. I'll even arrange a meeting with Anthea – but there is a condition.'

He opened his eyes and looked at her.

'You must promise not to talk to Anthea as openly as you've talked to me.'

'She doesn't know about Lawrie? What about Anthony?'

'She knows some of it. I'm not sure how much. I'm not sure how much she wants to know, so be careful.'

'You know, when Lawrie died, it was good to know that his wives and his family were in the world somewhere. It was all that kept me going. I'd have loved to have had a family. Kids ...'

Dear God, she thought. Could be she had even more in common with this man than she had with Anthea.

'I suppose the closest we've got to posterity, you and me, are Lawrie's daughters,' he said. 'So that's where my cut of the ranches is going when I shoot through, in case you were wondering.'

'I wasn't – but thank you ... Not a word to them about

327

Lawrie or about Anthony either. They know nothing, and that's the way it's to stay.'

'Right on,' he said, closing his eyes and resting his head against the back of the chair. 'Right on ... You have my word.'

Chapter Fifteen

Amy watched them from her chair by the fire, returning
Beth's smile whenever she looked at her from across the
room. It was warmer this week, the snow had melted, the sun
was shining, and sparrows were chittering and fighting as they
flew in and out of the eaves above the living room window.
Spring is coming, Amy thought, watching the group seated
around the big table eating lunch.

But in a way it was like Christmas. Anthea and Vivien were
here, but now, so too were Beth, Graham and Anthony's
friend, the man from Australia. Only Wanda and her Robin
were missing – and the pattern had now almost settled in its
new, rightful form.

Maybe Anthony and Lawrence were also here. She would
have expected them to be. But they had passed from this world
and, as Amy had been brought more firmly back into it since
her new found friendship with Beth, every day it was becoming more difficult for her to tell.

'How long will it take them to drive to Heathrow?' asked
Anthea, up to her elbows in soap suds.

Graham dried the antique china dinner plate carefully and
put it on the kitchen table. 'About three and a half, four hours,
I suppose.'

'Quite a drive, especially for Beth if she's coming back on
her own. What did you think of him?'

'He seemed a nice enough chap. A little unusual ...'

'Yes ...' she said thoughtfully, pausing to look out of the
window. 'He's certainly that.'

329

Frankly, he didn't want to say it, but he'd thought the bloke was damned odd. For a start, the way he'd raved about the dinner service, the delicacy of the china. Though Anthea had taken a great deal of trouble with the table and the meal, and as he'd hardly eaten anything, perhaps he'd been trying to make up for it by going on at length about the china. After all, there was no law about a man being interested in antique china, even if it wasn't what you'd expect of a shrewd, slightly rough, wealthy Australian horse breeder. Though, somehow, other than business, he couldn't see how the chap could have had too much in common with Lawrence, or with Anthea's brother, as far as he remembered him.

'He's very ill, of course, poor man,' Anthea said. 'Still, that's cancer for you, Lord help us all. Beth seems to think he's riddled with it. I must say, I'm terrified of cancer.'

'I think we all are. He's got a damned nasty cough.'

'He's still a ball of fire, all the same. Beth and I took him round the farm in the truck on Friday, and up over the moor as far as the beacon. He asked all sorts of questions. I think he really enjoyed it.'

'I'm sure he did,' Graham said, accepting another plate for drying.

'There was still quite a bit of snow lying in the gulleys up over the top.'

'I expect there was. It'll take a week or so for the drifts to go,' he said, his thoughts still with Tillotson. His height, the broad hands and shoulders, the long sheepskin coat, the elegant cut of his tweed jacket and twill trousers that hung off him since he'd lost so much weight, somehow just did not fit with the bright silk handkerchief, the chunky gold cuff links, the gold bracelet and the too large signet ring.

'Beth's looked after him for over a week. She's been very good to him,' Anthea said.

'She has.'

'Well, he was a good friend to Lawrence. And to Anthony.'

'Yes.'

'He kept calling the truck the ute.' She laughed. 'I got to quite like his accent and his funny way of talking.'

'Did you. Yes ...'

'Graham – are you listening to a word I'm saying?'

330

'Yes, of course.'

'Are you, indeed,' Anthea said, smiling as she presented him with a stack of red-hot dripping cutlery. 'You haven't taken in a word of it.'

It was what he thought he was seeing in his assessment of Tillotson that was bothering him. Still it took all sorts to make a world, he supposed – even if the women hadn't realised. And as for Lawrence – well, he'd been a damned good bloke, and there was no law about who one chose as a business partner beyond him being good at the job.

'You know, I'm so used to thinking of Beth as Carrothead or the bitch, it still seems a bit odd sometimes, to be calling her Beth and have her sitting opposite me across my table.'

He chuckled, liking her honesty. 'I saw Vivien watching you both and having a little smile to herself. Where is she? I thought she was staying on for a day or so.'

'She is. She's gone for a walk. I think she's still a bit upset about Wanda and Robin. That's why I didn't ask them to lunch. They met Wayne at Tivington over the weekend. And as for Wanda – the little madam ... This isn't how I brought her up, you know.'

'I wouldn't worry about it. There's nothing you can do about it anyway. She's over eighteen.'

'I know she's more suited to Robin than Viv was, and I know things have changed since we were young – but all the same, I really do not approve of her living with him before they're married.'

That's you told yet again then, Lang, he thought. *No nookie for you here without a ring.*

'I think I need a dry tea towel.'

'Left-hand drawer of the dresser.'

He opened the drawer and looked through the jumbled assorted contents.

'Right at the back,' she said. 'I must have a turn out of those drawers when the lambing's over. In fact this whole house could do with a turn out. I haven't had a spring clean for years. There's loads of stuff I don't need that could go to a jumble sale.'

'There'll be plenty of jumble sales begging for things to sell come the spring. I must go through my bookshelves. I've got

331

some books and magazines to turn out, and there's all manner of junk in the garage.'

'I love jumble sales. The bric-a-brac ...'

'Do you really? Yes, so do I. There's one in Porlock village hall on Saturday. We'll go if you like. If you've got time. Last year I found a spanking new sink top I needed. It only cost me a couple of quid.'

'I'll have more time now I can afford a lad to help on the farm. He hasn't been here a week yet, but it looks like he'll be good. He's a strong lad, none too bright, but he's willing, and he's Reg Pugsley's nephew. He's spent all his school holidays working on Reg's farm, so he knows what it's about.'

She emptied the washing-up bowl and started to dry her hands.

'All done?'

'Yes. Thanks so much for drying. You'll be pleased to hear I'm thinking about buying a dishwasher.'

'Oh, I never mind washing-up after a party. You can talk about your guests.'

'Nasty man.'

He laughed, and going over to hang the tea towel on the rail of the Rayburn he noticed that the gander was not in his box. 'Percy's out in the yard again, is he? Is he better?'

'Not much, but I thought now it's getting warmer the sun would do him good. I bring him in at night.'

Then, the rail being full of shirts and socks, as he pushed them closer together to make room for the tea towels – he suddenly saw them. A beautifully clean pair of very white cotton pants. Eureka ...! And beside them, half hidden under her working shirts, was the top half of a pair of men's striped pyjamas – and he was suddenly so pleased, so happy, so certain, that he turned, and learning against the rail as he watched her put the plates in the dresser, he thought back to the night he had slept here. The night of the snow – and before that the goodnight kiss he'd given her when they'd been to the dinner dance. He had wanted her then, and he wanted her now. He ought to at least consider the possibility of marriage.

'What are you looking at?'

332

'You,' he said. 'I was wondering if you'd mind very much if I kissed you.'

'Oh ...' she said, and shyly, 'Well – no. I wouldn't mind at all.'

At first the bloke on duty at the Quantas check-in – neat head, smooth medium brown hair, marvellous features – seemed suspicious of his single piece of luggage for a long haul flight. It was a fair-sized holdall, though as usual everyone else in the queue seemed to be travelling with the entire contents of their houses and most of the equipment from their local gymnasia. Tillotson preferred to travel as light as possible, and having covered millions of miles by road, rail, sea and air in the course of his job, he had got his packing down to a fine art.

He put his ticket and his boarding card in his shoulder bag, checked for his passport and medication, and went back to sit down on the faded plum-coloured bucket seats by the revolving door where he'd agreed to meet Beth when she'd parked the car.

She'd been damned good to him, had Lawrie's pretty wife. Both Lawrie's wives had been good to him. But on Tuesday and Wednesday, after such a day of it Monday, Beth had made him stay in bed. He'd been bloody crook on Tuesday, and she'd nursed him like a baby. That's about what he was now ... Just about as God damned useless as a baby.

Bloody humiliating too ... She'd had to do things for him he'd only ever had done at the clinic before. Bed baths when he sweated, and several times in the course of the twenty-four hours when he'd been too weak to make it to the dunny, she'd had to strip off his pyjamas and change the sheets. Christ ...

Though it had served a purpose. She'd been damned hostile to start with, and then there had been the beginnings of a detached, cool sort of truce which, in the two days she'd had to do everything for him, had begun to melt with the snow into something close to friendship. She'd kept her word and had arranged for him to meet Anthea and the daughters, and he had kept his. The youngest daughter looked like Lawrie; had his marvellous dark blue eyes. The eldest, from what he'd heard and observed, had his business brain and his push.

333

And today, as if Beth hadn't already done enough for him, she had insisted on bringing him to the airport for the evening flight, though he'd have been perfectly prepared to pay for a taxi from Somerset.

He could see her through the plate glass now, stepping out smartly in her long brown leather boots, her mane of bright auburn hair bouncing on the shoulders of her camel coat as she crossed the well-lit traffic lanes and ran towards the revolving door.

'Okay?'

'Fine,' she said, a little out of breath.

He took in her glossy hair, the perfection of her cream-coloured skin – and shivered. She seemed to have brought in the cold night air on her clothes. The last night he would spend in England. At Tarran Hills now, it would be seven o'clock tomorrow morning, daylight, and already the air would be warm.

How the days raced ...

Standing up, he said, 'The bar's upstairs. Or would you rather have coffee?'

'Coffee.'

'Right on, well let's go up then. There's a McDonald's. I'll buy you a Big Mac, if you're sure you won't let me buy you a proper meal.'

'No, really. I only want coffee.'

They went upstairs, and walked the length of the terminal past the shops to the cafeteria. Having talked all the way here in the car, they walked in silence.

For once the place wasn't too busy. He found them a table in the smoking section that looked out over the planes in their parking bays, and when he returned with two coffees, she was sitting, chin in hand, looking out at the night.

'I love airports. The smell of aviation fuel. That tingle of something about to happen,' she said, sitting back in her chair as he put the coffee on the table. 'I suppose you've travelled so much you don't even notice.'

'I never used to – but I know what you mean,' he said, hitching at the knees of his trousers as he sat down. 'Are you sure I can't even get you a sandwich? It's a long drive back.'

'No, really. This is fine.'

334

He watched her sip her coffee.

'I owe you a lot, Beth,' he said at last.

'No you don't.'

'You don't know how much I looked forward to this visit. How much it has meant to me.'

'Yes ... Well, I can't pretend it wasn't a shock, but I am glad we've had a chance to talk.'

'These days I'm not very good at goodbyes. Too bad I can't persuade you to come with me.'

'I've told you, Wayne ...'

'I know,' he said, lifting his hand to stop her. 'You're a nurse, not a company secretary or an accountant, and you don't know one end of a horse from the other. But like I said – I wish you were coming with me.'

In any case, it's a nurse I shall be needing more than anything before too long, he thought – and aware that to say it would be pleading, he looked away. Watched a man with a woman and three medium-grown children who were settling themselves down at a nearby table. Life didn't come with any guarantees of company, but on the whole the straight guys had it made. He really did not want to die alone ... What was more, if there was anything in this crap about reincarnation and he ever found himself queuing in a line to come back, he was coming back as one of the straight guys, sure as God made little apples. And the second he was old enough, the first thing he'd do would be to find himself the love of an affectionate woman and settle down and have kids. The man who was now at the counter ordering food for his family was about his age, though Tillotson knew that in the last few months his body and his face had become so ravaged that he looked at least twenty years older. Years older than the photograph in his passport ...

And over the past few days he'd been thinking about things like reincarnation and the possibility of an afterlife quite a lot.

'Pretty kids,' he said, nodding in the direction of the table to which they had returned to say something to their mother. 'Just think, if I had kids, one of them might be interested in carrying on with the business.' He considered again the idea of kids being one's eternity. Then he said, 'Look, it's no good ... Before I go, I've got to ask you. I know this is going to sound like I'm not quite the full quid – but do you by any chance believe in a life after death – anything like that?'

'I've come to believe in some sort of an afterlife. Something – somewhere.'

'Right ... Well I know how this is going to sound, but while you were nursing me ... I was delirious, hallucinating – right?'

'You were delirious some of the time. You might have been hallucinating. If you were, you didn't say anything. At least, not while I was in the room.'

'What about Thursday morning when you brought me that cup of tea?'

'You were better on Thursday. Your temperature was well down.'

'Right on, but I was hallucinating. I must have been. On Thursday morning for sure, though several other times as well, I was sort of half seeing things.'

'What things?'

'That room I was sleeping in. Was it Lawrie's by any chance?'

'It was his dressing-room.'

'I thought it might have been.'

'Why?'

'Okay. Look ... It's possible this bloody disease is starting to get at my brain – but when you brought in that cup of tea, I swear he came into the room behind you.'

She raised her eyebrows and put her cup back on the saucer. Though perhaps what surprised him most was that she didn't seem surprised at all.

'You didn't say anything.'

'Damned right I didn't,' he said. 'You wouldn't have let me out of bed if I had, and I'd already wasted three days.'

'You weren't hallucinating,' she said, meeting his eyes. 'If you saw him, he was there.'

'You reckon ...?'

'Why not? I've begun to sense him about the house quite often. He's at Luccombe as well.'

'You see him, do you ...?' he asked, uncertainly. 'Even though you're a nurse. Scientifically trained?'

'Even scientist's accept that they don't know everything.

336

And no, I haven't seen him, but I have sensed him, and I'm fairly sure Amy Kenworthy has seen him.'

'She's a very old lady.'

'She is, and she rambles a bit, but she's not senile if that's what you're thinking. The very old and the very young are often, well – sensitive.'

'Jesus ...' he said, and suddenly believing it, the skin over his scalp felt as if it had shrunk. 'Could be I'm going to break out in a sweat.'

She gave her gentle laugh. 'I should just accept it. I rather envy you. I haven't seen him.'

'Right ...' he said, still not entirely convinced but deciding to give it more thought. It seemed a damned odd conversation to be having in the austere surroundings of an airport. 'Right ...'

She took another sip of her coffee and pushed back her coat sleeve to look at her watch.

'If you want to get going ... It's a fair drive back down those roads to Somerset. I wish you'd let me check you into a hotel for the night. I'll be glad to pay for it.'

'No, thanks all the same. I'd really rather get back. Thanks for the coffee.'

'Good on you. Thanks for the car ride.'

He had a good two hours to wait before they'd start to call passengers to the plane, but he was going to have to let her go eventually – so it might as well be now. They had both finished their coffee. And perhaps it would be best if she left.

I've become very attached to her, he thought as he picked up his hat and watched her push back her chair. Bonded, like a kid to the only adult with whom he felt safe ...

And as he walked back with her through the terminal to the covered walkway that lead to the short stay car park, he wanted to touch her; take her hand. She understood about AIDS, so she might not even mind if he kissed her.

Or perhaps she would mind a great deal – and suddenly paralysed with shyness, instead he announced his intention of seeing her safely to the car.

'No way ... You stay here in the warm. I'll be fine.'

'Well – thanks again. And if you do change your mind and want to take a look at Australia, you know you'll be welcome. Just don't leave it too long,' he added, meeting her eyes.

'You're a fighter, Wayne, I'll give you that. Good luck ...'

All the days he'd spent with her, until now, she had always called him Tillotson. And suddenly she stepped closer, raised her hand, pulled his head forward, and kissed him hard on the mouth.

'Take care ...' she said as they hugged.

'You too,' he replied, the words thick in his throat, his head light with gratitude as he clung to her.

That's it then, he thought when they'd let go of each other and he was watching her walk away. He felt fitter right now than he had in weeks – though he'd fulfilled his last ambition. Where could he go from here ...? *A fighter*, he thought watching her cross the bridge. *But I respond to the crowd; fight best in front of an audience.*

Come with me, Beth Seligman – Lawrie's wife ...

I need you.

Without you, there's nothing left worth fighting for

He watched her until she reached the car park, and on the far side of the bridge she turned one last time to wave. He lifted his hand in reply, then refusing to allow any emotion to register, he turned and walked quickly towards the carpeted slope down to the departure desks, produced his ticket and his boarding card, passed the policeman at the barrier, and went on through passport control and the security scan into the departure lounge.

But the vastness of the lounge accentuated his loneliness, and he made for the men's room; locked himself in a cubicle; collapsed against the door.

Come with me, he begged silently. *Lawrie's wife – I need you*. Damn the farm where Lawrie grew up, the land, the business, the ranches, the horses, everything they'd worked for ... Damn it to hell. *It's me who needs you ... I'm a selfish bastard – but I'm scared. I really do need you.*

And turning to press his forehead against the hard cold tiles on the wall, he at last relaxed and allowed himself to sob.

He was, Beth thought, one of the bravest men she had ever met. He carried his illness like a sword, never brandishing it – yet although he was well kitted out for a fight, its weight

338

was pulling him down, and the fact was, he was going home to die.

He probably had six months to a year at the most. If he picked up some virus, flu or even a nasty cold, it could be much less. As little as six weeks or even six days.

Either way, he wouldn't see England again – and driving away from Heathrow towards the junction for the motorway, she tried to analyse exactly what she was feeling. For months she'd done everything to avoid any contact with the man. Then she had met him, come to admire him – and already she was missing him.

I'm a nurse, she had said to him ...

On Tuesday when he'd been at his worst she had wondered if he was going to make it. Had almost called an ambulance. Had very nearly telephoned the clinic in Sydney so that she could accompany him to hospital with details of his drugs and their specialised advice as to his treatment. But by mid-afternoon he had begun to recover, and gradually over the next couple of days she had seen his zest for life return until it shone in his eyes like a fire. His body was hardly more than a skeleton hung about with too much yellow skin, but in his eyes she had seen the man he must have been. Strong, sensitive, enthusiastic, determined. A man who, regardless of his illness, was still determined to summon all the strength he could muster to show an interest and to learn – and since Thursday lunchtime when she'd allowed him to come downstairs, he had all but exhausted her with intelligent conversation and his constant questions.

She could see why Lawrie had loved him, if only briefly – though she would never understand why or how the love had become physical. Nor did she want – or indeed need to. It was love itself that mattered now. The rest was irrelevant.

On the way to the airport, before it grew dark, she had noticed him taking in the scenery; every landmark, every thatched cottage and ancient village church. He had a thing about thatched cottages and small village churches – and she'd known he was stocking up a bank of good memories to draw on when the going got tougher in the months ahead.

'There are advantages, in knowing you are going to die,' he'd said on Thursday afternoon as they'd sat bundled into

339

their coats in the car on Minehead seafront. The sun was shining, the snow had already gone from the roads and the promenade, and they were eating ice-creams. 'I've been able to get things in order. And in many ways, I've never felt so alive. I seem to have found a whole new dimension. You probably think that sea out there is just muddy brown water. What I see is water soft and flat as silk, shining with light, and alive with the constantly changing reflections of the clouds. And the smallest things have become significant. Grass seems greener, snow whiter, trees taller. Until recently I never noticed – but have you ever looked at the bark of a tree? I mean really looked – and touched it, smelt it? There's a whole new world whole new dimensions to be discovered, just in the bark of one single tree – and every tree is different. For Christ's sake Beth – life is for living, so live it to the full. Through all your senses ... You know, I reckon I might even be able to paint now I'm seeing things so much clearer. Now I've actually learnt how to see. I'd love to paint that view from your lounge-room window. I've always rather fancied myself as an artist. When I get home, perhaps I'll give it a go before it's too late.'

'I had a go at painting once. I was hopeless.'

'You're a bloody good nurse though, I'll tell you that.'

'You're a very rewarding patient.'

This was the man who, two days before, she'd been so sure was about to die that every time he'd drifted into sleep she had stayed in the room with him, the phone nearby, the names and dosages of his eight different types of medication memorised, the bottles and cartons ready to grab and take with her in the ambulance if there was a change for the worse in his already laboured breathing.

The man to whom she had also been able to say, 'Thank God you call yourself a homosexual rather than gay. I really resent that lovely word being stolen from the English language.'

'Well I'll tell you something,' he'd said. 'Gay is actually the last thing that we are. Gay is what we like to think we are. What most of us actually are is Sads, Frighteneds and Lonelies. Why do you think we call you heterosexuals "straight" if we don't know we're the ones who're off track and bent?'

340

And I, she had repeatedly told him, *am a nurse*.

Every mile of the long drive home, those four words continued to haunt her like a few notes from a song. Because a nurse, of course, was now exactly what he needed. He'd been psyching himself up for this trip to England for months and was determined to squeeze the last drop out of every minute of it. Once he got home he'd probably give up and die.

And somehow, since she had nursed him, she felt a responsibility towards him.

'I do know how you must have felt,' he'd said over the weekend, 'because I suspect it was what I felt when Lawrie told me he intended to marry Anthea. You see, for me it was the other way about – I felt disgust at the idea of him wanting a woman ... I knew why he wanted to marry her. I just couldn't understand how he could bring himself to do it.'

'I think you will when you see her. She is very like Anthony. Your other lover ...'

'You are getting brave,' he said, tucking in his chin, mocking her gently. 'But Anthony wasn't my lover. I've told you. He and Lawrie were the couple, and although they were mad to have behaved as blatantly as they did, they were utterly faithful to each other. It was quite touching really, despite the chaos it caused at the ranch. And yes, when it came to Anto's death – I felt every bit as responsible as did Lawrie. Because I was the clear-eyed if somewhat jealous observer who could see the chaos, and should have guessed where it was likely to lead. I should have challenged Lawrie and insisted on sacking the lad – for everyone's sake. Instead I did nothing. So if anyone other than Anthony himself was to blame for his death, I guess it was me.'

'Oh, come off it, Tillotson. Anthony wasn't exactly a kid. He was old enough to make his own choices. You said so yourself.'

'Right on,' he said, taking a cigarette out of its packet and putting it in his mouth. 'But you always have a responsibility to your friends – and sometimes, like it or not, you also have a responsibility to their lovers.'

'You aren't seriously going to smoke that thing, are you? For God's sake, listen to your breathing!'

'Ah, come on, lady ...' he said gruffly.

341

'Listen, Tillotson, I'm your nurse, and I'm telling you – throw the bloody things away.'

A nurse ... Trained to take responsibility for the sick – let alone any responsibility she might have had forced on her because he'd been Lawrie's friend or his lover.

But as the car's headlights continued to cut a new road through the darkness, she decided that she'd done her bit while he was in England – and after months spent in a kind of depression, she now had plans of her own.

Walking round the paddocks with a torch Anthea checked the heavily pregnant ewes – and, closing the gate, looked across the valley. There were lights in the house at Tivington. Beth was back – and she too was safe.

It had been a strange week. She'd been a little nervous about meeting Wayne Tillotson, though she needn't have worried. Although he'd obviously been fond of both Lawrie and Anthony, he'd said not a word out of place.

And if it had been a strange week, today had capped it all. The lunch party – and then Graham suddenly becoming so frisky. Until Viv had walked in and spoilt it.

And then, sadly, Graham'd had to get back to the office ...

Early the next morning Viv pulled on her wellies and went out to the yard to talk to Anthea who was shaking out straw in one of the tiny walled concrete pens that used to be the piggery. At this time of year she used the old pig sties as lambing sheds and a nursery for sick lambs and orphans – though you'd never guess, given the number of lambs that seemed to end up in the kitchen.

All Viv could see of her above the wall was her head and her shoulders – and she was wearing one of Lawrence's jerseys from a bag of stuff that Beth had given her. Viv paused by the corner of the barn, steeled herself, then walked across the yard.

'I've given Gran her breakfast.'

'Thanks, love. Did you sleep well?'

Not really. She'd had too much on her mind. Things which Mum was not going to like hearing.

'Is that a lamb in there? It's very small.'

'Too small. This season's first, and by my reckoning it's a good week too early. Born to one of the young ewes, and she won't let it feed. She hasn't a clue. I hope it isn't going to be one of those years ...'

Viv slid her hands into the back pockets of her jeans. This wasn't the best time to say it, but Mum was going to have to hear it sometime.

'Mum, I've been thinking. I've decided to go to Australia.'

Anthea leant on the pitchfork and looked at her.

'I thought you were going skiing.'

'I don't mean for a holiday. I want to go out there and work. Now, before it's too late. You heard what Wayne said. He doesn't want to sell those ranches and have everything he and Dad worked for pass to some stranger. I want to go out there and learn how to run that business. Just think, if I can run it for another ten years that strain of Narong Creek horses could really be something to reckon with. As well known in Europe as they are in Australia and out East. I'd really love to help to achieve that.'

All the colour had drained from Anthea's face, and Viv knew what she was thinking.

'I know how you feel about Australia. Uncle Anthony and all that – but I shan't go for any walkabouts in the desert, I promise.'

'It's not that ...'

'I'll be home for holidays. And you can come out to visit. You might enjoy that. I want to run those ranches, I really do. It's just what I need. Something new and quite different. Something I can really get my teeth into.' She took her hands out of her pockets, flexed her fingers. 'Think of the challenge!'

'You're not going, Vivien. You are not going to Australia. You can't!'

'Mummy darling, if Wayne agrees I don't really think you can stop me.'

'It isn't only up to Wayne.' Her voice was rising together with her colour. 'Beth owns half those ranches!'

'I know that,' Viv said patiently, 'I'll have to talk to her, but I just wanted to tell you first.'

'Listen, Vivien, if your father had wanted you in Australia

343

he'd have said so. He didn't want you or Wanda anywhere near those ranches. After his death he wanted those ranches sold, he made that quite clear in his will. It's Wayne that wants those ranches kept. It was the business here that Lawrie wanted you to run.'

'I know. Mum, I'm not doing this for Dad. I'm doing it for me. All the same, I think he'd have rather had me involved in Australia than not at all.'

'Thanks so much for coming over. She's indoors. You'd better come in and talk to her,' Anthea said as Beth got out of the car. 'She can't go out there. Please, Beth – help me reason with her. Tell her you want those ranches sold. Tell her you need the money. Tell her anything. She can't go out there – you know that as well as I do.'

'Actually, Anthea, I'm not sure that I do.'

Anthea stared at her. 'She can't go out there. She knows nothing about race horses. Though that's the least of my worries ...'

'She can learn. Anthea – she's exactly what Tillotson needs. A business manager. He's got trainers and ranch managers.'

'Shut up!' Anthea yelled at the geese who had waddled over, protesting loudly about Beth's arrival. Percy was with them Beth noticed, but he looked old and listless and was trailing dejectedly a few yards behind.

'Beth, please ... Don't let her go out there – for Lawrie's sake.'

'What are you saying, Anthea ...?'

Anthea met her eyes. 'You know that as well as I do. And supposing they were your daughters? They are ... You treat them like your daughters, and they do look on you as a second mother now. Please – let them remember Lawrie as they thought he was?'

'All right ... And it will be all right. It'll be fine. Also, I can see why Viv wants to get away. It's not just because of Robin and Wanda. She needs a change. A new challenge.'

Anthea groaned. Shook her head. 'I could wring Wanda's pretty little neck ...'

'No – Wanda's found what she's looking for. That's part of the problem. But everything else we can handle. Wayne

344

assured me that there's no one on either of the ranches who remembers Lawrie or your brother. No one other than his little circle of friends in Sydney even knows about him.'

Anthea pursed her lips and watched the geese which had lost interest and were waddling away towards the pond. 'The skeletons this family has in its cupboard ...' she said, slowly shaking her head. 'Oh, Beth – can you really be sure Viv won't find out? How do you know Tillotson won't say anything?'

'Lawrie trusted him implicitly – you think about it. And anyway, I'll be there.'

'*You ...?*'

'Yes. I'll be living with Wayne in the house. I can't promise I'll hear every word he says to her, but when I ring to tell him I'm coming, I'll make his promise of silence the condition. He's a man of his word. He won't let us down.'

'But – you don't want to go to Australia. I heard you tell him that on Friday.'

'I changed my mind. It won't be for long. Twelve months at the very most. I wouldn't want to live out there, but he'll need a nurse, and I would like to see New South Wales, and the places where Lawrie grew up.'

See the places in the photographs – and after Anthea's phone call this morning, hearing that Viv was going, she had suddenly known, beyond all doubt, that she had to go too.

'Selling land you've worked and lived from is like selling part of yourself,' Anthea said thoughtfully.

'Well, there you are then. You know how Wayne feels. How Lawrie might have felt if he'd allowed himself to feel. Before I go I'll see you and Amy through the lambing, and I need to spend at least a few days with some friends in Scotland. By then, if Viv's serious, she'll have worked out her notice at Thanes and it should all fit in perfectly. We can probably travel out on the same flight.'

'Oh, she's serious all right,' Anthea said dubiously. 'Well, if you're quite sure, I suppose you'd better come in and talk to her.'

*

'Wanda!' Robin yelled from his office. 'Answer the phone for me, darling – please? If it's that bloody contractor from Dorchester about the decorators, say I'm not in.'

Damn it Robin, she thought, *why can't you answer it ... Get the damned mobile phone mended ...*

He never answered the phone or the door if he could help it, and she was trying to get a pie made for supper before cleaning the flat and going shopping – and by two o'clock she had to be at work.

Having climbed to the crest of the first hill Viv stopped to take off her body warmer and looked down at the valley. Basking in sunshine, the fields stretching away to North Hill were the tender yellowish browns and greens of early spring after snow.

She would always have a special feeling for these moors and the valley where she was born, but she was glad to be leaving.

She'd come to realise that she would never be entirely free of her father. That the values he had taught her would always be with her as the yardstick by which, in business at least, she would make many of her decisions and measure her successes and failures.

He would be pleased to know that, if nothing else, she was going to carry on the work he'd started at Tarran and Barrington – and, as she would be doing what she wanted to do, that she would never be free of him no longer seemed to matter.

'D'you want to go round again?' Beth asked.

Amy lifted her head to look at the garden and, one hand holding on tight to Beth's arm, the other gripping her thumbstick, she gave a curt nod. On such a lovely mild morning it was good to be out of doors.

'You're going on a journey then, you and young Vivien.'

'I don't think I shall be gone long.'

'No, I don't reckon you will,' Amy said.

And suddenly, as she continued to look around the garden for a particular plant, everything seemed to change. In the corner by the barn she saw her empty wicker chair, and around it the leaves which had not as yet appeared on the trees had already fallen, and were blowing across the lawn in a garden that bore all the signs of autumn.

'All the same, time's getting short and there's a lot I must teach you before you go. Come over here, my Beth,' she said, waving her thumbstick to urge them forward. 'There's a plant here somewhere that might even help 'ee with that there Australian.'

Chapter Sixteen

Viv looked at her watch. Gran had nodded off in her chair, Mum had gone to some jumble sale with Graham, and Beth was due to come over to sit with the old lady so that she could get back to Bristol and pack to go skiing. She was looking forward to that, as well as Australia. She had talked to Thane on the telephone, and yesterday she had posted her formal resignation. He'd been devastated. Flatteringly so – although he had well understood her wanting to take over the family business.

She heard the car pull up in the yard and got up to go to the door.

'Thanks, Beth ...'

'Hello, Amy, my love,' she said, following Viv into the living room.

Gran smiled and they squeezed hands. Those two had quite an understanding, and Gran, too, seemed to have taken on a new lease of life.

'I warn you, there were some more lambs this morning,' Viv said as she picked up her bag. 'Very unlike Mum but she seems to have got her dates wrong.'

'I know. She phoned me. I've brought my toothbrush in case there's a rush and I have to stay on.'

'Has Wayne phoned you again?'

'Twice.'

'Since Thursday ...?'

'He can't wait for us to get there.'

'How is he?'

'He's well – and all the better for knowing that we're going.'

'Have you talked to the agents about renting out the house?'

'I've decided to leave it. Mrs. Westcott and Stan are going to look after it. What about yours?'

'I'll talk to the agents when I get back from France, then Graham will handle it, and as soon as the market picks up he'll arrange for it to be sold.'

Beth nodded. 'Did Anthea say what time she'd be back? What about the animals?'

'Early evening. The animals are all taken care of. The new lad's in charge.'

'Fine. Well then, I'll see you when you get back. Have a nice time. Don't break anything.'

'Lord no – I hope not,' Viv said, laughing. Then, having kissed both Beth and Gran, she made for the door.

As she drove back to Bristol she thought over the events of the past few months. It seemed as if, before Lawrence's death, each one of them in their own way had been stagnating in a pool, but were now moving forward down the course of their own little streams. She was glad Mum had Graham looking out for her – she might not have felt so free to go off to Australia if she hadn't. Now, everything was in order. The books balanced perfectly.

With one exception ... Before she left for France tomorrow, she must make one last phone call.

They left the village hall and started back up the hill to Graham's house.

'What did you buy?' he asked looking at the large carrier bag in Anthea's hand.

'Six fruit cakes.'

'Six ...?'

'They'll all be eaten. Mother loves her bit of fruit cake at tea time, and they've come from a good clean kitchen. Mew's a wonderful cook. They'll keep in the deep freeze. And I bought one of her sponges for us.'

'Oh ... So did I. Well, a sponge anyway. I don't know who's kitchen it's come from.'

He opened the gate and they crossed the gravelled forecourt that had once been the front garden and which was now a parking area for his clients' cars.

'Tea,' he said as he opened the front door. 'I'm parched. It must be the dust from that infantry charge when they opened the doors. Some of those women would kill to be first for a bargain. You go on into the office, there's a fire in there. I'll put the kettle on and find a plate for the cake.'

The temperature was dropping rapidly now that the sun was starting to go down and the fire in the tiny grate was almost out. She stirred up the ashes, put on some coal, and waiting for him to come back she looked at the books crammed in on the shelves on the wall. He was a great reader ... In addition to reference books there were classics, travel books, and a good number of paperbacks – the sort that had covers illustrated with blood-stained daggers and smoking shotguns. There was also a hi-fi and, in the cabinet beneath it, a large collection of records. She twisted her head to one side to read the names on the spines – and noticed a book on the floor. A fat book that had fallen between the cabinet and the arm of the sofa and was lying open, its pages fanned out and buckled by their own weight. She picked it up and began to glance through its contents.

'Have you read all these books?' she asked, as he came in with the tray.

'I think I've read most of them.' He closed the door with his foot and put the tray on his desk. 'If there's any you like the look of you're welcome to take them.'

'Sorry ...?' She hadn't really heard him. Mainly because the book she was holding seemed to be about sex. And she had just noticed it's title. Was considering its possible implications.

'What have you got there?'

She held it up to show him. '*Relationships The Second Time Around.*'

'Oh that ...' he said, flustered. 'That ... Oh, that must have been one of Stella's.'

Stella's ...? Stella didn't need a book like this. Stella could have written this before breakfast with her brain in neutral. And anyway, even if it had been Stella's, he'd been reading it ... *And* it was too new to have been sitting on those shelves for ten years ... What was more, he had turned extremely pink around the ears.

350

He did want more from her than friendship then ...

And, love him, he so much wanted to get it right that he'd actually bothered to buy a book on the subject.

'Are you sure it was Stella's?'

'Umm ...?' He had cut two slices of cake, and was looking at her while making a big thing about licking the jam off his fingers.

'I would have thought that Stella could have written this herself. And a few more besides.'

'Yes, well ... Thank God you couldn't. It's a useless book anyway. Anyway – I don't need a book to tell me how to ask you to marry me.' He raised his eyebrows, put his head on one side. 'So – will you marry me ...?'

Hugging the book, she stared at him. 'What about my mother?'

'She can be bridesmaid.'

'No, you daft idiot. I mean, who's going to look after her?'

'We will of course. And the animals, and the chickens, the ducks and the geese. The whole Noah's Ark.'

'You'd come and live at the farm?'

'Why not? As long as you don't mind. I'll see you right financially. I'll sell this place, buy something smaller to use as an office and pay you the balance.'

'You don't need to worry about that.'

'I do. And I'll be paying the bills and the housekeeping.'

'You've got it all thought out.'

'Of course. I'm that sort of chap. I should warn you though, I've got some odd little habits. And I am a bit set in my ways.'

'You look all right from here.'

'Come over here then,' he said, smiling. 'Look a bit closer. Much closer – and put that book down so I can kiss you.'

'Who's going to answer the phone?' Robin asked hopefully.

'You are, or I'm warning you, we're about to have our first row. I'm fed up with answering your phone calls.'

'It's your phone as well as mine. It might be for you.'

'It might, but I doubt it.'

'Answer it, darling Wanda – please? It's probably that bloody contractor again. He's livid because I've sacked him and sent in my own decorators. I'm not going to argue with

351

him on a Saturday night. Just say I'm not here. I'll answer the phone all day tomorrow, and I'll get the mobile mended next week, I swear it.'

'Wonderful ... The damn thing hardly ever rings on Sundays anyway,' she said.

Idle sod, stretched out on the sofa ... The phone was still ringing.

'Oh, all right,' he said suddenly, sitting up. 'I'll deal with the bastard ...'

But Wanda was already on her feet, and passing the sofa she grabbed a cushion and threw it at him.

'Wanda?' said a familiar voice, if unusually diffident, from the far end of the line. 'It's Viv. Don't hang up ...! Listen – I'm going skiing tomorrow, and in case the plane crashes or something, I want you to know that I'm sorry.'

'What about?'

'Lots of things. For barging in on you and Robin, for a start. And for all the awful things I said.'

'You were pretty nasty.'

'Yes, well, I can be. You know that as well as anyone.'

'Are you all right ...?'

Viv never apologised. She didn't know how to.

'Yes – I'm fine. I've been staying at Luccombe this past week as you probably know, so I know you're nursing and that you've applied to Tor College. Mum says you're hoping to train at Musgrove so you can be in Taunton with Robin. Listen, Wanda, I know it's none of my business, but be with him as much as you can. He's got a thing about that.'

'I intend to. I want to be with him.'

'Yes. That's the difference between you and me, I guess. You'll put him at least on an equal footing with your career. And you needn't worry. I shan't be breathing down your necks. I'm off to Australia.'

Viv told her where and why she was going. And then there was another surprise.

'Has Mum phoned you this evening?'

'No.'

'Well, she'll be phoning you over the weekend, because sometime before Beth and I leave, she's going marry Graham Lang.'

'Graham ...? Viv – that's great! That's really brilliant.'

'Isn't it just? Don't you go teasing her though. She's really quite coy about it.'

It was over an hour before they'd finished talking, then Viv asked to speak to Robin and Wanda went back to the sitting room. She and Viv had said things tonight that should have been said a long time ago, but until now it hadn't been possible. Not even in the week after Dad had died. And waiting while Viv also apologised to Robin, hearing the murmur of his one-sided conversation from the hall, it occurred to her that perhaps Dad was still somewhere quite near – and that, once again, quite certainly he was smiling.

Chapter Seventeen

Beth drove down into the farmyard and got out of the car.
Save for the sheep dog flat out in the sun by the piggery
wall, the yard seemed unusually quiet for the middle of the
afternoon. At the far end, under the chestnut trees, the ducks,
grouped around the pond, heads under their wings, were
also sleeping. Even the two geese knew her now and took
little interest in her arrival. Beaks pointed skywards, they
stretched their necks, extended their wings and squawked
half-heartedly before waddling off to peck about amongst
the daffodils by the gate into the field. She had never taken
to those geese – though she had become increasingly fond
of old Percy who at times seemed almost human.

Enjoying the peace of what was a surprisingly hot afternoon
for April, she stood in the sun and, looking around,
remembered how grey and stark both the day and the
farm had been when she'd first come here in January.
The trees were beginning to green now, their leaves almost
open; the daffodils in their full, deep yellow glory; the
hedges around the yard, strewn with primroses – and, at
Graham's instigation, the house had been given a good coat
of paint and the window above the front door had been
mended.

Anthea and the lad, working around the clock when
necessary, had delivered close on a thousand lambs, most
of them twins or triplets, while Beth had acted as
housekeeper, cook, Amy's companion and pupil, and nanny
to ten or so orphaned lambs, most of which, at one time
or another, had joined Percy in an assortment of boxes

around the kitchen floor. She had never worked so hard in her life.

'I bet you didn't know you had it in you, did you?' Anthea had said with a shy smile as, reeking of lanolin and half dead with fatigue, she and Beth had passed on the stairs at six-thirty one morning – Beth going down to feed two sickly lambs, and Anthea going up to snatch a couple of hours sleep.

'No – but I always did enjoy working the children's wards.'

And then, after almost a month, the lambing had finished and Anthea'd had just two days clear before she had married Graham.

'Lord love us, that was cutting it fine,' she'd said, coming down to the living room when she'd dressed for the service. 'Look at the state of my hands! And I stink of lambing oil, I'm sure I do.'

'Rubbish,' Muriel said. 'You look lovely, doesn't she, Beth? A real sight for sore eyes. A transformation.'

'Well, he might as well get used to it,' Anthea said. 'And he does know he's marrying more mutton than lamb.'

'Will you stop putting yourself down,' said Muriel. 'Come on – let's see your hat!'

It was a sort of large, floppy beret that sat very well on her freshly tamed hair. The peacock blue of the beret matched her suit and, made of satin, matched the buttons and the trim round the cuffs and the lapels.

'Oooh ...' Muriel said, appreciatively – and it was indeed a completely new Anthea.

'All right?' Anthea asked, looking at Beth, although it was Muriel who had been appointed as her official dresser.

Heaven only knew what Muriel thought of Beth being there anyway – Anthea's enemy, turned accomplice. But whatever she thought, in typically local manner, she had kept it to herself, and since the day she'd first met Beth at the farm, had been nothing but friendly. In fact, Beth was beginning to wonder if perhaps, unless drop-ins and outsiders damaged property or left gates open, the locals were quite resigned to their presence and accepting of their strange if amusing city ways. That perhaps it had been the chip on

355

her own shoulder which had put the reservation and suspicion into their watchful eyes, and that, until they knew you, rather than sly, they were really quite shy.

'Yes,' she had said to Anthea, 'you look fantastic. Honestly.'

'As for later ...' Anthea had said. 'Well, thank the Lord, it'll be dark by then. If I hold my tummy in and remember not to lie on my side I'll probably pass as reasonable when he's turned the light out.'

Somewhat embarrassed by a certain memory, Beth threw back her head and roared with laughter.

'It's all right for you,' Anthea said. 'Those girls ruined my tummy muscles. Even years of heaving hay bales hasn't put that right.'

'Do stop flapping, Anthea, my dear. It's not nearly as bad as you think it is,' said Muriel. 'You should see my stomach when I let it loose on the world. And you've bought a lovely sexy nightie and some very fancy underwear. He'll like that. Men love a bit of silk and satin.'

'Lord love us,' Anthea said, sitting down on the arm of a chair. 'I'm tired just thinking about it. Never mind getting married, I could do with a week in bed.'

'Yes, dear,' Muriel said, making unnecessary adjustments to her own hat in the mirror above the sideboard. 'Well, you'll probably get it. That's what honeymoons are supposed to be about.'

My God, Beth thought smiling broadly. Shy ...? If Viv and Wanda could hear these two, they would never believe their innocent filial ears.

'Oh no, not with Graham,' Anthea said. 'I shouldn't think so. Would you?' She was looking at Beth.

'Well ...' she said, remembering, suspecting that Anthea might be in for a surprise. 'You can never really tell.'

And for a moment, as Muriel continued to fuss with her reflection, there was a silence as, almost certainly, both Beth and Anthea thought back to the honeymoons they had spent with the same man. 'Have you remembered to pack suntan oil?'

'Suntan oil ...?'

'For the sun,' Beth said.

356

What else ...? Though this conversation was going rapidly downhill. Right now, oil to Anthea meant oil for lambing, which Beth had recently discovered was put, with ewes in labour to a far more personal use.

'Oh that,' Anthea said. 'Yes, of course. Will I need suntan oil ...?'

'April in Tenerife, yes you will.'

And so to the wedding ... Minehead Registry Office, followed by a blessing in the church at Luccombe and a slap-up lunch for the families and a few close friends at a smart new restaurant across the valley at Selworthy – after which Beth had stayed on to look after Amy and Percy while Reg Pugsley and his nephew looked after the farm, and Anthea and Graham had escaped for a week away.

A week during which, now that Amy could command Beth's full attention, she had made sure that several hours of each day were set aside for learning. Every day, in a state of clear-brained determination, and for as long at each sitting as her seemingly renewed strength would allow, she had taught Beth about the numerous herbs and minerals she had used for healing, instructed her as to where each could be found, the methods for preparing them into oils, tinctures or potions, methods of application, and the ailments for which they must be used, either singularly or in combination.

By the end of the week Amy had dictated a good deal of the information she had acquired in her lifetime, and the thick, hard-covered exercise book she had instructed Beth to buy when they had started had been completely filled with notes which must one day be passed to Wanda.

True that after each session Amy had been drained and exhausted, but while they had worked Beth had been constantly amazed at the old lady's clear, astute mind. Envisaging a human body, she had started at the head and worked down to the toes listing every possible ailment, its diagnosis and its treatment. Beth had been amazed at her natural, untaught knowledge of the human anatomy, and it had been like taking down notes from some highly qualified professor of medicine at the peak of her career who was writing a textbook, the details and layout of which she had already prepared.

357

Yet Amy could do nothing more for Percy – and, listening to her concepts of death as a mere progression to other lives beyond for all living creatures, not just man, it became clear to Beth that for Percy, she no longer considered it right to do so.

'Everything all right?' Anthea asked, eyes alive with happiness, face tanned, nut brown arms encircling a huge straw basket when they'd returned.

'Fine,' Beth said. 'Nothing to it.'

'What about Percy?'

'He's still with us. Just about.'

By then, his constant presence in the box by the Rayburn where he had continued to lie week after week getting no better and no worse, had become a dark shadow in the lives of them all.

That night Beth had returned to Tivington where she had spent Sunday packing up both a suitcase and the house before leaving to fly up to Scotland on the Monday for her visit with Liz. It had been so good to see Liz and the family again, and the children had grown almost beyond recognition. Scotland, too, had been at its best in the spell of fine spring weather, and she knew that whenever she eventually returned from Australia, she would fly up to visit them again as soon as she could. Before the workmen moved in to start on the alterations at Tivington ...

But all the time Beth had been away Percy the gander had been there at the back of her mind – and she was concerned for Anthea for whom the death of that gander would mean the end of an era.

Thank goodness for Graham ...

And yesterday, the Tuesday after Easter Monday, as soon as Beth had returned from Scotland, Anthea had phoned her.

'Percy's still here, but it can't go on. I know you've got too much to do and there isn't much time, but when you can, do you think you could come over?'

'I'll come over tomorrow,' she'd said. 'About three o'clock when I've been to the bank.'

And, in spite of all the other paperwork and all the packing that had yet to be done before Wanda drove her and Viv to Heathrow at the weekend, she was here and on time. She

358

pushed herself away from the car against which she had been leaning and took one last look round the yard. Four more days, after which she wouldn't be coming here again for sometime. In the harsh, fly-ridden heat of Narong Creek, she wanted to be able to hold this little farm, this yard and the view down over Porlock Vale to the hills beyond in her memory as it was now, at this moment, green and pleasant in the soporific warmth of an English spring afternoon. Making a memory bank was a lesson she had learnt from Wayne and, in the months to come, although there would be others – Australian memories to be stored in a new, quite different account – while nursing him, she might very well need such memories that she could store from here and now.

'Hello, my dear ...'

Turning, she saw Muriel coming down the steps from the front door.

'We didn't hear the car. How was your holiday in Scotland? You'd certainly earned the change and a rest. Anthea's in the garden.' On the way to collect her bicycle that was propped against the wall, she passed close to Beth, patted her arm and added confidentially, 'She's a bit upset.'

If time had seemed to stand still, it now leapt forward, and as Beth walked across to the front door she seemed to know what was about to happen.

The house seemed dark after the bright sunlight in the yard. No fire was burning in the huge grate and although the back door and the windows were open, the rooms smelt of wood smoke. There was no one about, and knowing they would be in the garden she walked through to the kitchen – and was drawn towards the bright oblong of light that was the doorway.

On the doorstep she paused. Amy, the tartan rug over her knees, was asleep in her low wicker chair in the sunny sheltered corner of lawn by the barn wall. Behind her in the beds beneath both walls there were daffodils, their strong colour adding to the brightness of the light reflected from the sandstone. The whole garden seemed to be filled with yellow – and Anthea was sitting on her heels beside a large box on the lush green grass.

Beth stepped out into the sunlight and walked across the

359

lawn. The box was made of honey-coloured pine, and in it, lying listless and dejected, was Percy.

'Don't ask ...' Anthea said quietly so as not to disturb him. 'But it can't go on.'

'No ...'

He was a huge bird, and even now, rather than particularly old or ill, he just seemed to be tired of living and appeared not to know how to die. Caught in a sort of limbo ...

'He's not going to get any better is he,' Anthea said.

They both knew that he wasn't.

'What are you going to do about it?' Beth asked.

Anthea looked down at a syringe lying in the grass beside her. Then she looked up at her. 'Will you do it? I can't ...'

Beth looked at Percy. His blank blue eye seemed to be staring at her.

Lawrence, lying in the grass, looking up at her, the needle silver against his brown cord trousers, his eyes, accusing, horrified – then finally, accepting, forgiving, loving, as all sign of life faded ...

Dear God ...

'Can't Graham do it?'

'Not as well as you can. You must have given hundreds of injections. He did make the box. And he has dug the grave.'

Big deal ... Beth looked at the loaded syringe, and swallowed.

'Graham says if he does it he'll have to use a gun. Shoot him ...'

Beth looked at her.

'Yes, I know. Look, Tom's given me the stuff. I can't call him out just to inject it. He thinks I did this weeks ago. But I can't do it, Beth. And if I can't – please ... It has to be you.'

'Quick ...' Lawrie whispered, his lips barely moving. 'The antidote. In the shelter, on the straw.'

Yes ... It did have to be her ... Because, apart from anything else, it was time to finally lay the ghost – and without a word she sank slowly to her knees beside the box and held out her hand for the syringe.

'What's in it?'

'Pentobarbitone.'

She assumed it to be an extra large dose of the barbiturate

that would therefore act as a permanent anaesthetic ... Her hands were shaking, but slowly, holding the syringe up to the light, she eased the plunger into place. Then she looked at the gander. At the blue eye ... And rested her hands on her lap.

'You'll have to cover his head. I can't do it while he's watching me.'

'That's his blind eye. He can't see you.'

'I can see him.'

That bright, staring, all-seeing blue eye ...

So Anthea rested one hand over his head, and with her other hand, gently began to stroke his soft white wings.

Do it Beth, she told herself. *You are going to have to do it – so do it now.*

Slowly she rose on to her knees and leant forward over the side of the box; ran her hand lightly down the long neck, parted the feathers – and positioned the needle.

Percy flinched, and feeling the slight resistance of skin and muscle, she clenched her teeth – and watched the syringe begin to empty as she eased home the plunger.

Then, supporting the flesh with her thumb, she withdrew the needle; rubbed her thumb over the place; stroked his neck – and sat back on her heels to watch him drift slowly into his permanent sleep.

'How long will it be?' Anthea asked softly.

'Not long.'

Though longer than it had been with Lawrie, she thought as she laid the syringe on the grass. Much longer ...

She leant forward again to stroke the soft white feathers, and pressed her fingers on his neck to check for a pulse. It was very faint; almost gone – and the sunlit garden and its vibrant colours had become a sparkling blur of rainbow-tinged tears.

Yet, somehow, within herself she was already feeling lighter.

'Is that it?' Anthea said, when finally she took her fingers away.

'Yes. That's it.'

Neither of them wanted to leave him for a while, and sitting back to wait, Beth slid her hands into her trouser pockets. 'Where are you going to bury him?'

'By the paddock wall with all the others. And tomorrow I'll order a little stone plaque.'

In one of the pockets Beth's hand had closed around something soft, and she remembered the ball of hair. Remembered that she had been wearing these trousers when she'd sorted through Lawrie's dressing-room.

'You've seen Lawrie's tombstone?'

'Yes. I like it.'

'What will you put on Percy's?'

'I thought Loyal Friend and Guardian?'

'Yes – that's lovely. Would you mind if I buried something with him?' and taking her hand out of her pocket she showed her.

Anthea nodded. She didn't have to ask whose hair it was.

'Put it in the box.'

'D'you want to bury him now, or shall we wait until Graham comes home?'

'I think,' Anthea said, 'That we should do it now, don't you? Just the two of us ...'

Amy woke from her nap to see him standing amongst the dappled shadows of the lilac tree at the end of the lawn. His aura was so faint that in the bright sunlight, she could barely see him. But he did seem to be there – hands clasped behind his back, standing near the dip in the sandstone wall.

He was watching something in the paddock. Amy couldn't see what it was, though in the still afternoon air, she could hear what sounded like the shuffle and clink of metal against earth and stone.

And standing beside him there was a large white gander.

Both man and gander remained absolutely motionless, and after a while Lawrence's wives appeared by the wall and climbed back through the dip into the garden. Anthea was carrying a shovel and, engrossed in conversation, oblivious to any other presence, they passed by and walked on across the lawn to the back door of the house.

But, intrigued, Amy continued to watch and gradually, in the silence, she began to hear the distant beating of wings. A multitude of wings, beating powerfully and coming ever closer – so that, soon, she could hear the whip and whine of a billion individual feathers cutting air.

362

The man and the gander had heard it too – and as she watched, the gander rose to his full stately height and ran forward into the sunlight, huge white wings extended as he took off and climbed through the air to join the wild geese that were passing overhead on their flight north to their feeding grounds on the salt marshes of the coast.

And now that the air was still again, Lawrence seemed to be walking towards her – and suddenly she understood. It was time for him, also, to leave – and at last she knew what it was that he wanted of her.

'Anthony,' she called softly in her mind as, closing her eyes, she focused her concentration. 'Anthony, my son ...'

She believed then, that her senses rose to a heightened dimension, and that the light in the garden grew far brighter than that from the sun. She seemed to feel the touch of Anthony's hand on her shoulder and, looking up, was sure he was standing beside her. Saw him return her smile and watched him, her blond graceful son, move out across the lawn to stand beside Lawrence so that the intense light that surrounded him gave back to his friend both his power and his youth.

Then, slowly, the two young men smiled at her, turned away and, walking towards the wall, together they gradually faded into the shadows under the lilac trees.

It was almost as if, over the months, as Lawrence's aura had weakened, so had Amy grown stronger – but, for the present, she was so exhausted that when Beth brought her tea into the garden she no longer had the strength to lift her hand to accept the cup and saucer.

You have been reading a novel published by Piatkus Books. We hope you have enjoyed it and that you would like to read more of our titles. Please ask for them in your local library or bookshop.

If you would like to be put on our mailing list to receive details of new publications, please send a large stamped addressed envelope (UK only) to:

Piatkus Books, 5 Windmill Street
London W1P 1HF

PIATKUS

The sign of a good book